There were no tears at our goodbye. I kı͏̶ ͏̶ ͏̶ stand for it. Tears offended her more than just about any other wrong a person could do. "That's enough," she'd say, scowling and stomping her heel on the floor whenever my eyes showed the slightest sign of being wet. "American girls never whimper."

After Mrs. Wentworth led me out of the house, I heard Mama shut the door behind us, turning her key in the lock.

"Come now, Miss Fenwick," Mrs. Wentworth said, taking my hand and urging me down the steps to the street.

Looking back, I saw Mama's arm reaching to close the curtains on the front window, her figure changing to a silhouette. Led by the tired bend of her neck, she moved to turn the lamp down, making the room go dark.

Thirteen, I'd thought, would be my time to go.

Mama thought, *twelve.*

Ami McKay's debut novel, *The Birth House*, was a number-one bestseller in Canada, winner of three CBA Libris Awards, nominated for the International IMPAC Dublin Literary Award, and a book club favourite around the world. Previously a music teacher, Ami's literary career started with a year of writing thank-you notes to people she didn't know. Now every day is a writing day. Born and raised in Indiana, Ami lives in Nova Scotia. To find out more visit her website at www.amimckay.com

By Ami McKay

The Birth House
The Virgin Cure

The
Virgin
Cure

AMI McKAY

An Orion paperback

First published in Great Britain in 2012
by Orion Books,
an imprint of Orion Publishing Group Ltd
Orion House, 5 Upper St Martin's Lane,
London WC2H 9EA

An Hachette UK company

1 3 5 7 9 10 8 6 4 2

A CIP catalogue record for this book
is available from the British Library.

Text design by Kelly Hill
Map by Erin Cooper

ISBN 978-1-4091-3869-3

Printed and bound in Great Britain by
CPI Group (UK) Ltd, Croydon, CR0 4YY

The Orion Publishing Group's policy is to use papers that
are natural, renewable and recyclable products and
made from wood grown in sustainable forests. The logging
and manufacturing processes are expected to conform to
the environmental regulations of the country of origin.

www.orionbooks.co.uk

For Sarah Fonda Mackintosh–doctor, mother, rebel;
and for my mother, who never let me forget that
I came from such stuff.

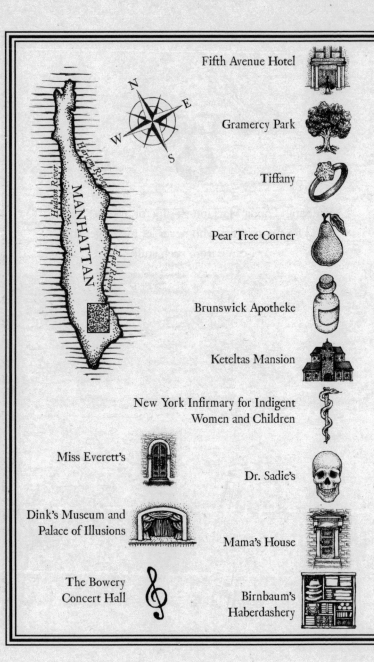

Fifth Avenue Hotel

Gramercy Park

Tiffany

Pear Tree Corner

Brunswick Apotheke

Keteltas Mansion

New York Infirmary for Indigent
Women and Children

MANHATTAN

Harlem River

Hudson River

East River

N
E
W
S

Miss Everett's

Dr. Sadie's

Dink's Museum and
Palace of Illusions

Mama's House

The Bowery
Concert Hall

Birnbaum's
Haberdashery

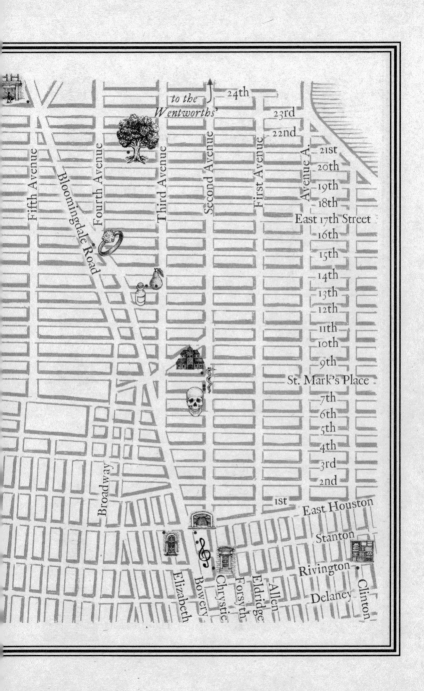

TO THE READER;

In 1871, I was serving as a visiting physician for the New York Infirmary for Indigent Women and Children. While seeing to the health and well-being of the residents of the Lower East Side, I met a young girl, twelve years of age, named Moth.

In the pages that follow, you will find her story, told in her own words, along with occasional notes from my hand. In the tradition of my profession, I intended to limit my remarks to scientific observations only, but in the places where I felt compelled to do so, I've added a page or two from my past. These additions are offered in kindness and with the best of intentions.

OCTOBER 1878

S.F.H., DOCTOR OF MEDICINE

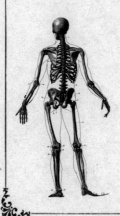

Recall ages—One age is but a part—ages are but
    a part;
Recall the angers, bickerings, delusions, superstitions,
    of the idea of caste,
Recall the bloody cruelties and crimes.

Anticipate the best women;
I say an unnumbered new race of hardy and
    well-defined
women are to spread through all These States,
I say a girl fit for These States must be free, capable,
dauntless, just the same as a boy.

                                        —WALT WHITMAN

Shrewdness, large capital, business enterprise, are all
enlisted in the lawless stimulation of this mighty
instinct of sex.

                            —DR. ELIZABETH BLACKWELL,
                            founder of the New York Infirmary
                            for Indigent Women and Children

PROLOGUE

I am Moth, a girl from the lowest part of Chrystie Street,
born to a slum-house mystic and the man who broke
her heart.

My father ran off when I was three years old. He emptied the rent money out of the biscuit tin and took my
mother's only piece of silver—a tarnished sugar bowl she'd
found in the rubble of a Third Avenue fire.

"Don't go . . ." Mama would call out in her sleep, begging and pulling at the blanket we shared as if it were the
sleeve of my father's coat. Lying next to her, I'd wish for
morning and the hours when she'd go back to hating him.
At least then her bitterness would be awake enough to keep
her alive.

She never held my hand in hers or let me kiss her
cheeks. If I asked to sit on her lap, she'd pout and push me
away and say, "When you were a baby, I held you until
I thought my arms would fall off. Oh, Child, that should
be enough."

I didn't mind. I loved her.

I loved the way she'd tie her silk scarf around her head
and then bring the ends of it to trail down her neck. I loved

how she'd grin, baring her teeth all the way up to the top of her gums when she looked at herself in the mirror, how she'd toss her shawl around her shoulders and run her fingers through the black fringe of it before setting her fortune-teller's sign in the window for the day. The sign had a pretty, long-fingered hand painted right in the middle, with lines and arrows and words criss-crossing the palm. *The Ring of Solomon, The Girdle of Venus. Head, heart, fate, fortune, life.* Those were the first words I ever read.

It was my father who gave me my name. Mama said it came to him at a place called Pear Tree Corner–"whispered by a tree so old it knew all the secrets of New York." The apothecary who owned the storefront there told my father that he could ask the tree any question he liked and if he listened hard enough it would answer. My father believed him.

"Call the child *Moth*," the twisted tree had said, its branches bending low, leaves brushing against my father's ear. Mama had been there too, round-faced and waddling with me inside her belly, but she didn't hear it.

"It was the strangest, most curious thing," my father told her. "Like when a pretty girl first tells you she loves you. I swear to God."

Mama said she'd rather call me Ada, after Miss Ada St. Clair, the wealthiest lady she'd ever met, but my father wouldn't allow it. He didn't care that Miss St. Clair had a diamond ring for every finger and two pug dogs grunting and panting at her feet. He was sure that going against what the tree had said would bring bad luck.

After he left us, Mama tried calling me Ada anyway, but it was too late. I only ever answered to Moth.

"Where's my papa?" I would ask. "Why isn't he here?"

"Wouldn't I like to know. Maybe you should go and talk to the tree."

"What if I get lost?"

"Well, if you do, be sure not to cry about it. There's wild hogs that run through the city at night, and they'd like nothing better than to eat a scared little girl like you."

My father had thought to put coal in the stove before he walked out the door. Mama held onto that last bit of his kindness until it drove her mad. "Who does such a thing if they don't mean to come back?" she'd mutter to herself each time she lifted the grate to clean out the ashes.

She knew exactly what had happened to him, but it was so common and cruel she didn't want to believe it.

Miss Katie Adams, over on Mott Street, had caught my father's eye. She was sixteen, childless and mean, with nothing to hold her back. Mrs. Riordan, who lived in the rear tenement, told Mama she'd seen them carrying on together in the alley on more than one occasion.

"You're a liar!" Mama screamed at her, but Mrs. Riordan just shook her head and said, "I've nothing to gain from lies."

Standing in front of the girl's house, Mama yelled up at the windows, "Katie Adams, you whore, give me my husband back!"

When Miss Adams' neighbours complained about all the noise Mama was making, my father came down to quiet her. He kissed her until she cried, but didn't come home.

"He's gone for good," Mrs. Riordan told Mama. "Your man was a first-time man, and that's just the kind of man who breaks a woman's heart."

She meant he was only after the firsts of a girl–the first time she smiles at him, their first kiss, the first time he takes her to bed. There was nothing Mama could have done to keep him around. Her first times with him were gone.

"God damn Katie Adams . . ." Mama would whisper under her breath whenever something went wrong.

Hearing that girl's name scared me more than when Mama said *piss* or *shit* or *fuck* right to my face.

The day my father left was the day the newsboys called out in the streets, "Victory at Shiloh!" They shouted it from every corner as I stood on the stoop watching my father walk away. When he got to the curb, he tipped his hat to me and smiled. There was sugar trailing out of a hole in his pocket where he'd hidden Mama's silver bowl. It was spilling to the ground at his feet.

Some people have grand, important memories of the years when the war was on–like the moment a brother, or lover, or husband returned safe and sound, or the sight of President Lincoln's funeral hearse being pulled up Broadway by all those beautiful black horses with plumes on their heads.

"Victory at Shiloh!" and my father's smile is all I've got.

The rooms I shared with Mama were in the middle of a row of four-storey tenements called "the slaughter houses." There were six of them altogether–three sitting side by side on the street with three more close behind on the back lots. If you lived there, there was every chance you'd die there too. People boiled to death in the summer and froze to death in the winter. They were killed by disease or starvation, by a neighbour's anger, or by their own hand.

Mothers went days without eating so they could afford food for their children. If there was any money left, they put ads in the *Evening Star* hoping to get their lost husbands back.

MY DEAREST JOHN, please come home.
We are waiting for you.

Searching for MR. FORREST LAWLOR.
Last seen on the corner of Grand and Bowery.
He is the father to four children,
and a coppersmith by trade.

MR. STEPHEN KNAPP, wounded in the war.
I'll welcome you home with open arms.
Your loving wife, Elizabeth.

They stood in the courtyards behind the buildings, pushing stones over the ribs of their washboards and sighing over the men they'd lost. Elbow to elbow they put their wash on the lines that stretched like cat's cradles over that dark, narrow space.

Our back court was especially unlucky, having only three sides instead of four. The main attractions were one leaky pump and the row of five privies that sat across from it. The walls and roof of the outhouses leaned on each other like drunken whores, all tipsy, weeping and foul. Only one of the stall doors would stay shut, while the other four dangled half off their hinges. The landlord's man, Mr. Cowan, never bothered to fix them and he never bothered to take the trash away either, so all the things people didn't have a use for anymore got piled up in the court. Rotten scraps, crippled footstools, broken bits of china, a thin, mewling cat with her hungry litter of kittens.

The women gossiped and groused while waiting for their turn at the pump, hordes of flies and children crawling all around them. The smallest babes begged to get up to their mama's teats while the older children made a game picking through boards and bricks, building bridges and stepping-stones over the streams of refuse that cut through the dirt. They'd spend all day that way as their mothers clanged doors open and shut on that little prison.

Boys grew into guttersnipes, then pickpockets, then roughs. They roamed the streets living for rare, fist-sized chunks of coal from ash barrels or the sweet hiss of beans running from the burlap bags they wounded with their knives at Tompkins Market. They ran down ladies for handouts and swarmed gentlemen for watches and chains.

Kid Yaller, Pie-Eater, Bag o' Bones, Slobbery Tom, Four-Fingered Nick. Their names were made from body parts and scars, bragging rights and bad luck. Jack the Rake, Paper-Collar Jack, One-Lung Jack, Jack the Oyster, Crazy Jack. They cut their hair short and pinned the ragged ends of their sleeves to their shirts. They left nothing for the shopkeeper's angry hand to grab hold of, nothing even a nit would desire.

Girls sold matches and pins, then flowers and hot corn, and then themselves.

By nine, ten, eleven years old, you could feel it coming, the empty-bellied life of your mother—always having to decide what to give up next, which trinket to sell, which dreams to forget.

The most valuable thing a girl possessed was hidden between her legs, waiting to be sold to the highest bidder. It was never a question of yes or no. It was simply a matter of which man would have you first.

There was a whole other city of us, on rooftops, beneath stair steps, behind hay bins, between crates of old shoes and apples. Rag pickers, hot-corn girls, thread pullers.

We got by, living on pennies from a lady's purse or nickels from men who paid us to let them look at our ankles or the backs of our necks for "just a little while longer." Some of us were orphans, most of us might as well have been. "Dirty rags," Mr. Alsop the fishmonger called us, as he stood there waiting with a long, thin stick, ready to crack our shins black. His stall was lined with barrels of salt herring—dried, chewy secrets with lonely little eyes.

In summer we slept sideways on fire escapes. In winter we fought rats and beggars for filthy stable corners.

We came from rear tenements and cellar floors, from poverty and pride. All sneak and steal, hush and flight, those of us who lived past thirteen, fourteen, fifteen years old, those of us who managed to make any luck for ourselves at all—we became New York.

1871.

BOARD FOR A YOUNG LADY.

A woman wishes to obtain board
in a private house of respectability
for her daughter,
where she would receive
a proper upbringing and firm supervision.

I.

Mama sold me the summer I turned twelve.

Everything stuck like corn silk that season—my dress to the small of my back, the catcalls of the bootblack boys, the debts Mama owed every man with a "Mister" in front of his name for five blocks around. There were riots just after the strawberries, and people went mad from the heat all June, July and August. Miss Lydia Worth, the seamstress next door, got sliced across the face with a knife by Mr. Striech, the butcher, just because she refused to marry him. The woman who lived above Mama and me, Mrs. Glendenning, hid her baby away in a stove-pipe when it died because she didn't know what else to do with it. I listened at our door when the police came to take her away. She'd only been able to afford swill milk and she was sure it was the milk that had killed her child. She wailed and sobbed, her cries of sadness filling the dark of the stairwell like the howls of a dying dog.

In the evenings, when it was too hot to sit inside, I'd leave Chrystie Street and walk up Second Avenue. Moving between pushcarts and passersby, I'd get as far away from Mama and our rooms as I dared. The journey was safe enough, even for a girl, alone, as long as I paid attention to the alleys and corners. Crossing Houston my heart would twist, not because there was any danger to it or Mama forbid me to go there, but because reaching the other side of the street always made me feel as if I were headed more towards home than away from it.

Peering through windows, I'd gaze into people's gaslit homes, keeping track of all the things I wanted for myself. Number 110 Second Avenue held a handsome gentleman, resting his arm on a mantel, mouth rounding into a satisfied O each time he puffed on his cigar. In the parlour of number 114, three little boys were sprawled out on their bellies across a flowery rug, rolling marbles in the channels of petals and leaves. At number 116, two lovers were sitting together on a settee, their elbows barely touching. A thin-lipped woman lorded over them, her arms crossed in front of her chest as if to say, *Don't you dare.* Glowing, moving pictures of ease, they made me want to lick my lips, my longing burning the sides of my tongue like I'd been lucky enough to have too much sugar.

Businessmen paraded by me in fitted, neat suits, their shoes perfectly black. Street vendors pushed and pulled their carts, the wares still looking orderly and fresh, even at the end of the day. The pigeon man came blowing a bosun's whistle, carrying braces of birds across his back. Shopkeepers cranked up their awnings and swept off their stoops, forcing clouds of dust to fly up around their feet.

They scowled as the dirt settled back down into the cracks between the cobblestones, staring after it as if it ought to be ashamed for coming too near their door. If it weren't for Mrs. Riordan once telling me you had to cross the East River to get there, I would have sworn I'd walked all the way to the beautiful place she called Brooklyn.

At the corner of St. Mark's Place and Second Avenue was a grand house on a large plot, rising five storeys above the street. Although the other houses surrounding it had been divvied up into *a*'s and *b*'s to accommodate the growing number of merchants who were setting up shops in the area, this house, with its blood-red brick and white marble trim, belonged to just one person, Miss Alice Keteltas.

Quite particular about the house and the gardens that surrounded it, Miss Keteltas had placed several notices on the lawn to keep strangers at bay.

Be advised, I am not dead and this house is not for sale. –signed, Miss Alice Keteltas.

All visitors without an appointment (good-intentioned clergy included) shall be turned away. –signed, Miss Alice Keteltas.

Curiosity seekers shall be met with suspicion and a stick. –signed, Miss Alice Keteltas.

Please, don't feed the peacocks. –signed, Miss Alice Keteltas.

Miss Keteltas generously donated her peacocks to the Central Park Menagerie two months after she acquired them. This practice was quite common with ladies who mistakenly wished for peacocks, or forty-two white swans, or perhaps a bear cub, or three sweet-faced monkeys. Thus, a zoo was born, to save the fine ladies of New York from their misguided game keeping and guilt.

Although the peacocks were long gone, the tall iron fence that had been erected around the gardens to keep the birds from escaping still remained. Menacing black spikes ran along the top and bottom of it, bayonets against the wild impulses of rioters, boys and dogs.

I liked to run my hand along the fence as I walked past, my fingers slapping the pickets just hard enough to make the metal hum. If I took hold of one of the posts while it was still singing, a delicious tickle would come between my lips, like paper over the teeth of a comb, or a whistle made from a blade of grass. I liked to think that this set the house to buzzing as well and that Miss Keteltas was somewhere inside, sitting at the dining room table or even reclining on her bed, suffering pleasant tremors of laughter without knowing why.

To the rear of the house one of the pickets was missing, leaving a space in the fence just wide enough for me to slip through. *It means she wants me here,* I told myself when I first discovered it. *It's a sign.*

Mama was always talking of signs to the women who came to our place to have their fortunes told. I'd watch from behind the curtains as she sat at her round-topped table with whichever woman had shown up at our door looking for answers. Putting a finger to the small, heart-shaped birthmark on her right cheek, she'd gaze into her witch's ball or stare at the lady's palms; then she'd give the woman the news. Sometimes good, sometimes bad.

I liked it best when a woman was willing to pay Mama enough to converse with the spirits. This called for both Mama and the lady to rest their fingertips on an upended glass. Then Mama would start humming and sighing, and soon the glass would go sliding over the wooden tabletop, dancing between the letters and numbers she'd painted there to help the spirits spell out fate. Even though the spirits said the same things time and again, it was still quite a thing to see. "You're gonna die young," Mama told every woman with fat wrists. "But that's all right. There will be flowers at your funeral and nobody will say a bad thing about you." Then she'd squeeze the woman's hand, tears coming to her eyes, making them shine. "We should all be so lucky."

The evening I decided to steal into Miss Keteltas' yard and across her lawn, a light shone from a wide window into the garden. No one had ever come out to stop me from touching the fence, and I'd never seen so much as a hint of Miss Keteltas or her stick. *All good signs,* I thought, *leading me to this very moment.* I decided that if I got caught, I wouldn't lie. I'd simply say, "There's a hole in your fence, Miss Keteltas. You really should have someone fix it."

When I reached the window, I could see into a parlour meant for the lady of the house. Miss Keteltas wasn't there, but right next to the window was a pair of birds inside a cage. They were brilliant green, like the first leaves of spring, all except for the feathers on their faces, which were a deep pink, making them look as if they were blushing.

I watched as one of the birds took a single seed from a bowl and fed it to its mate. The second bird kindly bowed its head and returned the favour. They went on like that, their stubby beaks pinching and putting, gentle and fair, until all the food was gone. Then they took turns preening and nuzzling each other's necks, stopping every so often to puff up their feathers in delight. Stout little things, they'd wobble apart and then together again, dancing along the length of their perch. Finally, the larger of the two seemed to tire of it all and closed his eyes. His mate tilted her head and stared at him while he slept, her wings folded tight behind her back. She looked just like Mrs. Riordan did whenever she was having a hard time hearing what I had to say.

Before long, a maid came into the room. As soon as I saw her, I went to my knees, crouching beneath the window and holding as still as I could. For a moment, I was certain I'd been caught, but then the light went out and the garden became dark enough for me to sneak away.

As I walked home, I didn't think about how late I'd be getting back to Mama. I just kept thinking of how much I wanted to be inside Miss Keteltas' parlour, with nothing to do but watch those lovely little birds. I won-dered if any two people had ever cared for each other like that. *Not my mother and father,* I thought. *Mrs. Riordan and her hus-band, perhaps.*

Lovebirds mate for life. Thus, pains should be taken not to separate an established pair. A lonely bird will engage in destructive behav-iours such as pining, biting and plucking out its feathers. If you are faced with a single bird, you must become what the bird longs for and lavish all your attentions upon it, lest it lash out at you.

Although Mr. Riordan died long before I was born, Mrs. Riordan still spoke of him often, her voice catching in her throat whenever she said his name. "Twenty years without my teeth or my husband and still it's Johnny I miss most."

Mama was on the front stoop when I got home, fanning herself with a folded newspaper. "It's too dark for you to be out," she said, glaring at me. "Go inside and get to sleep."

When she came to bed she didn't speak to me. Even though she didn't ask where I'd been, her silence on the other side of the mattress we shared made me feel as if somehow she knew. Maybe her glass and the table had spelled it out for her. *M-o-t-h w-a-n-t-s t-o r-u-n a-w-a-y.*

The next morning, my boots were gone.

"Shoes in summer are nothing but a waste," she said when I went crawling under the bed searching for them.

They weren't the nicest pair of boots in the world. The leather had begun to crack across the toes and they were nearly too small for my feet, but they were mine. I'd paid Mrs. Riordan a nickel for them. She'd gotten them off the body of a girl she'd dressed out for burial. The girl had died of consumption and her mother had told Mrs. Riordan that she should have the boots, it was the least she could do to thank her.

A girl with shoes can hold her head a bit higher. She can run away.

"Where are they?" I asked Mama.

"Gone."

"Where?"

"Mr. Piers . . . but don't bother asking him about them, he took them apart for scraps right on the spot."

A knife grinder by trade, Mr. Piers had a pushcart he wheeled up and down Chrystie Street. His hands were shiny–not greasy like a butcher's after handling lard, but slick with the oil that made a blade sharp and exact. Mr. Piers wore his hair in two long braids and his eyes were almost black. All the women thought he was the handsomest man they'd ever seen. I felt that way about him too, until he had my shoes.

Mr. Piers also shaved people's lousy heads, and sold bottles of Dr. Godfrey's Cordial. He'd sit on the street at night, his feet pumping the grinding wheel, sparks flying, looking like the Devil's man as he waited for women to come and ask him for his "best."

Mothers called the cordial "quietness," because their teething babies would stop wailing as soon as they rubbed it on their raw, red gums. A few drops under the tongue and the child would fall into a deep sleep. Mama said it did much the same for her, so she'd drink half a bottle of the stuff whenever she felt weary from life. I didn't see it quite like that. I thought it just turned her too tired to find her way around the room. I hated those square bottles, with their fancy, boastful labels.

Dr. Godfrey's Cordial–"a soothing syrup, concocted from the purest ingredients!" (*sassafras, caraway, molasses, tincture of opium, and brandy*). "For all manner of pains in the bowels, fluxes, fevers, small pox, measles, rheumatism, coughs, colds, restlessness in men, women and children, and particularly for several ailments incident to child bearing women and relief of young children breeding their teeth."

With the heat of summer, Mama's fortune-telling business had dropped off. "The hotter it is, the less people like taking a chance on getting bad news," Mama would say for every day that went by with no customers. "Come September, it'll pick up. You'll see."

When our cupboards got bare, anything we didn't need got sold to Mr. Piers. By July, Mama was taking things to him every few days, in exchange for a bit of money, or more often in trade for a bottle of Dr. Godfrey's. My boots had gone towards the cordial along with Mama's tortoiseshell hair combs and the amulet she wore around her neck to protect her from the evil eye.

"I'll get you a new pair," she told me. "Come September."

After that she started talking of other mothers who'd had great success in arranging positions for their daughters– as house maids or cooks' helpers, as seamstresses and laundry girls. Lingering over the details, she made them sound more like saints than servants. "They were nearly at the end, you know–no food in the cupboard, no money to speak of." Sighing with admiration, she'd go on, "It was the daughter that saved them. If she hadn't stepped up, the whole family would be dead."

Her stories were always the same. First, a sad, worn-out mother would manage to save up enough pennies to place a help-for-hire ad in the *Evening Star*. Then, a week later (no more, no less), the woman's daughter, "a bright and willing girl, mind you," would be plucked from the slums and miraculously placed in a situation that paid more than enough to keep her family from starvation. "She's living with a fine, well-bred lady, all the way up on Gramercy Park. Her mother says there are at least a dozen other maids in the woman's employ, and the house has too many rooms to count. Can you imagine?"

I could not. At least not in the way Mama hoped I would.

Whenever I tried to imagine a place that grand, I always wound up picturing myself not as a maid or a cook, but as the lady of Miss Keteltas' house, floating through ballroom and conservatory wearing a dress made from the finest silk. Sometimes the dress would be forget-me-not blue, sometimes it was a demure lilac. More often than not it was petal pink, with yards of black velvet ribbon looped around the hem. No matter the colour of the dress, the vision would end with me smiling and lying naked on a feather bed. The mattress was so deep I could hardly find my way out of it. Mama didn't know that her uptown mansion with too many rooms to count only made an appearance in my head if the house and all that was in it were mine.

Thirteen, I'd tell myself, any time Mama started to go on about servants' quarters and maid's wages. *I'll stay with Mama until I'm thirteen.* I hoped by then to find a way of becoming something on my own, something beyond Mama's expectations.

She came to me, pushing at my shoulder while I was asleep. Ignoring her, I curled myself into a ball on my half of our sagging straw mattress.

"Wake up, Moth," she nagged. "Get out of bed and get dressed."

Her voice wasn't right. It was thin and tight in the wrong places and all I could think was that there must be a fire.

Mama loved watching buildings go up in flames. We had a collection of sooty bric-a-brac on the front window-sill to prove it. She'd pulled things from the rubble of every fire she'd ever chased. A gentleman's shaving mug cracked in two; a blackened doorstop shaped like a dog; countless bits of melted glass—brown, green, blue; even a tiny porcelain chamber bowl meant for a dollhouse. It had words painted around the rim: *Piss or get off the pot.* Mama had a scar on the palm of her right hand from where the thing had burned her.

"You go on without me," I mumbled, my tongue feeling thick with sleep. "I don't need to see it."

"Get up," she insisted, twisting the fine hairs at the back of my neck until the pain of it made me sit up and open my eyes.

The hoops she always wore in her ears were winking at me, shimmering in the light of a candle she'd just lit. Reaching to the post at the end of the bed, she grabbed my dress and tossed it at me. Then she began taking my things out of our dresser drawers and throwing them on the bed: a pair of stockings with the toes worn through, my old petticoat, the ragdoll I carried around as a child and called Miss Sweet. The doll's arm came off in Mama's hand and the rest of Miss Sweet fell to the floor. She picked up the thin, limp body and looked at me.

"You still want her?" she asked.

"Yes," I mumbled, as I pulled my dress on over my head.

Mama took the doll and its arm and pushed them into an empty pillowcase. Then she held the case out to me and looked to the pile on the bed. "Put the rest of your things in this."

"What's happening?" I asked, as she reached around my middle to tie the sash of my dress. "Is there a fire? Are we in trouble?"

"There's no fire and there's nothing for you to worry about," she said, working my hair into a loose braid down my back. I heard the slither of a length of ribbon being made into a bow, felt the ache of it being pulled tight. She turned me so I was facing her and brushed a stray hair away from my brow. "You're going on a little trip, that's all. I've found you an excellent position, but you have to leave tonight." Putting the lumpy pillowcase in my hands, she took me by the arm and led me to the front room.

There was a woman sitting next to Mama's fortune-telling table, resting in our velvet rocker, one of the few things of value that Mama hadn't sold. She was wearing a fine, dark dress with a long matching cape that pooled around her in her seat. Her face was soft looking, her eyes moist and shining at the edges. The wide bow of her hat was tied under her chin, and the flesh of her neck folded against it as if she were made of butter and cream. Looking at me, she picked up the front of her skirts and shifted in her seat. I could see her shoes peeking out from her petticoats–black leather boots with scalloped trim around the buttons that reached far above her ankles.

"Say hello to Mrs. Wentworth," Mama said, as she pushed me towards the woman.

Still staring at her boots, I stumbled, nearly falling into the lady's lap.

Mama smiled at her apologetically. "It takes her a while to warm up to strangers. You understand."

Mrs. Wentworth stood and held her hand out to me. "How do you do, Miss . . . ?"

Speaking up before I could, Mama said, "Miss Fenwick will do." Then she looked to me and nodded as if she'd just named a stray dog.

Fenwick wasn't my father's name or even my mother's. It was the name on the label that was peeling off an old bis-cuit tin Mama kept with the rest of her fire souvenirs. The box had been painted to look like it was made of gold, and from a distance it seemed as if it were meant to hold some great treasure. Up close, the thing was a disappointment, with rusty holes eating away its underside, and a dented lid that wouldn't stay shut. *Fenwick Brothers Shortbread, a cut above the rest.*

Mrs. Wentworth took my hand in hers. "A pleasure to meet you, Miss Fenwick," she said. Looking me over with her large, watery eyes she added, "I'm sure we'll be very happy together."

Mama stared at me not with sadness, but with pleading. She was thinner than I'd ever allowed myself to notice, looking more like a child than a woman. I wanted to believe she knew what was best for me. I wanted to believe she was like every other mother and that she loved me more than I loved her. I hoped if I followed her wishes, I would finally make her happy.

There were no tears at our goodbye. I knew Mama wouldn't stand for it. Tears offended her more than just about any other wrong a person could do. "That's enough," she'd say, scowling and stomping her heel on the floor whenever my eyes showed the slightest sign of being wet. "American girls never whimper."

After Mrs. Wentworth led me out of the house, I heard Mama shut the door behind us, turning her key in the lock.

"Come now, Miss Fenwick," Mrs. Wentworth said, taking my hand and urging me down the steps to the street.

Looking back, I saw Mama's arm reaching to close the curtains on the front window, her figure changing to a silhouette. Led by the tired bend of her neck, she moved to turn the lamp down, making the room go dark.

Thirteen, I'd thought, would be my time to go.

Mama thought, *twelve.*

Mother, if you love her–
Mother, if you love her, keep her clean.
Mother, if you love her, keep her–

II.

I'd always felt my future was waiting somewhere else, far across Manhattan. It called to me in the *clip-clop* of the streetcar horses, begging me to chase after it. *Up on my back, off in a crack; Child, tell your mother that you won't be back.*

The notion that I was meant for something far beyond the slums had set up shop in my brain somewhere around the same time my heart started to beat. My life held great promise, I was sure of it, but finding my way there was another matter altogether.

The week before Mrs. Wentworth took me away, I'd dared to bring out Mama's witch's ball for a secret consultation. Cradling the thing in the palm of my hand while she was asleep, I'd stroked and flattered it, telling the bubble of blue glass that I believed in its magic more than I believed in my own mother. When I asked it to reveal what was in store for me, it just sat there, reflecting my questioning eyes– too scared to give anything away for fear of upsetting Mama.

It knew as well as I did that if she were to catch me with it, she'd throw a fit. *What questions could you possibly have? To be taken into the house of a true lady, that's what you want–even if it's only to wash her stockings and serve her tea. Now that would be a lucky fate, indeed.*

As Mrs. Wentworth's carriage took me away from Chrystie Street, I wondered what the witch's ball might have shown me if it had been brave enough. Would I have seen Mrs. Wentworth sitting in our chair? Would I have noticed the great relief that came over Mama's face as I was led away? I couldn't help but long for answers. How many other girls were already in Mrs. Wentworth's employ? Was she kind to them? Would they become friends, or enemies?

The velvet curtains in the cab of the carriage were tied shut, leaving me with little sense of where I was headed. I tried noting the turns, left or right, east or west, counting hoof-beats along the way, but I soon lost track. The farther I got from Chrystie Street, the more I struggled to decide which was worse—my fears of what lay ahead or my regret over having stayed with Mama too long.

In the end, I chose to push them both aside and wish myself into a pleasant dream. I closed my eyes and re-imagined everything that had happened, from Mama shaking me out of my sleep to sitting now across from the silent Mrs. Wentworth in the dark of the cab. I told myself it was simply fate's way of playing a trick on me. In my musings, the woman sitting across from me wasn't named Mrs. Wentworth at all. She was, instead, Miss Alice Keteltas, come to take me home at last. She'd even arranged to have a welcome party waiting, at this late hour, with ladies in evening gowns and men in coats with tails, all lined up to meet the girl who was named by a pear tree, the girl who knew how to make a house hum and sing.

"You're to go right to bed," Mrs. Wentworth announced

as the carriage wheels rolled to a stop. "I want you rested for tomorrow."

"Yes, ma'am," I answered, startled out of my dreaming by the sharpness of her voice.

As the door to the cab opened, cool night air rushed in and clung to my skin. Clutching the pillowcase Mama had given me, I followed her from the carriage to the house. Shuttered and dark, the building looked nothing like Miss Keteltas' mansion. It most certainly was not a home to cheerful gardens and sweet-faced lovebirds.

Inside, the place was dimly lit, with only a few lights flickering on the stairs and in the hall. Even so, I could see it was a house made from great fortunes: the floor of the entry-way was tiled in marble, and the ceiling, piped with plaster ribbons and roses, soared far above any practical height.

We were greeted by a man dressed in a fitted coat and handsome silk tie. He was a proper-looking gentleman in every way except for the terrible scar that ran across his left cheek. Long and curved like a frown, it looked as if whatever had caused it had also come close to cutting the man's lip in two. Gone white and catching light, it spoke of another life, of knife fights and bloodied ears. It reminded me of the knots the roughs around Chrystie Street all sported on the bridges of their noses. "Billy bumps," they called them with a puffed-up sense of pride, because they'd gotten them as the result of tangling with the police.

I bowed to the man, assuming he must be Mr. Wentworth.

Looking down at his shoes, the gentleman cleared his throat and waved me up.

My face went red with embarrassment. I hadn't even considered Mrs. Wentworth might have a butler.

"Nestor," Mrs. Wentworth said, as she motioned for him to assist her with her cloak. "This is Miss Fenwick. Please show her to the servants' quarters, and make certain she's comfortable."

"Yes, ma'am," he responded.

No sooner had he taken the cloak off her shoulders, keeping a polite distance from the sweep of her skirts, than she was making her way towards the wide staircase that curved up from the entrance hall.

The banister that graced the stairs was made from handsome, polished wood and was decorated with aloof-looking cherubs that stood guard at every landing. Six angels in all, they balanced frosted globes of gaslight on their chubby shoulders. It was all I could do not to reach out and touch the cherub closest to me, to stroke its smooth, perfect toes. Appearing and disappearing as she passed them by, Mrs. Wentworth's tired face glowed turnip yellow in the lamplight.

After she was gone everything was still, except for the ticking of a tall clock in a nearby alcove, its pendulum glinting as it slipped back and forth. According to the clock's face it was quarter past one. I imagined there must be an army of maids asleep somewhere under the roof, and I was glad I'd soon be joining them.

"This way, Miss Fenwick," Nestor instructed, as he lit an oil lamp that was sitting on a marble-topped table. "Time for you to get some sleep." The lamp sputtered when he took it up, giving off a trail of greasy smoke.

Following the butler down a long corridor, I did my best not to brush up against the thin-legged stands and scallop-edged tables that lined the walls. Each one held a delicate-looking vase or some precious object that needed to be kept safe under a glass dome. Paintings of gentlemen and ladies from days past hung on the walls, their dour faces making me feel as if they'd caught me walking on their graves.

"Watch your step," Nestor instructed as we came to a second staircase at the rear of the house, this one unadorned, narrow and steep. He held the lamp to one side as he went up the stairs, so I could better see the way.

The shadow of his figure crept beside us—a looming, faceless version of himself. It made me think of all the frightening stories I'd heard that summer, told on front stoops and in back courtyards, of girls being snatched up and dragged away by strangers. They were true tales that had happened right in the heart of the city, printed in the newspapers and weeklies for all to see. It was the fair-haired, well-off girls gone missing who'd made the headlines of the *New York Times* and the *Evening Star,* but there were plenty of poor girls with immigrant blood who'd disappeared as well. (*Of non Americanized parentage,* the papers said when referring to them, hushing them away in the tight, distant columns of *Police Briefs* and *News From Neighbours.*)

Eliza Adler was thirteen years old and lived only two doors down from Mama and me. She'd been gone for three days when her body was found floating in the East River. At first they thought she might have done

There is much talk, even today, about what it means to be an "American girl." One well-known English writer defines her as: "a little under medium height; hair the colour of spun gold to golden brown; eyes a violet blue; cheeks and lips rosy; teeth whiter and brighter than pearls; hands and feet extremely small and well-shaped; figure petite, but exquisitely proportioned; toilette in the latest mode de Paris; and above all, bearing that marvellous bloom upon her face, ...

herself in, but her mother swore that she was a happy girl who had never wandered far from home. After the police took a close look at her body, they saw she'd been beaten and strangled to death. One week after Eliza was found, another girl's remains turned up, this time buried in a haystack at the stables in Central Park. She'd come from some town in Pennsylvania to be a servant girl on Fifth Avenue and now she was dead.

In both cases, there were signs the girls had been spoiled by a man just before they were killed. There was the tearing and bruising and blood to prove it.

... which American girls share with the butterfly, the rose, the peach and the grape, unequalled by any other women in the world."

Sentiments like these may seem flattering, but they have also served to fuel the denigration of many an immigrant's daughter. Are they, too, not American?

"Everything all right?" Nestor asked when we were halfway up the stairs, nearly causing me to miss a step. "You're awfully quiet back there."

"I'm fine, sir," I answered, hoping he hadn't seen me flinch.

It was common knowledge that newly hired servant girls were often taken aside for personal indulgences—by the butler, or the footman, or even the master of the house. It was assumed it was their right to have the girl, a natural part of the domestic economy, but I hadn't given up anything to anyone yet. I hadn't had my first blood or my first kiss, wasn't sure of how to meet a man's expectations outside of Mama once explaining to me, "All you need to know about men is this—they have a great need to put their cock into whatever holes they find

In August of 1871, a man was caught attempting to drag a young girl away near her home on Delancy Street. He later confessed to murdering four other girls, including Eliza Adler.

fitting. The more you're grown, the less it'll hurt. So, until you're ready, stay out of their way."

I can trip him, push him down the stairs if I have to. I can run away.

Mama would never forgive me.

More and more, I'd felt men gazing at me, licking their lips when they thought they might get me alone. Mr. Goodwin, the grocer, made no secret of his fondness for little girls. Mr. Cowan insisted on calling me "princess" every time he came to collect the rent. Pensioner Peter Rutledge was kind and had a roaring laugh, but he was thirty-three and had no legs or prospects because of the war.

Unsettling as their attentions were, I understood (as most girls in my circumstance did) that I could, if careful, get quite a lot from a man before having to give any of myself away. A look, a word, a nod was an invitation to a game. *What's in it for me?* I'd learned to ask myself. *How far can this go before it's too late?*

I'd smiled at Mr. Goodwin, let him run the back of his rough hand across my cheek so he'd give me half-a-dozen eggs instead of the three or four Mama's pennies would buy. A winning smile and a lingering nudge of my shoulder against his arm, had, on occasion, meant a new ribbon for my hair. There were dangers to such games of course—one false move and I might end up ruined, or worse, like poor Eliza—but the rewards that came when I moved cautiously and correctly were too tantalizing to resist.

This was the sort of path Francine Grossman had taken all the way to London, and then to Paris, and then back again to New York. Now known as the Baroness de Battue, she'd once been a Chrystie Street girl herself. She'd played her cards right and become a *courtesan* rather than a whore, a woman of consequence rather than a corpse. All the girls from Five Points to Rag Pickers Row had, at one time or another, tied strands of oyster shells around their necks for jewels, waltzed in the dust with broomsticks for princes, and pretended to be her. Every ten-cent whore on the Lower East Side cursed her existence, insisting *that should've been me.* Eliza had planned to follow in Francine's footsteps, but had somehow lost her way. I wasn't about to let that happen to me.

Nestor's voice was gentle, and he'd struck me as a thoughtful man, somewhat like Reverend Osgood, the minister who came on Sunday afternoons to say prayers with troubled souls in the slums. I wondered if perhaps Nestor had been his own man in his youth, but somewhere along the way had fallen on hard times, leaving him to depend on serving others for his livelihood.

His eyes had gone soft when he'd looked back at me, sympathy held like a pearl in the furrow of his brow. I hoped he was the kind of man whose heart could be touched by pleading. *Please, sir, not now*—I'd beg, if he approached me. *I'm too young.*

Reaching the top of the stairs, he shone his lamp into the gloom of a small, dark room where it revealed the figure of a woman stretched out on a mattress in the middle of the floor. Her breathing was steady and low, her mouth agape. Our footsteps echoed on the wooden floor, but she didn't stir.

"That's Caroline," Nestor said. "She cooks and keeps house." Shining the light in the far corner of the room he added, "And that's your bed, Miss Fenwick. Good night."

"Good night, sir," I said, sighing in relief.

After he was gone, I lay down on the mattress, still in my clothes, holding fast to Mama's old pillowcase. I could feel the lonely arm of my ragdoll through the thin cloth. So many times I'd patched her up, plumping her again with sawdust and peanut shells I'd gathered from the doorstep of a beer hall, sewing her together with thread made from my hair and the needle I kept hidden in her belly.

Staring at the shadow where the slant of the roof came down to meet the floor, I put my nose to the pillowcase, breathing through the cloth like a baby nuzzling the sleeve of her mother's dress. It smelled of rosewater, Dr. Godfrey's cordial and money-drawing oil. Mama had taken to anointing herself with the latter, believing that the musty-smelling concoction would bring customers to our door.

Before taking me away, Mrs. Wentworth had placed a small, velvet bag in the middle of Mama's fortune-telling table. Tied up with a drawstring, its contents had sweetly jangled as it came to rest. It was Mama's payment for letting me go, a sum of good faith.

I wondered what the weight of the bag would feel like if I held it in my hand, and if any coins had spilled on the floor when Mama untied the string. Had a penny rolled into a crack between the boards, causing her to curse? Had she put the coins to her face to feel their coolness on her cheek?

By the age of five, I was stealing buckets of coal and bundles of sticks for Mama's tiny, rusted stove. I'd pumped bucket after bucket of water in the middle of our muddy, stinking courtyard, scrubbed other people's clothes and hung them up to dry—all the while hoping I'd wake up one morning to find my father had come back to us and Mama had turned into the lady on the side of the Pure and True

Laundry Flakes box. She was a round-faced mother dressed in calico, with a clean white apron around her waist. Her eyes smiled as she puckered her lips, forever kissing the top of her little girl's head. Along the hem of her skirt a slogan was written: *Mother, if you love her, you'll keep her clean.*

Mama must've had an amount in her head she wanted for me, a sum she considered right and fair—more than she'd got for my boots or her tortoiseshell combs or the trinket she wore around her neck, enough to buy the largest bottle of *Dr. Godfrey's* Mr. Piers had locked away in the old sea chest he strapped to the back of his cart.

How much did you get for me, Mama? I whispered in the dark.

8 am–the lady of the house rises for tea in her boudoir

Half-past eight–she dresses for breakfast

9 am–breakfast is served

10 am–the lady retires to the drawing room for correspondence

11 am–the lady dresses for luncheon

Noon–luncheon is served

Half-past one–the lady retires to the drawing room for reading and rest

3 o'clock–the lady dresses for afternoon promenade

Half past three–promenade commences

Five o'clock–the lady dresses for dinner

Six o'clock–dinner is served

Quarter past seven–the lady dresses for evening

Ten o'clock (or at the lady's leisure)–she is to be prepared for sleep

On **Tuesdays,** she receives callers

On **Thursdays,** she goes out

III.

I woke to see Mrs. Wentworth's housekeeper, Caroline, pouring water from a pitcher into a deep, waiting bowl. She glanced at me when she heard me stir, but didn't say a word.

Setting the pitcher aside, she stared at her reflection in a mirror that was hanging in front of her on the wall. The silver backing was cloudy and pitted, so that one half of her face– her neck, her mouth, her nose–was a streaky blur. One eye, steely and clear, blinked back at her, one cheek blushed ruddy in the morning sun that shone through the room's narrow skylight. The calico kerchief on her head wasn't nearly as fetching as the silk scarf Mama always wore, but the field of tiny cornflowers suited her, their cheerful blue petals making a welcome halo of softness around her stern countenance.

Thin-lipped and flat-chested, she bore all the signs of a woman whose labours had added to her years. Her hands were wrinkled, her nails ragged, her neck veined with impatience.

I watched as she scrubbed her face, as she slipped a drippy sponge under her skirts and up between her legs. After she finished, she gave a short nod in my direction indicating my turn at the basin.

"Thank you," I said, smiling and hoping for a smile in return. I wanted to get on her good side, since I was all but certain she'd be the one ordering me to scrub floors and polish silver.

As I went to the basin I introduced myself, but she ignored me, pretending to be busy with pinning a small tear in the hem of her skirt. When I asked how many other girls were in the house, she merely rolled her eyes and grunted.

"Lady's got herself another green one," she grumbled as she walked past me to the other side of the room.

Just by being here, it seemed, I'd already gone wrong.

Opening the door of a large wardrobe, Caroline brought out a maid's dress. Practical looking but pretty, it had a row of shiny buttons up the front, and matching lace collar and cuffs. She inspected the garment front and back and then laid it across my mattress. Going to the wardrobe a second time, she fetched a pair of boots from the bottom drawer and then placed them on the floor next to my bed.

"Thank you," I said again, making my voice as sweet as I could, hoping she'd forget herself and say something in reply. She did not.

Pulling the dress over my head, I caught the faint smell of sweat from the girl who'd worn it before me. *Who was she? Where was she now?*

Even second-hand, the dress was nicer than anything I'd ever owned. I couldn't help but admire the cut of it, how the pleats came racing down the front of the waist, how the buttons sat in a straight, neat row after I'd fastened them. Caroline gave me a sideways look, clearly trying to discern if the dress would suit. I turned in place, smoothing the brushed cotton cloth against my belly. She needn't have worried. The dress fit fine.

The boots, however, were another matter. Although they were polished and whole, the leather was stiff and unforgiving. As I slid my feet inside them, my toes poked through the holes in the ends of my stockings, rubbing against the boots, threatening to blister even before I stood up. Laces loose, they still felt tight. I took them off and put them on again, and then did it again, each time tugging at the ends of my stockings until the holes were tucked under my feet. Still, my toes found their way out to rub against the leather.

"Lady's got to have her tea by eight," Caroline said, heading for the door.

I gave up on the stockings and hurried to tie my boots. I followed her down the same flight of narrow stairs I'd come up with Nestor the night before, this time descending past the doorway to the main floor of the house and into the kitchen below.

Nestor was there, tending a fire in one of the three large stoves that lined one wall. "Good morning, Caroline," he said, greeting the housekeeper with a cheerful voice.

She responded with a distracted, "We'll see."

"Good morning, Miss Fenwick," he said, now turning to me, "I trust you slept well?"

"Yes, fine, sir," I replied, relieved to find he hadn't changed his ways towards me because of Caroline's attitude.

I looked around, thinking I might find at least one other maid preparing for the day, but there were only the three of us, Nestor, Caroline and me.

I watched as Caroline took a loaf of bread from a basket and began tearing it apart. She placed three metal soup bowls in front of her and put several hunks of bread into each one. When I stepped close and offered to help, she jabbed a sharp elbow into my ribs and shoved me aside.

Wincing, I decided to act as best I could on her nods and shrugs until she saw fit to direct me with her words.

Once the bowls were filled with bread, Caroline went to the cupboard and brought out a large, heavy crock. After removing the crock's lid, she took up a ladle and plunged it through the thick layer of fat that sat across the top of the pot. "One for you, one for you, one for you," she whispered to herself as she deftly poured ladlefuls of broth into the bowls. The ragged pieces of bread melted with the weight of the liquid, turning moist and brown. Caroline looked at the last bowl with a great deal of satisfaction. She hadn't spilled a drop.

"Have some, Nestor," she called out to the butler, presenting him with his serving before I could get to it.

Nestor took the bowl from her hands and then sat down at the wooden table in the centre of the room. Catching my eye, he gestured for me to do the same. I hesitated, and shook my head, thinking I should wait for Caroline to take hers first.

The mere sight of food had started my belly rumbling. The thought that bread could be kept in a house with no danger of it summoning a pack of rats was nothing short of a miracle to me. *How much food was there?* It seemed to be coming out of every cupboard and corner and I imagined that if I could steal into the kitchen without anyone knowing, I could take whatever I wanted. Sitting in the middle of the floor, I'd eat until crumbs and grease were dripping from my chin.

"I took the liberty of filling the kettle for the lady's tea," Nestor informed Caroline before lifting his bowl to his lips. "It should be plenty hot by now."

"That's fine," she replied, bringing out a silver tea service and placing it on a tray at the other end of the table.

I waited for a moment when I might be of use to her. This, however, only caused more trouble. The next time she turned around we were nose to nose and I could see by her scowl that my persistence had angered her. She brushed past me in a huff, and I gave up, taking one of the remaining bowls of bread and broth and sitting down across from Nestor. His eyes crinkled into a smile as I settled in my chair.

Free from my hovering, Caroline glided between table and cupboards, artfully arranging delicate bowls and plates, filling them with sugar and milk, grapes and pears. Now that there was distance between us, I could see she had a sense of grace about her. Like the tiny wooden woman who inhabited the cuckoo clock in the window of the jeweller's shop on Second Avenue, her waist was constantly moving in sympathy with her skirts, turning round first this way, then that.

"Where'd the lady get to last night?" she asked Nestor as she snipped at the stems on a bunch of grapes with a small pair of scissors.

"Chrystie Street, I believe," he answered, looking to me for confirmation.

I gave him a nod before taking a sip of broth. It tasted of beef, rich with salt and onion, so good I forgot myself. Gulping and slurping, I carried on until every bit of the bread had slithered down my throat.

"Went slumming again, did she?" Caroline asked, one eyebrow arching. "You think she would've learned, after the last one . . ."

Staring at Caroline, Nestor tipped the edge of his bowl against the table with his finger. The last of its contents spilled out from it, running in a stream, straight towards a folded, white napkin that the housekeeper hadn't yet placed on the tray.

"Chrystie Street," she muttered as she scrambled to rescue the napkin. "Never heard of it . . . sure hope it's better than *Ludlow*."

If she'd bothered to ask me, I would've said with great confidence that it was. I would have told her that the people on Chrystie Street were a cut above, that everything they did was a matter of pride, and that if she'd never been there, she was all the poorer because of it.

I would've been lying, of course. While Ludlow and Chrystie streets both had their share of falling-down tenements, Ludlow had sewers and Chrystie Street had none. All slums are not created equal.

When Caroline turned away, Nestor nicked a pear from the bowl of fruit sitting on the tea tray. Cutting it into slices with his pocket knife, he offered me a piece. Made bold by Caroline's disdain, I took it.

The fruit was sweet and juicy in my mouth, not like the mealy, past-ripe pears sold on street corners or at Tompkins Market. Those pears floated in buckets of syrup for weeks at a time, young girls selling them with false promises of "fresh firm fruits from the farm—just picked today . . ."

As Nestor's long, sly fingers came towards me with another slice, I thought of my father. He, too, was a thief. Mama always swore that he'd stolen both her and a horse from right under my grandfather's nose in broad daylight. "Stealing a horse from a Gypsy is no easy feat," she'd say, closing her eyes in bliss and sadness whenever she brought the memory to mind. I'd supposed all kinds of things about my father when I was young. In my dreams, he never appeared on Chrystie Street. Instead, he was always dancing around the apothecary's pear tree, pouring sugar from Mama's silver bowl down between the tree's roots. "I like my pears sweet," he'd say just before he would disappear.

As I reached to take the last slice from Nestor, I caught sight of Caroline's hand coming towards me, a wooden spoon clenched in her fist. Before I could move, she smacked the spoon on the table, so hard it made me jump. "Damn fly," she said, staring right at me.

Nestor let out a nervous chuckle and said, "Poor thing never had a chance."

Sour-faced, Caroline had opened her mouth to scold him, when she was interrupted by three sharp rings coming from a row of bells strung along the wall by the stairs. Each of the bells had been labelled for a room in the house— *parlour, study, dining hall, foyer, master's chamber, bath, library, conservatory* . . . When the ringing came again, I saw that it was from the bell marked *lady's chamber*.

Nestor stood and took up the tea tray. "Three bells are for the lady's maid," he said. "Come along, Miss Fenwick. That's you."

My toes burned inside my boots as I got to my feet, making me feel as if the shoes had gotten even smaller in the short time I'd been sitting at the table. Caroline's gaze followed me as I moved to join Nestor.

"Good luck with Chrystie Street," she called to the butler, still holding tight to her spoon as we went out the door.

The elite do not wear the same dress twice. If you can tell us how many receptions she has in a year, how many weddings she attends, how many balls she participates in, how many dinners she gives, how many parties she goes to, how many operas or theatres she patronizes, we can approximate somewhat to the cost and size of her wardrobe. It is not unreasonable to suppose that she has two new dresses of some sort for every day in the year, or seven hundred and twenty. Now to purchase all these, to order them made and to put them on afterward consumes a vast amount of time. Indeed, the woman of society does little but doff and don dry goods.

–George Ellington, *Women of New York: or, Social Life in the Great City, 1870*

IV.

Mama's bustle was an old flour sack stuffed with straw that she'd coax into shape whenever she was going out to see Mr. Piers. She didn't have many dresses to choose from, but she always saved her best for him. It was cotton chintz, with a long row of buttons up the back. I loved seeing her bring it out, because it meant she would need me to help her dress.

After I'd fastened the last button, Mama would take her cracked hand mirror and sit with me on the edge of the bed.

Pointing to her reflection, she'd show me how a person's eyes dart to the side when they lie. "Beware a woman who's slow to smile, she's sure to be holding a grudge."

I didn't much care about what Mama had to say, I was just happy to be near her without thinking I was about to catch it, glad to look at her dark eyes and the sureness of her mouth. After a while she'd go quiet and stare at her face like it wasn't her own. "See that spot there on my cheek? That mark was given to me when I was born. It means I was meant for something great." Then she'd touch the spot with her fingertip. "It's fading now," she'd whisper. "I'm fading away."

The daily grooming rituals Mrs. Wentworth undertook were to remain, as best as I could manage, invisible. "Still," Nestor explained as we climbed the stairs to her bedroom, "if one observes carefully, you can see the subtle fruits of a maid's labours displayed on her lady's person. It's in her visage, the confidence she carries on her face. If her hat never loses purchase on her head, it is a tribute to you. If her skirts brush the toes of her shoes without ever tripping her up, then you may rest easy at the end of the day.

"Your role is quite simple," he said. "Comb the lady's hair, read to her, serve her tea, help her dress: be whatever she requires,

Helpless to the whims of fashion, a true lady always requires assistance in dressing. She must have at her disposal (at the very least) a second pair of willing hands. A woman without the means to properly look after herself might as well withdraw from society, for she will never be "looked after" by her equals or by any self-respecting gentleman. One public gaffe, or ill-managed piece of attire and she is left to embarrassment, sentenced to make her way between parties and parlours, alone. Each new day, every new gown, presents the opportunity of elevation or disgrace.

whenever she requires it. You, my dear, are the foil behind the button."

I stopped short in the middle of the corridor, thinking I could never live up to such high expectations. Mama must have misunderstood what it was that Mrs. Wentworth wanted in a girl. Had she known, I was sure she wouldn't have sent me away.

"Miss Fenwick?" Nestor said, turning back with a look of concern. "Are you all right?"

"Yes, sir," I answered, palms sweating, feet aching. I'd assumed I'd be cooking and cleaning, not seeing after Mrs. Wentworth's personal needs.

"You'll do fine," Nestor reassured me. "Much better than the last girl, I'm certain of it. Miss Piggott she was called. The poor thing was always at a loss, even when it came to the simplest of tasks. I can't blame Caroline for the cruelty she inflicted on that one. I assure you the child brought it upon herself. She put Mrs. Wentworth in a terrible state, making Caroline's life even more difficult than it already is."

Looking at the floor, I tried to will the queasiness in my belly to stop.

"Come now, Miss Fenwick, don't worry," Nestor said. "What Caroline put you through this morning was nothing but a test. She'll come around, you'll see. Besides, Mrs. Wentworth's the one who put Caroline out of sorts, not you. In all the years that she's served in this house, the poor woman has never once been considered for the position of lady's maid. She gets passed over for the job every time, and it upsets her beyond belief. I've told her she mustn't dwell on it, that it's simply a matter of Mrs. Wentworth preferring to have a younger, more impressionable girl by her side, but she won't hear it."

As we approached the door, Nestor lowered his voice and gave me a final list of instructions. "Be sure to add hot tea to her cup whenever she lets it rest for more than five minutes. Place her napkin in her lap, folded in half, tip to tip, the point facing to the ground. Mrs. Wentworth doesn't approve of having it the other way around, she says it makes her feel like a dagger's coming right for her. Always inquire as to how much sugar she'd like in her tea, even though her answer will always be the same—*none*. Assure her that Caroline is happily preparing her eggs just as she likes (poached, with an inch of moon around the yolk) and that there will be toast points to accompany them, and marmalade, and—"

My face must have shown the trouble I was having in trying to commit Nestor's words to memory, because he stopped mid-sentence. "Forget the marmalade and the toast points. Don't fret, my dear, morning tea is easily pantomimed. The only thing you need remember is to have a bit of grace and common sense."

Mrs. Wentworth was sitting in a chair next to her tea table when I entered the room, her hair pulled back in a tight bun, her mouth set in a frown. The taffeta dressing gown she was wearing rustled with her every movement, echoing her impatience. "Place the tray on the stand," she ordered. "I want only dishes on the table."

"Yes, ma'am," I replied, following her directions as best I could.

Like every other little girl in the world, I'd often played at tea-time and again, making a watery *shoosh* between my lips while pouring steaming make-believe brew out of thin air, or pinching the handle of an invisible cup between my fingers as I chatted about the weather with Miss Sweet and Mama's iron dog doorstop.

Like Caroline with her broth, I spilled no drops, made no mistakes. I smiled and bowed and spoke softly to Mrs. Wentworth, thinking all the while that if Caroline had been there to witness my performance, her hatred for me would've caused a bitter stream of words at least a mile long to issue from her mouth.

The hardest task in it all was keeping my mind on my duties while standing in the most glorious place I'd ever seen. Mama's rooms on Chrystie Street could've fit inside Mrs. Wentworth's dressing quarters three times over. There was enough space in the bedroom alone for two fainting couches, a table with three chairs, a dressing table with a large, round mirror attached, and an enormous, canopied bed, with spiralling posts that soared clear to the ceiling. Dressed in every possible shade of pink—rosebud, blush, salt-water taffy, tip-of-the-tongue—the bed was laden with pillows and blankets of quilted silk and satin.

Embroidered velvet curtains lined the room's tall windows, the heavy panels pulled shut against the outside world. The mantel of the fireplace was decked with a row of twinned treasures: a pair of porcelain pheasants with clocks in their bellies, two matching ginger jars, two lamps with rose-coloured globes sparkling with the steady glow of gaslight. The whole room was filled with beautiful things, every last one of them perfect and right. If Mama had known about this place, she would've prayed every night for it to go up in flames, just so she could tiptoe through the embers and take whatever was left behind.

"I've gone to the trouble of setting out my morning attire," Mrs. Wentworth announced after finishing her tea. "I'll do this with my wardrobe for the rest of today, but starting tomorrow, you'll be responsible for my *toilette* in its entirety. Do you understand?"

Still staring at one of the pheasants, I wondered what it would be like to wake up one morning and find your insides ticking away.

Mrs. Wentworth cleared her throat and repeated her question. "Do you understand?"

"Yes, ma'am," I replied, looking at the heap of clothing that had been carefully piled on one of the couches. I'd been able to make fair guesses with the tea, but all that tulle and lace was daunting. I wasn't quite sure where to begin.

"My corset," Mrs. Wentworth ordered, taking off her dressing gown and revealing that she was already wearing pantaloons and a chemise. Lifting her arms above her head, she waited for me to fetch the thing and bring it around her body. I pushed at the stays from the sides, working to fasten the corset's clasps up her front.

Her breasts were huddled and heaving before I'd even tied the satin bow at the top, but when I turned to fetch the next piece of clothing, she scolded me and called me back to her. "You must tighten the laces," she said, as she took hold of a bedpost for support.

I went behind her and tugged at the laces one by one, working my way from top to bottom. A quiet creaking could be heard, the sound of shifting bone. I began to sweat, not knowing if the sound was human or whale, living or dead.

"Don't be so cautious, child," the lady scolded. "You can go tighter, much tighter. I didn't spend years corset training for nothing. Strict lacing afforded me this figure and I dare say my husband as well."

"Yes, ma'am," I replied.

"Perhaps you should pick up the pace," she complained. "I fear it will be supper hour before I get into my breakfast clothes."

Several mounds of ruffled cotton and silk still remained on the couch, all a prelude to her dress.

"They aren't choices," Mrs. Wentworth said with an impatient sigh.

As I picked up the underskirt that I thought should come next, Mrs. Wentworth shook her head, clucking her disapproval.

When I tried again, but made yet another wrong decision, her face flushed and she said, "Your mother told me you knew how to dress a lady."

"Please, ma'am," I said, taking up the last petticoat and clutching it in my hands. "I can learn."

Certain that I'd already disappointed her beyond a second chance, I waited for her to dismiss me and turn me out of the house. Instead, her gaze softened, and a gentle smile spread across her face.

"Kiss my cheek and all will be forgiven," she said as she bent towards me.

Mama had never allowed me to kiss her. She said that kissing was something people took far too lightly, and that the genuine affection that was meant to occur when lips met flesh had long ago been lost. For a moment, I wondered if Mrs. Wentworth, like Caroline, was giving me some sort of strange test.

"Go on, child, do as I say."

My lips touched her pillowy cheek, and I found myself inhaling the heady scent of flowers. It wasn't like Mama's rosewater or her lavender soap. This was spicy and strong, like nothing I'd ever known.

Next to the broth Caroline had served, Mrs. Wentworth's perfume was the only other scent that had gotten my attention since I'd arrived. The house seemed almost without smells at all, pleasant or foul, leaving me to wonder if the upper class existed on a different sort of air from the rest of the world, a breeze piped into their homes from above the clouds, so clean you had to pay for it.

As I made to move away from her, Mrs. Wentworth reached out and took my chin in her hand. "What a face you have," she said. "So willing and so full of promise."

She fixed her gaze on me, but I couldn't bring myself to return it. Instead, I settled on looking at the ribbon that trimmed the edge of her corset. The entire garment was adorned with pink lace and ruffles of a shade that matched the canopy over her bed. The longer I stared at it, the more I wished it were mine.

I'd asked Mama a hundred times for a corset. "Even the kind with rope for stays would do," I'd begged. But Mama knew as well as I did that a corset was the surest way to turn a girl into a woman before her time. It brings the body into a desirable shape, taking a girl's breath away,

While many women believe in the powers of the corset—to create a diminished waist, heaving bosoms, and an accentuated female form—science has proven that this insidious garment is no friend to the fairer sex. Constipation, indigestion, shortness of breath, and fractured ribs, are the least of the injuries caused by the device. Over time, it causes internal organs to become misshapen and displaced, greatly diminishing the volume of the lungs and pressing the liver violently upward, threatening imminent bisection." –from *Against the Corset*, by Dr. S. Fonda (See figure 1.)

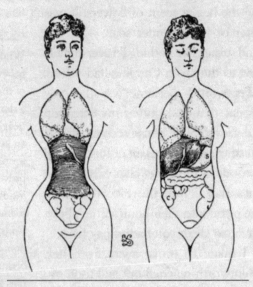

Fig. 1

causing her to dream of whirling around a dance floor or riding a galloping horse–her only chances to fly.

All the dresses I'd ever worn had been made for a girl, with buttons up the front, or a short row down the back that could be fastened easily at the nape of the neck. They were second-hand dresses bought a bit too large, with hems that could be taken up, and later let down. The frock I'd brought with me from home was one I'd found sticking out from between two crates behind Mr. Goodwin's shop. I'd spotted the skirt first, its sad ruffle coming apart, snaking down into a muddy puddle. Both the sleeves had been torn as well, but aside from the mottled way the fine-checked gingham had faded, there was nothing that couldn't be repaired. Much to Mama's dismay, I'd filled it out nicely, my breasts looking like more than two knobby lumps, my hips almost round enough to rest a basket on when I walked.

"You favour your mother," Mrs. Wentworth said, still staring at me. "You have her lovely dark hair and eyes." Trying to get me to look up at her she asked, "Tell me, who were her people?"

The ladies who went slumming on Chrystie Street often asked the same question of me. Perfectly fashionable and modestly snobbish, they came from parish halls and ladies' societies or on behalf of Miss Jane Clattermore's Home for Wandering Girls to peer into our windows and our lives, one hand holding the front of a skirt, the other keeping a peppermint-scented handkerchief to the nose. "Poor little dears," they called us children, as they dropped pennies into our hands, taking care not to touch us.

I hated them almost as much as I hated the surly, knock-kneed boys who hissed at me and called me "dirty little Gyp." They'd yell after me from down the street, telling me to wash the ugly off my face and go back where I came from. I'd run home feeling sad and angry, and scrub my face with salt until it burned, wishing that at least one of them would fall in love with me and that all the rest would die.

"Just stay away from them," Mama would say, throwing up her hands at my tears. "And stop stealing my salt. You're never going to be a golden-haired Alice with a long neck and freckled skin. You've got the Black Dutch in you."

I'd liked the way the words had sounded coming out from Mama's mouth, *Black Dutch*–rude and proud all at once, like her. The Jews and Gypsies and Swarthy Germans all claimed Black Dutch for themselves. It meant that however they looked, they could be whatever they liked, that they had good beginnings and acceptable blood.

"Don't be shy now," Mrs. Wentworth urged. "You can tell me."

Mama's voice echoed in my head, but the words that had once seemed so defiant, so sure, now felt like they had little to do with me. My skin and my heart were never the same as hers. They were fairer, perhaps even weaker, somewhere in between her Gypsy blood and my father's unknown roots.

"Black Dutch," I answered. "My mother's Black Dutch."

Dearest Mama,

I am doing my best to please Mrs. Wentworth.

I hope my wage proves to be enough.

Did you know I was to be a lady's maid?

It's better than serving in the scullery, but more

difficult than you can imagine.

I have much to learn.

I miss you.

I miss hearing my name.

Your daughter,

Moth

V.

Mr. Wentworth's portrait graced the wall of Mrs. Wentworth's sitting room—a grand-looking likeness of the man, set to stare at his wife's back while she was seated at her desk. The collar of his shirt was stiff and high, wrapped round with a tie so full it nearly covered his chin. What the tie couldn't conceal (even under the careful hand of the artist) was the weary slant of Mr. Wentworth's jaw. The dour-faced gentleman's eyes were dark and searching and had far more to say about regret than accomplishment. Seated in a chair that was larger and more imposing than the one paired with his wife's desk, Mr. Wentworth had a walking stick in his hand and an eager-faced hound at his side. Both the dog and its master were curiously absent from the house and Mrs. Wentworth's life.

The first time I entered the sitting room was to serve the lady her afternoon tea. I found Mrs. Wentworth standing and gazing at the painting. Before taking her chair she approached the portrait, touched the edge of its frame and said, "I'm waiting." Her voice was steady, her lips not quite turned into a half-smile.

Halfway through the hour, Mrs. Wentworth took up the fan that was dangling from her wrist and tapped it on the arm of her chair. After gaining my attention, she touched the tip of the fan to her cheek. I thought she meant to show me a drop of tea that was lingering there, so I quickly reached for a napkin and moved to wipe her face.

Waving the napkin away as I came near, she shook her head with disapproval. "You're to kiss me, not clean me," she scolded.

"Yes, ma'am," I replied, giving a short bow before bending to bring my lips to her cheek. It was a kiss given in haste, and far less gentle than the one I'd placed on her cheek that morning.

Grabbing me by the arm she held me fast and said, "You should've known what I wanted."

"I'm sorry, Mrs. Wentworth," I whimpered, hoping she'd soon let go.

She did not.

My awkward and tardy show of affection had caused her to lose all patience and she meant to punish me for it.

"Kneel down and bare your wrists," she ordered, her eyes narrow with anger.

Frightened by this change in her, I pushed the sleeves

of my dress past my elbows, knelt and held my arms out.

"It's the soft of them I want," she complained, circling her fan in the air to show she wished for me to turn them over. "And you're to keep your hands open, no fists."

Unsure of what might happen if I refused, I did as I was told.

"That's better," she said, as she raised her hand, the fan tight in her grip. Then she brought the thick of the fan's guard down on my arms, so hard I couldn't help but cry out. I knew she didn't mean to stop.

"Please," I said, wincing from the pain the blow had left behind. "I'll do better, I promise—"

But she paid no attention to my pleas. Five, six, seven stripes appeared as she continued to smack the tender part of my wrists, red lines burning in a row. Mr. Wentworth and his dog looked out from the portrait, eyes blind to the cruelty that was being heaped upon me and the tears coming down my cheeks.

Mrs. Wentworth had chosen the fan that morning out of a drawer filled with gloves and garters. It was a beautiful thing, the sticks and guard made of bone, the image of a dragon painted on its silk—tail snaking around, eyes wide, tongue lashing out.

The look on the dragon's face had reminded me of a dead horse I'd once seen on the side of the street when I was small. Two men had been arguing over the animal—one grousing over who should have to dispose of it, the other muttering of secret poisonings and evil deeds. A gang of guttersnipes soon gathered, pushing and shoving, daring one another to touch it, take its eyes, even piss in its mouth. The horse's head was nearly larger than the whole of me, but I walked right past the bickering men and sat down next to the poor creature. Curling up in the curve of its neck, I shooed away the flies so I could marvel at its eyelashes and stroke its velvety nose. My bare knee touched its skin, rubbing against the wormy scars that had been left behind by its master's whip. "Sleep well," I said to the horse thinking it deserved at least a bit of kindness.

When she was done, Mrs. Wentworth ran her hand along the length of my arm, fingers gliding over my stinging flesh. She clasped her hand around my wrist and pushed her thumb into one of the marks she'd made. "Now you'll know better," she said, as she tightened her grip and watched me flinch.

"Yes, ma'am," I said, salty tears on my lips.

The imprint of her fingers blossomed white after she let go, then faded away.

"I'd like some shortbread now," she said, straightening her shoulders and picking up her teacup.

Afraid to stop to wipe my eyes, I stood up, the room blurry before me. I fumbled to place the plate of biscuits in front of her so she wouldn't have to reach for them.

Rather than taking one of the squares, she folded her hands in her lap and stared up at me. "From *your* hand," she ordered, making it clear she intended for me to feed her. "I don't like getting butter on my fingers."

"Yes, ma'am," I said, picking up a piece of shortbread by the edges and bringing it to her lips.

To my dismay, she chose to make a meal of it, nibbling at the biscuit in tiny bites, licking at my fingertips for the last of the crumbs. When she was finished, she smiled and said, "I quite like forgetting where I end and you begin."

From then on, with her every complaint, out came the fan.

I was the one to dress her, so I was responsible for making certain it was always on her person, secure around her wrist. She'd strike me with it whenever it pleased her to do so. If I winced, or made any sound at all, she'd hit me again, twice as hard. The more attention I gave her, the more she required. I was to hold her hand until she fell asleep at night, wash every inch of her when she bathed. Turned-down sheets and pinned-up ringlets (no matter how deftly placed) never satisfied her for long. She wanted more. Without any gentle words on her part, she expected to be showered with affection. "Show your devotion, Miss Fenwick," she'd say several times throughout the day, pointing the fan to her cheek. She had a Sybil's sense for detecting half-heartedness, and try as I might, my attentions were never soft or sincere enough to please her. She did not hold back in showing her disappointment.

The insides of my arms grew raw, and soon became mottled in shades of yellow, green and blue. According to how many times she'd hit me the hour, the day, the week before, spidery lines of purple and red formed like lace around the edges of my bruises.

Mama had, on occasion, left a dark bruise on my ear or in the fleshy part of my arm where she'd pinched me too hard, but even at her worst, she'd never been set on hurting me like this. Every time Mrs. Wentworth came at me, I thought of Mama. I prayed she'd walk through the door and put a stop to Mrs. Wentworth's meanness. I dreamed she'd take the woman by the hair and give her a fierce pounding–cursing, spitting and screaming, "I won't let you treat my girl that way."

But Mama could never know. I was tied to Mrs. Wentworth now. The wage they had agreed upon was meant to keep Mama alive. If I ran away, I feared Mrs. Wentworth would come after Mama. She'd be left with nothing–no clothes to wear, no place to sleep, no food in her belly. My bruises were a small price to pay.

Caroline still hadn't seen fit to speak to me directly, and although Nestor had told me time and again not to worry about it, I couldn't help wishing she'd change her mind. "Maybe Chrystie Street can get that for you," she'd say whenever Nestor asked her to pass the pitcher of milk from across the table, not quite speaking to me, but almost. Calling out in the dark whenever she thought I was listening to her talk herself to sleep she'd grouse, "Chrystie Street should mind her own business."

I missed the kind of talk that went on between women– over the course of an hour's worth of chores, at the clothesline in the courtyard, on front stoops in the evening. The women of Chrystie Street were generous with their stories and their gossip, even when there was no fondness between them. Fast friends one minute, enemies the next, it made no difference to them.

Nestor did his best to make life bearable. We did not talk of Mrs. Wentworth's cruelty or of the things she did to me behind closed doors. Instead, we spent late nights in the kitchen after Caroline had gone to sleep, raiding the larder and bragging about our "worsts"–the worst fight he'd ever been in, the worst thing I'd ever found rotting in a trash barrel.

He said he'd been raised on Old St. Nichol Street in the East End of London, a place where rats dine better than people, a place that sounded an awful lot like Chrystie Street to me. He went on to say that the only thing that had saved him from ending up in the gutter like the other St. Nichol lads was "meetin' my dear Polly one evening at church."

His girl's name was Miss Paulette Saxby, and according to Nestor, she was the prettiest and kindest soul he'd ever met. "Don't know what she sees in a sod like me," he liked to joke, his hearty laughter there, then gone, as memories of Polly took over his thoughts.

Not long after the pair met, Nestor decided to make his way across the Atlantic to America. Hearing there were untold riches to be had in New York and points farther west, he convinced Polly that his going was their best chance to start a new life together. As much as he'd hated to leave her behind, he knew it was better she stay with her family until he got settled in a place they could call their own.

He wrote to her nearly every night, penning letters to be sent out in the next morning's post. *I'll bring you here one day soon, my love, I promise. Until then, thoughts of you warm my bones and my heart as I write, as I wait for your reply.*

I'd known how to read for as long as I could remember, having figured out, first, the words Mama used on her notices, and then others as she read me ads from the paper. She'd run her finger along the text and say the words under her breath—*curious, clean, lily-white, good, sweet, amazing!* I soon knew all the words that got painted on signs or the sides of buildings, and anything to do with soap or baked goods, yet

I'd never learned to use a pen. The only writing I'd ever done was to make my name in the dirt with a stick. Lines and hatches beside a game of hopscotch, M-O-T-H written to the right of the numbered court, my O looking lopsided and strange next to Eliza Adler's graceful script that swirled inside the arch at the top spelling out the word *Home*.

Sometimes Mama would tell a woman who came to have her fortune told to write something down on a piece of paper. It was usually the name of a man, one whose affections might be turned, or who had wronged her, or who owed her money. The bits of paper she used for the ritual were tiny enough to hide inside a pocket-watch or, in the case of needing to forget the man, to be burned in a candle flame.

Pen and ink were luxuries, so Mama guarded them, even from me, keeping them locked inside an old wooden tea caddy. The box was one of her fire treasures, found intact but without a key. To open it, she'd insert a bent hatpin in the keyhole and give gentle tics with her wrist until it unlocked. There, nestled between the bottle and nibs were three small rolls of paper she'd cut from the margins and edges of the *Evening Star* and then carefully wound onto empty thread spools. Delicate and creamy, one edge evenly (barely) scalloped, it looked just as beautiful as fine French ribbon.

The paper Nestor used to write to Polly had been given to him by Mr. Wentworth. Each sheet was perfectly square at the corners and embossed at the top with a proud, weighty *W*. The envelopes had the same mark on the flap. It seemed to me that London was a terribly long way for a letter to travel, but Nestor assured me that far lesser paper had made the journey there and back. He showed me one of Polly's letters to prove it, her words of love scrawled across sheets so thin the ink had bled through to the other side, making them nearly impossible to read. *The day will come, my dearest, when we will have no use for pen and paper. We'll be too occupied with being in each other's arms. Your adoring Polly.*

After Nestor finished his letter to Polly for the night, he'd guide me through lessons in penmanship. He watched over me as I looped *L* after *L, O* after *O,* learning to connect letters together.

I felt guilty when I dipped the pen, thinking I should offer him something for his kindness. I had only bits of myself to give (a kiss, a touch), but he asked nothing in return. He smelled like pipe tobacco and Macassar oil, of warmth and somewhere far away. At first I wished he were my father, then, later, I wished I were his Polly. Neither thing was right or good, but my affection for him knew nothing of manners.

In Nestor's company, I forgot Mrs. Wentworth and the pain she gave me, at least for a little while. I'd stay at the table long after I should've been in bed, turning my name into a feat of curves, the pen never coming off the page until the final upturn of the *h,* trying to impress him.

There is much to be learned from the ebb and flow of a lady's script. No matter her words—all her hopes, schemes, aspirations, and inclinations are coded within her hand. Aside from the obvious cues of station set forth by the quality of the paper and ink, the writer gives further indications of her identity away when she puts pen to paper. Swift, short lines indicate distraction, bold strokes given to words such as *Dearest, Yours,* and *until* are hallmarks of true affection. Shakiness of script often portends weakness of constitution or mind.

"She'll like it, won't she?" I asked him, before gently blowing sand off a letter I was writing to Mama. In my heart I knew it was the sort of thing she'd find to be a waste of time, but it meant everything to me, the words having come from my heart to my hand to the page, a bit of myself about to be folded square and sent back home.

"I should think she'll like it very much," Nestor answered, his voice filled with confidence and perhaps even a little pride.

Standing behind me, he placed a hand on my shoulder and looked down at my work. I'd turned the cuff of my sleeve back so as not to smudge the ink, and when I glanced up at him, I caught his gaze shifting from the page to the bruises on my wrist.

"You're not hers," he said, staring at the marks on my arm. "She doesn't own you."

I'd once watched Mama work a spell to help a woman break free from a bad situation; the woman's man had beaten her, and she said he simply wasn't the same to her anymore. Out of a page from the *Evening Star,* Mama made a charm for the lady to take home and burn in a candle's flame—a perfect heart within a heart, cut from the centre fold of the newsprint and marked with the man's name. "Repeat the words *I'm not yours* while the heart burns away. Don't stop until it's turned to ashes, or all will be ruined."

After the woman left the house, I crawled under Mama's table and collected all the scraps of paper that had fallen to the floor. I took the largest piece and used it to make a string of wishing dolls. Folding the paper back and forth, I wondered if there was enough of Mama's magic left on the page to make a wish come true. With rusted scissors I cut through the folds, curving the paper around, whispering my heart's desire until the figure of a girl appeared. Taking her tiny arms in my fingers, I pulled a dozen sisters between my hands, each one passing my wish, one to the other, secretly multiplying my chances of success. "I don't want to belong to anyone," I told the fluttering string of paper girls before hiding them under a loose floorboard by Mama's bed.

"I can get you out of here," Nestor now whispered in my ear. "Just tell me when you want to go, and it's done."

His words made my heart race. A kindness like that would require everything I had to give. Even if he didn't ask, I would have to offer. I thought of him holding me and stroking my hair and giving me warm, soft kisses along the nape of my neck. I'd let him call me Polly. I would never tell.

"Miss Fenwick, did you hear me?" he asked. "I'm offering my help."

"I can't leave," I said, pushing away from the table. "My mama needs me to stay here."

In the prison cell I sit,
Thinking Mother dear of you,
and our bright and happy home so far away.
And the tears they fill my eyes,
spite of all that I can do,
though I try to cheer my comrades and be gay.
–from *The Prisoner's Hope*, George Foot, 1864

VI.

Mrs. Wentworth's punishments grew worse. In addition to smacking my wrists, she took to slapping me across the face, turning the large agate ring she often wore to the inside of her hand before letting loose her anger. "You need discipline," she'd explained over my tears, "if you wish to become a perfect maid."

She never went out and no one came to call. All the drapes were drawn, and every room was kept in a constant state of shadow. The only traces of sunlight I ever saw were the slanted rays that came through the skylight in the quarters that Caroline and I shared. Our view was a clueless bit of sky that told me nothing of where I was, and refused to show me anything outside of predicting the threat of rain.

Nestor hid his feelings well in Mrs. Wentworth's presence, but it was soon clear

Women of certain station make a point of leaving the city (preferably by the end of May) to avoid the unpleasantness of summer. Outings to Macy's and dinners at Delmonico's are abandoned, replaced by botany walks in the countryside and . . .

64

to me that he despised her. He could hardly mention her without some tic of disdain—his leg restlessly twitching under the table, or his nose wrinkling up as if he'd just gotten too heavy a whiff of dung. He'd gone so far as to say she'd done something terrible in her husband's eyes, but had refused to discuss the matter any further.

"She's been an embarrassment to him."

"What sort of embarrassment?"

"The sort that causes a gentleman to loathe even the sight of his wife."

"Please, Nestor, go on," I'd begged, wanting to know if Mrs. Wentworth had committed a crime worse than anything she'd done to me.

"Being an honourable man, I find her actions too coarse for conversation. To say she acted poorly is enough."

"But . . ." I wanted him to tell me more.

"That is all, Miss Fenwick," he said.

As punishment for his wife's mysterious misbehaviour, Mr. Wentworth had demanded that she cut her summering short. She could plead sickness, or say she was visiting relatives abroad, or whatever she liked, so long as the house had the appearance of being empty for the summer. All the doors to the outside were kept locked from within and only Nestor was allowed to have the keys. "The lady is required to carry out the illusion that she has not yet returned home," he explained. Only upon Mr. Wentworth's arrival

. . . endless hands of whist. The spring of 1871 brought news of "Paris gone wild," and many ladies' long-planned European tours were cancelled. The unrest in France soon became an inviting (and fashionable) excuse for any change in a woman's social calendar, bringing on stories of visits with long-lost cousins and reunions with "old friends." Still, there were enough Baronesses (real and imagined) both in New York and elsewhere, who were only too happy to reveal the true whereabouts of any lady who was inclined to manufacture the truth.

would Mrs. Wentworth be permitted to officially declare herself to be "at home."

Until then, she would have to spend her days fretting and wandering through the house.

Weeks passed, and still, despite my efforts, I failed to please her. Although I'd chosen not to make anything more of Nestor's offer to assist me, I couldn't help but entertain thoughts of escape.

I'd sent several letters to Mama, but hadn't gotten a reply. Her silence made me wonder if something had gone wrong. Lying awake at night I imagined her belly-up in a gutter or dizzy-headed on the roof, half gone on a bottle of Dr. Godfrey's cordial. I longed for her to send word that she was now making ends meet, so I could walk out Mrs. Wentworth's door, my head held high.

> *Dearest Mama,*
> *I am anxious for your reply. I trust that you are well—*

One night, when Mrs. Wentworth sent me to retrieve a book of sayings and quotations for her, I'd discovered a silent, dusky room hidden on the other side of a pocket door in the back of the library. Compared to the lady's sitting room it was a small space, but its panelled walls and bearskin rug made it feel important nonetheless. The scents of stale tobacco and a hearth gone cold filled the room. I'd stumbled into Mr. Wentworth's study.

For a brief moment, I settled myself in the chair behind his desk and clutched the ends of its arms. They were carved in the shape of an animal's paws, a lion or tiger perhaps, so large my fingers nearly disappeared in the spaces between the wooden claws. Sliding open the drawer that was in front of me, I peered in, inspecting its contents. A few pens rolled to the edge of the drawer, out from under a scattered pile of letters and receipts. Sticking out from the mass of papers was the end of a ribbon, pink and soft and sweet. When I took it from the place where it was hiding, I found it was made from a wide band of velvet with a large bow fixed to the centre. I couldn't imagine Mrs. Wentworth ever wearing such a thing in her hair: it was made for a girl rather than a woman. Stroking it, I wondered if Mr. Wentworth had known his wife all her life, or if perhaps they'd had a child, a little girl who was now gone. Either way, the man had tucked the ribbon away for safe keeping, hidden from sight, but not forgotten. I carefully returned it to its hiding place.

Several books were stacked on the edge of Mr. Wentworth's wide desk with a large globe sitting next to them. I put my hand to the globe's yellowed surface and spun it around on its stand as I read the titles of the books. *Tribal Peoples of the World, A Gentleman's Companion to New York City, The Witches of New York* . . .

A Gentleman's Companion was a mystery. The insides of the book had been mangled and every second page was missing. *Tribal Peoples* was an album of cabinet cards, mostly picturing women, bare chested and frowning. A ribbon had been placed partway through the collection and its red dye had bled, leaving a mark on the tissue paper that was meant to protect the image underneath. *Estelle Lavoraux* was the name of the young woman beneath the thin page. Wearing a woven band across her forehead, she had a proud, confident look about her and menacing eyes. I could tell by the oily smudge at the picture's corner that Mr. Wentworth favoured her image over the rest.

The Witches of New York was the book I'd found most intriguing. Listing addresses from Broome to Nineteenth Street, it claimed to be a reliable guide to the soothsayers of the city. I put it on the top of the stack, planning to come back for it later to search for Mama in its pages.

Later that evening Nestor and I were sitting at the table in the kitchen, engaged in our ritual of letter writing. I put my latest note to Mama aside for a moment and turned to him. "When will Mr. Wentworth come home?" I asked.

"Whenever it pleases him," Nestor replied, as he smoothed another piece of paper out in front of him on the table, the second page for Polly. "Why do you ask?"

"Just curious," I said.

But Nestor guessed there was more to my query than I was willing to say. "Don't put your hopes on your lady's husband," he warned. "It will only end in disappointment."

My darling Polly, It won't be long now. Perhaps a year, at most.

We impart information that is not generally known, even to old denizens of the city. We give the reader an insight into the character and doings of people whose deeds are carefully screened from public view. We describe their houses, give their locations, supply the stranger with information which he stands to need.

Not that he ever desires to visit those places.

Certainly not.

He is, we do not doubt, a member of the Bible Society, a bright shining light."

–A Gentleman's Companion to New York City, 1870

Mr. Wentworth's weary gaze staring out from his portrait had made me think I might be better off if he were here, in the flesh. I thought his homecoming might serve to pacify his wife, turning her heart soft to everyone around her, including me.

This, along with the notion that he had even a passing interest in fortune tellers brought me hope. Mama had often told those who sought counsel with her that the very act of sitting at a mystic's table made a person more susceptible to curses and spells. "Once you open yourself up to me, you open yourself up to everything," she'd say, before offering to part, for a fair price, with the protective charm she was wearing around her neck. "It works against everything from hexes to the evil eye." The top drawer of her dresser was filled with an endless supply of the charms, for just such opportunities.

I'd always thought it was a bit of humbuggery on Mama's part, done to make an extra dime, but the growing number of bruises on my arms and face had me changing my mind. I hoped, if Mr. Wentworth was a believer in things mystical and strange, that I could practise a bit of Mama's magic to lure him home sooner rather than later. Cutting wishing dolls out of Mr. Wentworth's stationery, I prayed Mama was right.

Late mornings Mrs. Wentworth would nearly wear out the carpet in the sitting room waiting for the post to arrive. No letters from Mr. Wentworth had come for her in all the time I'd been there, and according to Nestor, his last correspondence had left her in such a state that "we should be glad there has been nothing more."

Nestor came to the door of the sitting room every morning at half past ten to deliver the post. Mrs. Wentworth would sort through the cards and letters one by one, anxiously searching for any word from her husband. She'd throw aside the notices of appreciation from various shop-keepers (*Mr. Macy looks forward to your return, Mr. A.T. Stewart is happy to meet all your needs, Mr. Tiffany knows your heart's desire*) and file away any invitations for the upcoming season (*the pleasure of your company is requested on . . . , a dinner is being held in honour of . . . , nuptials will be celebrated for . . .*) all the while growing more and more agitated.

Two weeks after I'd fashioned my wish with paper and scissors, an envelope arrived bearing the familiar *W* of Mr. Wentworth's stationery. Mrs. Wentworth turned it over several times before taking up her letter opener to slice along the edge of its flap. Her eyes widened as she unfolded the single page that was nestled inside. She read the message, mouthing the words. When she'd finished, she held the letter to her breast, then tucked it away in the top drawer of her desk.

"Two weeks, and he'll be home," she said, smiling.

I smiled as well, thinking there must be something to Mama's magic after all.

Mrs. Wentworth began at once to make plans so that everything might be perfect for her husband's return. Flowers were to be ordered, menus prepared, rooms that had been closed for months aired out and set right. "Where did you get that brandy you were so fond of last Christmas?" she asked her husband's portrait, her brow pinched with not remembering.

Refusing to take lunch, she stayed at her desk and penned dozens of notes—orders to be carried out within the fortnight. When the clock chimed three, I thought she would decline her afternoon walk as well, but she turned to me (as she always did) and declared, "It's time for promenade, Miss Fenwick."

Mrs. Wentworth's daily promenade was, of course, confined to the corridors of the house. I was to dress her in the appropriate attire at promptly three o'clock, and then, with parasol in hand and reticule dangling from her wrist, she would commence to walk.

It seemed altogether pointless to me, but Mrs. Wentworth took the ritual seriously, even going so far as to pause every few steps to look through the ceiling at the blue of an imagined sky, or to gaze past the walls into the shop windows of her memory. I followed her, pacing the hallways and up and down the stairs, taking the same tired path every day.

At the end of the main floor hall was an enormous mirror. It spanned floor to ceiling, its gilded frame a gaudy tribute to turtledoves and fruit. Mrs. Wentworth took great care to watch herself as she approached the glass, straightening her shoulders, adjusting the angle of her parasol, raising her chin a bit in order to make a good impression on her own reflection. The day she received Mr. Wentworth's letter, she went right up to the mirror until her nose touched the surface. When her short, laced-up breaths began to leave a foggy circle, she took a step back and

In appropriate weather, the proper ladies of New York engage in the tradition of taking an afternoon promenade. This, I can assure you, is quite a sight. In fine walking suits and feather-laden hats, they parade along Lady's Mile at the prescribed orchestral gait of seventy-six beats per minute. Always andante, never allegretto. The purpose of this activity is not (as some may purport) to rejuvenate a lady's constitution, but rather to allow her to practise setting her sights on the triumphs and inadequacies of others with discretion and ease.

resumed appraising herself. "My hem," she said, looking down, motioning for me to fix a slight wrinkle in her skirt.

After seeing to the turn in the fabric, I got back to my feet and caught sight of myself in the mirror. My cheeks were covered with bruises, the skin around my eyes gone dark. The girl who'd peeped through the windows along Second Avenue, who'd longed to lie on her belly on an oriental rug, who'd wanted just one wink from the man with the big cigar, who'd dreamed of fine silk dresses and of lolling in Miss Keteltas' soft feather bed, had all but disappeared.

Reaching out, Mrs. Wentworth stroked the top of my head. She ran her hand down the length of my braid, her fingers softly tugging it, counting each twist under her breath as she went. " . . . five for silver, six for gold, seven for a secret."

I pulled away, unable, for once, to bear her touch.

"Get back here," she scolded, reaching again for my hair and yanking my braid. "You'll move when I tell you to move."

"Please let me go," I begged.

Dropping her parasol to the floor, she took my arm in her other hand and forced me to the sitting room.

"It's for your own good," she told me as she took a pair of scissors from her desk and minced the blades together in front of my face. "He would have favoured you too much. No matter how many bruises I give you, I can't stop your beauty from coming back. I swear it mends in your sleep just to torment me."

Day by day she'd been moving towards madness. Now, it seemed, she had arrived.

Holding me tight, she sawed at my braid. "I don't know how to manage it any other way. It's not your fault, of course, dear girl. You've been the most loyal of all—"

"Don't," I cried. I put my hand up to try to stop her, and she stabbed my fingers with the sharp scissors, turning my hand into a throbbing, bloody mess.

"Be sweet for me, Miss Fenwick," she cooed then, as if what she'd done hadn't hurt me in the least. "Let me finish. Let me keep my husband."

Soon she held the length of my hair in her hand like a prize. The ribbon I'd tied to the end of my braid that morning dangled, looking worn and shabby against the perfect folds of her dress.

Cradling my hand in the front of my skirt, I bowed my head, dizzy and sick with pain. Crimson drops spilled to the floor, a pale, yellow flower in the carpet now ruined with my blood.

Mrs. Wentworth looked first to her husband's portrait and then to me. "He can't be trusted," she said, her voice shaking. Then she went to the servant's bell and rang it over and over again, crying out, "Nestor! Nestor, come quick! I need you!"

Please, Nestor, come.

Sort the tress, which is about to be used, into
lengths, tie ends firmly and quite straight with
pack thread, put the hair into a small saucepan
with about a pint and a half of water and a
piece of soda the size of a nut, and boil it for
about a quarter of an hour to twenty minutes;
take it out, shake off the superfluous moisture
and hang it up to dry, but not near a fire.

–from "How to Prepare Hair for Jewellery
Work," *Godey's Lady's Book,* 1850

VII.

"Never let a stranger get hold of your hair," Mama
would scold as she'd gather up the strands that
had fallen from my brush. "Powerful magic can
be done against you by the person who finds it." After collecting it all, she'd roll the hair between her palms and form

it into a ratty-looking ball. Then she'd tuck the thing into the little cloth pouch she used for a hair receiver. She'd fashioned the pouch from one of my father's handkerchiefs, sewing the square of cloth into a point and attaching a length of ribbon to the corners so she could hang it from a nail over the head of the bed.

"Remember Mrs. Deery?"

"Yes, Mama, I remember."

"Remember what happened?"

"Yes, Mama."

Mrs. Deery was dead. Mama said it was because the woman's sister got angry with her, stole her hair and gave it to a bird. The bird flew off to a hole under the roof and then set about weaving Mrs. Deery's hair into its nest. While the bird sewed the hair round and round, back and forth, between sticks and spiderwebs, Mrs. Deery fell into madness. She got so she couldn't think straight anymore. She was sure that everyone was out to get her. She walked the streets, turning in circles and forgetting her name.

One day she spun herself right off the curb and was hit by a delivery wagon. There was nothing the driver could do. As barrels of fish tumbled off his cart, Mrs. Deery cried out from under the wheel, "She put a curse upon me! She wished for me to die . . ."

Whenever Mama's receiver got too full, she'd take the hair and use it to fill her pincushion. It kept her needles and pins shiny and free from rust. When that hair got old, she'd take it out of the cushion, recite a charm over it and throw it into the fire.

Mama's hair was so black it was almost blue. She could've sold it to Mr. Darling the wigmaker over on the

Bowery and gotten enough money to last us a good month or more. Even when our bellies growled so loud they kept us from sleep, Mama refused to give up her hair.

Once, when we'd gone three days without eating, I begged her to let me go see Mr. Darling.

"Go on, if you like," she'd said, shrugging and rolling her eyes. "But when you're mad with not knowing who you are, don't expect me to remind you."

Hungry and out to prove myself, I went straight to Mr. Darling's door. I was sure it was Mama's vanity, rather than Mrs. Deery's ghost, that kept her from parting with her hair. She'd leave one long curl dangling down past her cheek whenever she went to see Mr. Piers, or when she knew Mr. Cowan was coming to collect the rent. Twirling her hair with her finger, she'd stare at them with crazy eyes as if she meant to hold them under a spell. Sometimes, if she caught me watching, she'd give me a sly wink as if to say, *This, Moth, is how it's done.*

I wished Mama hadn't felt she had to conjure up poor Mrs. Deery to get me to behave. I loved her, I wanted to please her any way I could, but most of all, I wanted her to trust me with the truth.

Standing outside Mr. Darling's shop, I watched the women come, then go, scarves wrapped tight around their heads to hide their sacrifice. One woman, after catching her reflection in a shop window, began to tug at what little hair was left on her head. She pulled it from under the sides of her scarf and then smoothed the short wisps down in front of her ears. Crowning glory gone, by magic or necessity, she'd been defeated.

I didn't let Mr. Darling take my hair. I went behind the

stalls at Tompkins Market and showed my ankles to Mr. Goodwin instead. For two bruised apples and half a loaf of stale bread, I let him rub his bristly beard against my leg.

I went home, handed the bread to Mama, and said, "I'm not a child anymore."

Soon after Mrs. Wentworth rang the bell, Nestor came rushing into the room. "You called, ma'am?" he asked, then frowned when he spotted the blood that was dripping from my hand to the floor.

Slipping my braid inside her desk, Mrs. Wentworth motioned for Nestor to approach and spoke to him as if she were sharing a confidence. "As you can see, there's been an accident. The girl has made an awful mess. Take care of her, won't you?"

"Yes, ma'am," Nestor answered, bowing politely before turning his attention to me.

"And tell Caroline I wish to speak with her immediately," Mrs. Wentworth added. "There's much work to be done."

"Of course," Nestor replied. Placing his hand on the small of my back, he said, "Come along, Miss Fenwick."

Once we were on the other side of the door, I began to sob.

"Shh, quiet now," Nestor whispered. "If she hears you, it will only make things worse."

After leading me to the kitchen and sitting next to me at the table, Nestor rinsed my hand in a bowl of water. I watched the blood cloud and swirl, turning everything red. I feared, any moment, that Mrs. Wentworth would come tearing down the stairs, scissors in hand, ready to slice my dress open and cut out my heart.

"Dry your hand," Nestor instructed, offering me a clean, white tea towel. "Hold it fast to the cut until the bleeding stops. Then I'll dress it for you."

I nodded to him but didn't speak. Unsteady without the rudder of my braid nagging at my neck, I felt there was nothing left for my head to do except wobble. I had no weight for it to carry, no purpose or pride.

"It looks like we've reached the end of Chrystie Street," Caroline announced as she came into the room. She'd been to the parlour and back, no doubt returning with a long list of orders from Mrs. Wentworth.

"Hush, Caroline," Nestor scolded as he began to tear a piece of linen into long, thin strips. "There's no need for that."

Sulking, she went to the cabinet where she kept all her spices and pulled out a large, brown bottle. "Soak the cloth in Foucher's before you put it on," she said to Nestor as she set the bottle on the table. "It'll keep the wound clean and help it heal."

Nestor caught her by the arm and smiled. "Why, Caroline, how kind," he teased. "I didn't know you had it in you."

She put her hand on her hip and scowled. She looked as if she were about to let loose on him, but catching sight of the towel I was using to soak up the blood, she stopped herself. "There's no sense to it," she muttered as she turned to go back to her chores. "No sense to it at all."

Unable to bear the thought of facing Mrs. Wentworth again, I whispered to Nestor, "Help me get out of here. I'll do anything you ask."

"I will, but now is not the time."

"She means to kill me," I told him, my voice now shaking. "I know it."

"Patience wins the day, my dear," he whispered back.

When he'd finished tending to my hand, he walked me to my room and told me to stay there until he returned. "I'll come for you soon, I promise."

I paced from corner to corner for the longest time. Reaching under my mattress, I fished out the charm I'd made to call Mr. Wentworth home and tore it to bits. My hand still hurt, but the dressing Caroline had suggested had soothed it enough that the pain was now a dull ache.

Three times I climbed on top of the wooden stand of the washbasin, trying to reach the skylight. Neither the stand nor the ceiling's height ever changed, and no matter how I stretched, my hand never got any closer to the glass. I attempted to push the wardrobe across the floor, first with my shoulder and then my back, but found its weight too much. I'd hoped I might scale the thing to freedom.

When there was nothing else for me to try, no furniture left to move, I stood at Caroline's streaky, pitted mirror and stared at the damage Mrs. Wentworth had done. I'd pulled my hair away from my face every morning for most of my life, but what I saw now was altogether different. Covered in bruises, I was boyish and ugly, so square-faced and lopsided I was sure even Mama wouldn't know me.

Running the tips of my fingers through what was left of my hair, I turned my head one way and then the other. Even the lowest working girl—the thread puller, the pin maker, the scullery maid—can think herself pretty if she has the winding twist of a bun or a long braid at her neck. She knows that at the end of the day she'll let it loose, tresses falling down around her shoulders, covering her breasts. She'll comb her hair over the edge of her hand, imagining what it would be like for someone else to perform the task for her. Such pleasures would not be mine again for quite some time.

The room had gone dark with evening before Nestor returned. I ran to the door as soon as I heard his hand on the latch.

"I'm ready," I said, holding the pillowcase Mama had given me when I'd left home. Everything I owned was stowed safely inside it. Miss Sweet was snug in one corner so there'd be no chance of my losing her.

"Not yet," he said, entering and shutting the door behind him.

I stepped away from him, guessing what he might be after. I feigned innocence, hoping to put him off a little while longer. "I know I should give back the dress," I said, walking quickly to the wardrobe. "But there are at least a dozen more in here just like it, you can see for yourself . . . and this one suits me so well. I doubt my old one even fits anymore—"

"Quiet, Miss Fenwick," he said, moving towards me.

Desperate to be free from Mrs. Wentworth, I'd planned on letting him have any favour he asked of me. Now that he was standing here, I wasn't sure I could see my way to it.

"I've n-never . . ." I stammered.

"And you won't," Nestor said, shaking his head in dismay. "Certainly not by my hand. I should hope you'd think better of yourself and of me, Miss Fenwick."

"I'm sorry," I said, apologizing. "It's just, I want so badly to leave, and when you shut the door, I thought–Please, Nestor, I want to go home."

Looking to me with a grave face, he said, "Mrs. Wentworth has requested your company."

"No," I replied, tears coming to my eyes. "I can't go to her. I won't–"

"I'm afraid you must," he said. Then he put his arm around my shoulder in a gesture of comfort. "She says sleep won't come to her without you there. And I can't set you free until she's asleep."

"Don't make me . . ." I pleaded.

Taking a handkerchief from his pocket, he handed it to me and said, "Dry your eyes and listen carefully. You must do exactly as I say."

Mrs. Wentworth was sitting at the tea table in her room when I arrived, concentrating on some sort of handiwork. A man's top hat was perched on the edge of the table in front of her, long threads dangling from its flat surface, a handful of pins keeping them in place. Each strand was weighted with a wooden bobbin, the kind that grandmothers and legless men in dusty storefronts used to make lace. The bobbins clacked together as Mrs. Wentworth's fingers moved, and stopped each time she checked

Hair Work! Hair Work! We cannot recommend this artistic pastime highly enough to all ladies. It is the only means by which the precious remains of a cherished child, husband, or mother can be indefinitely preserved. For, at the moment of a painful bereavement, what can be more piously kept than their hair? Enjoy the inexpressible advantage of knowing that the material of your handiwork is the actual hair of the loved and gone. The benefits of doing your own hairwork are many. Those who learn the craft for themselves are free from nightmares of . . .

. . . body snatchers and anatomists (devils of the night who seek to turn profit from remains not long in the grave). Many believe the power of these personal effects has no limits. We have received several reports testifying that upon completion of a necklace, bracelet or watch chain, the spirit of a loved one was felt near – their strength, their vibrations, their life-force all present. Although we make no claims as to the veracity of these statements, it cannot be denied that, through these precious objects, something of a life that was lost belongs, once again, to the living.

her progress in the small book she was holding in her lap.

"Miss Fenwick," she said, without looking up from her work. "Come see what's become of your beautiful hair."

Scared that she might be planning to lash out at me again, I moved towards her with caution, holding onto Nestor's words for courage. *You must hold back emotion, refuse impulse. Act according to plan.*

This was not the first time he'd instructed a girl on how to break free from Mrs. Wentworth. According to him, there had been two other maids before me, one who'd been left with a scar on her cheek from Mrs. Wentworth's signet ring, and another who had lasted only a week.

"Lovely so far, isn't it?" she said as I came close. She was criss-crossing the strands of my hair to form the beginnings of a bracelet. Although it had been prepared in such a way that it now looked more like embroidery floss than my hair, it was all I could do not to tear it from her hands. "It's this one, here," she said, holding up the book and pointing to the page. "The Maiden's Wreath."

NO. 27—THE MAIDEN'S WREATH.

This bracelet makes for an exquisite tribute
to a dear sister or daughter parted from us too soon.
Gentle lobes are fashioned into lacework,

like delicate tears, then intertwined to
create a symbol of everlasting love.

Every injustice Mrs. Wentworth had ever heaped on me came to my mind—all the times I'd held my tongue, all the thoughts I'd had of striking out at her. *It will soon be over,* I told myself. I just needed to find the strength to wait a little longer.

"Would you like me to turn your bed down, ma'am?" I asked, hoping she didn't have plans to complete the bracelet before going to sleep. Some evenings she'd stay awake for hours, poring over the latest *Harper's Bazar* or *Frank Leslie's Illustrated News.* By the time I'd get down to the kitchen, Nestor would be dozing in his chair.

"Yes, of course," she answered, waving me away with an air of irritation. "I just want to finish this portion so I'll have a decent place to start when I come back to it." She took the ribbon that had once tied my braid and placed it between the pages of her book.

Patience wins the day, Miss Fenwick.

Despite not being allowed in Mrs. Wentworth's sleeping quarters, Nestor knew every gem, bangle and ring that lay inside her jewellery box. He'd catalogued the trinkets in his mind, keeping track of his master's generosity each time he'd presented his wife with a gift at home or sent her something precious from abroad.

With each maid's departure, he'd instructed the girl to dip her fingers into the box's drawers and take two pieces of jewellery—one for the girl and one for him. The items he chose were ones he knew Mrs. Wentworth had reserved for the social season later in the year. They were expensive pieces, laden with diamonds and other jewels, ornaments that looked best in the sparkling candlelight of dinner parties and winter balls. Mrs. Wentworth hadn't yet noticed that other pieces had gone missing, and with any luck, she wouldn't become aware of my thievery until long after I was gone.

"Miss Fenwick," Mrs. Wentworth called after sliding herself under the sheets. "It's been such a trying day. Won't you sing me to sleep?"

"Yes, ma'am," I said, sitting down on the edge of her bed. She'd requested I sing to her on several occasions, ordering me to hold her hand until I was sure she'd drifted off. Out of all the chores I performed as her maid, this was the one thing that never felt like a bother. I liked knowing that my voice was the last sound in the room, that my footsteps, my leaving, would be unknown to her.

"What would you like to hear?" I asked, reaching for her hand.

Tracing the edge of the bandages that covered my wound, she said, "Anything is fine, so long as it's not one of Mr. Pastor's songs. His sentiments don't sit well with me."

So I sang "Tenting Tonight," and then all the verses of "Beautiful Dreamer." Finally, halfway through "Hard Times Come Again No More," her hand went limp and her lips parted with dreaming.

"Why don't I just take it all, Nestor, and you can leave with me?"

"Oh no, Miss Fenwick, that would never do. My dear Polly needs me to be wiser than that. I'm no good to her if I'm locked away in the Tombs. Besides, who would save all the sweet little girls like you?

There's a pale drooping maiden
Who toils her life away
With a warm heart whose better days are o'er:
Though her voice would be merry,
'Tis sighing all the day–
Oh! Hard Times come again no more.
'Tis a song, the sigh of the weary
Hard Times, Hard Times, come again no more;
Many days you have lingered
Around my cabin door
Oh! Hard Times, come again no more.

VIII.

My going was much like my coming had been– footsteps echoing on the tile of the front hall, the sound of the clock ticking in the quiet of the night. I bid farewell to the cherub on the stairs, this time touching its cheeks, its wings and its toes while Nestor waited impatiently by the door.

The most troublesome aspect of stealing the jewels had been putting the key back without waking Mrs. Wentworth.

Be sure to return the key to where you found it. Touch wood, we'll both be on to better things by the time she figures it out.

Although she kept the box in the dressing room, she hid the key inside a small ginger jar that sat on the bedside table. I knew the whole of the room by heart, so even in the dark, *taking* the key was easy.

But afterwards, Mrs. Wentworth's jewels stuffed deep inside my pockets, I moved too fast. The key slipped from my bandaged fingers and fell, jangling against the bottom of the jar. As Mrs. Wentworth's breathing hastened, I froze, thinking for certain she'd wake. Thankfully, she only let out a sigh and turned in her sleep.

Nestor had wanted a collar of pearls and diamonds with a heart-shaped pendant. Sometime soon, he'd said, he'd take it to be fenced, handing it over to a shopkeeper on Clinton Street in exchange for cash. He'd add the money to the rest of the savings he was putting aside for Polly's passage to New York. Caroline was to receive a share as well—a reward for being at the ready to distract Mrs. Wentworth if needed and to forget everything that had happened when all was said and done.

My reward was a heavy gold bracelet, coiled three times round and made to look like a snake. It had rubies for eyes and the length of its back was set with a line of brilliant green stones. "A token of affection from Mr. Wentworth," Nestor had said. "Christmas 1869." The couple had gotten into a terrible row that year over Mr. Wentworth requesting lemon tart instead of Mrs. Wentworth's family's traditional pudding. Mrs. Wentworth hadn't worn the trinket since.

In the course of my seeing to her daily attire, I'd held several pieces of her jewellery in my hands, usually only long enough to fasten a clasp around her neck, or to slip a bangle over her wrist. Before I left her quarters that night, I loosened my sleeve and slid the bracelet past my elbow and halfway up my arm. It was then I understood why wealthy women demanded such ornaments from their lovers. It wasn't about the way the thing looked or the number of gems that spotted it—it was how the gold felt on my skin. Even though I knew I'd have to give it up, for Mama's sake as well as my own, feeling that precious metal turning warm against my flesh was a delicious victory all its own.

Without Nestor's knowledge, I took something else from Mrs. Wentworth's dressing room. He may well have supported me if I'd asked, but I wanted the thing so badly I didn't dare risk his refusal. Fastening Mrs. Wentworth's fan to a ribbon around my neck, I slid it under the collar of my dress and let it rest between my breasts. Whether I'd choose to sell it or keep it remained to be seen, but at least I could be sure it would never again be used for cruelty.

"Won't she come after me?" I asked Nestor, after we'd left the house. I was worried that even if I got away, Mrs. Wentworth would rage down to Chrystie Street and force me to return.

"She'll complain bitterly. She'll say good help is hard to find and that charity is a useless endeavour best left to clergymen and nuns, but rest assured, by the day's end she'll have another girl to take your place."

Closing my eyes, I wished the girl well, whoever she might be.

Nestor pointed to a horse and cart waiting down the street. "It's not Mrs. Wentworth's carriage," he said apologetically. "The driver she's been using isn't a steady enough fellow for me. I don't trust him."

For a moment I thought that this would be our good-bye, but Nestor walked me to where the wagon stood. After a brief conversation with the man who owned the cart, he helped me to the driver's seat and then hopped up and settled beside me, taking hold of the reins.

"Mr. Gideon Hawkes . . . now there's a good man," Nestor said, snapping the reins to start the horse moving and then nodding to the gentleman who was now walking away. "He delivers every kind of household item you can imagine in this rig—precious cargo mostly, statues, paintings, porcelain vases taller than you. He's offered me a share in the business when I'm ready—Hawkes and Coates, movers, at your service." Smiling at me, he asked, "How's that sound to your ears?"

The houses were dark, the street almost empty. The only light came from street lamps that flickered along the sidewalk. Although I'd only been there a month, it seemed a lifetime since I'd been out in the air, outside the walls of that wretched house. Steam rose off the pavers—they'd seen rain within the hour. Leaves, wet and turning in the crease of the curb, heralded the arrival of autumn.

"Second Avenue will take us there," I told Nestor after he'd inquired as to the best way to get me home. As we approached Miss Keteltas' house, I asked him to go slow so I could look into the shadows of her garden. Even though I couldn't see much, I imagined her birds at the window, singing to me, inviting me to crawl through the fence once more.

A shiver went through me as the cart's wheels chattered over Houston Street. A group of men crossed in front of us, swaying this way and that, leaning on one another as they walked. I was sure they'd come from the Bowery, howling their way from dance hall to brothel to home. There were fires in barrels on the curbs. Boys and men crowded around them, their faces lit up with sparks and the glow of the flames. Two youths were picking up dried clods of horse dung in the street and pitching them at a barrel to feed their fire.

Then I could feel the wheels of the cart gumming up with Chrystie Street muck. Beggars and children were sleeping on steps, or huddled in storefronts. Lamps and candles lit up windows here and there, crooked panes of glass with red shades drawn. I rubbed my hands together and breathed warm air into them, my belly twisting.

Mama was sure to be angry with me. I only hoped she'd listen long enough for me to explain the reasons for my departure and to tell her that I'd found a better way for the both of us.

It had occurred to me, while picking through Mrs. Wentworth's jewellery, that my actions, so long as they remained undiscovered, might be the start of something much bigger. The idea that I could get away with thievery (countless times perhaps) thrilled me to no end. My success at stealing would be my defence against the anger Mama was bound to show me. Stealing, I would argue, was the remedy for all our troubles.

She'll come around, I thought as the cart came ever closer to her door. *I just have to get her to listen.*

Mrs. Devlin James, I would begin. *You'll be like Mrs. Devlin James, Mama.*

Mrs. James lived over on Orchard Street and visited Mama from time to time to discuss matters of the heart. She had been married to Mr. Devlin James (a.k.a. Patrick Silver, a.k.a. Patrick Gold, a.k.a. Patrick Dymond, et cetera). The couple, unremarkable in their lives (he swept the streetcar tracks and hoisted bricks for masons; she made paper bags, folding the brown sheets, one, two, three, and creasing them with sticky, smelly glue), carried on much like everyone else, until the day Mr. James decided that he was going to make the most of the war.

The Union had kindly provided a way out for men who did not wish to serve. For the sum of three hundred dollars, a gentleman could be freed from his duty. The only catch was he also had to provide a substitute to take his place. As the war dragged on, bounties for substitutes soared, often reaching as high as a thousand dollars or more. Agencies specializing in the brokerage of such agreements set up shop throughout the city and across the whole of the North. Every other block soon boasted a substitute broker, a tin-type dealer, and an embalming service, all for the sake of the soldier.

One morning in the spring of 1863, Mr. James kissed his wife goodbye and walked into one such office on Third Avenue. He signed the paper with an *X,* a document which promised him "sufficient consideration" for his service. He sent the bounty home to Mrs. James, who promptly stuffed the money inside her mattress. Over the course of the next six months, Mr. James repeated this same process several times over, slipping away before reaching the front line, disappearing from telegraph-line repair duty, getting captured by and escaping the enemy—while Mrs. James waited patiently at home.

Then, during one of Mr. James' self-appointed furloughs in the city, he chose to visit a woman on Mott Street rather than going straight home to his wife. Mrs. James, in her scorn, became something of a patriot, and did not hesitate to turn her husband in for bounty jumping. "I know a man," she announced to a policeman stationed at General Dix's office, "who has deserted his country and his wife several times over." Two weeks later her husband was executed by firing squad at Governor's Island.

After crying over his body and making arrangements for his remains, Mrs. James took her mattress, moved to Ohio and changed her name. Within a year, she had become Mrs. Frederick C. Mills. Not long after, she sent Mama a letter to say that Mr. Mills had bought her a three-storey house with a mansard roof in a town called Cincinnati.

"I'll do all the work," I'd promise her. "I'll take on whatever position you find for me. You can sell me away as many times as you like." I imagined myself coming home again and again with whatever I could get my hands on–silver, jewels, money, gold. All Mama would have to do was sit on her mattress and wait. If anything went wrong, there was always Ohio.

"It's just up there," I said to Nestor. "You can let me off any time."

The horse's ears were turning, catching my words and then letting them go again. The leather straps in Nestor's hands gently moved up and down with the horse's gait.

"All right then," he said, looking at me with concern. "I'll stop at the corner and wait until you get inside."

"You can't," I told him. "The boys here don't sleep. They'll swarm the wagon if they see the quality of your clothes. They'll take your hat and tear off your coat. They'll cut the straps on the horse and take her too."

"I have to see you safe," Nestor argued.

"Circle around if you must, but don't wait for me," I said. "You needn't worry. I've got somewhere to go if she won't take me back."

Nestor nodded, giving a gentle tug at the reins. The horse let out a snort.

"Be well, Miss Fenwick," he said, reaching out to touch my hand.

I wondered for a moment if I was making a mistake. "Will she be different when Mr. Wentworth comes home?" I asked. "Would things have gotten any better?"

"No, my dear, they would've gotten worse."

Then, with a grim expression, he added, "The last time Mrs. Wentworth was in the same room as her husband, she took her anger and a length of rope and strangled the dog."

Shocked by his words, I pulled my hand away from his and tugged at the collar of my dress. There was no more room for doubt. I'd been well on my way to ending up like Mr. Wentworth's dear hound.

Seeing my distress, Nestor tried his best to calm my fears. "You must know, dear girl, I wouldn't have let it come to that. I had plans to get you out from the very start."

"I know," I said, nodding to him, thankful that Nestor had been there at all.

Leaving him was more difficult than I'd imagined. My cheeks burned and my throat swelled with not knowing what to say. I hoped that he'd be at least a little bit lonely without me.

Jumping from the cart, I landed square on the street.

"My name's Moth," I told him, not waiting for him to say anything more.

Someone I hold in great esteem would one day explain to me that Nestor's actions (although meant to save me) were just as criminal as Mrs. Wentworth's.

His motives were not pure (enough).

True.

He asked you to commit a crime.

True.

He allowed harm to come to you in order to serve his needs.

Perhaps.

September 25, 1871
The New York Infirmary
for Indigent Women and Children
128 Second Avenue, New York, New York.

They are everywhere I look—girl after girl left behind by their mothers, their families, and society.

Mandy Clarke, sixteen years old, looking as aged and tired as a Fulton Street whore, sores and chancres covering every inch of her body.

Penny Giles, thirteen years old, ruined by her uncle.

Fran Tasch, nineteen, her face badly burned by the carbolic she drank to end her life.

Girl Unknown, approximately nineteen to twenty-five years of age, her corpse found stuffed inside a trunk at the Chambers Street station. Her death was caused by an abortion gone wrong.

These were just the girls I saw today.

S.F.

WANTED! WANTED!

Wanted at once!

1000 Substitutes!

Able bodies!

To Whom the Highest CASH Price

will be Given.

Apply to HARDY and KELLY by

the first of the month.

IX.

I tried the latch but found it bolted. I knocked, first quietly rapping at the door, then pounding hard with my fist.

"Mama?" I called, but there was no answer.

I called again, this time louder, figuring she must've tipped back too much Dr. Godfrey's before bed. "Mama, are you there?"

When the door finally came open, the face that greeted me wasn't hers. A stranger stood in her place, a fair-haired woman holding a lamp, her cheeks lined with sleep. She wore a black-fringed shawl wrapped tight around her shoulders just like Mama's.

"I'm looking for my mother," I told the woman as I tried to see past her into the front room.

She scowled at me and said, "You a beggar—go away."

Her voice was throaty and mean, as if she meant for the words to stick in my ears. She was, like so many of the women in this part of the city, filled with distrust. The language of her homeland had not been welcomed by strangers. *A-mer-i-ca* had turned out to be a false friend.

Mama still had her mother's tongue locked up inside her head, but refused to use it. Every so often I'd catch her whispering strings of unknown words to a dress or skirt she was mending. They sounded tender and haunting to me, like someone telling a secret.

"Teach me to speak like that," I'd said one night, settling down next to her while she was sewing.

"No," she said, biting thread between her teeth.

"Don't you miss having someone to talk to?" I asked.

"Let me be lonely, Moth," she answered. "You don't need to learn more words for sorrow."

As the woman moved to close the door, I stepped forward to stop her. "Please," I said, quickly pointing to Mama's fortune-telling sign still sitting in the window. "Do you know where she is?"

"Gypsy of Chrystie Street," the woman said, nodding as if she'd understood.

I could hear the wheels of Nestor's cart behind me in the street. He whistled to the horse to pick up her pace, and drove on. I hoped he could see that I wasn't in the clear and that he'd choose to keep circling for a bit longer.

"The Gyspy is my mother," I said to the woman. "Where has she gone?"

The woman shook her head and frowned. Motioning to the sign and then to herself she said, "Fortune teller— that's me."

A man's voice echoed from the dark of the backroom. "Lottie," he grumbled. "Come to bed!"

She pushed me out to the step. "No Mama here," she insisted, and shut the door.

I looked around, wondering if I'd forgotten where I'd lived. Perhaps Mama had been right all along about the dangers of not keeping track of my hair.

Standing on the curb, I waited on Nestor for as long as I thought safe, but he was gone. He must have thought the woman on the doorstep was my mother and that all had ended well. The streetlight closest to Mama's door was just the same as when I'd left—glass cracked on two sides, the post leaning as if it were too tired to stand straight. In its faint glow, I saw that Chrystie Street, too, was just as it had always been—dark and hungry, waiting to devour the weak.

I picked up a piece of broken brick from a pile of rubble and hid it in the palm of my hand.

Head up, eyes ahead, move fast, don't run.

"She's gone, dear," Mrs. Riordan explained after she'd let me through her door. "You didn't get word?"

"No." I sat down on the wobbly stool she'd offered me. The death notices of a hundred paupers came to mind. *No one has come forward to claim the body and it is probable she will be buried in Potter's Field.* The back page of the *Evening Star* was never without them. "Was she sick? Did someone hurt her?" I tried to push away the thought that Mama had come to a terrible end.

Mrs. Riordan took my hand. "Oh, no, dear child," she sighed. "That's not what I meant. It's just she left Chrystie Street some time ago and I don't know where she's got to."

After I'd gone, Mama had strutted around for a week, bragging about the fine lady who'd taken me into her house with too many rooms to count. And then she'd disappeared. Her place was nearly empty when Mr. Cowan came to call, nothing in the rooms to speak of except an old frying pan sitting on the rusted stove. It was clear she'd planned to go.

"He wasn't too pleased, as you can well imagine. He claimed your mother robbed him blind, that she hadn't paid rent since July. Make sure you watch for him when you're about. He'll take what she owes him out of your hide if he can catch you."

Staring at me with sympathy, Mrs. Riordan asked, "Have you any place to stay?"

"No," I replied. I had no one in the world but myself.

"Then you'll stay here with me," she said. "There's not much room, I know, but it's a place to rest your head. Get a proper night's sleep and in the morning you can begin again."

Mrs. Riordan's house was nothing more than a shack–one in a row of makeshift shelters that had been tacked on to the back of the tenements. Mostly let by immigrants fresh off the boat, they were an easy way for landlords to make fast cash. People got out of them as quickly as they could, moving to a spot on the floor of a distant cousin or friend–a place with proper walls and perhaps even a window or two. Poor Mrs. Riordan had travelled in the opposite direction. Her status had slipped away bit by bit, until this shack, crumbling and sad, was all that remained between her and the street.

"I'll take the wall side, dear," she said, pulling back the tattered quilt covering her bed.

I curled up next to her, unsure of our closeness, but thankful to have a place to sleep. She smelled of fish and smoke, and every time she exhaled there was the slightest hint of turning milk in the air.

As I tried to settle down, I heard the twitchy *pinch-pinch-pinch* of rats in the wall. Mama always said that rats would eat anything, including the fingers and toes right off a person's body while they were sleeping.

I'd brought home a stray cat once, thinking it would help keep the rats away. He was sleek and black, with ears so thin they looked like bat's wings. I called him Soot. I named him before I caught him because I thought if he had a name, he'd be more likely to stay in one place. Mama scolded me as soon as she saw him and then she threw him out the door. "Shame on you, Moth," she complained. "You know proper Gypsies don't keep cats."

In a single year, a female rat can produce two-hundred-and-eighty-five offspring. The best rat-catchers in New York are revered for their talents. At dawn, they rise like tricksters from beneath the finest hotels, twirling their bags with deft wrists, carrying hundreds of squirming rodents.

Whenever she heard a rat in our rooms, she'd stomp around the place with a broom, banging the end of the handle on the walls, floors and ceilings. Then she'd pass the rest of the night in fits and starts, bolting up in bed and saying, "Ssst. Did you hear that? Damn rat. Oh, Moth, did you hear it?" I would lie next to her, listening hard, fighting to keep my eyes open. I hoped that if a rat did try to eat me, I'd be strong enough to beat the hungry, chattering thing to death.

There was a rat inside Mrs. Riordan's mattress, moving underneath me. I felt it come up through a hole at the end of the bed, slither past my ankle and tug at the hem of my dress. Not wanting to startle my host, I grabbed hold of my skirt and shook it, desperate to scare the rodent away.

"Shh, child, don't be afraid," Mrs. Riordan cooed in the dark. "They'll settle down soon enough. You'll see. They're sweet, like children. The more you don't want them around, the more they wish to be near you."

I gave up trying to sleep. I lay there in the dark trying to figure out why Mama had gone. Before she'd sent me away, she'd grown devoted to staying put, sometimes not leaving the house for days. She'd sat in her chair by the window, talking through memories of her youth and of travelling with her father's medicine show, of horses pulling beautiful caravans and days spent rafting along rivers from place to place, stopping to camp when the moon was full. That life had sounded better to me than any other I could imagine—even the one where our rooms and clothes and Chrystie Street were new again and my father had never gone away. "Let's go to the river tonight, Mama," I'd begged. "We'll find the Gypsies and go with them. I won't be any trouble, I promise."

Shaking her head, she'd told me no. Her face had turned pale as she said, "As soon as I leave this spot—that will be the moment your father will come home. This city is filled with too many women, each one waiting to take another's place. If I'm not here, some other woman will be here to open the door. She'll welcome him, she'll feed him. He'll forget all about me and take up with the new one. You know Mrs. Peale from two doors down? Well, I can tell you for certain that weren't the same Mrs. Peale who was there a year ago. Where's that first Mrs. Peale, the one I knew?"

Mrs. James, Mrs. Deery, the first Mrs. Peale–all the women who came to Mama ended up asking the same question, *Does my man love me?*

Mama would never tell them yes or no. She'd just look her petitioner in the eyes and ask, "Does he watch you when you walk away? Not with lust, mind you, but with care. As if he's worried you might just up and disappear."

At that, the woman would either sigh with relief or break down in tears. Then Mama would collect her fee and show the woman the door.

I'd often wondered if Mama's test for love held true for everyone, even for mothers and daughters. The night Mrs. Wentworth took me by the hand and led me down the steps, I'd hoped to turn and see Mama wave one last goodbye. All she did was pull the curtain shut and turn down the light. She didn't watch me walk away.

My heartbreak that night was terribly polite. It let me know it was coming for me, even when I insisted on ignoring it. *This won't end well,* a quiet voice whispered from the centre of my head. Then my hands went moist, my mouth went dry, and my ears whined and buzzed with the warning of what was to come next. *Nothing good.*

September 25, 1871.   THE EVENING STAR

A TALE OF TWO STOREFRONTS

In the part of the city known as "Dutchtown" (or, as it is called by local residents, *Kleindeutschland*) there is a stately building that is said to be one of the most formidable destinations in New York. Round shouldered against the corner, five stories tall, its large storefront windows boast the words FANCY GOODS AND HABERDASHERY. The rest of the floors are reserved for the private, familial rooms of the store's owners, including a lovely parlour, a well-appointed dining room, a vast ballroom, and a sprawling kitchen in the basement.

The Proprietors, long ago immigrants from Prussia, deal in fine goods for gentlemen and ladies alike. The lady of the place, as grand in stature as her residence, is well-liked by many prominent figures in society. Mrs. B_., or "Marm" as she is known to friends and family, is often praised for her sensibility in fashion and her impeccable taste in decor. Her lavish dinner parties are attended by judges, politicians, Wall Street gentlemen and their wives.

Her husband, Mr. B_., in his pin-striped waistcoat and tortoiseshell spectacles, is a pleasant-looking man, bearded and grey with a wink full of wrinkles around both eyes, but not a line across his brow. He is noted for having a keen eye for business and an intelligent, but a wry sense of humour.

Outside, passersby admire the shop windows that are always dressed according to the season. Inside, a rack of ivory-handled parasols spans floor to ceiling. Spools of ribbon are lined up like a rainbow behind the counter. Two large glass cases (one for the ladies, one for the gents) hold pair after pair of gloves, all flat fingered and waiting for someone to slip them on for the first time. Handsome dandies purchase gaudy silk ties there, and mother after mother comes in with her giggling young daughters to buy collars and cuffs and gloves of lace. The customers come and go through the store's painted door, a string of brass bells jangling all the day.

An East Side Secret

What most upstanding citizens of this city don't know is that the building and its owners are harbouring a secret.

To the rear of the building is a small dark door with no glass and no bells. This is where the real business is done. The craftiest of the city's lady shoplifters come knocking there—Big Sarah Cox, Mother Roach, Miss Nelly Flowers—bringing goods they've pilfered from A.T. Stewart's and the like. An endless parade of house thieves trade over flour sacks filled with dinner silver that's to be melted down into shiny lumps of profit. Known in the dialect of crime as a *fence,* the Proprietors are the best friends these criminals have. As receivers and traffickers in stolen goods, it is their function to guard the plunder taken by thieves until it can be worked back into the channels of legitimate trade. The whole of thieving Manhattan is at their beck and call.

A Guttersnipe Speaks

"When it comes to fencing goods, they're tops," one scrappy-looking pickpocket explained as I followed him down a dark alleyway at night. "They runs a smooth shop from front to back, top to bottom, the best in the city."

Trained in the Fagin school of the building's basement, the young boy, all of thirteen years of age, says he's learned his trade from "the best." By this he means, the resident thieving master of the place. A former lieutenant in the War Between the States, the man now leads a platoon of guttersnipes from his quarters in the cavernous reaches of Mr. B_'s cellar. Holding up straw gentlemen and ladies on sticks, he teaches the littlest boys (some as young as four years old) to try their first "touch." Once they have command of that trick, he rewards them with hunks of rock candy and moves them on to "real marks," enlisting any of the older boys who might be loitering around to let the lads have a go at their pockets.

His Future Looks Bright

The boy who laid bare these secrets to the *Evening Star* may look like any other ragamuffin, but he is far from destitute. He's got money enough in his pocket for food as well as a place to sleep whenever he needs shelter from the elements. "I used to thieve for a Mr. G_. over on Third Avenue, but I had to get away from him. He don't care if his boys live or die. He'd just as soon cut off your ear or your fingers or gouge out one of your eyes if he thinks it'll turn people soft to you and bring him more money.

"These people ain't like that. They do fair by all the street boys and a lot of the girls too. If you can get in with them, you're set."

X.

*P*ound, tap, tap. Pound, tap, tap. Pound, tap, tap, pound . . .

Mama used to sing a song with a rhythm that went just like that. It was a pretty little tune about a ladybird and her young. She sounded happy and free when she sang it, even when she got to the part where the ladybird's babies burned.

> *Ladybird, ladybird,*
> *fly away home.*
> *Your house is on fire*
> *and your children all gone.*
> *All except one,*
> *and that's little Ann,*

and she has crept under
the warming pan.

Pound, tap, tap. Pound, tap, tap. Pound, tap, tap, pound.
I beat my fist on the wooden door in the alley behind the
Birnbaums' shop. *This is how you let them know you're wait-*
ing, Nestor had said.

I'd left Mrs. Riordan's early that morning, before she
was awake. The scratching and nibbling of the rats was
more than I could bear. No matter how kind she was, she
was a spectre of everything I didn't want to become. I'd
vowed to go back on occasion, bringing her a twist of
roasted peanuts or a pail of flat beer to repay her for her
kindness, but I'd never stay with her again.

"Good day," came a man's voice from above my head.

I looked up to find spectacled eyes peering down at me
through a peephole that had opened near the top of the door.

Standing straight, I greeted the man with a polite smile.
"Good day, sir."

Nestor had told me how things should go with Mr.
Birnbaum, explaining that the man's customers all addressed
him as "Herr" Birnbaum and that only his friends and business acquaintances were allowed to call him by his first
name, which was "Wolfe." The boys who worked for him
called him "sir" and never "boss." His wife simply called
him Lieb, because he cared for her more than anyone or
anything else. "She's the one you have to please," Nestor
had warned. "It's not easy to get on Mrs. Birnbaum's good
side, but once you're there, you're set."

"We have business, I take it?" Mr. Birnbaum asked, staring down at me.

I was alone in the alley, but I'd passed a group of roughs on my way here and I couldn't help thinking they might not be far behind. They'd been loud and rude, smacking their lips and sucking kisses from the air when I walked by. Although they couldn't have known about the bracelet, I was worried they'd followed me anyway, just to see me run. Reaching up my sleeve, I pulled Mrs. Wentworth's golden snake down far enough that Mr. Birnbaum could see it.

He pushed his face farther through the hole, his eyes tick-tocking as he looked at the bracelet. "Yes, yes, it would seem that we do."

I reached for the handle on the door, but Mr. Birnbaum stayed put, still staring at me. Finally, he cleared his throat and asked, "Who sent you here, dear girl?"

"A friend called Nestor," I replied.

"And your name is?"

"Miss Moth Fenwick, sir," I answered, trying to sound as proper as I could.

"May I assume you're here because you assisted Nestor in some way?"

"Yes, sir," I answered.

Mr. Birnbaum slid the peephole shut and I heard him turn lock after lock after lock. Once the door opened, it led right to another. Behind the second door was a landing where you could choose to go up a flight of stairs, down a flight of stairs or straight ahead into the backroom of the shop.

Gaslights glowed along the walls, making it seem far too cheerful a meeting spot for thieves. Boxes and barrels were stacked neat against the sides and there wasn't a scrap on the floor. There was a bright copper spittoon in the corner and when I looked down into it, I could see to the bottom. The inside of the thing was just as shiny as the rest. There was a funny little sign on the wall above it with a picture of a woman chasing after a man holding a rolling pin high above her head. The man's face was red and his cheeks were all puffed out, his eyes bulging. There was writing on it too, but it was in the fancy, fat script of the kind that was on so many of the signs in the shop windows of Dutchtown. From the look on the woman's face, I guessed the sign said something awful, something mean enough to make a man think twice before doing any spitting at all.

Mr. Birnbaum had the same kind eyes and warm smile as Mr. Bartz, a shopkeeper on Stanton Street, only Mr. Birnbaum still had all his hair on his head and Mr. Bartz had none. Mr. Bartz sold bread, cheese, sausages, beans, beer, hot soup, and two kinds of pickles from two great glass jars—one for sour and one for sweet. His potato soup was three cents a cup, and once in a long while, when Mama'd had a really good day, she'd let me go down and fetch some to share.

Mr. Bartz would ladle the steaming soup from the black of the pot, and then go behind the counter and bring out a large loaf of pumpernickel bread, the crust shining and dark. He'd always cut the end off and hand it to me. I'd shake my head, trying to refuse it, but he'd take my hand and place it there, insisting in his deep, kind voice, "Take it, dear girl. You're nothing but a wisp."

Mama said that Mr. Bartz would be ruined one day, because he cared too much for making things right and keeping people happy. I hoped that she was wrong. To me, it was because of Mr. Bartz that things kept going as right as they could in our part of the city. In the spring, when the crusts of dirty snow melted, the great puddles that were left behind in the street got kicked and splashed by the horses and streetcars. Storefronts and houses were soon plastered with a vile slop of chicken innards, bits of wet newsprint and stale dung. Mr. Bartz scoured every bit of it off his place. He sent his goodness through the handle of his broom like a shock of lightning, casting the dirt off his steps while the rest of the street fell to the rats. He took rags and vinegar water and rubbed round and round at his windows. His place would be clean even if it killed him. He would not give up.

I planned to go straight to his shop when I was finished here to order myself a bowl of soup and to make certain he was still there.

"This way," Mr. Birnbaum said, as he led me into the backroom. "I'll take you to Marm."

His wife was sitting at a large table, moving a pen across a wide ledger. The puffs on her sleeves brushed the pearls dangling from her ears, setting them to swinging. Looking up from her work she stared at me, making me feel as if I was doing something wrong just by breathing. No woman I'd ever seen, not Mama, not Mrs. Wentworth, not even one of Miss Clattermore's ladies, could compare to her in their presence or style. She and the folds of her dress filled up her chair so much that if it weren't for the carved, high back of it, I would have thought that she wasn't resting on anything at all. The smooth, black curls at her temples lay perfectly flat against her cheeks, telling the world that she was the kind of woman who wouldn't stand for anything or anyone she didn't like.

Seated next to her was a young man, his clothes slightly ill-fitting, his shirt collar loose at his neck, his coat sleeves just shy of his wrists. Despite the comical way that one of his ears sat much lower than the other, he had an air of great seriousness about him. His honey-coloured hair was slick with oil and his garments were clean and whole, without any tears or shine to them at all. Hanging on a hook behind him was a brown wool cap with a short brim. It, too, had a rightness about it. This was not a boy from Chrystie Street. This was a boy who cared how things ended up, a boy who'd never allow his hat to touch the ground.

"Please sit," Mrs. Birnbaum said, closing the ledger and pushing it aside. "I'll get to you in a moment."

I sat down on a stool at the table and waited.

All around her were piles of trinkets—watches, hatpins, necklaces, rings, brooches. To her left was a small bucket labelled "Herr," to her right, a bucket labelled "Frau."

The boy pushed the hair off his forehead with the palm of his hand, his long, slender fingers making straight rows through his well-kept mane. I touched my face when he looked at me, self-conscious about my bruises and the mess of my hair. I must've seemed a sad rag picker to him.

"'$20 REWARD,'" the young man read out loud from a newspaper in front of him on the table. "Lost on Monday morning while riding the Fourth Avenue street car—A Lady's Honeymoon pin. Gold crescent with bee and blue gem flower. The above reward will be paid and no questions asked if returned to No. 14 Irving Place.'"

Mrs. Birnbaum scooped one of the mounds of jewels towards her and began sorting through it with her thick fingers. Two watches (one with a chain, one without), four stick pins, and a sweet, gold pinkie ring with the initial *L*. When I saw the ring, I thought it looked the right size to fit my finger. It would have made my hand look gentle and fine, and when I wore it I could say that my name was Lucy or Laura or Lydia or Lily.

Mrs. Birnbaum kept at the pile until she found the pin the boy had described. Taking hold of a special lens she had clipped to a metal band that circled her brow, she flipped it down over her left eye and twisted at it until she was satisfied. It made her look lopsided and strange, like one eye was right and good while the other had been plucked from a fish. She held the pin to the light and peered at it through the lens, humming a little tune while she stared at it. I didn't mind the wait, however long it might take. I liked being close to that pretty little ring and watching this big, fish-eyed woman sing to bits of gold and silver.

Mrs. Birnbaum's eyes went large and soft as she looked at the pin, and for the first time I could see why Mr. Birnbaum must love her. There was something sweet about the way she gazed at it, as if she had the power to make the pin more precious just by the touch of her glance. "Sapphires for the petals, and a pearl in the centre," she said. "How lovely."

She turned it over once, then twice, and then positioned the lens in front of her eye again. "'Forget me not,'" she whispered, reading the sentiment on the back of the pin. "How dear." Then, clucking her tongue against her teeth, she shook her head. "But I'm afraid twenty dollars isn't quite enough for the owner to get it back. It looks like Mr. Birnbaum gets this one." Arching an eyebrow, she smiled at the young man and added, "One must always consider the sum of the parts."

Mouth firm, he nodded in agreement.

I took a moment to glance around the room. In the corner was a large, bamboo birdcage with a magpie sitting on a perch inside it. The bird seemed to nod at Mrs. Birnbaum's words as well. The door was wide open, so the occupant could come and go as it liked. The bird tilted its head and looked at me for a moment, then turned away to preen itself. Its long, black feathers made me think of Mrs. Wentworth and the way her cape had hung down off her shoulders the night she took me away from Mama's. I anxiously wondered if all the wealthy ladies in New York knew one another, and if Mrs. Birnbaum knew Mrs. Wentworth, and if somehow my being here meant that she would try to put me back into Mrs. Wentworth's hands.

Making a sweet cooing sound, the bird flapped to the back of Mrs. Birnbaum's chair. Taking the pin from her hand with its beak, the bird hopped to the corner of the desk and dropped the pin into the bucket marked "Herr." It nodded again, whistling and then jeering out what sounded like a question. "Cake-cake-cake?" Then the bird repeated the word once again, this time so clear it sounded like a baby begging its mother. "Caaaake?"

Mrs. Birnbaum scolded the bird, "Soon, Jenny Lind, soon."

My empty belly grumbled at the thought of any kind of food, so loud I was sure Mrs. Birnbaum, the boy and the bird must have heard it.

The young man went on to read more queries for lost things–a heart-shaped pendant, a ruby ring, a handful of pocket watches. As he read, Mrs. Birnbaum located each item, almost as if by magic, then deemed it either worthy of the reward offered or for Mr. Birnbaum's pot. Any "found" jewels were placed in small boxes and labelled, to be returned to their owners "posthaste."

$100 REWARD. Lost on Friday last,
while strolling along St. Mark's Place–
a man's gold ring in the shape of a
lion's head with rubies for eyes.
The above reward will be paid and no questions asked
if returned to No. 75 Washington Place.

Voices came from behind us at the door. When I turned to look, I saw two boys talking to Mr. Birnbaum. They seemed much like the other guttersnipes I'd seen, trousers torn at the bottoms, worn-out soldier's caps crooked on their heads. Mr. Birnbaum spoke to them in a cheerful tone, inviting them to go downstairs.

"I believe Barber Jim is in the cellar with a few other lads. Maybe you'd like to join them?"

The boys answered together, "Oh yes, sir, we would." Then they tipped their hats and disappeared down the stairs.

"Caaaake!" Mrs. Birnbaum's bird complained.

The woman turned to the bird and held out her hand. "Oh, my dear Jenny, I haven't forgotten you. Come here."

The bird hopped along the table and right into Mrs. Birnbaum's lap. As fast as Mrs. Birnbaum could bring spongy bits of cake from her pocket, the bird gobbled them out of her hand. I could smell the cake from where I sat, the odour of sweet cherries reminding me of times I'd snuck Mama's empty kirsch bottle out of the cupboard and under the blankets of the bed. I'd opened it up and breathed what was left of the scent until I could taste the liquor in the back of my throat.

Stroking the magpie's feathers, Mrs. Birnbaum bent over and kissed the top of its head. The bird looked lovingly up at her and cooed. When it had finished, Mrs. Birnbaum guided it with her hand to perch on the back of her chair.

> Magpies never push their offspring from the nest. The mother carries her baby down to the ground instead, staying with her, watching everywhere she goes until she learns to fly.

"Let me see it," she said at last, turning away from the bird and holding her hand out to me. "Show me what you've got."

I pulled the bracelet from my wrist, all the while wishing I could keep it. I knew it wasn't for me, but that didn't change my desire to have it snug and warm against my skin.

Mrs. Birnbaum's eyes widened as she placed the bracelet on a set of scales at the far end of the table. She stared at the weights, one finger to her lips as if it helped her to think. Picking the bracelet up again, she turned it in her fingers, looking at it all the way around, inside and out.

"Anything else?" she asked as she slipped the bracelet over her hand and up her arm.

Unsure of what she might offer me, I thought of Mrs. Wentworth's fan. I could feel it against my chest, poking at my skin with every breath. I guessed that Mrs. Birnbaum would be glad to take it, but in the end, I chose not to show it to her. It wouldn't fetch the same sort of price as the bracelet, and I wanted something to remind me that Mrs. Wentworth didn't win. It would be there if I got desperate for something else to sell.

"No, ma'am."

"Do you still have entrance to the house where this came from?" she asked, stroking the bracelet with her fingers.

"No, ma'am."

"Pity."

Leaning close, she whispered in the young man's ear. He nodded to her and opened a wooden box that was sitting on the table. Picking out a few coins, he handed them to Mrs. Birnbaum, who in turn handed them to me.

"For your trouble," she said, her smile revealing one gold tooth at the corner of her mouth.

"Thank you," I said, gazing at the coins in disbelief.

"I can take some of it back, if you like," she said, reaching out her fat fingers, ready to pinch a dime away. "Perhaps I gave you too much?"

I closed my hand and shoved the coins deep into my pocket. "No, ma'am," I said, unsure whether she'd meant what she said.

Seeing my confusion, she laughed at me. The bird laughed right along with her, raucous and long, and then asked for more cake.

"There's no bickering over price or pay with Mrs. Birnbaum," Nestor had said. "Don't ask her for anything and when she gives you your share, don't you dare count it. It shows you trust her and she can trust you."

Thinking she was done with me, I moved to get up from my stool. Before I could stand, she held up a hand to stop me. "Don't leave just yet," she said, pushing back her chair and exiting the room.

When she returned she came to my side, holding two shawls, one in either hand. The first was delicate and lovely, made of figured silk with lace along the edges. The second was fashioned from wool, and although its plaid had faded in one corner the garment was sturdy-looking all the way around. It was long and thick, and would make for a cozy blanket on cold autumn nights.

"Which one do you prefer?" she asked.

"Oh, I can't afford to buy anything, thank you," I said.

She chuckled at me again. "Then I guess I'll have to let you steal it from me, eh, little thief?"

Accepting her invitation, I reached out and touched the wool shawl. "This one."

"Wise choice," she said, nodding with approval.

"Thank you, ma'am."

"And I thank you," she said, holding up her arm and shaking the bracelet around her wrist. "Do come back if you ever find anything else."

Nestor had said that the Birnbaums were the best fences in town. They were hidden in full view, and benefitted from a long-standing friendship with the police. "It's the murderous, hotheaded crooks the cops want–the type of criminals who disrupt the day-to-day of the city. New York would be a far worse place without the Birnbaums. They understand the importance of being fair."

As I went to leave, Mr. Birnbaum came in with a young woman who was unfastening her cloak to reveal large, deep pockets in its lining. Reaching into one of them she pulled out a silver comb. "There's plenty more where that come from," she boasted, teasing Mr. Birnbaum with a wink.

I nodded to them as I headed out the door. Then, slipping my hand inside my pocket so I could feel my share of Nestor's plan, I found four quarters, three nickels and a dime—tiny and thin and mine.

The vagrant and neglected children of the city, if placed in a double file, three feet apart, would make a procession eight miles long. From Castle Garden to Harlem Meer. From Wall Street to Fort Washington. Nearly thirty-thousand little souls.

—DR. SADIE FONDA,
The Annual Report of The New York Infirmary for Indigent Women and Children, 1871

XI.

A nickel would buy a plank in a crowded basement. Six cents would buy a night in the girls' Christian lodging house on St. Mark's Place. It was four cents more if you wanted a plate of pork and beans. I wouldn't have minded spending the four cents, but then, while my mouth was full, they'd go and tell me I was nothing but a sack of sin.

The lodging house ladies called every girl they met an orphan. It made perfect sense to them, even if it wasn't true. If a girl had no family, then they had an excuse to catch her and treat her soul like it needed fixing. As soon as all those wretched *r*'s started coming from between their lips—*refuge, reform, religion*—I would be out the door. The lodging house ladies could keep their prayers *and* their pork and beans.

For three pennies I could get a place on a floor. *Tin on the door, open floor.* A cup, a can on a string, a colander, an old kettle hanging on the latch—those were the things that told any wanderer they'd found a house with room to spare, a place to lay their head for the night. Even Mama had tied Papa's dented mug to the handle of our door whenever we needed to collect extra pennies to make rent.

We'd get as many as a dozen women in one night, some with children in tow. In the morning, I'd see them sleeping on the floor, or leaning with their eyes closed against the walls of our front room. Even asleep, there was sadness in their faces. Maybe they had no home, or the mister was angry, or somebody had held tight to the handle of an iron skillet while saying something they shouldn't have. Mama didn't ask. All that mattered was that they had three pennies and no place else to go.

The money I'd gotten from Mrs. Birnbaum bought food, a bit of time off the street, a kerchief for my shorn head, a knife for my pocket and a new pair of boots. The kerchief was a square of Turkey-red calico, and the knife, although rusty and dull, made me feel secure. The boots were second-hand, of course, from a cobbler's stall at Tompkins Market. I'd picked them off one of the long poles the shoe man had propped up along the back of his place. He slid fourteen pairs off the end of the ladies' stick before he got to the ones I wanted. They were black with red leather at the toes, and while not pretty, they fit me far better than the pair Caroline had given me to wear at Mrs. Wentworth's. I'd gladly traded that pair for the cobbler's, sure that the new ones would be sturdy enough to last me through the winter.

October arrived along with empty pockets and the need to think ahead with every step. Mama had always said

October was her favourite month of the year. "Another fine month ending in an *r*, safe to eat all the oysters you want without having to worry about a troubled gut." I'd loved autumn for different reasons–for sunsets and candlelight coming sooner every evening, and the way people forgot all the terrible things that summer made them do–but this year, October's uncertainty, its days of rain with no end in sight, and first fires in dirty chimneys sending homes up in flames, worried me to no end.

Hot-corn girls sang on every corner, their baskets perched on their hips.

> *Hot Corn! Hot Corn!*
> *Here's your lily white corn!*
> *All you that's got money,*
> *poor me that's got none,*
> *come buy my hot corn,*
> *and let me go home!*

They were sweet-looking girls around my age and I hoped I could become one of them. I envied their steady pay and their ability to carry a tune while being badgered by sporting men and roughs.

"*I'll come home with you!*"

"*I got some hot corn for ya, girlie!*"

"*How about some butter for that* corn?"

The men gladly paid their three cents an ear, but it wasn't the corn, harvested dry and bloated back to life by boiling, that they were after. Blushing cheeks, hot with embarrassment, were what they craved.

Arnica Liniment.
Add to 1 pint sweet oil, 2 table-spoonfuls tincture of arnica; or the leaves may be heated in the oil over a slow fire. Good for wounds, bruises, stiff joints, rheumatism and all injuries.

I went to Mr. Pauley, the man who hired the girls to sell his corn, but he had no interest in taking me on. My kerchief covered my hacked-off hair, but the bruises hadn't yet faded from my face. He took one look at me and told me to go away. "I need girls with fresh faces, not pathetic-looking waifs."

Mr. Finnegan, the flower girls' boss, said the same.

My first night on Chrystie Street, I slept on the roof of Mama's building, relying on its bricks and mortar to give much-needed warmth in the chilly autumn night. I knew I should've gone away from there, but I found great comfort in being close to the place I'd once called home. In summers past, Mama had let me tent on the roof. I'd used piles of newspaper for my mattress, and an old sheet thrown over a wire as a shelter for my head. I knew where the handholds were in the brick on the side of the building, which ones were loose and which ones weren't. I knew just where to catch the fire escapes to make it the rest of the way to the top.

That night I spotted a wooden barrel on the next building over. Making a bridge with a stray board across the space between the two rooftops, I rolled the barrel back to my spot. Putting bricks on either side to keep it steady, I made my nest inside the thing by lining the bottom with newspapers and mouldy burlap bags I found in the rubbish. Other people came and went from the roof, mostly boys looking for a spot of their own for the night. The knife I'd bought from the junk man wasn't sharp enough to do much harm, so I kept a length of board by my side to use as a weapon. It had three nails sticking from one end and I named it Pride, hoping it would swing true before a fall.

In the mornings, I'd sit at the edge of the roof, watching for things to start squirming under the garbage that overflowed from the bins along the street. I'd make guesses as to whether something was a rat, a cat or a baby. Even if a bin was a little too far away, I could still make a pretty good guess as to what was inside it. A rat will wiggle and crawl all around, but then hold dead still if it's startled. A cat will dig and stop, then dig and stop, keeping at whatever it's after for quite a long time. A small child almost always goes straight in, trying to reach one precious thing. If they can't get to it, or can't find their way back out, they break down and cry.

I spent my days begging on the Bowery, only a short walk from Chrystie Street. Mama had always discouraged me from going there, saying it was a terrible place for a girl or anyone else for that matter. "If you've money in your pocket when you arrive, you can be sure it'll be gone when you leave." But I didn't have any money left to lose, so the thieves and temptations of the lively, broad thoroughfare didn't worry me.

Every building on the Bowery was flashy and loud. There were dance halls, third-class hotels, variety theatres, concert saloons and any number of amusements. Shooting galleries opened up to full view, shadow men and beasts waiting under striped awnings to get shot through the heart. One popular spot boasted a cut-out of a lion that let out an awful roar when fatally wounded. The place was always busy, scores of barefoot boys lined up to try their luck. A shiny knife would be their prize if they hit the bull's-eye painted on the snarling creature's chest.

Ragged organ grinders scolded their monkeys for chattering too much. Sad-faced boys sat on stoops, leaning on banjos or harps, plucking one string at a time and holding out their hats for a reward. "Copper, sir? Spare a penny?" they cried. An old man played the fiddle and danced, his eyes squinted shut to make people think he was blind. He could play just about any tune anyone asked of him, making his fiddle sound like ten. When he was finished, he'd laugh and smile and talk to himself, his mouth all gummy—not a single tooth in his head. I thought if anyone deserved charity, it was him. I promised myself that someday when I had money enough to share, I'd find him and put at least a quarter in his hat.

It takes equal parts of desperation and courage to beg well. Passersby look at you and think there must be laziness in your blood, that you've a secret sense of ease and glee with every penny that comes your way. Oh, if only that were so. There were as many kinds of beggars on the Bowery as there were storefronts, each one—man, woman or child—merely looking for a way to get through to tomorrow.

Some were lonely grandmothers worse off than Mrs. Riordan. Some were soldiers who'd been injured in the war. Most of them were missing at least one limb. Mr. Dillibough's right leg was gone all the way to his thigh. He had a polished wooden replacement the government had given him to help him get along, but he left it at home when he was working the Bowery because, as he liked to say, "Empty trouser legs have more appeal."

Maggie the Borrower paid young mothers for the use of their children. She could fetch quite a lot of sympathy with a babe swaddled in her arms, half again as much if she had a second child toddling along at her side, holding fast to her skirts.

Mr. Tomas was a weeper. He came out from the alley-ways at night, a dark cloth covering his face. He'd whisper in a hoarse voice, "Don't come near, I'm a leper." Then he'd ask for spare change. "You can drop it on the sidewalk. God will bless you for it."

Old Beckie was my favourite beggar of all. She was jolly and bright, and knew the hallmarks of any malady you could imagine. She'd fall ill on a street corner at the drop of a hat. Writhing in pain, holding her head or clutching her belly, she never asked for money. What she wanted was to be taken to the nearest hospital (preferably by swift horses pulling a doctor's carriage) and to be given food and shelter and attention for the night. I found it hard not to send her off each time with a round of applause.

I tried my hand at picking a gentleman's pocket, thinking that because I'd gotten away with stealing from Mrs. Wentworth I might have some natural affinity for thieving, but my first time at it, I got caught. The gentleman whose money clip I'd lifted took me by the arm and shouted, "Thief! Thief!" at the top of his lungs. Frantic and scared, I dropped the money, and squirmed out of his grasp and ran away. No policeman had been near enough to hear his cries, but his anger had frightened me so much that I vowed not to try the trick again.

After that, I fashioned myself into a nibbler. I liked the gambit because it wasn't a trick or a lie. I simply had to make my hunger visible for everyone to see.

Late mornings I'd buy an apple from Mrs. Tobin's green-cart. Sitting on a nearby stoop, I'd eat the thing down to the core. At the noon hour, I'd sit myself on the curb in front of the windows of Mr. Mueller's bakery. Clutching the shawl Mrs. Birnbaum had given me, I'd stand there, looking sad, sucking and gnawing on my nicely browned apple core. Customers and passersby who felt sorry for me put pennies and nickels in my hand.

Once, I spotted the crooked-eared young man who'd been sitting next to Mrs. Birnbaum the day I'd visited her. He was moving through the crowds, elegantly tipping his hat to people along the way. He even stole a watch from the pocket of a gentleman who was bending over to give me a penny. His fingers dipped under the man's coat, the watch chain glinting, slithering out of its pocket like a golden, charmed snake. The boy looked at me and winked, then was gone like a ghost.

Every other day (precisely at one, according to the clock in Mr. Mueller's window), a pair of girls would come to fetch a large box from the baker. "Hey there, what's your hurry?" the bootblack on the corner would shout each time they strolled by, ever confident, even though the girls never bothered to look his way. They were far more interested in the gentlemen at the oyster bar two doors down from Mr. Mueller's.

The girls wore their hair piled on top of their heads, curls pulled out from under their hats here and there to make them look knowing, yet sweet. Their dresses had been cut to make them look like ladies, but their faces still held the freckled innocence of youth. I'd watch them pass by, admiring their flounced skirts, Nestor's voice sounding in my head. *I should hope you'd think better of yourself and of me . . .*

Did he know how little I'd get from Mrs. Birnbaum or how fleeting the money would be? Those girls had nice dresses and, I was certain, soft beds. They were the ones thinking better.

The lodging house ladies often paraded behind them, handing out broadsheets to all the girls on the street. In thick black letters across the top, the notices read, *Girls, don't go with strangers! WHITE SLAVERY IS REAL.* Underneath was a picture of a girl standing behind a barred window, pleading for her life. *Dear God, if only I could get out of here.* Staring at the girl from the shadows was a man, the brim of his hat crooked, a cigar held tight in his smirking lips.

I took one of the sheets back to the roof and hid it between the newspapers in my barrel, not because I was worried someone would try to steal me away, but because I thought the girl in the picture looked beautiful, even in her fear. She was neat and clean and there was something about the lace along the neck of her dress that said it wasn't too late for her. Before I'd fall asleep at night, I'd practise being like her, clasping my hands together at my heart and rolling my eyes up to heaven.

One morning, just three weeks after I'd come back to Chrystie Street, a man grabbed me tight around the waist as I was climbing down from the roof.

"Gotcha!" he said as he pulled me to the ground.

I struggled, but his hold was far too strong.

"Where's your mother?" he asked, his breath hot in my ear.

Mr. Cowan had found me and had come to collect the rent.

"Let me go!" I twisted in his arms to face him, my back against the brick, my arms pinned so I was unable to reach my knife.

He put his face close to mine. "I knew it was you, Princess, sneaking around on my roof." Then he licked my cheek and hissed in my ear. "Tell me where your mother's got to."

He used to visit her on the last day of every month, like a hungry tick. He'd show up, his big liver-coloured dog at his heels. Mr. Cowan and the dog looked alike–both of them shovel-faced and wheezing–only the dog's eyes were yellow, which meant he couldn't hide in the dark. Mama would lead Mr. Cowan to the corner of the room, leaving me to sit with the dog. The dog and I would watch each other for a while, the animal pacing and sniffing the air between us. Then it would settle down in the middle of the rug to growl and whine at me.

"Such a pleasure to see you, Mr. Cowan. Is it the last of the month already?" Mama would ask, sidling close to him. "I'm afraid I'm a bit short today, but if you come by on Friday, say around supper hour? I'll give you the rest then. I'll cook you up a plate of sausages and cabbage for your trouble."

He sat at our table and ate our food a few times. Twice he'd gone with Mama to our backroom.

I'd looked through the keyhole once and seen Mama on her back, the weight of Mr. Cowan pressing her down into the tired straw mattress. He had pushed and grunted, and Mama's head had lolled to one side, turned away from his breath. I could've sworn she was staring right at me. Her face looked just like it did when she was counting the coins in her pocket with her fingers, or remembering her way through a nursery rhyme she half knew—*Oh that I were where I should be, Then I would be, where I am not; But where I am, there I must be* . . .

I'd closed my eyes to the dark arch of the tiny hole and thought, *"And where I must be, I cannot."*

Not long after that he told her he was tired of her.

"The end of the month is the end of the month," he'd say, before putting the tip of a pencil to his tongue and making marks in his thick black book. The only time I saw him come close to smiling was when he was writing in its pages, his long, dark beard bristling against his collar. "I'll be back tomorrow to collect the balance, plus a quarter's penalty, for my trouble." Before leaving, he'd rouse the dog with his cane, and say to me, "Penny and penny, laid up shall be many. Who will not save a penny, shall never have many."

Now Mr. Cowan's dog circled my legs and sniffed at my skirts.

"I don't know where she is."

Rubbing his body against mine, he kept at me. "How about you give Mr. Cowan a fuck?" he said. "Then we'll call it even."

I tried to scream but nothing would come.

From the other end of the alley came the shrill sound of a policeman's whistle.

Feeling Mr. Cowan's grip go loose, I thrust my knee between his legs and ran.

Many well-dressed and comely females whose ages range from fourteen to twenty-five years walk the streets of New York unattended by the other sex. They are Nymphes de Pave, or, as they are more commonly called, "Cruisers." Dressed in the best style, they are smart, good looking, fairly educated, and predisposing in appearances. All strangers in our city would do well to keep a bright lookout for this class of girls. They are to our public street what sharks are to the ocean.

–A Gentleman's Guide to New York, 1871

XII.

It wasn't the police who saved me from Mr. Cowan, it was a girl.

I nearly ran her over as I raced out of the alley, Mr. Cowan's dog giving chase, barking the whole way. The girl's sudden appearance caused me to trip on a crooked stone and fall.

"Hey!" I heard the girl shout.

Turning to look at her, I saw she'd put herself between me and the dog.

The animal stopped cold and stared at her, its body tense, foamy drool stringing from its jowls.

Hiking up her skirt, the girl kicked the dog square in the head. The animal yelped, tucked its tail between its legs and ran away.

Dressed in a fashionable frock with matching wrap and hat, the girl was a strange sight for Chrystie Street, yet somehow familiar to me. Even from the ground, I couldn't help but admire the buttery boots on her feet, and a skirt that boasted five rows of ruffles before reaching the hem. As I looked up at her, I recognized the rusty-red curls under the brim of her hat and her pale, freckled cheeks. She brought the Bowery and the scent of fresh-baked bread to mind, even though she wasn't holding one of Mr. Mueller's boxes in her hands.

"Are you all right?" she asked, leaning over to help me up.

As she did so, I spotted a shiny silver whistle dangling from a chain around her neck. It was shaped like a fox's head, the hoop for the chain clenched in its snarling teeth.

"I'm fine," I answered, waving her hand away and getting to my feet on my own, afraid she might consider giving me a kick if I soiled the white kid gloves that fit tight to her fingers. Still shaken by what had happened with Mr. Cowan, I looked over my shoulder to see if he'd decided to pursue me.

"He's gone," the girl said, giving me a knowing smile. "I saw him limp off the other way."

She'd saved me from my predicament, but I couldn't guess why. No matter how grateful I was for what she'd done, I figured she wouldn't want to be seen with me. "Thank you," I replied as I turned to make my way up the street.

Following close she said, "Wait—let me walk with you."

Her name was Mae O'Rourke, she was fifteen years old, and she'd come to the city from Patterson, New Jersey, by way of a marriage broker who'd claimed she had found the perfect gentleman for Mae to marry. "A doctor," she said, jangling her whistle on its chain, twirling it one way and then the other around her finger. "A well-respected gentleman wanting a runaway for a wife—I should've known the woman was lying. The man didn't mean to marry at all, or even keep a mistress. He just wanted a girl he could ruin and toss to the street."

"You got out of it, I guess?" I asked, desperately wanting to learn how she'd gone from being hoodwinked by a dishonest matchmaker to wearing fine clothes and carrying large boxes of baked goods.

"I did indeed," she said, grinning. "Our parting was much like your farewell to that gentleman in the alley."

I laughed at her remark in hopes that she might continue with her tale, but instead she asked me, "Have you got a name?"

"It's Moth," I answered. I felt embarrassed by the thin, homely sound of my tongue hissing too long between my teeth.

"How'd you get a name like that?"

"My father gave it to me."

"Not your mother?"

"She wasn't for it."

Pulling a clump of peppermint drops from her pocket, Mae worked to break them apart, then handed me a piece to suck on before popping one into her mouth. Clacking the candy against her teeth, she said, "I know a place on the Bowery that serves the best oyster stew. Graff's Oyster Bar—want to go there?"

I had a nickel in the bottom of my pocket but I needed

it to buy an apple from Mrs. Tobin. "I can't," I told her, looking to the ground. "I have somewhere I need to be."

She took me by the arm. "I'll pay," she said. "It's the least I can do after all you've been through."

My dress was tattered from all the times I'd put my boot through the edge of the hem while climbing to the roof, and the passes I'd made at washing myself at court-yard pumps hadn't made much of a difference to the filth that had taken up residence on my clothes and skin. I'd become so dirty I'd given up trying to keep clean. On the rare occasions I'd had extra money to spend, every shop-keeper I approached had turned me away before I got through their door. I knew Graff's had a cellar where a rougher crowd gathered from lunch until midnight, but the one time I'd tried to get in, I hadn't been welcome. "I'm sure they won't take me," I told Mae. "You're bound to get looked over if I'm by your side."

"Nonsense," she said as she began to steer me towards the eatery. "We'll visit the stand and eat in the beer garden— no one will mind. I know one of the oyster stabbers there. I'll tell him you're with me."

The scent of roasted peanuts and steamed oysters waft-ing from nearby vendors' carts nagged at my belly, making it impossible for me to refuse Mae's invitation.

By the time we got to Graff's, the courtyard was busy with people milling about, mostly men who'd come to drink beer and play checkers. A few women were there as well, tending to small children or babies they'd brought out for a stroll.

I recognized the gentleman standing in line in front of us as a regular. From the place where I sat at Mr. Mueller's to do my nibbling each day, I'd watched the lanky, well-dressed gent come and go from Graff's, his countenance always fairer after his belly was full. He'd sometimes dropped a penny at my feet on his way past the bakery door, but he'd never bothered to look me in the eye.

"The usual, sir?" the oyster opener asked him when it was his turn at the stand.

Pulling a shiny two-pronged fork from his pocket the gentleman flashed it at the stabber and said, "Yes, indeed."

"A dozen Blue Points, clear, coming right up," the opener declared.

The gentleman watched as the stabber began slinging oyster after oyster with his knife. "You're the chief surgeon of stabbers, my friend," he teased.

Deftly plopping the half-shells in a basket, the stabber boasted cheerfully, "Straight from the bi-valvery institute . . ."

The round-faced oyster man's smile grew even broader when he saw Mae approach. I wondered exactly what she'd meant when she said she was friendly with him.

"Two bowls of the best oyster stew outside of Dorlan's," Mae announced to the opener as we stepped up to his stand.

"Best oyster stew *anywhere*," the stabber replied. Ladling milky hot stew from a pot, he gently scolded Mae. "A pretty girl like you has no business being down by the river. When you want a belly full of oysters don't you dare go to Dorlan's. You come see me."

Mae winked at him and paid for the two steaming bowls of stew. Then she gave him another handful of pennies for a plate of beans and some crackers.

"It's all Shrewsburys in there, I'll have you know," he said, his cheeks pinking up with the touch of Mae's gloved hand.

"Little oysters are the sweetest and in every way better," she replied.

The oyster man took her money, returning her wink, and then gave me a terrible frown. For a few, all-too-easy moments, I'd forgotten my place on the Bowery. In an instant, the oyster man's disapproving gaze brought me back down to where he thought I belonged.

"She's all right," Mae told him, giving him a pout. "She's with me."

Buckling to Mae's appeal, he motioned for the two of us to go into the garden. "Go on, take a seat," he said, waving us through. "I won't charge you nothing for it."

It was a lovely day, with a gentle breeze and a sun so warm you'd almost think summer was trying to come back for an encore. An *oompah* band was playing away under a half-tent in the corner of the garden, the musicians' cheeks puffed fat with every note. I walked beside Mae, forgetting the state of my dress and the oyster man's stare. One look from her had made it easy to pretend life was perfect.

As we settled ourselves at the end of a long table she asked, "How old are you, Moth?"

"Twelve," I said, reaching for my bowl of stew.

"I would've guessed fourteen, maybe fifteen," she said. "You seem much older than twelve."

Slurping a hunk of oyster down my throat, I croaked, "Thanks."

"Do you sleep on that roof every night?"

"Most nights."

"You can't go back there now, though," she said. "Not after what happened."

"No, I guess not."

As it was, I rarely slept the night through on the roof. Tucked inside my barrel, I'd stay awake listening for voices and footsteps that came too near. I feared someone might give the barrel a shove and roll me off the edge of the building, or at the very least try to oust me from my spot. When I did manage to fall asleep, visions of Mrs. Wentworth haunted my dreams. She'd cackle and scream as she tried to strangle me with the ribbon that secured her fan around my neck. Gasping, I'd wake, crying out for Mama.

"I know someone who can help you make a new start," Mae said, pushing her bowl aside. "She'll put you in new clothes, give you a place to stay—"

The cut of her dress, the quality of her boots, the winning smile she'd given the oyster opener all pointed in one direction.

"Are you a whore?" I whispered, interrupting her before she could finish.

My question, blunt and awkward as it was, didn't seem to bother her in the least. Tugging at the wrists of her gloves and pulling them taut, she looked me in the eyes and replied, "Almost."

THE INFANT SCHOOLS OF GOTHAM

Hidden among the more legitimate venues in New York are any number of establishments providing lesser, baser entertainment. These days, even the loftiest and most sensible of our citizens are aware of the scourge of gambling houses, concert saloons, rat-fighting pits and brothels—both high and low—that thrive in the metropolis.

The latest such business to make its home in our city is far more disturbing and deceptive than all the rest. Worst of all, it is kept from view in such a way that even if you were searching for it, you might not know it was there. It is an establishment known to sporting men simply as an "Infant School."

Maidens are kept there—in the rooms above—as young as eleven, twelve, thirteen years of age. They are being "raised" by a worldly matron, after being sold off by their parents or having come there by invitation from a girl who has already been "educated" on the premises. They are pampered and groomed, and then "certified" as *virgo intacta* and set on a path to their demise.

An Infant School off the Bowery

One such place exists near the Bowery and Houston Street. By looks, it is certainly not the detestable hellish place one might imagine. It is a home, with parlours and rooms both warm and bright. It is fashionable and comfortable in the kindest, bohemian sense.

The men who come there specifically seeking out "fresh maids" are of surprising ilk. They are often gentlemen of high station who believe their appetite for virgins to be in keeping with their important lives. Like-minded men sit at the club, sharing the information of location, quality and purchase price as readily as they exchange stock tips. When asked, "What of your dear wives?" they claim that their spouses wait patiently for them at home, fully aware of their transgressions. Their women gladly turn a blind eye, feeling it is better their husbands start fresh each time they are unfaithful, rather than indulge in the company of a seasoned lady of the night.

Miss E_., the matron of such an infant school, boasted that one particular gentleman's habit of procuring maids had grown to the point that each Sunday he sends his wife off to church and then has a girl delivered directly to his house for his enjoyment.

The matron shows no remorse for her dealings. She says she is proud of how she "raises" her girls and that "they are far better off under the roof of my fine home, than out on the street."

Miss E_. went on to explain that the girls are brought into the trade gradually, with care and consideration for their tender age. Men are required to court them, in a sense, buying the girl of their choosing candies and gifts as an overture to their deflowering. "My position here is as a watchful mother. I make certain the men who come for my girls are well-looking and kind. None of my girls has ever been hurt, or stolen away, or used as a virgin cure."

A Virgin Cure?

"It's a lie of the most terrible and monstrous sort," the matron explained. "The notion that a man can be cured of French pox or any other disease by laying with a virgin is preposterous. And it's nothing but a thorn in the sides of all who wish to protect young girls and raise them up right." The disdain in her voice was evident. "None of my girls, not one," she insisted, shaking her head. "I keep my girls safe."

No. 73 East Houston Street
(on the corner of Houston and Elizabeth)
Miss Emma Everett – Five lady boarders

Miss Everett, the dashing brunette whose smiling face is ever ready to welcome her patrons, keeps this house. "Little Emma," as she is generally called, has five young lady boarders whose cheerful dispositions tend to drive away the blues. The bewitching smiles of the fairy-like creatures who devote themselves to the services of Cupid are unrivalled by any of the fine ladies who walk Broadway in silks and satins new.

There is a regular physician attached to this house, and every attention is shown to its visitors. It is a first-class place, quiet and orderly—comfortably fitted up with French mirrors, Brussels carpets, rosewood furniture and superb bedding.

BY APPOINTMENT ONLY.

A Gentleman's Companion to
New York City, 1871

XIII

Mae confided that after she'd gotten out of the situation with the false marriage broker, she'd called on the only person she knew in the city, a young woman named Miss Rose Duval. Also from Patterson, New Jersey, Miss Duval was a distant cousin of Mae's who had once shown promise as a stage actress, but through a chain of unforeseen events wound up a whore instead.

"I didn't know any of it until I saw her again," Mae said. "Even her mother had no inkling she'd become a belle of the boudoir rather than a star of the stage."

Mae had begged Rose to help her, explaining that she had her reasons for not returning home, the greatest of which was the terrible beating she'd get from her father if she dared to show her face again at his door. Seeing Mae's distress, Rose promised to find a way to assist her.

"He's not my real father," Mae said, after noticing the concerned look on my face. "He's just the man my mother married after Papa didn't come back from the war. He loves her and hates me. It's as simple as that."

I knew when it came to love or bruises, nothing was ever simple. Still, I chose not to press Mae to talk further about her family.

In 1871, under common law, the age of consent was ten years of age. (In Delaware it was seven.)

The young girls of New York understood (for better or for worse) the value of declaring themselves to be of a palatable age to gentlemen. Twelve sounded far too young to the ears of any man with a conscience or heart. Sixteen, even when uttered by honest lips, inevitably brought the girl's purity into question.

Of the years left between, fifteen was declared to be the ideal number.

I didn't want her asking after mine, and her past wasn't nearly as important to me as the fact that she was now a girl-in-training at a first-class brothel on Houston Street.

"There's whores and then there's near-whores," Mae said, as we walked together up the Bowery. "And only the best madams in the finest brothels know how to make something out of the difference between the two."

Motioning to the stoop of a clean, modest-looking house just ahead of us, she said, "You wait here. I'll go in and get Miss Everett to come meet you."

"All right," I replied, taking a spot halfway up the steps.

"Oh, and remember," Mae added, turning back. "You're fifteen years of age—fourteen if she doesn't believe you." Then she opened the door and disappeared inside the house.

The bevelled glass in the door reminded me of the entrance to Mrs. Wentworth's, and although Mae had seemed honest enough to me, it was hard to shake the memory of being caught in a situation with no way out. I thought of Eliza Adler, her body floating in the river. I stuck my hand in my pocket to feel for my knife. *If I die today, at least I'll go with a full belly.*

Mrs. Riordan had often reminisced about her childhood, saying, "We was poor, but we didn't know it." But she'd had a family and a mother who'd bothered to care for her— she'd had love. I hated being poor. Mama never did anything to make our life seem better than it was. She'd spend her days making something out of nothing for everyone else, but when it came to inventing happiness for me, it was too much trouble. *I won't be like you, Mama. I won't fade away.*

Laughter came from the other side of the door along with the voices of at least three young women. Although

I couldn't make out much of what they were saying, I could tell they were having a high time teasing each other. "It's true!" one of them exclaimed, amid more fits of laughter. I was all but certain it was Mae.

Over our stew, she'd told me a fair bit about the matron of the house, Miss Emma Everett. Mae had explained that she knew of any number of madams across the city who'd be glad to take me on, but that none of them cared about their girls half as much as Miss Everett did hers. "Those other women only care for profit," Mae said with an air of disgust. "They allow men to line up halfway around the block and wear out their girls' bodies just so they can fill their pockets with more cash.

"Raising girls to be gentlemen's companions, and highly paid ones at that, is Miss Everett's business. She'll start you off slow and smart, teach you to keep company like a lady, and how best to attend to a gentleman's needs. No agreement is made until she feels a girl's ready, and even then, only if the gent's willing to pay the right price. Miss Everett's girls live freely and generously. We drink, eat and sleep like royal mistresses, and care for nobody on earth."

I could tell she was being careful to put things in a way she thought would sound best to my ears, but I kept quiet and let her finish. I was just so thankful to be seen as more than a sad-faced girl in a ragged dress.

Not long after the sound of the girls' laughter died away, the door to the house opened and a woman appeared. Petite and attractive, she stood above me on the steps, wearing a blue satin dress that dipped low at the neck and gathered tight at the waist. Her hair was pulled back and tucked inside a pretty snood, its long ribbon hanging gracefully behind her right ear. The lace gloves she wore on her hands matched it perfectly, down to the ties at her wrists.

"Miss Fenwick?" she asked.

"Yes, ma'am," I replied as I got to my feet, regretting I'd not stood up as soon as I'd heard the latch move in the door.

After looking me over from head to toe she said, "You may address me as Miss Everett."

"Yes, ma'am," I said with an awkward bow. Then, stumbling to find a more proper greeting, I added, "Pleased to meet you, Miss Everett."

By the lines at the corners of her mouth, I could see she was past the age for bridal gowns and babes in arms. The telltale wrinkles on her powdered, heart-shaped face gave her a look of constant seriousness.

"This way, Miss Fenwick," she said, holding the door open for me.

The house was far more lavish on the inside than out. It was just as well-fitted as Mrs. Wentworth's home, yet more comfortable and bright. Rather than having tiles in the entryway, carpets had been laid the entire length of the hall, so thick I thought I was about to sink into the floor with every step.

Miss Everett led me to the front parlour and invited me to sit. "Wait here while I arrange a few things, then we can discuss matters further."

I nodded, but before I could reply she turned her back on me.

Mae was there in the parlour with another girl, the two of them seated on a couch with plum-coloured velvet cushions. Fresh bouquets of flowers had been placed on every table, and the air in the room was thick with the scent of roses. A piano filled one corner, a gilded harp another, and fine paintings covered nearly every inch of the walls. There was a picture of a cabbage rose opening up to beams of sunlight, and a scene of a river winding through countryside making its way to a forest glen. Hanging over the piano was a portrait of a young girl holding a basket of fruit. Her blouse had fallen to reveal one shoulder, and her hair tumbled in loose curls around her neck. So serene was the expression on her face, I guessed she hadn't a care in the world. The brass plate attached to the frame read, *The Gypsy Girl's Bounty*. From the room's tasselled curtains to its chandelier, to the tea cart that was parked in front of the couch, I wanted it all.

The cart was set with a silver service and three round trays piled high with perfect, tiny cakes. There were round ones, and square ones and even little cakes shaped like hearts—all frosted with sugar ribbons and icing flowers of yellow, blue and pink.

"Tea?" Mae offered, reaching for the teapot.

"Yes, please," I answered, hoping that it might take my mind off worrying over whether Miss Everett was going to take me in.

The girl next to Mae stared at me, her blue eyes bright and sweet, as if she were still a child who could easily be impressed. Her hair was the colour of clean straw and the dress she wore was even nicer than Mae's, a beautiful pink frock with a princess neck and velvet trim. She was shapely and pretty, but didn't act as if she knew it.

"This is Alice Creaghan," Mae said, handing me a saucer with a steaming cup of tea.

"Mae brought me here too, when I had no place to go," the girl confided. "She spotted me running for my life and stepped up to save me."

Alice had the same crazy-eyed zeal when she talked about Mae as the missionaries I'd seen up on their soapboxes along the Bowery, shouting for people to come to them to be *saved*. They pounded their fists against their bibles and read lengthy passages about temptation and hell to anyone who'd listen. "When she brought me to Miss Everett's," Alice said, "I thought I'd died and gone to heaven."

Reaching for one of the little cakes on the tray, Mae said, "Who knew heaven was a brothel." She winked at me as she bit into the treat with her shiny white teeth.

I reached for one of the cakes as well and stuffed the whole of it in my mouth at once. The thick icing stuck to my tongue, its sweetness melting and humming down my throat.

"Mae came in through Miss Rose Duval," Alice continued. "Miss Duval has her own room and a steady gent. He brings her anything her heart desires and pays for her to be seen by only him. There's even talk he's planning to put her in an apartment soon, in the Fifth Avenue Hotel. He's Chief of Detectives, you know."

Shaking her head, Mae frowned at Alice. "You shouldn't have said that last bit."

"What's the harm in it?" Alice complained. "Moth will soon be one of us."

"If Miss Everett agrees to it," Mae said, taking another cake.

"And if the doctor says you're clean," Alice added, then smiled at me reassuringly.

Doctors rarely came to the slums of Chrystie Street. The people there either couldn't afford their care, or were too scared to call for them. I'd grown up hearing stories of the bad things that happened when the doctor came. Aside from the pain and tears he'd likely bring to your door, the bill he'd leave behind would take you straight from the sickbed to the poorhouse.

Mrs. Popovitch's on Broome Street was the place most people went when they needed healing. Using remedies from the old country, she'd help women when they didn't want to have babies, or when the babies they did want got stuck. She yanked out bad teeth and knew how to *cup* away disease. She was a quiet woman, with large, strong hands, and hair gone white before its time. I liked walking past her house, especially on sunny days. She kept her cups sitting upside down in her window. They sparkled there, on a long, lace runner, waiting for Mrs. Popovitch to heat them up with a flame and stick them on a person's back. She claimed they'd suck the sickness right out of a person's body.

But Mama didn't trust physicians or Mrs. Popovitch. She said that if a person couldn't be cured by drinking a bit of tonic and taking to bed for a day, then maybe they weren't meant for this world after all.

When Alice mentioned the doctor, my cup slipped in its saucer, hot tea sloshing over the edge of the cup. "Don't worry," Mae said, shaking her head. "The doctor is a *lady* physician. She looks over all us girls."

Belly rumbling, I wondered if a lady doctor was any better than a man, and if I dared reach out and take a second cake for myself. The meal I'd shared with Mae felt like it had been days ago, and I longed for every last one of those cakes.

Mae pinched two cubes from the sugar bowl with a pair of silver tongs. Letting the cubes fall one after another into her cup, she gave me a sly grin as she reached back to the bowl once more. "Two makes it sweet enough, but I always add a third . . . just to make myself happy," she said. The last cube splashed into her cup, making the tea jump, but she didn't spill a single drop. She placed the tongs in front of me. "What makes you happy, Moth?"

I didn't pick up the tongs or take any sugar. I drank my tea fast, feeling the heat of it going down my throat, warming my belly.

Mrs. Wentworth's gold bracelet circled around my arm. A handful of coins in my pocket. Sugary cake melting on my tongue.

"Plenty," I told her, taking another sweet from the tray and popping it into my mouth.

With clasping arms and cautioning lips,
With tingling cheeks and finger tips.
"Lie close," Laura said,
Pricking up her golden head:
We must not look at goblin men,
We must not buy their fruits:
Who knows upon what soil they fed
Their hungry thirsty roots?

       –from *The Goblin Market*,
       Christina Rossetti, 1862

XIV.

While I sat waiting with Alice and Mae, two of the other young ladies who lived in the house came into the parlour. Half dressed, in flowing silk robes, hair tied in rags, they each filled a napkin with tea cakes and then wandered off again, busy, I assumed, with the task of preparing themselves for the evening ahead. One of them, a willowy girl with a mole on her cheek, nodded to me and smiled, but neither she nor the young woman at her side said a word.

"Miss Emily Sutherland and Miss Missouri Mills," Alice said, after they were gone.

As I saw Miss Everett coming down the hall to fetch me, Mae whispered, "Make sure you're quiet on the stairs– Miss Rose Duval's still sleeping."

I followed Miss Everett to the topmost part of the

house. I worried as we went, every step reminding me of the first night Nestor had led me to the servants' quarters at Mrs. Wentworth's.

Miss Everett ushered me into a room with three spool beds lined up the middle, each one dressed with soft-looking quilts and clean, fluffed-up pillows. Three dressing tables sat along one wall, pages from magazines picturing ladies in expensive-looking gowns pinned like wreaths around their mirrors. Hat boxes were stacked five and six high in the corners, piles of colourful hair ribbons draped over their tops. Compared to the space I'd shared with Caroline, the room was a warm, bright nest of girlish wonders. Closing my eyes, I imagined myself asleep here, my cheek resting on the pillows, my eyelids fluttering with dreams.

Miss Everett shut the door behind us. "Dr. Sadie will be joining us shortly," she announced, "but for now it's just the two of us."

I nodded to her, my belly turning. Graff's oyster stew and too much cake were threatening to make a terrible return.

"Strip off your dress," she said, arms folded, making it clear it was a command rather than a request.

I reached into my pocket and held tight to my knife. What if Mae was just leading me on, and there was a man waiting to take me right then and there.

"I assume you've a blade there," Miss Everett said, staring at the spot where my fist was clenched under the folds of my skirt. "You're welcome to keep it in your hand if it brings you comfort, but please remove your dress."

I'd wanted to seem confident, as if I understood everything that was going on, but it was too late for that. Letting go of my knife, I fumbled with the buttons at my collar, loosening the dress. When I was finished, the dress fell, the knife along with it, to the floor.

"You needn't worry," Miss Everett said, bending down, fishing in my pocket for the rusty blade. Placing the handle of the knife in my hand, she said, "If I was the kind of person who meant to hurt girls, you'd already be ruined and back on the street." Circling around me, she took hold of the edge of my worn, thin chemise and rubbed it between her fingers. "How old are you?" she asked.

"Fifteen."

"Good."

Discovering the ribbon I was wearing around my neck, she tugged at it, threatening to pull Mrs. Wentworth's fan from under my garment.

I put my hand to my chest to keep the fan in place.

"Shh," she said, "I only want to have a look."

I gave in to her request, and allowed her to draw it out.

"What a lovely thing," she said, turning the fan in her hand. "Where did you acquire it?"

"It was my mother's," I answered, praying she wouldn't detect my lie.

"I see," she said, as she let the fan drop. "Is she living?"

Not wanting to bring bad luck by saying Mama was dead when I didn't know it to be true, I simply said, "She's gone."

"Please take off your kerchief," Miss Everett said. "The doctor will need to check for nits."

Pushing the calico scarf off my head, I felt the greasy slick of my short hair. It had grown since leaving Mrs. Wentworth's, but was nowhere near being an acceptable length, especially for a whore.

Miss Everett let out a frustrated sigh. "You sold it, I suppose?"

"Yes, ma'am," I said, stacking yet another lie, neat and close to the rest, like sticks bundled for burning.

A quiet knock came at the door, followed by a woman's voice. "May I enter?"

"Yes," Miss Everett answered. "Come in."

The doctor came in, carrying a large, black bag. It sank into the quilts when she placed it on one of the beds. I wondered if there was anything in it that might stop my belly from lurching.

"I'm Dr. Sadie," she said, giving me a short nod as she took a bright red bar of soap from her bag.

Looking down at the floor, trying not to get sick, I replied, "I'm Moth."

She was dressed in black from head to toe, the fabric of her dress expensive, the cut so fine I was sure it had been made just for her. The buttons down the back of her collar and at her sleeves were silver, each one made to look like a tiny rosebud. They pointed to wealth and good breeding, but her forthright attitude said she didn't want anyone to make too much of it.

Untying the ribbon on her hat, she pulled it off to reveal dark brown hair, braided and pinned in a bun. After setting the hat on the edge of a washstand that was against the wall, she folded back the sleeves of her dress and went

There are many choices to be made in the daily life of a doctor's work. When faced with the choice to participate in the care of the residents of 73 Houston Street, or to dismiss said inhabitants as unworthy of my consideration, I chose the former.

My intention was not, as some have outrageously assumed, an attempt to satisfy depraved desire or base instincts on my part. It was, quite simply, for the sake of the young women who lived there and for the benefit of science. I've logged many pages of case histories, noted many valuable observations while visiting there.

about washing her arms and hands in the basin. The smell of the soap was as harsh as tar.

When she'd finished, she came back to her bag and took out a crisp, clean apron. Pulling it over her head she tugged it into place and then tied the strings around her waist. "I'm sorry," she said, apologizing before she'd even started. "I'll try to make this easy."

Miss Everett patted the edge of the bed closest to her and motioned for me to sit.

My legs, weak from nervousness, nearly buckled as I took my place. I wondered for a moment if I'd ever be able to stand again.

The doctor took a flat piece of silver from a chain at her waist. It looked something like Mrs. Wentworth's letter opener, but with rounded edges instead of coming to a point. I pulled back when she came at me with it.

"I need to see inside your mouth," she said, gesturing for me to open up, the tool still in her hand.

I did as she asked and she pressed the thing against my tongue and peered at my teeth, telling me to say "ah." Then she removed the thing from my mouth and set it on the washbasin. Gently tugging at my eyelids she stared at my eyes. Spreading the hairs apart on my head, she checked for nits, Miss Everett hovering the entire time. Thankfully I'd been spared them.

Then she had me lie back on the bed so she could feel my arms and legs and all around my belly with her fingers. After that, she asked Miss Everett to leave.

The woman seemed disappointed by the doctor's request, scowling at her all the way to the door. "I'll be waiting right outside," she said.

In a soft voice, Dr. Sadie explained, "I'm going to have to lift your undergarment now for an internal examination. I don't mean to hurt you. Please spread your legs wide and do your best not to move."

Feeling trapped and confused, I put my hand between my legs and held my knees tight together. As a child I'd held myself there in my sleep, one hand nestled, fingers cupped over the softest part of me so I'd feel safe. I'd thought nothing could harm me as long as I could feel the warmth of it, holding, holding, holding.

"Don't," I said, ready to run from the room. "I won't let you."

"All right," the doctor said, pulling my skirt back down over my knees before sitting herself at the end of the bed. "How old are you?" she asked, her voice filled with concern.

"Fifteen."

"How old?"

"Fourteen."

Shaking her head she said, "You're welcome to tell Miss Everett anything you like, but I ask that you not lie to me. I'm here to be of help, if you'll allow it. Your proper age, please?"

I refused to answer.

She took a small book from her bag and began to write in it. "Have you any family?" she asked, pencil in hand.

"My father left when I was young."

"And your mother?"

"She left too."

"How long ago was that?"

"It's been a while now."

The pencil was in a pretty ivory holder, carved and spiralled around like a ribbon.

"Do you have regular courses?"

"I don't know what that means."

"Have you had your first blood?"

"No."

"You've never lain down with a man? Never been put upon or seduced?"

"No."

"You understand what that means, and what Miss Everett expects from you?"

The thought of being with a man was frightening. Though I'd seen her that once with Mr. Cowan, Mama had explained very little to me about how things should go, saying she thought it was best a girl get her start not knowing any better.

"Do you understand?" the doctor repeated.

"Yes."

What I really knew was that, like the bracelet I'd stolen from Mrs. Wentworth, my virtue was a dangerous thing to keep, especially on the street. I'd never felt this more keenly than when Mr. Cowan had his hands on me, his breath greedy and hot against my cheek. It was inevitable that I should part with my innocence but at least under Miss Everett's roof I hoped I might get the chance to give it up for a fair price.

Putting aside the book, the doctor said, "If you haven't any other place to stay, there's a girls' lodging house over on St. Mark's Place–"

"I know it," I said.

"I'd be happy to help you get a spot there."

"No, thank you, I'm fine," I insisted.

In medicine, there is always the matter of practice before friendship. One tries to make oneself as human as possible.

I liked the girl the instant I met her. There was not a shred of nonsense about her (unlike so many girls her age). Even at her lowest, she knew who she was. In that way, we were more alike than different.

The doctor sighed. "The nights are getting colder now and the beds there will be harder to come by. They serve hot meals every night and hold classes to teach reading, arithmetic and sewing."

"I already know how to read and I'm staying here."

She stared at me, her eyes moving back and forth across my face. "You had bruises around your eyes, not so long ago. Did someone hurt you?"

Like a Gypsy, like a witch, like Mama, she knew how to see things in a person that they'd just as soon forget. Turning away from her, I refused to answer any more of her questions. I stayed silent until she was gone.

THE DOCTRESS OF THE BOWERY

BY MR. DANIEL CHARLES, special to *The Evening Star*

I first met the young doctress at an evening soiree held at the home of the esteemed Mr. Thaddeus Dink. I watched the graceful young woman from across the room, not knowing who she was. The other ladies in attendance gave her brief, polite smiles and then swiftly moved on to talk of china patterns or the latest fashions from Miss Demorest's closet. She seemed such a pariah, that had she not been as modestly and elegantly dressed as she was, I would have assumed she was the courtesan of some notorious gent. Needless to say, I was captivated by her from the start.

She is a rare creature, a lady physician working and striving in a society where many would just as soon she'd disappear. Some have called her unfeminine, while others have gone so far as to say she is more monster than woman. Still, she carries on. For the sake of her anonymity, I shall call her "Doctor S_."

It is obvious to anyone who makes her acquaintance that she comes from good breeding. Her beauty is of a refined nature, her stature delicate, yet full of vigour. How it is that she hasn't been married off is still quite puzzling to me. When I asked her why she had chosen the path of medicine over marriage, this was her reply.

"Medicine is my first love. It would be wrong of me to ask any man to stand second to it."

It Is Her Choice

While attending lectures at both the Women's Medical College of the New York Infirmary for Indigent Women and Children and the renowned Bellevue College of Medicine, Dr. S_. gained great sympathy for the less fortunate souls of our fair city. Although graduating in the top of her class, winning the medal for excellence in physiological studies, she has chosen to continue to carry out her practice on the meanest streets of this city. "I've seen many things I'd rather forget," she tells me, stopping herself from saying too much for fear of offending. "But my work here goes on."

October 16, 1871

Rounds were made to the usual boarding houses today. (Two cases of diphtheria, one infant with catarrh. Preventative powders and tracts on venereal diseases were given to young women at 111 and 112 Spring Street, as well as 97 Mercer.)

A new boarder has arrived at Seventy-three East Houston.

"Moth" Fenwick, allegedly fifteen years of age. After examining the girl, I would estimate her age to be closer to thirteen years at most. She's far too young in body and heart to be any older.

When I told Miss Everett as much, she argued that the child is fifteen and old enough to know her mind. "Malnourished," she insisted when I made note of the girl's undeveloped physique. As proof, she went on to say that she'd seen the girl begging on the Bowery on several occasions. Which begs the question—did Miss Everett entice her?

"She came of her own free will."

For my part in today's deceptions, I lied when Miss Everett asked about the girl's internal exam. (She got the news she wanted, nonetheless.) The girl is *virgo intacta*, but I didn't need to touch her to know it. I've seen enough girls in the infirmary, in orphanages, in lodging, boarding and whore houses to know whether or not a child has been had by a man.

She's too young. She's not bled yet. She has no family, no home.

I've been visiting that house for nearly a year, but

had never encountered a girl of such tender age. To the child's credit, she's intelligent and bold. I only wish she'd allowed me to find a place for her elsewhere.

Miss Everett was quick to remind me that I've nothing to offer a girl that can compare to what she's got to give. "A spot in a house of refuge? A position as a scullery maid or thread-puller? What sort of life is that?"

A life free from the threat of disease and the hardship of being put upon by men.

"Remember Katherine Tully," she retorted.

How can I forget?

S.F.

XV.

Miss Everett chose to take me on. "You'll do fine,"
she'd said, putting her hand on my shoulder after
the doctor was done with me. "I'm sure of it."

At first blush, life in the house seemed near perfect. Vases
filled with pink buds of affection graced every room. Boxes
of chocolates and bottles of wine sat crowded together on
a marble table at the bottom of the stairs, the cards attached
to them addressed to *Miss Sutherland, Miss Mills, Miss Duval.*

Even the house's cook, Mrs. Coyne, was everything a girl would want her to be, friendly and warm—the opposite of Caroline. She welcomed me with a bowl of chicken stew and a hearty "Pleased to meet you, miss," the minute I sat down for the first time at her kitchen table. The stew, made from the better parts of a bird, fresh carrots and peas, wasn't quite as tasty as the dishes Caroline had served Nestor and me, but it was still far above anything I'd ever gotten at home. I tipped the bowl to catch the last drops of broth in my spoon, not wanting to leave them behind.

"Save something for the rag-woman's pot," Miss Everett scolded, suddenly appearing at my shoulder.

I dropped the spoon in the bowl, handle clattering against the rim. "I'm sorry, ma'am."

Bristling at my clumsiness, she reached out to take the bowl. "Manners over appetite," she chided. "Grace knows no hunger."

Mrs. Tuesday was the rag-lady who'd come knocking at Mrs. Wentworth's kitchen door once a week. The hunched-over woman collected leftovers and rags in exchange for the buttons and spools of thread she carried in her two-wheeled cart. Her rig was pulled by a pair of Swissy dogs wearing collars of bells that jangled as they walked. On Tuesdays, Nestor took care to save the bones from Mrs. Wentworth's plate so he could give them to the woman's dogs. In good weather, he and Mrs. Tuesday would share tea on the basement steps. Before leaving, the rag-lady would sing a song for him, her voice rising up the bricks of the house and over the roof, filling the air with sadness and despair. I wondered if the woman who came to Miss Everett's back door could sing like that.

After I'd finished my meal, a young man came into the kitchen carrying a basket filled with boots. The pungent scent of blacking came with him. When he saw Miss Everett he set the basket down and pulled the faded soldier's cap he was wearing off his head. "The girls' boots is shined, Miss Everett," he said. "Anything else you need?"

His voice was strangely rough compared to his clean-shaven, soft-looking face. His brows, thick and dark, shaded large eyes with long lashes. Sleeves rolled up to his elbows, his sinewy arms hung down at his sides, their length putting his age somewhere between boy and man.

"Draw a bath for Miss Fenwick in Rose's room, won't you, Cadet?"

"Yes, Miss Everett," he responded. Taking two buckets from hooks on the wall, he set to work.

A tin washtub near the kitchen door was what Miss Everett said would normally be used for my bathing, but for my first bath in the house I was to use Miss Rose Duval's copper tub. "It was a gift from her lover," Miss Everett explained with pride, "delivered as a surprise for her seventeenth birthday."

I lost count as Cadet carried bucket after bucket of water from the heated boiler attached to Mrs. Coyne's stove, his hands turning red as he gripped their rope handles. His hair fell in his eyes and sweat dripped from his brow, and I felt terrible about the effort he was making on my behalf. If I'd had the courage I would've asked Miss Everett to tell him to stop, that surely he had carried enough hot water, but I was afraid to question anything she said for fear she might turn me back out onto the street.

Rose's room was warm with the glow of fire and lamp-light when we arrived. There was a bouquet of red roses on her dressing table along with a collection of perfume bottles and a silver brush and comb. Gilded mirrors–round, oval, oblong and square–covered an entire wall, reflecting the image of the plump-lipped, dark-eyed beauty waiting to greet me. With her dressing gown open at the neck and her dark hair spiralling around her shoulders, I could see why she'd thought to be an actress. Even half dressed Rose was something of a star.

"I'll leave Miss Fenwick to you," Miss Everett said to Rose.

"Certainly," Rose replied. Shutting the door after the madam had gone, she turned to me and said, "Right this way."

"Thank you, Miss Duval."

"Please, call me Rose."

Taking a small blue bottle from her dressing table, she pulled the stopper and shook a few drops of lavender-scented perfume into the bath. "Don't be shy," she said with a sweet smile. "Modesty makes the water turn cold."

The tub was near the fireplace, half hidden from the rest of the room by a tall, three-panelled screen. Decorated with scenes from the Orient, the screen reminded me of Mrs. Wentworth's fan, the creatures painted on it staring at me with fierce, hungry eyes.

Handing me a cake of soap, Rose directed me behind the screen. "You can undress back there."

I brought the soap to my nose and inhaled the strong, spicy scent of carnations. It had yet to be used–the cake's edges were still square. The innocent lump of lye and fat seemed quite a luxury, especially compared to the slivers

Caroline used to have me fetch from Mrs. Wentworth's bath for us.

"I'm here if you need me," Rose called from the other side of the screen.

I'd watched mothers dunk their babies into washtubs in the courtyard on the hottest days of the summer. The children would squeal from the shock of it, then giggle with glee. Mama had turned her nose up at the sight of them, so I was sure she'd never done the same for me. She had strict ideas about how to stay clean and tried her best to keep the water she used running like a river, according to Gypsy law. She only washed herself straight from the pump or with water poured from a pitcher over her skin, and never allowed the water in the shallow tub under her feet to collect past her ankles. "Baths breed sickness," she'd say, shaking her head.

The tub was large enough for me to stretch my legs nearly straight. Sinking into the warm, steaming bath, I scrubbed the oily sourness of the city off my skin, and then slid down until I could rest my head on the smooth, rounded edge of the tub. Comfort, ease and hopefulness conjured by the water, I would gladly have spent half the night lounging there. Mama could keep her superstitions.

"This is for when you're finished," Rose said, as a dressing gown appeared over the top of the screen. "There's no hurry, though. Mr. Chief of Detectives is busy keeping the peace tonight, so I've got the room to myself."

Muslin clinging to my skin, I came from behind the screen to warm myself by the fire. I flinched when I spotted my reflection in Rose's mirrors. The bath had caused my hair to spring into a curly halo that stuck out every-which-way from my head. It would be months before it would fall past my shoulders and I could plait it into one long braid.

"Come sit," Rose said, patting the seat of the dressing table's chair. "Let me see what I can do."

Settling there, I watched as Rose took up a bottle of Circassian oil and poured a generous amount of the sweet-smelling liquid into her hand. The bottle's label featured a winsome girl gazing at a bird in a cage. Her long, wavy hair, nourished and tamed by the magical lotion, flowed to the ground. After rubbing the oil into her palms, Rose stroked it into my hair, calming my curls.

"I swear by the stuff," she said. "I use it morning and night."

Opening a porcelain box that sat next to her brush and comb, Rose took out a rat of hair that had been fashioned into a sausage-shaped twist. "I had nits as a child and my mother cut my hair more than once. I save every strand now for fear I'll lose it again."

With combs and patience and the rat of her hair, Rose went about making it seem like my locks were as long as they'd ever been. No matter how I turned my head, it looked as if I'd simply chosen to pin my hair up into a sweet, lovely bun.

"I'll take extra care with the rat, I promise," I told her, touching her creation lightly to see that it was secure.

"Don't worry, I've got others," Rose said with a smile.

While I was certain Mama's tales about Mrs. Deery's madness had been more show than truth, I planned to do my best not to think any ill thoughts while wearing Rose's hair on my head. It was the least I could do.

"You got a first name, Miss Beautiful?" Rose teased,

as she watched me admire myself and her handiwork in the mirror.

"Moth."

"Moth?" She shook her head. "Miss Everett's never going to let you keep that. You'd better change it before she changes it for you."

Thinking she was making a joke, I didn't respond.

"I was *Ruth* before I was Rose," she confided. "Miss Everett said Ruth was far too biblical. I can just guess how she'll feel about a girl being named after a bug. She'll turn you into a flower or a state without a second thought. If you don't want to be called Iris or Georgia, you'd better find something to call yourself instead of Moth. That's certainly not your real name—what was the one your mother gave you?"

"Oh," I said, pausing to think. "It's Ada."

"Ada," Rose repeated, stretching the name out, her mouth wide open. "*Aye-dahh* . . . I like it. It has appeal."

Putting a finger to my chin, I looked in the mirror and tried pouting like Mae had done with the oyster man. *Moth. Moth Fenwick. Miss Fenwick. Miss Beautiful. Miss Ada Fenwick, beautiful girl.* For the first time in my life I actually felt pretty.

"You've done wonders, Rose," Miss Everett said as she came into the room, catching me still staring at myself in Rose's mirror.

"Ada made it easy," Rose replied, giving me a wink.

Coming to my side, Miss Everett whispered in my ear, "Careful with your pride, dear. You've still a ways to go."

My face fell.

"That's better," she said, smiling. "Much better."

The Bowery Concert Hall

257 Bowery

A fine resort for sporting men.

Nightly dances. Fun and frolic prevail.

Ladies enter free.

"An hour cannot be spent more pleasantly
than at this establishment."

–from *A Gentleman's Companion to
New York*, 1871

XVI.

A girl had one month's grace before Miss Everett expected her to lie down with a man. "Give or take a week, depending on your willingness," Mae explained. "If your training goes bad, or Miss Everett loses interest in you, then it's back to the street." If a girl did well, then the clothes and anything else she'd been given (so long as the bounty paid by the gentleman who took her maidenhood covered the cost) were hers to keep. As far as pocket money was concerned, Miss Everett didn't pay a girl a penny until after she'd been had by a man.

Running a brothel wasn't a lawful occupation, but Miss Everett and the other madams of the city had the advantage of numbers on their side. Manhattan was bursting with businessmen from near and far with large bank accounts and even larger appetites. Those who ruled the city from the private rooms of Tammany Hall turned a blind eye to their cravings. Boarding house matrons who catered to the needs of Mr. William Tweed and his friends were not only favoured by the mayor's office but rewarded for their efforts with protection by (and from) the law. Rose's ongoing affair with the Chief of Detectives was proof of that.

"She all but told me she's leaving to be kept by the Chief," Mae announced to Alice and me as we sat talking in our room a few days after my arrival. Primping in front of her dressing table mirror she added, "After Rose is gone, her room will be open for whichever girl's next."

There was overwhelming confidence in Mae's voice, in her posture and her attitude. She was certain that she was going to be the next girl. With only space for three full-time whores in the house, most girls who got their start at Miss Everett's didn't stay in her employ. They went on to work at brothels (of equal standing or better), their services bought by madams who hadn't the ability or patience to deal with the delicacies of brokering a girl's first time.

"Missouri Mills says sometimes Miss Everett will double up girls in a room if she thinks they merit keeping," Alice chimed in. "There might be room for all of us."

We three near-whores, Mae, Alice and I, shared the upstairs quarters—the room where Dr. Sadie had examined me. There was teasing and rivalry of course, and sometimes sharp words, but, in the short time I'd been there, there'd been more kindness than cruelty. We were sisters of a sort— with Miss Everett acting as our strange, sly mother.

Mae had been at the house three weeks, Alice, half that. It had only been five days since I arrived, and already I'd been given three sets of undergarments, several pairs of stockings, two day dresses with petticoats, a pair of boots, a soft bustle and a corset. I'd accepted the clothing without question, but after Mae made it clear how things worked, I'd begun to keep a list of everything Miss Everett put in my hands. Recording each item in the margins of an 1868 *Harper's Bazar* I found under my mattress, I was determined that my accounting would match Miss Everett's, line for line.

No matter how things added up, I was glad to be a pampered girl without a care. Miss Ada Fenwick had nice dresses, a full belly and a soft bed. Better than that, she had prospects and a chance at a life I'd never known.

My biggest trouble so far had been adjusting to my corset. Made from English leather and lined with muslin, it featured a system of buckles woven around it to supply added strength to the laces down the back. "You're to wear it day and night, until further notice," Rose had said as she fitted the stays to me, tightened the buckles one by one, then pulled hard on the laces.

Excited by the comeliness of my reflection in her many mirrors, I'd said "yes" to her pulling the laces ever tighter. The crush of the corset around my ribs was stifling, but I kept my shoulders back and my body upright in an effort to cooperate with the garment rather than struggle against it. I wasn't about to let something that had seemed so simple for Mrs. Wentworth defeat me.

"Here, Ada," Alice said, coming over to where I was sitting on my bed, "shall I let you loose for the night?"

Each evening Alice had taken pity on me and loosened my corset so I could sleep. She'd worn one since she was really young, and her torso was wonderfully curved, her waist small from years of training. Miss Everett didn't require her to wear a corset at night, which, it seemed, made her all the more sympathetic to my pain.

"Yes, please," I said, turning my back to her, anxious for relief.

Rather than getting ready to retire, Mae was donning a fresh dress, and adorning herself with her favourite hat and a drop of neroli oil behind each ear. She had plans to go to the Bowery Concert Hall, a nearby saloon that offered free admission to pretty young girls. They held dances there every night, including Sundays. Although Miss Everett had made it clear that we weren't allowed to go out after dark, Mae, having climbed out of (and back into) the window the week before without being discovered, was determined to try her luck again.

"You're going out again?" Alice asked, shocked at Mae's behaviour.

"*Amantes sunt amentes,*" Mae declared in a flirty voice. "Lovers are lunatics, my dear."

Alice shook her head and sighed.

"Stop fretting," Mae scolded. "I'll be home long before the house wakes."

"If Miss Everett discovers what you're up to she'll put you out on the street."

Taking Alice's hand, Mae stared at her with wide eyes. "But she won't find out, now, will she?"

Pulling her hand away, Alice muttered, "No."

"I only want to dance with some pretty gents before I'm sent to Rose's room," Mae complained. "Have you seen Mr. Chief of Detectives?"

"Rose likes him just fine," Alice argued. "He takes her

to the theatre, and to Delmonico's for steak and oysters, and to Sunday dinner parties at the Birnbaums.'"

"Mrs. Wolfe Birnbaum, on Clinton Street?" I asked, picturing Mrs. Birnbaum's magpie squawking through her mistress's parties, begging for cake.

"That's the place," Mae answered, giving me a curious look. "You've been there?"

"Only in the shop," I answered, and said no more.

Telling the truth about why I'd been at the Birnbaums' might have gotten me some respect from Mae, but now that I'd chosen whoring over thieving, I didn't want there to be any reason for Miss Everett not to trust me.

"Rose says Mrs. Birnbaum's dinner parties are over-the-top affairs," Alice said as she changed into her dressing gown. "Her tables are set with fine china, linens, silver and crystal, all stolen from the richest homes in the city.

"The sideboard's crowded with sweets and pastries, wine flows from a fountain, and Piano Charlie, the best-dressed house thief in the city, sits at the keys, playing whatever Mrs. Birnbaum requests, all night long. There's always at least one duke, princess, baroness, lord, lady or senator in attendance, as well as the finest safecrackers, jewel thieves and confidence men."

Ignoring Alice's prattling, Mae came to me and pointed to the ribbon around my neck. "Let me borrow it," she said, gesturing to Mrs. Wentworth's fan.

I shook my head. Though we'd begun to share things, trusting combs and hatpins to each other's care, the fan was off limits. "You know I always keep it with me."

"You owe me, Ada . . ."

"Then I'll have to keep owing you."

Alice intervened, trying to make peace between Mae and me. "It was her mother's. It's her good luck charm."

Giving up and heading for the window, Mae said, "I don't need it. I make my own luck." Then she was gone.

"Don't let Mae fool you," Alice said after the other girl had disappeared into the night. "She's as soft-hearted as you or me."

I wasn't sure that anyone could be as soft-hearted as Alice. At sixteen, she bore the innocent air of a much younger girl. Fate had dealt her a terrible blow—her parents and her sister had died from the tailor's cough in the space of a year—but she hadn't let it break her. She'd sold her family's belongings (her mother's silver spoons, her father's pocket watch, her sister's best dresses) in an effort to survive. When everything of value was gone, she went to work at Mr. Mueller's bakery, fixing sugar roses and bows to cakes with pink apple jelly. One bow, one rose, one bow, one rose. It was simple work, and she understood how it should go, but haunted by hunger, she'd turned into a thief by the end of her first week. Crumbs on her cheek, icing sugar on her lips, she'd told Mr. Mueller she couldn't help herself. "I understand," the baker said, and then, slapping a rolling pin against his palm, he stood over Alice and told her that she wasn't to return. That's when Mae came to her rescue.

"Mae got a fair bit of pocket change the last time she went to the concert hall," Alice said, climbing into her bed. "She didn't steal from the men there, or ask for anything outright, she just made mention of forgetting her reticule and needing to pay for the streetcar. The gents she was with were more than happy to oblige."

"She wasn't afraid of getting put upon by them?" I asked. I'd seen the sporting men who lined up outside the concert hall each evening on my way to the rooftop on Chrystie Street. I was sure things there weren't as jolly as Mae made them out to be.

"She says she's an anything-but-girl and that she knows how to turn a gent away before things go too far," Alice said with a shrug. "I'd tell on her in a heartbeat if I thought it was as simple as her just wanting to have a bit of fun, but she needs the money. Mae has her heart set on buying a coffin plate to send to her mother, sooner rather than later. Not a tin or copper one, but silver, with lots of fancy scroll-work around the edges."

Mae's mother had once carried a baby boy in her belly for nine long months, only to have the child die at birth. In her grieving, she'd had the coffin plate that bore his name, *Timothy O'Rourke*, removed from the tiny casket before it was laid in the ground. "She keeps the plate in a place of honour, next to a silver pitcher her grandmother brought all the way from Ireland. Those two objects are her pride and joy. She kisses them every morning after her prayers and then again after she kneels to pray at night."

Not wanting to remain in her mother's memory as for-ever missing, Mae hoped that sending a memento of her own death, a lie engraved on a shining, silver plate, would, in time, heal her mother's heart.

"Room and board are enough for me for now, so long as the man who gets me first falls in love with me," Alice said, wistfully leaning on her pillow. "Perhaps he'll even ask me to be his wife."

"I hope he does," I said, thinking Alice's desire to be even more ambitious than Mae's. I brushed the oil Rose had given me into my hair, counting out the strokes, *one, two, three, four, five, six,* impatient to reach *one hundred.* Not knowing if it was Rose or Miss Everett who'd purchased the oil in the first place, I stopped what I was doing and added it to my list, just in case. *One bottle of Circassian hair oil–large.* Then, *one pen, one bottle of ink, two packets of paper and a five-cent stamp.*

The stamp was to go towards sending a few things I'd been collecting in my dressing table drawer to Mrs. Riordan– an almost-full box of chocolates that Missouri Mills hadn't thought good enough to finish, a woollen scarf Rose found too scratchy for her neck, a pair of gloves Mae refused to wear anymore because she'd lost a button from one of the wrists. I planned to mail the parcel to Mr. Bartz's shop on Stanton Street and ask that his delivery boy take it on to Mrs. Riordan's. Not wanting Mr. Cowan to discover my whereabouts, I would pen a letter to Mr. Bartz as well, asking him to not reveal my address to anyone, even Mrs. Riordan.

"Ada?"

"Hmm?"

"Have you ever kissed a man?"

"No, have you?"

"Yes," Alice answered, smiling. "Well, a boy, anyway."

"What was it like?"

"Moist," she said, biting her lip, "and soft." Her face turned red as she offered, "I can get Cadet to kiss you so you can see for yourself. Mae teased him into kissing me."

Mama had told me I should never let myself get kissed, especially by a boy. She said kissing a man was also a risky thing, but at least you could usually get something out of him. "Of course, if you're not careful, you can stumble from whatever game you're playing right into something else and before you know it—nothing makes sense. You know what that something else is, don't you, Moth?"

"No."

"It's love, and it's exactly what you don't want to fall into with a man. If you end up loving them, then no matter how rich or fine they are, you'll just want more, and nothing they give you will ever be enough. You won't be able to keep yourself from telling them you love them, you need them, you want them—and in the end, they'll hate you for it. Stay away from kisses, Moth."

Alice thought Cadet to be a handsome young man, and she said that he was gentlemanly too, in a shy sort of way. He'd been hired not only to do chores around the house, but to act as guard as well. By day he travelled most places with the girls, and at night, he stood in the hallway outside Rose, Emily and Missouri's rooms, arms folded across his broad chest. Since he escorted Miss Everett's girls most of the time when they were out in public on their own, Alice had gotten to know a bit about him while walking at his side. "His mother died the minute he was born," she told me, shaking her head. "Isn't that just the saddest thing?"

I nodded, thinking I'd heard sadder tales, but wanting her to go on telling me what she knew of the boy.

"His poor father was left to raise him with the help of the barmaids at Sportsmen's Hall." Best known for its eight-foot-square rat pit and its bare-knuckle boxing matches, the Water Street establishment was run by a man named Kit Burns. "Cadet's father was the official bloodsucker there," Alice said, her eyes wide.

"A bloodsucker?"

"His job was to suck blood from the fighters' wounds so bouts could go on as long as possible."

"Oh," I said, feeling queasy at the thought.

Alice turned her talk back to Cadet. "You really should let him kiss you sometime. He's gentle and sweet, and, I suppose, its good practice for what lies ahead."

Alice's words lulling me, I thought of Cadet as I drifted off, and the way he stuck the tip of his tongue between his teeth whenever he worked to tie the laces on his boots.

The next time I opened my eyes, Mae was on top of me, her boozy breath in my face. "You should've seen the gents," she chirped. "Every last one of them was handsome, and so attentive."

"Go to sleep, Mae," I mumbled, wanting to go back to my dreams of kissing a bloodsucker's son.

Although the Bowery Concert Hall prides itself on being a respectable business, it is common knowledge that members of the criminal underworld frequent this establishment. Planning their crimes and foul deeds between dances, they laugh in the faces of the doctors, judges and lawmakers who sit at the next table. Many a girl of promise and education has been started on the road to ruin at that place. Missing maidens take in astonishing amounts of drink, until their judgement gets cast aside in favour of a single night's worth of carnal pleasure. Their fate should be noted as a terrible warning.

THE LEGEND OF STUYVESANT'S PEAR TREE

BY MR. DANIEL CHARLES, special to *The Evening Star*

Peter Stuyvesant planted a pear tree. The year was 1647.

Its magic began not long after, when the tree was but a stopping place on a winding path to the community well. Each day, a young maid, Miss Abigail Fish, would pause there to rest under the tree's branches. On her return home, she would pour a gentle splash or two of water on its trunk, and bless the tree with a simple verse or a song. Soon she was greeting the tree both coming and going, treating it like a long-lost friend, confessing all the dearest and secret desires of her heart.

One day, the maid dared to ask the tree a question: "Will I meet a handsome lad one day soon?" In the rustling of its leaves, the girl swore she heard the tree answer, "Yes." So amazed she was, she asked the question again. The tree again answered, "Yes." She asked a third time. Again, the same reply. She closed her eyes and thought to herself, "Three times a charm . . ."

Miss Fish ran straight home and told her mother of the wonder she had just experienced. Her mother moved to the door and bolted it. She went to her daughter and covered the girl's mouth with her hand. "Listen to me, daughter. You have always been an honest and good child and so I have no reason to doubt you. But you must never tell a soul what has happened to you at Governor Stuyvesant's tree. Please, swear it."

The girl did swear to her mother that day, but her oath did not last. When a handsome young lad, Master Willmott Rudd, asked to escort her to the well, Abigail couldn't help but tell him all. When she was done, she begged. "Will you keep my secret?"

"For a kiss," Willmott teased.

Abigail Fish closed her eyes and allowed Willmott Rudd to kiss her.

The next morning, the boy's father, Mr. Thomas Rudd, came knocking at her door.

"Good morning, Mr. Rudd," Mrs. Fish said in greeting.

"How I wish I could say the same to you. My only son has fallen ill with a fever, and I'm afraid your daughter is to blame."

"My daughter? How can that be?"

"Answers to a few simple questions should put the matter to rest. May I see the girl?"

Without waiting for permission, Mr. Rudd bulled through the house and laid hands on Abigail. As he dragged the girl out of her house and down the road, Mrs. Fish followed. When Mr. Rudd threw Abigail into his barn to stand trial in front of a judge and twelve men from the neighbouring area, Mrs. Fish sobbed.

"Did you, Abigail Fish, stand with Willmott Rudd at Mr. Stuyvesant's pear tree yesterday morning?"

"Yes."

"Did you, Abigail Fish, put your lips to those of Willmott Rudd?"

"Yes."

"Did you, Abigail Fish, tell Willmott Rudd that

you have had divine conversation with Mr. Stuyvesant's pear tree?"

"Yes."

"Do you, Abigail Fish, take the wisdom of a tree over the wisdom of God?"

At this, Abigail paused. She looked to her mother, her eyes laden with apology, and answered, "I believe their wisdom to be one and the same."

That was the end of Abigail Fish.

Within the charges against one Abigail Fish it is confirmed that she, having not the fear of God in her eyes, wickedly, maliciously and feloniously used, practised and exercised certain detestable arts called witchcraft and sorceries upon Master Willmott Rudd. It is also suspected that the accused has tortured, afflicted, consumed, wasted, pined, tormented and bewitched Master Rudd to the point of causing him great hurt. Let it be known that we, convened on the lands of Mr. Thomas Rudd, in the presence of the law, do find Miss Abigail Fish guilty. We therefore advise that these charges do crave Justice. The girl will be hanged for her crimes.

Some said the girl's soul, when denied entrance into Heaven, was taken up by the tree. People came, first in secret, then in the open, to have counsel with her. Some even tied their requests to her branches. People of all ages, all creeds, all races, all stations in life went away saying the same thing—that the tree could speak. There was magic to be found there, if one only listened.

Nearly half a decade has passed since a fierce February storm and the fateful turn by a runaway wagon brought the tree to its demise. It was still bearing fruit the summer before, bending with full branches–even when, like everything else in this city, its heart had been born in another place, its roots buried many times over. Peter Stuyvesant's beloved tree, this goddess of Gotham, had been brought across the ocean and planted in hopes that something of The Netherlands would survive even though New Amsterdam had been lost. Two hundred and twenty years of defiant growth she lasted, from a shady spot on a winding path, to a beloved landmark–now, just a memory. All that's left to us is a selection of artist's views, postcard sketches showing how the apothecary's storefront was once shaded by her branches–progress and history side by side.

Some say the tree held all the secrets of New York. Every grandmother in this fair city has, at one time or another, testified of its wonders while pushing memories and cabbage around in the bottom of a soup pot. The day the tree went down, there came a collective refrain: "Let it be known, that this was the day Old New-York was lost to us forever."

A section of Stuyvesant's beloved tree can still be viewed at the museum of the New York Historical Society. At the time of the accident, the rest of the tree's carcass was quickly carted away, fated to become fuel to stave off what was left of winter's chill, or fodder for walking sticks, napkin rings, paper weights and other mementoes.

TO THE YOUNG LADY
in the blue dress on the
Third Avenue Streetcar.
You whispered PERSONAL to me
this Tuesday last.
Would you like to meet for
agreeable conversation?
It was 2 o'clock when you got on
in the neighbourhood of Houston Street–
I got out just before Tenth.
I am an adventurous fellow,
seeking acquaintance with an
unconventional young lady.
If this is you, please respond to:
Mr. E.M.V. Box 473, HERALD office.
To prevent mistake,
please mention some particulars.

XVII.

*O*ne, two, three, four, five, six, seven, eight, nine. I
marked my days in the margins of the magazine
alongside a growing list of items that now
included a new garment Miss Everett had insisted I accept.
One silk walking suit, with matching hat, gloves and boots.
The dresses she'd given me my first few days in the house
had been lovely in their own right, but the suit, made

from fabric the same shade as the lilacs that bloomed along Miss Keteltas' fence in the spring, was finer still.

It was presented to me along with an afternoon of lessons on how to move about in it. Missouri Mills acted as my tutor, leading me to the parlour in a suit even more elaborate than mine, lace parasol resting on her shoulder. "Lift your chin, mind the hem," she instructed, her words and figure moving along in a graceful Southern lilt.

With shining red curls and bright green eyes, she was in perfect company with Rose Duval and Emily Sutherland. Rose was dark, Emily, fair, and Missouri was the ample-breasted belle who sat between them. Miss Everett had liked everything about her except her given name of "Martha," so she chose to rename the girl after the place where she was born. "Missouri suits me fine," she said after I'd asked her if she minded what Miss Everett had done. "Martha's a name for housekeepers and dusty old presidents' wives."

When we got to the parlour, we found Cadet moving furniture to the centre of the room, making an open path around the outside of it for us to travel. He was leaving as I was coming through the door and my shoulder brushed his arm as he passed.

"If a gentleman won't wait for you, then you must show him his mistake," Missouri

This pretty suit consists of a walking skirt, tunic, and basque waist, with revers collar. The walking skirt is of lilac silk, trimmed on the bottom with two ruches of the same material. The tunic is of violet silk, pointed on the sides and open in the back, with an apron in the front, and is edged with a ruche of lilac silk. The Pompadour basque waist of violet silk is worn over a plain waist of lilac silk. The flowing sleeves of the under-waist and the basque waist are lined with silk ruche. Lace under-sleeves. Violet silk hat, with lilac feathers. Lilac gloves. Lilac boots.

–*Harper's Bazar, 1870*

said, throwing Cadet a haughty look behind his back. "Next time, stand outside the door and watch until he's through. If no apology is offered, then he's not worthy of your time."

I hadn't minded what had happened, even if it was a mistake. My cheeks were flushed with something more than embarrassment, and as far as I was concerned Cadet had done more right than wrong.

Although Mae and Alice had already mastered the art of walking in such attire, they'd been asked to come to the parlour to act as models and walking companions for me. Ushering them into the room to join us, Missouri announced, "We'll practise strolling first. Mae and Alice side by side, Ada following behind."

I tried my best, but found it difficult to match their steady strides. Not allowing enough distance between us, I came far too close to Mae, catching the back of her skirt with the toe of my boot.

"Twice wasn't enough?" Mae groused the third time I tripped her up.

"Sorry, Mae," I apologized.

Turning from me, she resumed her promenade with Alice, her chin thrust high.

When I began to step after them again, I was overcome with nervous laughter, the picture of Mae's prideful strut jerking to a halt playing over in my mind.

Alice, too, fell into a fit of giggles. Holding our sides, we both stopped short while Mae continued strutting around the room. Afraid of being sentenced to promenade the house for days on end, I'd wanted to do well, but Mae's arrogance over the simple task of walking had made a comedy of the whole affair.

"Perhaps you'd like to demonstrate walking with a pail, Mae?" Missouri requested, trying to bring things back to the lesson at hand.

"I'd be happy to," Mae replied.

Three pails, the size of the growlers Mr. Bartz used for serving beer at his shop, were sitting on a table along the wall, each one half-filled with water.

Throwing a mean look at Alice and me, Mae went to the table, lifted one of the small pails and placed it on her head. As she took her hands away from the pail and began to move, Miss Everett came into the room.

"Alice, please join Mae," she said, taking the place next to Missouri on a nearby settee.

Mae whispered to me as she went past, the pail trembling. "This is how it's done."

Alice came next, moving more slowly than Mae, her cautious gait keeping her pail steady and straight.

"That's how it's done," Miss Everett said, leaning over to me.

I'd known a woman on Chrystie Street who could dance while balancing her laundry basket or a bucket of suds on her head. She called herself Aunt Chickory. She'd been a slave in Georgia and her skin was as dark as a roasted nut. Every morning, she'd dance through the slippery muck-strewn alley, all the way to the back court. *"I'm gonna take the cake,"* she'd sing as she went, *"Master's missy's gonna say I'm the best."*

One morning when I'd stared at her too long, she grabbed me by the arm and made me dance with Mama's egg basket perched on my head. My admiration for her along with my fear of what Mama might do if I broke her eggs made me a fast study. *"Take the cake, child. You gotta take that cake."*

Without being told, I went to the table now and put the last pail of water on my head. I walked a slow circle around Mae, shrugging and grinning like Aunt Chickory had taught me to do.

Arms folded and staring at me with disapproval Miss Everett brought my fun to an end. "That's all for today," she said. "Change out of your suit, Ada. You'll want it fresh for your outing tomorrow."

The next morning began with a visit from Dr. Sadie. It had been over a week since I'd seen her and I took a great deal of satisfaction in the look that came over her face when she saw me again. She actually let out a small gasp, staring at me as she made her way from the door to where I was sitting on my bed.

Placing her physician's bag next to me she said, "I hardly know you, Miss Fenwick."

She wore the fine but plain dress she'd worn when we first met, and she went about doing things much as she'd done then. She washed her hands, donned her apron, and asked me to "open wide" so she could inspect my mouth. The only thing she didn't do this time was request I spread my legs.

There was a softness about her if you were careful to look for it. She had a pair of modest pearl earrings in her ears and her hair was arranged in a neat, perfect twist. It was evident that she cared about the way she looked, her gaze flitting to her reflection in my dressing table mirror every so often, as any other lady might have done.

When she was finished, she sat on the end of the bed, her modest bustle pressing awkwardly against the small of her back. "You're still committed to Miss Everett's plan for you?" she asked, frowning.

"Yes," I answered, wishing she'd leave the subject alone.

"If you're having doubts—"

"I'm not," I insisted.

Dr. Sadie's kindness was well intended, but if a place in a house of refuge was all she had to offer, then she must have known I'd turn her down. Working long hours at a factory or spending my days bent over a sewing machine was not what I wanted.

Smoothing a wrinkle in my skirt I said, "I've no wish to leave."

"The Children's Aid Society runs an orphan train that matches homeless children with couples who are eager to start a family," she continued, placing a hand on my knee. "Most people are looking for healthy boys to help out on the farm, but there are others who long for a girl to make their lives complete. I could inquire at the Society on your behalf," she said. "I know someone there who travels with the children on the train. He'd make sure you got into a good home." Before I could reply she added, "Perhaps you and Alice could be placed together. Miss Everett mentioned the two of you have become quite close."

It was true—the more I'd gotten to know Alice, the more I liked her. She was kind and quick to smile, and good company at mealtimes and at the end of the day. Even if she hadn't possessed such qualities, I also could see that Miss Everett was starting to favour her somewhat over Mae, and I'd thought it best if I did the same.

"Alice wants to leave?" I asked.

"I don't know for certain," Dr. Sadie answered as she got up, removed her apron and tucked it away in her physician's bag. "But I thought if you both were having second thoughts, then perhaps the two of you might be better off somewhere else."

The idea of leaving New York made my stomach turn. It was one thing to have escaped Mrs. Wentworth, but it would be quite another to be stuck in a lonely pasture with nowhere to go. People in the city often thought of country folk as hayseeds, ignorant bodies made from naïveté and corn, easily parted from money and sense. I saw them differently. To me, they were the shadowy figures dotting the canvas of the painting in Miss Everett's front parlour, strong enough to push a terrible-looking blade through the earth, hard creatures who could withstand the heat of a punishing sun.

"Thank you, but I'm fine," I told Dr. Sadie. "Put it to Alice if you like, but I know my mind."

Looking defeated she said, "As you wish." Then she picked up her bag and headed out the door.

Alice had been especially nervous that morning, as she was to have her first luncheon date.

"It's only tea and sandwiches in the parlour," Mae said as a pink blush crept up Alice's neck, threatening to turn to hives. Any talk of accepting an invitation to meet with a man seemed to send her from fret to itch in a matter of minutes.

Smitten with the notion of falling in love, she could never be like Mae. I worried over Alice the way I'd worried about Mama, but I didn't have the heart to tell her that love was the most dangerous thing on which to pin your hopes.

"You'll do fine." I gave her a quick hug and an affectionate peck on the cheek.

With Alice otherwise engaged, Miss Everett paired me with Mae for my first outing. The thought that Cadet was to accompany us, that I'd be so near him on our walk, had caused me to toss in my sleep. *Stay away from boys*, Mama's voice had hissed the moment Cadet had entered my dreams.

The paths Miss Everett had her girls take on their outings were chosen with care. Mueller's Bakery, where the madam had a standing order for tea cakes and *madeleines* was three doors down from a gentlemen's club. Members of the club reserved the front window on Wednesdays at noon, fully aware of the schedule Miss Everett's girls kept. "It's a regular pastime for some," Mae said with laugh. "You should see them lowering their papers to stare. I can't smell the scent of baked goods without thinking of well-groomed men."

My first public outing was to a pharmacy at Thirteenth Street and Third Avenue. We were to walk all the way to Fourteenth Street first, pass by a cafe on the corner, and then stop in at the pharmacy and collect whatever items Miss Everett had on her list of ladies' necessities as we made our way home. It was a brisk but bright day, and I was glad for the cloudless sky, since I didn't wish to brave rain or puddles in my new suit.

"Let's catch a horsecar," Mae suggested when we got to the Bowery. "I'll pay."

Cadet didn't argue with the idea, but I wasn't so sure about it. The streetcars that ran down the length of the Bowery and all the way up to Central Park were rattling, dirty transports, pulled along by burdened horses. They were generally filled with gentlemen and roughs, strangers from the country, and a few doubtful women. Mama had refused me permission to board one, ever. "Nothing waiting there for you but a groping," she'd said.

Remembering what Alice had said about Mae having her heart set on buying a coffin plate for her mother, I asked, "Don't you think you ought to keep your money?"

"It's a long way there and back, and if your feet don't hurt now, they will."

Mama's warnings aside, I didn't want some rough to step on my skirts. "I don't know—"

"You're not scared, are you?" Mae bullied.

Arms folded, Cadet let out a snort.

"No," I said, feeling my resolve turn in my gut like a worm.

Mae arched an eyebrow, knowing she was close to getting her way.

"Fine," I said with as stern a face as I could muster. "We'll ride the car there, but if my suit gets soiled, I'm walking back."

When the streetcar arrived, Mae took three nickels out of her pocket and handed them to Cadet to give to the conductor. The sight of the coins passing from her hand made my heart twist with envy. She was so at ease with it, just as she'd been the day she'd taken me to Graff's for oyster stew.

BEWARE OF PICKPOCKETS, read a sign above the step.

"For me and the two ladies," Cadet told the conductor, gesturing towards Mae and me.

The man let Cadet go by, then leered at Mae as she boarded the car, his gaze going up and down the length of her. "I believe there'll be a seat towards the back there for ya, miss," he said, reaching out to touch the small of Mae's back in an attempt to guide her along.

"Thank you," she said, briskly shouldering her way among the standing passengers.

The conductor tried to do the same with me, but I stuck close to Mae, reaching out to hold her sleeve. I'd lost sight of Cadet in the crowded car and was determined not to be parted from Mae as well.

The smells of pipe tobacco, liquor and sweat mingled with the occasional waft of horse dung from the bottom of a working man's boot. As the car began to move, I took hold of the pole nearest me. Grabbing a spot too high for my reach, I stood on tiptoe, hoping to keep my skirt clean.

A man wearing a sack coat took the spot to the other side of me. His grey beard was streaked with tobacco stains, and I watched, helpless, as he closed his eyes and put his face near my hand, the scent of my perfumed glove sending him somewhere else, someplace he longed to be.

The businessmen on board were spending a great deal of effort to make as little contact with the other passengers as possible. It was an absurd kind of dance, and Mae, giving smiles and flirty glances to the men around her, looked quite happy to be in the middle of it.

As the streetcar slowed for the next stop, she stumbled into the embrace of a handsome young man. He was wearing a smart-looking hat and frock coat, his long, sleek sideburns pointing like arrows to the corners of his wide, red lips. There was a mole to the right of his nose, so perfect and round you'd swear he'd painted it there himself. Mae's face brushed his shoulder as he slipped his arm around her waist to steady her. Knowing how Mae felt about Mr. Chief of Detectives and the other men who visited Miss Everett's house, I was certain she'd made a point of singling the young man out from all the men on the horsecar.

Clearly enthralled by Mae's charms, the young man puffed his chest out like one of the birds in Miss Keteltas' parlour.

The next stop was his, but Mae wasn't about to let him get away without giving him a sign of her interest. Glove to the side of her mouth, I heard her whisper, "Personal."

French imported male "safes" (made from skin or India rubber) are a vast improvement over *onanism*, yet often shunned by men at the moment of need. Preventative powders are another solution to undesired conception, primarily made of Pearlash or corrosive sublimate. A woman must, however, find the proper moment to implement them (the sooner the better). In the end, womb guards are, perhaps, the most discreet way for a woman to prevent conception.

When we got off at our stop, Mae rushed to Cadet's side and slipped her arm through his. "Why, there you are," she said with innocent eyes. "I thought I'd lost you."

He let her take his arm, but the sour look on his face said he didn't care much for her company. Happy to see this, I paid little attention to the windows of the café or the gentlemen seated there. It wasn't until we reached the pharmacy that I really took in my surroundings.

BRUNSWICK APOTHEKE, the shop's window read, in large, painted letters. MR. WILTON HUBER, PROPRIETOR.

As we entered the pharmacy, I looked over the items on Miss Everett's list. *Preventative powders, toilet vinegars, lavender water, Macassar oil, sea sponges, smelling salts, Bouquet de Rondeletia, extract of patchouli, Grosvenor's Tooth Powder, cherry bounce, anisette.* They were the trappings of women, and in this case, of whores. Seeing the list didn't bring on thoughts of my impending fate—that day still seemed far-off, almost unimaginable. The note did, however, hold a notion I hadn't yet considered. With the correct choices, it seemed a girl might have success in bending anyone's will (stranger, friend, or foe) to her own.

Camphor rub, quinine, milk of roses, love-drawing oil—every useful potion you could think of was lined up on the shelves of the pharmacy, set between yellowed globes and maps of the world, exotic beetles with pins stuck through their shiny middles and bowl after bowl of gold-speckled fish swimming around in circles.

Mr. Huber's name was on the shop, but Mr. James Hetherington was the apothecary who ran it. Mr. Hether-ington was smart and proper looking, with a short spade beard and eyes so blue it seemed as if their colour had been dropped into them from a twilight sky. The part in his hair was messy and honest, not like the false, straight lines that ran down the centre of so many men's heads, splitting them in two.

Aside from the bottles and jars of remedies, soaps and liniments he had for sale, countless shelves and shadow boxes were crowded with colourful dead spiders and butterflies. I figured that maybe Mrs. Hetherington, if there was one, didn't want the things he'd collected cluttering up her house.

Wearing a long crisp apron, his shirtsleeves rolled up just past his wrists, Mr. Hetherington nodded to Cadet. Greeting Mae with a smile he said, "Miss O'Rourke, how may I assist you?"

Mae motioned for me to hand Mr. Hetherington the list, and said, "The usual, if you please."

"It would be my pleasure," he replied as he took the list from me. "And who might you be?" he asked.

"Miss Ada Fenwick," I said, giving him an awkward smile.

"Pleased to make your acquaintance, Miss Fenwick," he said.

"And I'm pleased to make yours as well," I replied, returning his kindness as Miss Everett had instructed me to do.

Cadet headed over to study one of the apothecary's globes.

Mae hummed a tune as she spun a lazy Susan of perfume oil samples that sat on the countertop. She looked back and forth between me and the whirl of the vials as they went round. "Lavender, no. Cardamom, no. Neroli, no. Hyacinth–yes." Pulling out the rubber stopper on the glass tube, she waved it under my nose.

"Try this," she urged. "I think it's right for you."

I took one sniff and my head went dizzy with the stifling-sweet scent. Backing away, I said, "I'm going to look at the fish."

"Suit yourself," Mae replied.

As I watched the goldfish swim, their feathery tails gracefully waving in the water, I wondered if the bowl was large enough to please such a beautiful creature. I wished I could box one up and send it to Mrs. Riordan. She would've marvelled at the way a fish never tired of turning round inside its tiny world.

"You may feed them if you like," Mr. Hetherington called out as he moved between cabinets and shelves, collecting the items on the list. "Just pinch a few grains from the jar that's next to the bowl and let it float on the water."

I did as he instructed and the fishes swam straight to the surface, nibbling and puckering away at the food. Was their only pleasure swallowing bubbles with every bite?

Cadet soon came to me and said, "I'm going outside, under the awning. You can join me if you like. I'm sure Mae will be awhile still."

My hands went clammy inside my gloves. "All right," I said, nodding.

I went to Mae, who was still investigating the perfume display, and said, "I'm going out front for some air."

"Mm-hmm," she murmured, dotting her wrist with carnation oil and lifting it to her nose.

I found Cadet reading a collection of handbills that had been posted on a board in front of the shop. After the way Alice had gone on about his kisses, I was nervous to be alone with him. The only other boy I'd ever spent any time with was John the Witcher. He'd stolen a teacup I'd found in an ash barrel, so I trailed after him calling him a thief. The sooty, flowered treasure was still useable even without its handle and I'd intended on giving it to Mama. John grinned at me when he snatched the cup from my hands but never gave it back, even though we spent the afternoon together, playing.

"Ever been there?" I asked, pointing to a notice for Dink's Museum.

"Many times," Cadet said with a nod.

The museum was joined to the theatre where most of the gentlemen who came to call at Miss Everett's house took her girls for an evening's entertainment—both buildings were just a short walk from the concert hall Mae liked to sneak out to at night.

In my days nibbling on the street, I'd caught glimpses of the freakish performers who stood out front of Dink's to entice passersby, but had been disappointed to find the place was *for gentlemen only*. Bricks painted in outrageous colours and boasts, I'd wanted to enter the building at first sight. A man with long, stretched-out legs was pictured there, standing as high as the first storey and holding a crystal ball in his spidery hand. MAGNIFICO, THE WORLD'S TALLEST ILLUSIONIST! Next to him was a woman's head with orange-red flames bursting out of her mouth. LADY MEPHISTOPHELES, MISTRESS OF FIRE! Images and words went up the side of the building and around the corner, melting into the brick. There was a two-headed goat, a woman with a snake wrapped around her body, a man sliding a long silver sword down his throat. LOOK! MYSTERIOUS PEOPLE FROM EXOTIC PLACES! SEE! MAGICAL TREASURES FROM EVERY CORNER OF THE WORLD!

While I was trying to think of something more to say, Cadet bent down to pick up a penny he'd noticed stuck between the cobblestones. He brushed my skirt with his fingers as he stood up.

My heart fluttered as I wondered if he'd meant to do it or if it had just been an accident. "Alice told me your father's a bloodsucker," I said, making another awkward attempt at conversation.

Putting the penny in his pocket he replied, "He was, until he died."

"Oh, I'm sorry," I said, feeling terrible.

"He's been gone two years now," Cadet said. "His last

words to me were 'I hope I get to heaven so's I can bite off Gabriel's ear.' That was my pa."

Picturing a man tearing off an angel's ear with his teeth made me want to laugh, but Cadet's face was sombre when he spoke of his father and I didn't want to offend him now that he seemed to have more to say. I listened, taking in his every word as he talked of boxing matches, bloodied faces and catching rats.

After his father had passed, he'd gone to work for a man named Dick the Ratter. Still scrawny and small, he was able to get into all the twisty, tight spaces the rat-catcher couldn't go. He'd cover his hands with sweet oil to attract the rats, then light a torch and wave it around, flushing out the vermin, right into Dick's waiting bag.

"After you've got them, you've got to keep the bag moving," he explained as he circled his arm round and round, an imaginary sack of rats hanging from his fist. "If you don't, they'll chew their way out so fast you won't even know they got away."

It had been a decent job, affording Cadet and his boss the opportunity to collect pay on the rats not once, but twice. "Fancy hotels need to keep their rat troubles quiet, so there's good money right there. Then you take the rats straight from the hotel and sell them, either to somebody who wants to put another man out of business, or to a man who needs them for a pit. Mr. Burns used to give the best price when he was still in the game. Good rats were worth ten dollars a hundred to him. He took bets on which of his dogs would catch and kill a rat first. When his best terrier, old Jack, died he had him stuffed and mounted over the bar. That dog caught a hundred rats in less than seven minutes, a true American record."

Mr. Burns threw all kinds of things into his pit—roosters, dogs and cats, as well as rats. Once, Cadet watched him put four dozen rattlesnakes down in the pit, the reptiles having been brought in special from someplace out west. "A man named Tinley was paid to walk through the pit between all the hissing, mean serpents while everyone placed wagers as to whether the man would get bit or not, and also, if he did get the fangs, whether he would live or die. You can always count on men to put money down on anything that's life or death."

Just as Cadet was about to recall Mr. Tinley's fate, Mae came out of the pharmacy with a large parcel in her arms. "Telling Ada about the rattlesnakes, I suppose," she said, handing Cadet the box. "How many were there this time, four, five or six dozen?"

Ignoring her, he began to walk up the street.

I chose to ignore Mae, too, in favour of catching up with him. "Did he die?" I asked, my flesh still crawling with the thought of having that many snakes at my feet.

"Who?"

"The man in with the snakes."

"No," Cadet answered, grinning. "And a lot of men still hate him for it, too."

October 29, 1871

I attended a meeting of the New York Committee for Women's Concerns this evening, Miss Jane Clattermore, the guest speaker. She is the matron for the Home for Wandering Girls, so I was curious to hear what she had to say about the plight of the young women of our city. Sadly, she demonstrated no real understanding of them at all.

"A girl has no instinct of purity to defend her."

"Her body and brain are weak from the start."

"She often lacks moral fibre to such a degree that any attempt to reform her presents a troublesome situation that most often turns out to be a waste of everyone's time."

"For the girl there is less chance in every way."

Because of these terrible and mistaken assumptions, she refuses to take girls who are over ten years of age into her care. She's given up on older girls, and proceeded to tell the women in attendance that we should do the same.

"How did you know where to draw the line?" I asked, anxious to see her try to defend herself.

She did not reply.

I'm frustrated too, I wanted to say, but I knew she wouldn't listen.

The law is in bed with the brothel keepers, corruption all around. The idea of a girl selling herself horrifies me, and yet I find myself in the middle of that world. Where is the line? How young is too young?

I believed Emma Everett when she told me she needed a doctor to examine her prostitutes, someone to educate them on matters of hygiene and signs of disease. Seeing Moth Fenwick again yesterday made me realize that things there have gone too far. That girl is too young—and surprisingly, given the world she's grown up in, still an innocent. Is Emma looking after the girl's interests, or is she merely in the business of selling virgins?

"If I turn her out, she will sell herself on the street," Emma threatened when I put the question to her.

Confident that the girl will choose her way over mine, she invited me to say whatever I liked to her. "Given the choice between wooden slats or feather beds, which would you choose?"

Dr. B_. says the infirmary cannot afford to get involved. Funding is difficult to come by and the words "whore," "disease" and "prostitution" send benefactors running, their purse strings pulled tight.

Still, the girls of this city need someone to insist there's another way. I can't stop thinking of dear Miss Fenwick. A girl should command attention, not suffer it.

S.F.

Face to face and nose to nose
Smick, Smack, Smuck and away she goes
Lay her eyebrow on your collar
Hug her so that she can't holler;
Tell her that you're always true
Squeeze her till her face turns blue
Keep it up for fifteen hours
Then begin anew.

—J.P. SOUSA

XVIII.

The private rooms of Rose, Missouri and Emily were located on the second floor of the house. Late nights, upon returning from an evening at the theatre, they'd lead their gentlemen up the stairs, giggling and cooing the whole way. They were, as Mae liked to say, "about to play Cupid's game."

One night, after we'd changed into our dressing gowns, Mae coaxed me into eavesdropping on Rose with Mr. Chief of Detectives, directing me to put my ear to the vent in the hallway of the third floor, warning me not to make a sound. "How else are you going to learn how the game should go?" she teased.

Remembering Mr. Cowan in bed with Mama, I figured hearing had to be better than seeing.

I'd spent a fair bit of time with Rose, helping her don her evening attire and mending her petticoats. Seeing to her needs was much like the work I'd done for Mrs. Wentworth, but far more enjoyable. She was the sweetest of Miss Everett's full-time girls. Tugging gently at my hair while I was adjusting her clothes, she'd measure its length between her fingers and say, "It's only a matter of time until you're a full-fledged minx like me."

From the sounds that came through the vent, Rose was far more cordial and free with Mr. Chief of Detectives than Mama had ever been with Mr. Cowan. Her every movement, translated through the strained creaks of her bed, brought about a response from her lover. "Yes, Rose," he said repeatedly, his voice growing ever more like a growl. Rose's replies were mixed with moans of *lover, baby, child, mister, please, more, now.* Putting my hands over my ears, I regretted saying yes to Mae.

Mae grinned at me, amused by my distress over the lover's play below.

She was well on her way to becoming more beautiful than Rose, Missouri and Emily put together, and made no secret of her desire to surpass them all. "I intend on having ten times their lovers and becoming ten times richer than them as well."

My dreams of owning a house like Miss Keteltas', with the softest bed money could buy, a pair of lovebirds in my parlour, and two pug dogs at my feet, seemed woefully ordinary compared to Mae's. Still, I was determined to do whatever it might take not to go the way of poor Eliza Adler—or Miss Nellie Lynch, a girl who let Chrystie Street roughs take her into dark cellars for a nickel.

Hearing footsteps on the stairs, Mae and I ran into our room and shut the door. Alice was at her dressing table, rolling rags in her hair before bed.

"Tie the back for me, won't you, Ada?" she asked, waving a piece of flannel in the air.

I took the rag and began twirling a strand of her wet hair with my finger.

"I always have trouble with the last bit," Alice said.

Mae sprawled on her bed and flipped through the pages of the *Evening Star*. "Anyone up for blind man's bluff?" she asked, raising an eyebrow over the edge of the paper.

"What—you're not sneaking out?" Alice asked.

Ignoring her, Mae proposed, "I say we play in the dark."

I knew from watching children play the game in the streets that it called for at least three players, or "the more the merrier." I had never been asked to play, even when Eliza was part of the group. I didn't blame her for leaving me out. The one thing the mothers of Chrystie Street seemed to agree upon (all except dear Mrs. Riordan) was how they felt about Mama. They'd go on and on, saying she was nothing but a deceiver, a seller of false hopes. Even those who believed in her magic (when they needed it), the ones who came to our door begging for charms and advice, would sneer behind her back and call her witch if it served them to do so. Mrs. Kunkle, as wide as she was tall, was the worst of the lot, often serving out her judgment of Mama on me. "The child of a Gypsy is the Devil's child too," she'd hiss, squinting at me through the space where her sheet dipped between two clothes pegs. "Stay away from me, girl. You're bad luck." She'd set her son Thomas on me, and laugh as he chased me down the street.

"I'll be It first," Alice volunteered, taking a scarf that was hanging off the side of her mirror and tying it over her eyes.

Lamp smoke drifting through the room, Mae began to spin Alice around in circles. "No hands," she commanded, before setting Alice free.

I moved on tiptoe, put my back against the wall and held my breath. The sounds of the house came up the stairwell—creaking floorboards, muffled laughter, the ticking of a clock.

Alice stumbled around, her hands clasped in front of her like she was praying. Feeling her way with her elbows, she bumped into one of the beds and nearly tripped headfirst over a pair of Mae's shoes.

"Trying to kill me?" she asked, hoping to fetch laughter.

Mae called to her, "Right behind you in the corner, by the window," then scurried across the room in the other direction.

"Gotcha!" Alice trapped me against the wall with her arms. Nuzzling my neck, she took the ribbon from my fan between her teeth and said, "Eeee-dah." As she lifted the scarf from her eyes she exclaimed, "I knew it was you!"

"Ada's It," Mae sang out.

"Help me get Mae," I whispered to Alice as she tied the scarf around my eyes.

Mae insisted on spinning me several times more than she had Alice. By the time she was through, I was so dizzy I thought I'd fall over. Forgetting the rules, I reached out, fingers spread to find my way.

"No hands," Alice scolded from somewhere across the room.

I heard footsteps, both heavy and soft. Voices whispered all around me.

Ada

        Ada

Ada   *Ada*

Stumbling towards where I thought I'd heard Mae, I ran straight into someone else.

"No hands," Mae's voice warned from behind me.

Rubbing my cheek along the person's front like a cat, I felt the scratch of a wool waistcoat, smelled the distinct scent of bootblack. Cadet.

"Let me kiss you," he whispered, taking hold of my arms so I couldn't get away.

I'd dreamed it, secretly planned how I might go about making it happen, even picturing myself alone with him in the kitchen, or sneaking into his room at night to steal a kiss while he was asleep. But those were only the brave notions of a girl's imagination. In my dream world, I was Miss Ada Fenwick, fully formed, with beautiful breasts and long flowing hair. Standing here in the dark with Cadet so near, I was only Moth, my mother in one ear telling me to stay away from boys, my father in the other asking, "How could you let them take your name?"

Cadet leaned in close and then his lips pressed to mine for what seemed a lifetime, our breathing shallow and warm, nose to cheek.

Laughter came from opposite corners of the room, breaking the spell.

Mae pulled the scarf off my head. Alice lit a lamp. Cadet was gone.

The salt-sweet taste of him still on my lips, I didn't hear a word Mae or Alice had to say the rest of the night. For the first time in my life, I understood what hips, thighs, breasts, sighs, touches and thoughts were meant for.

"No man is allowed through these doors unless he's a gentleman through and through," Miss Everett reassured me the morning I was to make my first appearance in her "quiet room." "He must have an honourable pedigree and an upstanding reputation. He must come with references in hand."

Gentleman callers weren't allowed in the house before noon, except on Sundays. On Sunday mornings, at half past eleven, a handful of invited men filed through the doors to see Miss Everett's near-whores take off their clothes.

The idea was to raise a gentleman's interest. If all went well, he'd request an invitation to meet. Chaperoned luncheons were then followed by an evening at the theatre, and after that, an offer for a private engagement. Miss Everett assured me it was an orderly process and that I'd be watched over every step of the way.

There were two parlours in the house. The main parlour was the one at the front where Emily played the harp or the piano while Missouri and Rose read to each other from magazines and story-papers. Their gentlemen callers waited for them there, bearing flowers or a box of chocolates or some other gift. If they came empty-handed, Miss Everett sent them away.

The second parlour—the one Miss Everett called her "quiet room"—could only be gotten to through a pocket door in the panelling on the far wall of the front parlour. Comfortable-looking chairs were lined up in a row, their seats and backs covered in deep red velvet.

The chairs were placed up close to a latticework screen that ran the length of the space, dividing the room in half. On the other side of the screen was a low stage that had been set back a ways so that all the men could have a full view of it. It was wide enough to move about on without feeling confined. To the right of the stage was a large music box that worked by setting brass discs to spinning with a wind-up crank. It would *plink, plink, plink* out tunes, chiming along like rain on a roof.

Although I knew I'd be far enough away from the screen that I wouldn't fully see the men behind it, I was still nervous about them being there. Even if I could get past the notion that strangers were watching, I felt less than confident about the way I looked. I wasn't nearly as developed (in the places that mattered) as Mae and Alice, and the traces of Mama's Gypsy blood made me far less American-looking than them.

"It's just a matter of pairing you with the right man," Miss Everett told me. "There are plenty of gentlemen who are seeking more exotic fare."

Alice had gone to the quiet room twice before and she could hardly bring herself to talk about it. "You might think if you can't see them, it wouldn't be so bad, but it's . . . awful."

Mae acted like it was merely an inconvenience. Her month of training was nearly up, and she had other thoughts on her mind. She'd soon be going to the theatre, and then on to Rose's room.

"Ask Miss Everett to play 'Beautiful Dreamer,'" Alice advised later that morning as she fixed a satin ribbon in her hair. "It's the shortest of the songs. You can get away with making things go a bit faster that way, and then you're done."

"Not too fast, mind you," Mae warned, "or you'll be standing there in your pantaloons for what feels like eternity."

I watched as Mae gazed at herself in the long mirror by the window, getting ready for her turn in the second parlour. Tending to a button on her waist that she'd missed, she was enviably calm about it all. *Easy for her*, I thought.

Alice came at me with a tin of rouge in her hand. "To make you look as if you're always blushing," she said as she went about dotting it on my lips and cheeks.

"To make you look more a whore and less a girl," Mae added.

But I am a girl.

"There are men who chase after children," Alice said with a shudder. "I've seen them watch the schoolgirls of St. Patrick's skip rope and play tag down Prince Street. It's as if they think that if they stare at the girls long enough, they'll find a way to steal their joy for themselves."

Shaking her head, Mae said, "Emily had one of those. He brought her a schoolgirl's dress to wear in her room for him so she'd look like she spent her days listening to nuns and carrying her books home in a leather strap."

"Did you know he was a priest?" Alice asked, her voice hushed.

"Better Emily than a child," Mae said.

"Yes."

Yes.

When Miss Everett gave the sign, I came into the parlour and took my place on the stage. After she started the music box spinning, she opened a curtain that was draped in front of the latticework. This was the sign that I was to take off my clothes. "Just like you would at the end of the day," she whispered. "Very simple. Not too fast."

I could smell the stale cigar smoke on the men's breath. From the sound of a few scattered coughs and their movement in their chairs, I guessed there were four, five, six of them, maybe more. I tried not to think of them. I knew they couldn't touch me, and that Cadet was standing just outside the door, but it brought little comfort.

My fingers numb with fear, I trembled as I began to undress.

Miss Everett had requested I wear my walking suit for the occasion, so it was gloves first, then my hat, then I let loose the clasps on my tunic, and unbuttoned the buttons on my waist, starting at the collar, allowing it to come away from my shoulders.

Shh, little sweetheart. Don't be afraid, one of the men hissed through the screen. The other men began to talk to me too, their voices low. *Take your time. Over here. That's it. Good girl.*

I looked to Miss Everett, but her face was calm, as if she hadn't heard a word of their rude coaxing. I couldn't tell if she was standing too close to the music box to have noticed it, or if she was simply choosing to ignore it.

I saw one man's fingers curve through a space in the lattice, a gold band circling his ring finger.

Tears in my eyes, I turned away.

"The door stays closed until you're done, my dear," Miss Everett whispered. "You must face them and continue."

Your skirt should fall down to the floor in a frilly heap. Once untied and pushed past the hips, your petticoats will slide free to join the rest. All that should be left is your corset and pantaloons.

I'll be nearby to help if any tie has a stubborn knot or any clasps get caught.

And so I turned towards the screen once again. I kept my eyes straight ahead and removed my clothing down to my undergarments. Then I stood there.

When the song from the music box finally came to an end, Miss Everett closed the curtain, and ushered me from the room.

"Let your dress go slowly next time, my dear," she said. "And lower your eyes as well. I dare say that determined gaze of yours may have frightened the lot of them."

Putting a dressing gown around my shoulders, she added, "I've got wonderful plans for you, Ada. If all goes well, you might turn out just like Rose."

All that night I cried in my pillow.

Alice came to the side of my bed and whispered, "You should pray. That's what I do. Ask God to take your pain away."

Alice believed that when she got down on her knees, put her hands together and spoke to the air, angels came and took her worries straight to heaven. "I wouldn't lie about something like this," she said.

I'd spent my whole life longing for someone to want me—for Mama to say she loved me, or for my father to reappear at the door. It seemed unfair that what went on in Miss Everett's parlour was the kind of wanting I'd get instead. I doubted that I'd be any better off letting God know I was here.

The body of an unknown woman was found yesterday floating in the East River off the docks at the old William H. Webb shipyards. By the Coroner's observations, the deceased met with an accident and expired by drowning. Foul play is not suspected. Guessed to be between forty and fifty years of age, the woman was wearing a simple dress with a silk scarf still tied around her head. The deceased could not be identified, and, upon the Coroner holding an inquest, the body was sent to Potter's Field for interment.

—*The Evening Star*, November 5, 1871

XIX.

From the time I was old enough to remember the number on our door, Mama had left me alone at night. She said she had things to do that she couldn't do in the day and that it was just the way things had to be. Before she'd go out, she'd put me to bed and tell me to stay there. I'd sit in the dark, dreaming up a Good Mother to come care for me until Mama returned.

My Good Mother wasn't anything like Mama. She was fat and happy, with her flesh all round in rolls underneath her dress. When she put her arms around me I could hardly breathe for the warmth of her embrace. She wasn't bothered by anything and her teeth shone white when she smiled, except for the hole where one was missing, right in the front. She'd whistle and hoot silly tunes through that little hole just to make me laugh. At the end of my pretending, my Good Mother would put me to bed, tucking Miss Sweet under the blanket with me. She'd wait with us, wondering, as I did, if this was the night Mama wouldn't come home.

Now she came to me, pushing at my shoulder while I was asleep.

"Wake up, Moth."

But it was Miss Everett calling my name, wanting me to get out of bed. "Just wrap yourself in a quilt, dear. There's someone waiting for you downstairs. It's urgent. "

I got up as she asked and followed her to the parlour, wiping sleep from my eyes.

Mrs. Riordan was sitting on the couch, her lips set in a grim line. Clothes dingy and mismatched as ever, she made for quite a sight next to Miss Everett's perfect, upholstered furniture. I greeted her with a kiss on the cheek. The last time I'd seen her was the day before Mr. Cowan cornered me in the alley. Mr. Bartz wouldn't have told her where I was without good reason, so I knew that something must be terribly wrong.

"I trust you're well?" I asked.

"Well enough," she replied. Giving me a strained smile she said, "Mr. Bartz sends his apologies."

Miss Everett looked at me with sympathetic eyes from where she stood in the doorway. "Mrs. Coyne is in bed for the night," she said. "But I'm happy to make a pot of tea for the two of you if you like."

"That would be much appreciated," Mrs. Riordan said, answering for the both of us.

Miss Everett nodded to her and then went off to the kitchen to fetch the tea.

"My dear child," Mrs. Riordan began, her voice weaker than I remembered it to be. "I have news of your mother." Reaching out, she took my hand in hers and squeezed it tight. "She's passed on, Moth," she announced, her eyes watery and sad. "They found her drowned in the river not three nights ago. A gang of boys fished her out from under the docks."

Tears burned my eyes. My heart hurt. I couldn't help but think perhaps Mama was hiding somewhere, looking on to see if I still cared for her.

"You're . . . certain it was her?"

She gave a solemn nod. "Yes."

Word of Mama's death had travelled mouth to ear, wharf to street, alley to stoop, by way of several different people, including Mrs. Kunkel and Mr. Bartz, to get to Mrs. Riordan. I could only imagine what they'd said.

"Did you hear about the woman who got pulled from the river last night? They say she was a Gypsy."

"I know for a fact it was that fortune teller who sold away her daughter, the one who used to live on Chrystie Street."

"She was nothing but a thief and a liar. My guess is she got what was coming to her."

"I'm afraid I couldn't find you in time to claim her body at the morgue," Mrs. Riordan lamented. "She's gone to Potter's Field already."

I broke down, as visions of Mama's sad, waterlogged body came to my mind. I'd been trying to forget her, wishing my

Eight to twelve hours after death, post-mortem staining occurs. Skin forms new shapes, accentuating the body's most prominent bones. Rigor mortis spreads over the body, muscle by muscle, and then retreats. Hence the saying "after the rigor, before the rats."

memories away bit by bit, and now she was gone, almost as if I'd meant for her to die. All the love I'd had for her came back to me now, hand in hand with the sorrow of her sending me away. There could be no forgiveness between us and no goodbye.

Reaching into her pocket, Mrs. Riordan brought out a balled-up handkerchief and laid it in her lap. She pulled at the corners of the cloth to reveal a small silver spoon and an oblong bottle the length of her finger, a chain attached to its neck. "Catch as many tears as you can this wretched night, and spoon them into the bottle, like this," she said, showing me how. "Stopper the bottle when you're through. As the days go by your tears will disappear along with your sorrow. Then you'll know your mourning's done."

Handing the spoon and bottle to me she said, "These were mine when my Johnny died."

"I can't accept them," I told her, trying to give the tear-catcher back.

"You must," she insisted. "I won't be happy until you do."

Putting the bottle and spoon aside, I thanked her for her kindness. I'd missed her gummy smile and comforting presence. I only wished she'd found me for a happier reason.

"There's something more I need to tell you," she said, her voice falling to a whisper.

Lachrymatories, or tear-catchers, were worn by brides during the war. The women were to fill the bottles with their tears as a sign of devotion to their husbands while they were away. Many men never returned from battle, and thus their wives were left to pour their tears of loneliness on their husbands' graves.

Today the practice of tear catching is more widespread, and is performed during periods of celebration as well as mourning. There has even been one account of a woman carrying her tears to dispel her love for an unattainable man.

"I have it on good authority that her eyes was open when they found her."

She knew as well as I did that a corpse with open eyes was the sign of a curse. It meant the person's soul was not at peace when they died and that they intended to haunt family and friends until they found another soul to drag down with them to the grave.

I'd sung the song of Mary O'Day enough times to know that a daughter was usually an unsettled mother ghost's first choice for haunting.

Mary O'Day got carried away
The day her mother died
For you see, she couldn't flee
Her Mama's open eyes!

"Here," Mrs. Riordan said, bringing out another gift. "I took the liberty of properly stuffing your poppet."

"Thank you," I said, clutching Miss Sweet to my chest.

Mrs. Riordan stayed with me the rest of the night, holding me in her arms while I rocked the doll in mine.

In the morning, Miss Everett had Mrs. Coyne fill a basket from the pantry and even called for a carriage so Mrs. Riordan didn't have to walk back to Chrystie Street. The gracious way she treated the old woman, a complete stranger to her, meant more to me than I could say.

"Get some rest," Mrs. Riordan advised, giving me a last hug. "You've had a long night, and there will be more to come. Don't lose faith. Eventually your mama's spirit will tire. Then she'll slip away to wherever God sees fit to put her."

After she'd gone, Miss Everett took me by the hand and led me to my bed. She told Alice and Mae, who were already awake, to get dressed quietly and leave me alone to rest.

I spent most of the morning crying in sadness, anger and confusion. Exhausted at last, I fell into a dream, grief conjuring Mama to my side.

Her ghost stood at the foot of my bed wearing nothing but a pair of pantaloons and an old, frayed corset. She had oyster shells tangled in her hair, and several of Mr. Hetherington's goldfish flopped about her feet, gasping for air. Dirty water flowed from between her fingers, then turned to blood as it pooled on the floor. Her mouth was dark with death.

"Did you know I loved you, Mama?" I asked her ghost while clutching the blanket to my chest. "I loved you enough for both of us . . ."

Floating towards me, her arms outstretched as if she meant to make things right between us, she came nose to nose with me, then stopped.

"Who took your hair?" she asked, her face stricken with horror.

Frantically tugging at the ends of my curls, I said, "Mrs. Wentworth did, but it's coming back, Mama, see? Every day, it's coming back."

"She'll take your mind next . . ." Mama moaned, repeating the words again and again as if she were casting a spell. *She'll take your mind, she'll take your mind, she'lltakeyourmind . . .* And soon her face began to change, turning round, plump and healthy, and looking for all the world like Mrs. Wentworth.

Holding a pair of scissors over her head like a dagger, she cried, "You're still mine, Miss Fenwick!"

And so, Johannes, fully determined on this promising scheme, began to cast about him for a
medium who was acquainted in the spirit sphere,
to introduce him to some of the eligible ghosts.

—Q.K. PHILANDER DOESTICKS,

The Witches of New York, 1859

XX.

For a short time, Miss Everett showed a great deal of
thoughtfulness towards me. She allowed me to sleep
the day away, and in the evenings she had Mrs.
Coyne prepare hot milk and oatcakes for me to eat in bed.

Alice, careful not to upset me, seemed eternally interested in discussing the latest news in necklines and fabric
choices as shown in the fashion plates of *Godey's Lady's
Book*. "I do hope the princess cut will hold over for 1872,
don't you?"

Mae, on the other hand, was more direct. "If I'd known
Miss Everett could turn so sweet," she smirked, "I'd have
paid some old bag weeks ago to deliver the news of my
own ma's death." Her bitterness was, of course, expected–
Miss Everett had discovered (or at the very least strongly
suspected) Mae's outings to the Bowery Concert Hall.

Mae had made a bumpy entrance through the window
the night after Mrs. Riordan's visit, and Miss Everett had
stormed into our room and informed Mae that if she
couldn't keep herself safe and secure, she had no choice

but to see to the task for her. "You're not my child," she'd scolded. "You're my whore."

"Near-whore," Mae had spitefully whispered as soon as Miss Everett had gone out the door.

After that night, Cadet had been assigned to hover over Mae during the day and to stand guard on the rooftop at night until the concert hall was closed.

I felt jealous that she had him so near, and I felt sorry for Cadet out there in the cold, his collar turned up against the wind. Mae tried to get him to go to bed by promising him an hour's worth of affection for every night he turned in early. She'd climbed out the window and gone to him wearing nothing but her dressing gown. Holding it open so he couldn't help but see her naked body, she entreated him: "Take something of me then let me go!" Cadet just stared straight ahead, as if by a miracle, he was immune to her charms.

Three days after I'd got the news about Mama, Miss Everett's sympathy ran out. Sunday morning arrived and despite my tears, she wasn't about to excuse me from my turn in the second parlour.

Taking me by the arm, she led me down the stairs.

"Please," I begged again, "don't make me strip off for them today."

"If you can't perform this simple task, Ada, perhaps you're not meant for my house."

After it was over, she took me upstairs to my bedroom and told me to stay there with no food or company for the rest of the day. "Think about it, Miss Fenwick," she said. "Don't let grief be the end of you." Then she took Mrs. Riordan's tear-catcher from where it hung by my bed, placed it in her pocket and walked out the door.

The next morning, when Dr. Sadie arrived for her weekly visit, I overheard her having a disagreement with Miss Everett in the parlour. I pressed my ear to the door in order to hear what they were saying, but I still couldn't make out their words. In the end, all I learned was that Miss Everett was "severely disappointed." Then I heard Dr. Sadie, as she approached the door, say, "I'll do what I can."

"Miss Everett would like you to come with me for the day," Dr. Sadie said after she'd finished with my examination. "She feels the fresh air might do you good, and I could use another pair of hands on my rounds. There'll be no talk of orphan trains, I promise."

Worried that Miss Everett was about to put me out on the curb, I accepted her invitation. Truth be told, I was anxious to get out from under the madam's watchful eye.

Walking up Third Avenue, we came to a row of tenements that looked much like my home on Chrystie Street. "I've got house calls today," Dr. Sadie said as she took hold of a fire escape ladder at the side of the corner building. "Up we go."

I followed her up the rungs and then across the roofs of building after building. It was amazing to see how well she got around, lifting the heavy black skirts of her doctor's dress with ease, and using abandoned crates and boxes as steps to get over the edge of one roof to another. She told me she visited most of her patients this way, finding it easier to get where she needed to go if her feet never touched the ground. "My nightmares are made of tenement stairs," she said with a shudder. "I avoid the rat-infested dark of them as much as possible."

Many of her patients lived in crowded rooms at the tops

of buildings, sweating away while they did piecework–
rolling cigars, gluing envelopes, or sewing shirt after shirt
after shirt. Sickness made itself at home in their close,
dark rooms, disease thriving in the absence of windows
and hope.

We climbed in to see them through skylights and fire
escapes. We looked in on a widow who had no one to care
for her, and weary mothers who had far too many children
to tend to on their own. We found people lying in their
beds, wasting away from some illness or from not having
proper food to eat. With every room we entered, I thought
of Mama, and how bitterly she'd always complained about
not having enough.

While Dr. Sadie treated coughs and fevers, lanced boils
and stitched up cuts, I did my best to get the children to
smile, taking them into my lap for a game of "to market"
or playing peek-a-boo with a tattered blanket. In their company I felt shame for having left Chrystie Street behind,
and guilt over the comforts I had now.

We worked through noon and late into the afternoon.
Finally Dr. Sadie stopped to rest on a rooftop, sitting down
to lean against a chimney. She pulled two apples from her
bag and handed me one. "Put your back to the brick," she
said. "It will help keep you warm." The day had started out
with bright, warm sun, but the cold, damp winds of a late
November evening were coming on fast.

Whenever she caught me glancing at her hands, she
promptly folded them in her lap. They were chapped and
raw from the soap she used to keep them clean, the struggle between science and beauty evident in every pore. Her
worry over her appearance was plain to see no matter how

much she tried to hide it, showing me that even the most serious of women still suffer under vanity's harsh rule.

"We've one more stop to make and then we're through," she said.

I nodded as I took a bite out of my apple. "That's good," I said after I'd swallowed, hoping that I didn't look as exhausted as I felt. Twirling the apple by its stem, I thought of my time on the Bowery. No matter how guilty I felt for the comforts I'd gained in Miss Everett's care, I hoped I'd never go back to begging for pennies on the street.

Dr. Sadie's last visit brought us to the door of a Miss Katherine Tully.

"Come in," a weak voice called out to us after we'd knocked.

The small single room was cold and dark, and smelled of stale urine. Miss Tully was lying in her bed, wearing what must have been every stitch of clothing she owned. She had two patchwork blankets wrapped around her feet but was still shivering so violently her bed frame chattered with sympathy.

Handing me a tin of matches from her bag, Dr. Sadie instructed, "Get a lamp lit, Moth. Let's make things a bit cheerier for Miss Tully, shall we?"

As I hurried to light the wick before all daylight was gone from the room, Dr. Sadie sat on the edge of the bed and spoke to Miss Tully in quiet tones. I watched as she wrapped her fingers around the woman's thin wrist and counted her heartbeats.

The dim light made it difficult for me to guess Miss Tully's age or what was ailing her, but clearly her sickness was doing its best to take whatever life she had left. She and Dr. Sadie kept company more like friends than doctor and patient, and Miss Tully even laughed as the good doctor made light of their shared spinsterhood.

"Just two old maids, aren't we?" Dr. Sadie said with a wink.

"Happy as can be," Miss Tully replied with a sigh. Then in a softer voice, she asked, "Nothing's changed in your situation?"

Answering the question with a shake of her head, Dr. Sadie reached for a medicine bottle that was on the bedside table and held it up to the light. "It doesn't look like you've taken much of the remedy I brought you," she said. "Didn't you understand the directions?"

"I did," the woman replied, smiling meekly. "I understood just fine." She motioned for Dr. Sadie to hand her the bottle. Pointing to the label, she read, "Take only after meals."

"I see," Dr. Sadie said, getting up from the bedside and going to Miss Tully's cupboards.

"Don't bother," Miss Tully said. "You'll not find anything there."

"Katherine," Dr. Sadie sighed. "I suppose there's no coal either?"

"No–"

"Why didn't you mention how bad off you were the last time I was here?"

"Leave me my pride," Miss Tully answered.

Unburdening herself of every coin she had in her pockets, Dr. Sadie directed me to take them to the nearest grocer and bring back all the food I could carry. "A bag of rice and a sack of oats . . . bread, milk, apples, beans and two of whatever meat pies he's got in the case. The shopkeeper's name is Mr. Hannigan. Tell him we need coal delivered today. If you say Dr. Sadie sent you, he'll take care of it."

Not long after I returned with the groceries, a delivery boy appeared with a bucket of coal. Having a fire in the stove instantly made the room seem a far happier place. I kept it stoked while Dr. Sadie prepared a pot of porridge and apples for Miss Tully's supper. We stayed with her until she'd eaten it all.

After spooning a dose of medicine down Miss Tully's throat, Dr. Sadie sat herself on the edge of the bed and began to brush the woman's hair. Making long strokes with a silver-handled brush she'd found in the drawer of Miss Tully's small table, she tended to the young woman as if she were a queen.

"I had a baby once," Miss Tully said to me as Dr. Sadie wove her hair into a loose braid. "She was a tiny thing that didn't live past two days. I called her Olivia, after my mother. She would have been a beauty, just like you."

"Thank you," I said, hanging onto the last of her words so I wouldn't have to imagine Miss Tully holding a dying baby in her arms.

She had no ties to me through family or friendship, so I saw her sadness quite clearly. Every hesitation in her manner, large or small—in her breathing, in her words—brought the overwhelming desire to go to her and say *all will be well*, even when I know it wouldn't be.

The sky was completely dark when we left that room. Dr. Sadie scolded herself under her breath as we walked down the street. "I should've checked the cupboards last time. I should've made sure she had something to eat."

Rain began to fall, coming down in heavy sheets, and we were without proper wraps to keep us from the weather.

"My room's closer than Miss Everett's," Dr. Sadie shouted over the downpour. "We'll go there until it stops."

Her garret was above the place where she'd been taught how to be a doctor, and only steps from Miss Keteltas' mansion. In all my wandering up and down that street, I'd never noticed the building before, or the sign above the door that said, THE NEW YORK INFIRMARY FOR INDIGENT WOMEN AND CHILDREN.

"I'm sorry the room's so small," Dr. Sadie said as she creaked the door of her stove open to poke at the makings of a fire. "I don't often have house guests."

Her room seemed fine to me. There were beautiful things all around—a basket of apples, a shadow box that held a collection of striped, spiralled seashells, a white cambric nightdress draped over a chair. There were books scattered everywhere, lined up on the shelves and on the desk, and still more of them piled in tall, crooked stacks.

She had a collection of morbid drawings pinned to the wall beside her bed—picture after picture of arms and legs, bodies and faces, made to look as if a person's flesh had been cut open for all to see. Jars of pickled creatures sat here and there on the mantel and between her books. Bloated frogs and twisted snakes peered out at me through murky glass, their eyes glowing, green, yellow and red.

"Would you like something to eat?" she asked, reaching high on a shelf for a tin of biscuits.

"Yes, please," I answered. I hadn't had anything to eat that day except the apple she'd given me.

As her hand went towards the box, I caught sight of a rat sitting next to it. I was about to scream when Dr. Sadie grabbed hold of the thing by its tail and set it aside. It stayed stiff and silent in her hand, its glass eyes twinkling. Opening the biscuit tin, Dr. Sadie offered me first pick.

"Have as many as you like," she added.

As I took a handful of biscuits, I suddenly noticed the skeleton hanging from a hook in the corner of the room. Held together with wire, it wavered ever so slightly whenever Dr. Sadie passed near it. I could have sworn it was staring at me from where its eyes should have been.

When she caught me looking at it, she said, "Oh, don't mind her, that's just Miss Jewett." There was a hint of pride in her voice, almost as if she'd known the girl and turned her to bone herself.

"Mr. Dink gave her to me as payment for coming to the rescue of a young lady who was performing in a production at his Palace of Illusions," she explained. "The girl had lost her voice and it was up to me to get it back for her. Saltwater rinses along with lemon and honey were the first order of business."

"Who was it?" I asked, far more interested in discovering the identity of the actress than in Dr. Sadie's remedy for croup.

"Oh, I don't think I should divulge her name," Dr. Sadie said, shaking her head. "Mr. Dink is very discreet when it comes to his players and his business." To make up for her disappointing me, Dr. Sadie playfully draped one of the skeleton's arms around her shoulder and then rattled the entire thing by the ribs. "Poor Miss Jewett," she sighed. She put her head on the skeleton's shoulder, adding, "You're the best friend I've ever had . . . I never have to cook for you, and you never complain about a thing, not even the weather." She grinned at me and beckoned me towards her. "You can take a closer look at her if you like, she won't bite."

There was a nasty hole in the side of Miss Jewett's skull, yet her mouth was open in a wide, toothy grin. I reached out and wrapped my fingers around one of the long bones of her arm. It felt smooth in the palm of my hand. I could see that someone had carved words along the length of it and darkened them in with ink. *As you are now, I once was. As I am now, so you shall be.* I let go of the bone and stared at the skeleton, afraid she might set her ghostly sights on me.

"You can sleep here tonight if you like," Dr. Sadie said, bringing out an extra pillow from a blanket chest and fluffing it into shape. "Miss Everett knows you're safe here."

"Thank you," I said, grateful not to have to walk back to the house in such terrible weather. Going to the window I watched the raindrops and listened to them tapping at the pane. I followed a single drop with my finger as it nagged down the glass.

"Did you meet Mr. Dink through Miss Everett?" I asked.

"No," Dr. Sadie said. "It was the other way around. I've known Mr. Dink for years."

"Really?"

In 1865 a fire broke out at the New York Medical College on Fourteenth Street. Housed therein was a vast collection of medical oddities, having once belonged to Dr. Valentine Mott (a late professor in the College of Physicians and Surgeons, New York). Numbering over one thousand items, nearly everything was lost. What remained of Dr. Mott's collection was shortly thereafter given to the doctor's widow. A few, select items were donated to a Bowery museum that specialized in anatomical specimens.

"Oh yes, I've been seeing to his performers' health for quite some time."

I tried to imagine Dr. Sadie attempting to look inside the mouth of the World's Tallest Illusionist. *That*, I thought, *would be a sight worth seeing*.

"Why did you want me to come with you today?" I asked.

Slumping into a chair next to the bed, she put her feet up on a pile of books. The shadows of the room made her seem less a lady and more a girl. Her voice sounded different too, softer and more relaxed.

"I needed to know that you were going to be all right, now that your mother is gone."

"Wouldn't it have been easier to ask?" I wondered out loud, still confused.

"Words are an unreliable way to measure the heart," she said. "I'm more inclined to trust what I observe rather than what someone tells me."

"Miss Tully will die soon, won't she."

Meeting my eyes, Dr. Sadie said, "Yes, Moth. She will."

"What's the matter with her?"

"She's got an illness with no remedy."

She told me that Miss Tully had caught one of the meanest things a person could get. The English blamed it on the French, the French blamed it on the Italians, the Dutch blamed the Spanish. No one was sure why it did what it did, but it came like a wolf in sheep's clothing, and just when you thought

There may not be any signs of the disease when you first encounter a gentleman with syphilis.

It tends to go into hiding for long periods of time. Men think they're safe, when they're not.

If a gentleman appears to have a grey-blue complexion, suffers from sore gums and excess saliva, or bears a scent akin to fried potatoes – you can be sure he's taking mercury to try to hold it back.

When the mercury fails, many men get desperate. Some turn to virgins thinking that their innocence holds a cure.

it was gone, it would turn up again, uglier than ever. After the rash faded, hair loss, muscle aches, and a pronounced limp were sure to follow. There was even a chance your nose might fall right off your face. If it didn't kill you sooner rather than later, it was quite possible you'd go mad from it. It was so awful it had a whole handful of names—the Grandgore, the Lues, the Great Pox, Cupid's disease.

Dr. Sadie had been chasing after it for quite a while and the one thing she knew for certain was that dishonesty spread it worst of all. Just like any other lie, once you'd passed it around, you couldn't take it back. It didn't care if you were a baby or a whore. There was no cure.

Sickness often took a terrible toll on the people of Chrystie Street. Mothers worried over their children with every new wave of typhus or cholera that descended on the slums. In the swelter of summer, whitewashed coffins got stacked tens high and tens across in the back of the gravedigger's wagon, mothers keening after it as it rolled away.

I wished I could forget ever meeting Miss Tully, and every sobbing mother I'd ever seen. I wished my father had come back to Mama and me, bringing happiness instead of sorrow to our door. I wished it was easy to do all that Miss Everett asked of me, and that Dr. Sadie's kindness would just disappear and she'd leave me to my fate. I got up and wandered over to the window. Pressing my nose to the pane, I tried to see down the street to Miss Keteltas' house, but it was impossible to make it out in the darkness and rain.

November 10, 1871.

Yesterday began with Miss Everett complaining that Moth (or Ada as she calls her) had been acting sullen and uncooperative. She said she was at her wits end over how to shake the girl from it.

"Isn't there something you can give her to even out her temperament?" she asked.

Loathe to blindly prescribe the type of cure she was suggesting, I asked if she'd tried talking to the child to get to the heart of the matter.

"It's beyond that," she said, quick to dismiss me.

"She's too young for this," I argued (once again.)

"Clearly the girl knows her own mind."

In the end, I suggested I take Moth with me on my rounds for the day to see if I could do her any good. Much to my surprise, Emma agreed to it. "She's all yours," she said, leaving Moth to my care.

I took her to see Katherine Tully.

I thought it an idea with small risk, and perhaps great rewards. I'd hoped that introducing her to Miss Tully might sway her thinking. It was wrong of me not to be honest and tell her the whole of Katherine's story, but I was desperate to have her turn away from Emma and turn to me, instead.

As the day went on, I was touched by the tenderness she showed my patients and her willingness to help. There were moments of true confidence between us, I'm sure of it, but sadly, it seems, they weren't enough. Although she spent the night curled up and sleeping in my bed, she was all too eager to leave the next morning.

She ran from me when we got to the house, straight up the stairs without saying goodbye.

It seems all I've done is remind myself of the mistakes I made in the past. Perhaps I'm not meant to take risks after all.

S.F.

May 5, 1870

Three weeks after getting Katherine Tully out of Miss Everett's and into a spot at a refuge house, she came to my door, begging to be let in.

She'd been seduced against her will.

The man had first approached her a fortnight before as she was walking home for the evening. He strolled with her on three occasions, each time handing her a few coins at their goodbye and then making her swear she would keep his kindness a secret between them.

The third time they met, he told her that he knew of a situation where she might be brought on as help for a party in a private residence. He said she would earn a dollar for her efforts and that she need only sign an agreement of employment and he would take care of the rest.

"What did the agreement say?" I asked her.

"I don't exactly know. I don't read so well."

They travelled by carriage to a fine house in a nice part of town. The man kept the curtains drawn on the windows, so she wasn't sure of where they ended up. She could only say that they were in the cab for what seemed like a long time.

When they arrived, there was no one there to greet them except the man of the house. She was escorted to the parlour and told to sit down. She recalled that there was a pianoforte in the room and when she told the man how pretty she thought it was, he sat down and played a song. After he was finished, he came after her.

She hid in the draperies and cried, begging him to leave her alone, but he grabbed her from where she was hiding and forced himself on her.

"Do you know the name of your seducer?"

"No."

"What is the name of the man who arranged it all?"

"He said his name is Mr. Jones."

No doubt an alias.

"Was there anything special or unusual about Mr. Jones that you recall?"

"He was a tall man with dark hair, and he had a handsome smile. He wore a nice suit, fashionable and bright. He didn't have a beard or moustache, only sideburns. He seemed respectable enough."

Upon showing me a painful chancre that had since appeared after the incident, she asked, "Is there something you can do to make it go away?"

A mercurial ointment will dry it up in a few days' time, but I'm certain the sore is a sign of a greater disease.

S.F.

15. How many lovers shall I have?

16. The one that I love, what does he really think of me?

17. Ought I believe the tender vows that are breathed to me?

18. The person that I am thinking of, does he love me?

19. The person that I am thinking of, does he think that I love him?

20. What ought I do, to make him (that I love) love me?

–from *The Ancient and Modern Ladies' Oracle*
by Mr. Cornelius Agrippa
(Infallible Prophet of the Male Sex)

XXI.

Mae came to my side and put her chin on my shoulder to see what I was looking at through the window of our room. "Why don't you go keep him company," she teased, pointing to Cadet, who was standing sentry on the roof. "Maybe he'll give you another kiss."

Lantern at his feet, he was standing guard as usual, waiting for Mae to try to escape.

Shrugging her away, I said, "He only kissed me because you told him to. The whole game was just a ruse so I wouldn't see it coming."

"Perhaps," she said. "But I never told him to enjoy it. He did that on his own."

I blushed at the memory of his lips against mine but didn't move from my spot at the window.

"If you don't go out there, I'll send Alice instead," Mae warned.

Giggling, Alice fetched my wool cloak and put it around my shoulders. "He'd rather see you than me," she said, giving me a little push.

More and more, things weren't as they'd seemed when I first came to the house. Alice had gotten into the habit of praying every night, begging God to bring her a husband rather than a seducer. Rose had grown short with everyone, impatient to leave. Three mornings in a row, I'd heard Emily crying in her room. When Missouri caught me listening at the door, she said, "It's nothing that concerns you. She'll be fine."

Miss Everett hadn't seen fit to return Mrs. Riordan's tear-catcher to me, but I was sure the tears I'd managed to trap within the pretty vial hadn't dwindled in the least. My dream of Mama's ghost had been false, and I'd not had any sign that she was truly near. I'd been waiting to smell the scent of Dr. Godfrey's on her breath when there was no one in the room, or to feel her fingers tug the hairs at the back of my neck, but nothing had come. Her passing had brought me more sadness than any lie she'd ever told. Betrayals can be forgiven and forgotten. Nothing changes death.

Only daydreams of Cadet relieved the anxious knot I often had in my stomach, and although I would've preferred to keep my longing for him to myself, there was no way I could fool Mae, or even gentle Alice.

"All right," I said, giving her a playful scowl. "I'm going. Help me out the window."

Pulling on the window frame, Alice and I got it open wide enough for her to help me scramble through.

It was cold on the roof, and the wind sliced through my cloak, making me shiver. Cadet smiled when he saw me coming; Alice had been right to send me out.

Taking a flask from his pocket, he twisted off the lid and held it out to me. "To take the chill off," he said.

The liquor had a far more agreeable odour than the stale beer Mama used to drink to chase down her Dr. Godfrey's, but my memories of her stumbling around and crying drunken tears on my shoulder kept me from accepting.

"No thank you," I replied with a frown.

"Suit yourself," Cadet said, then tipped back the flask and took a long draw from it. Seeing the distaste on my face, he wiped his mouth on his sleeve and said, "It's a bad habit, you're right. It's what took my pa's life. I guess I got used to sharing drink with the boys I lived with when I worked for Dick the Ratter. We slept in a cellar underneath a store on Third Avenue, in nothing more than a pick- and shovel-scarred cave. It got cold down there at night."

Spotting Mae and Alice still at the window, he said, "There's a sheltered spot behind the chimney stack over there—come on, let's get out of the wind."

I followed him to where he'd pointed and found he'd made a private place for himself with a box to sit on, out of sight. Once we were settled together, neither of us knew what to say or do, and our silence stretched awkwardly between us.

"Do you like it here?" I finally thought to ask, even though I was fairly certain I already knew the answer. The opportunities for a strong, young man like him were many. Surely he was only biding his time until something better came along.

"It's all right," he said.

"If you could go anywhere you wanted, where would you go?"

"Out west," he answered without hesitation.

"And leave New York?"

"In a heartbeat." He took another swig from his flask. "People find their fortunes out west every day. When I get enough saved, I'm going to get on a train and make my way to California. I'm going to make a new life, maybe change my name."

My heart fell at his words. I'd not guessed that his plans would take him so far away.

Putting a finger under my chin he lifted it until our eyes met. "Kiss me goodbye?" he said with a grin. "You never know when I'll be gone."

I closed my eyes and once again felt the softness of his lips. Reaching for his hand, I held it tight, wanting him to know how much I'd miss him.

He must have taken my affection as an invitation, because he slipped his hand out of mine and opened the clasp on my cloak. Sliding his fingers between the button-holes of my shirtwaist he felt my breast where it met the top of my corset. His kisses growing more insistent, he became less like the Cadet of my daydreams and more like Mr. Goodwin, wanting to touch whatever he could in exchange for a few eggs or a half-loaf of bread. I'd wanted so badly to be alone with him, but I hadn't imagined anything more than our sharing a kiss.

"Don't," I said, pushing him away.

"It's all right," he said. "I won't tell. No one will know."

Unsure of what he wanted, I stood up, ready to bolt.

"I thought you meant for me to," Cadet said.

"I only meant for you to kiss me, not take advantage."

"I'd never do that," he insisted.

"How was I to know?"

"You shouldn't play at things you're not sure of."

"You shouldn't play with the hearts of girls."

I waited for him to say something more, but he turned from me instead, and took out his flask for another drink. Feeling angry with myself and him, I crossed the roof and climbed back through the window for the night.

Alice was sitting on her bed, waiting. Mae was gone.

"She dared me to go steal us some biscuits from the kitchen," Alice said. "When I came back, she had snuck out."

"She's tricked us both, Alice," I sighed, realizing Mae's deception.

"Should we go to Miss Everett?"

"No, we can't tell on her—Cadet would lose his job, and you and I would be in our own share of trouble."

"For the longest time I pitied her for the things she told me about her mother," Alice said. "I even gave her the few pennies I still had to my name after she brought me here. But it doesn't seem fair that she gets to be so thoughtless. I'd love to go dancing, to laugh and twirl in the arms of a gentleman at least once before I become a whore. It must be quite nice to never care for the consequences."

Cadet caught Mae that night, sneaking back over the roofs after the house was dark and she thought he'd gone to his bed.

"You mustn't tell Miss Everett," she told him, her voice whiny with drink as she came through the window. "She needn't know that I'm so very clever."

"Conniving bitch," Cadet muttered before Mae pulled the window shut.

The next day, he turned his face away from me as I passed him in the hall.

I stopped and whispered, "It's not your fault Mae got away."

"Don't I know it," he said, looking at me and frowning.

Realizing he thought I'd had some part in Mae's plan, I said, "I didn't know she meant to leave—"

"I see," he said, then turned his back on me once again.

Another Sunday came and went, and although I didn't fall apart during my turn in the second parlour, Miss Everett still wasn't pleased with my performance.

"I don't mind if you have sad eyes, or even tears in them—some men like that sort of thing. But you need to make more of an effort to appear willing. Be more like Mae."

When Mae got dressed for Sunday mornings in the quiet room, she'd fix her hair into two long braids and pin them up beside her ears in two perfect loops. Tying bright blue bows to the top of her head, she'd make herself into the picture of sweetness and purity. "When I get in there, though," she said to me once, "I don't hesitate. I give the gentlemen what they're after."

I'd thought she was one of the most beautiful and clever girls I'd ever seen, but now that she'd put Cadet, Alice and me in the middle of her deceit, she didn't seem half so lovely or smart. I didn't want to be anything like her. And I wondered if the madam was as pleased with her now as she'd once been. Though a few gentlemen had shown interest in Mae, and met her in the parlour, only one of them, a Mr. Greely, had extended an invitation for her to accompany him to the theatre. After their first night out, he hadn't called on her again.

"Mae was too bold for him," Alice whispered that night as we were getting ready for bed. Then she confided that she'd met the man in passing in the hall, and that he'd asked Miss Everett if he could visit with Alice instead.

"But isn't her time up?" I asked, wishing that Mae would soon be out of our room and on to being a full-time whore, where her boldness might serve her well without hurting us.

"Miss Everett must still be looking for the best offer," Alice said.

"I suppose."

As Alice knelt for her evening prayers on a pillow by her bed, she said, "I'm in no hurry for Mae to move on. The longer it takes for Miss Everett to find the right gentleman for her, the longer God will have to bring the right man to me."

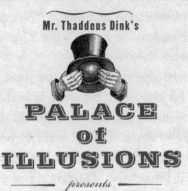

Mr. Thaddeus Dink's

PALACE
of
ILLUSIONS

presents

The Ladies of the
TABLEAUX VIVANTS!

With special appearances by:

Lady Mephistopheles

AND *the alluring* **Miss Suzie Lowe!**

PLUS a multitude of exciting

CURIOSITIES, too numerous to mention!

Friday, November 20 · 7 o'clock in the evening.
the corner of Houston and Bowery.

XXII.

I n preparation for a first visit to the theatre with a gentleman, each of Miss Everett's girls was to attend an
evening's performance at Dink's Palace of Illusions with
the madam herself. An invitation from Mr. Greely was all
but certain for Alice in the near future, so she was fitted

for an evening gown and taught how to enter and exit a carriage with dignity and grace.

Much to my surprise, I was given the same treatment alongside her. "Invitations are many and seamstresses few this time of year," Miss Everett said. "I'd rather have you ready and waiting, than be caught unprepared."

Draped in a delicate gown of canary yellow, Alice floated around our room like she'd been born wearing silk and jewels. I, on the other hand, found my dress to be almost more than I could manage. Made from the palest pink lace, it was a beautiful creation with ribbons and roses sewn all about, but it also had a troublesome train. Ruffles dusted the ground behind me this way and that—the thing seemed to have a mind of its own.

Rose, on a rare evening apart from Mr. Chief of Detectives, had agreed to assist Alice and me in dressing for our outing with Miss Everett. "You must think of your train as a loyal pet," she instructed while showing me how to sweep it to the side for sitting. "If you look on it with affection rather than annoyance, it will never trip you up."

Smoothing the lace between my fingers I hoped that she was right.

Evening Toilette—skirt of pink-coral grosgrain, trimmed with three pinked flounces of the same material, which extend up the front. Overskirt of point lace, draped behind *en panier* by means of two grosgrain ribbons of the same shade as the dress, tied in a bow. Basque corsage of pink coral grosgrain, with vandyked bertha, opening in front over a white lace underwaist, and confined by a cluster of pink roses. Wreath of pink roses and leaves in the hair. Necklace of pearl beads, with pink coral medallion. Pink coral and pearl bracelets.

—*Harper's Bazar*, 1870

Although the theatre was only a short walk from the house, Miss Everett insisted we travel there by carriage. Cadet, dressed in a clean suit, oil combed through his hair, accompanied us on the ride. The skirts of my gown threatened to drown him as he sat next to me in the cab, and I apologized more than once for taking up more than my share of the seat.

"Stop your simpering," Miss Everett scolded, after the third time I'd told Cadet I was sorry. "Beauty never apologizes."

Alice, sitting across from me, put her hand to her mouth and stifled a laugh. Cadet just stared out his side of the carriage. And so I stared out mine.

The Bowery was a marvellous sight to see at night, and Miss Everett must've thought so too, because she instructed the driver to go out of his way to take us up and down a good portion of the avenue before we stopped at the theatre. The horsecars had lamps dangling from front and rear, and the street was lined with glowing lights. Most of the shops, especially those places that boasted evening entertainments, had coloured glass lanterns hanging over their doors beckoning to passersby with their shards of rainbow light.

The Palace of Illusions was an enormous building with steam rising up from the sidewalks surrounding it, making it look like it was going to blow up any minute. Two buildings—the Palace and the dime museum next door—took up a great portion of the block, even turning the corner onto Houston Street.

The museum was said to hold strange exhibits and curiosities from around the world, but the theatre was no less enticing. It was there people came to see Mr. Dink's own troupe of players, a collection of the oddest beings he could find. Alice said it made her uncomfortable to think of a legless man walking on his hands and reciting poetry or a fat lady singing Stephen Foster songs, but I told her that I'd known two fine men with stumps for legs and that they were just as gentlemanly as any fellow with all his limbs intact.

As Cadet helped me out of the carriage, I spotted a man, only half Cadet's size, standing near the theatre's entrance on a stack of boxes. A sign on the box under his feet read, THE AMAZING MR. DINK! He had a stovepipe hat that was almost as tall as he was, and a long, dark walking stick that he waved around, passing it from one hand to the other, pointing it this way and that.

"Step right up!" he shouted, his voice croaking loud over the sounds of the street.

He beat his stick on the side of the box like it was a drum. "Be amazed by the magic of Magnifico!" he called out. "Be shocked by Lady Mephistopheles' dance of fire! Be thrilled by the beautiful Miss Suzie Lowe! All real, all live, all under one roof! Get your ticket now, there's only one show TONIGHT!"

When a young man stepped close to get a better look, Mr. Dink used his cane to prod him towards the door. "That's right, young lad, step up to the booth there and see our lady of the house, the strange and glorious Miss Eva Ivan. It's only a quarter to take in the show *and* the museum. Curiosities and monstrosities! Two thousand models of the human body—in health and disease—collected together at a cost of over twenty thousand dollars!"

Turning back to the street, he shouted, "Just one show tonight, my friends! Dink's is the only place in the Metropolis you'll find the exquisite Ladies of the Tableaux Vivants!"

Alice had stopped in the middle of the sidewalk to stare open-mouthed at the little fellow.

"Come along," Miss Everett told her, pulling at her arm and leading us through the massive front doors of the place.

The theatre was dressed all in red, from flocked paper on the walls to the heavy, tasselled curtains pulled shut across the stage. Gilt-covered creatures peered out from every nook and cranny—snakes, birds and goblins lurking about the ceiling, hiding behind columns and doors.

There were all sorts of people in the crowd, from the working class in their Sunday best, to cocksure dandies in striped trousers and bright vests. A young girl on her mother's arm looked at my dress with envy as I walked past.

You don't know me, I thought when our eyes met. *I'm just a girl, like you.*

Cadet guided us up three tiers and settled us in comfortable chairs at the front of the private box Miss Everett had arranged—first the madam, then Alice, then me.

I took up a pair of opera glasses Rose had loaned me for the night and began to peer around the theatre. "Take a good look while you can," Rose had teased. "The time will soon come when you'll be too busy to enjoy the scenery."

I spotted Missouri and Mae in a box directly across from us with two gentlemen. For Mae, it was to be her last visit with a man before she went to bed with him. She didn't seem nervous in the least. Waving at the crowd below as if she knew everyone in it, she leaned so far over the railing I thought for sure she would fall.

"Look there," Miss Everett said, pointing to the box below Mae's. "It's the Baroness."

"The Baroness?" Alice repeated, squinting through a pair of glasses of her own.

"The Baroness de Battue," Miss Everett said. "Isn't she magnificent?"

It was the first time I'd ever seen Miss Everett so clearly filled with awe.

I almost laughed out loud when she gushed over the Baroness's lavish scarlet gown and again when she tried to count the rubies and diamonds that sparkled in the diadem around the young woman's head. I recognized the Baroness, after all, since she'd started out as Miss Francine Grossman, just another girl from Chrystie Street.

Before long, Mr. Dink appeared at the front of the curtained stage. He tapped his cane on the boards three times and the band in the pit started playing a hearty version of "Tenting Tonight." Calling out above the music, he announced, "A song for all soldiers, dead and living!" Then he motioned for the audience to sing along. Raising his cane high in the air, he waved it like a conductor, keeping our proud, rowdy voices in time with the band.

How many times had I sung that song to Mrs. Wentworth as she was falling asleep? Whoever had written the words had taken great care to be wonderfully cruel, setting some of the saddest words I'd ever known to a jaunty, happy tune.

The lone wife kneels and prays with a sigh
That God his watch will keep
O'er the dear one away and the little dears nigh,
In the trundle bed fast asleep.

*Tenting tonight, tenting tonight, tenting on the old
    campground,
Many are the hearts that are weary tonight
Wishing that the war would cease.
Many are the souls that will die without light
Before the dawn of peace.*

As the song ended, there came a great round of applause from the crowd. Mr. Dink stood alone on the stage for the longest time, his chest puffed up, his eyes bright.

Then he began to usher in his acts, one after another in quick succession—a thin man who balanced spinning plates on long sticks, a fat lady who'd trained a dozen dogs to jump through hoops, three young girls from the Orient who could tuck their legs behind their heads and walk on their hands, scuttling around like crabs. With one flourish of his cane, he'd set the place booming, casting a spell over the audience and players alike.

After a performance by Magnifico, in which the long-legged illusionist went about making rabbits, doves and a pretty albino woman disappear, Mr. Dink returned once more to centre stage. Clearing his throat he said, "Tonight I am pleased to welcome a performer who is as accomplished and, might I add, far prettier than our esteemed magician. Coming directly to the Palace of Illusions after engagements in both London and Paris, our guest is undoubtedly the greatest performer—*in the exotic style*—New York has ever seen!"

Cheers broke out in such a roar that Mr. Dink had to hold up his hand until quiet returned. Then he announced, his voice lowered, "Ladies and gentlemen, I must warn you . . . do not to be alarmed by this fine lady's state of dress. Please let me assure you, the dangers of her talent demand it."

The young men in the front row hollered so loud, Mr. Dink had to rap his cane on the stage and start the band playing again just to quiet them down. As the music swelled, he exclaimed, "Good patrons of the Palace, I give to you the lovely and talented . . . Lady Mephistopheles!"

The curtain opened, and a woman appeared balancing a bowl of fire on top of her head. Dark and beautiful, she wore a long braid down her back and chain upon chain of tiny bells draped around her neck, wrists and hips. There wasn't much more to her costume than that, except where she'd wrapped the scandalous bits of herself in gauzy cloth.

Dancing to the front of the stage, she twisted and rolled her belly, snaking her arms this way and that. Then she lifted the bowl from her head and set it down at her feet, flames leaping high above the rim. She smiled as Mr. Dink came rushing to her side to present her with a long, thin torch. After blowing her a kiss, he scurried back off the stage.

Lady Mephistopheles put the end of the torch to the fire and set it alight. Holding it high above her head, she slowly lowered the flame to the tip of her waiting tongue. She touched it there, just for a moment, and then pulled it away as the drums in the orchestra pit faded to a low growl. Again and again she did this, until, at last, she plunged the fiery torch deep into her open mouth.

Alice gasped. "How has she not hurt herself?"

"Shh!" I put a finger to my lips, just as shocked as Alice was by the woman's trick. "I'm sure she knows what she's doing," I whispered, and then held my breath, hoping I was right.

Sure enough, the lady removed the torch and bowed to us all, unharmed.

Mr. Dink returned, this time carrying a large bottle on a silver tray. Lady Mephistopheles drank from it, holding the liquid inside her mouth. Mr. Dink put his hand over his eyes and took several steps away, peeking through his fingers, pulling for a laugh. Holding her flaming torch steady, Lady Mephistopheles blew the liquid out, causing fire to explode in a great, long flash. The flame reached clear past the edge of the stage, nearly scorching the top of the bandmaster's bald head. The crowd stomped and whistled for several minutes after that and the woman catered to their applause, breathing flames that were brighter and longer with every flash of her torch.

As she took her final bows, the crowd rose to its feet, applauding wildly. Lady Mephistopheles responded by standing in the middle of the stage, her chin held high, glaring out at the audience as if she'd just as soon set us all on fire.

At intermission, Cadet led us to the private reception room for those who sat in the boxes. He then took up his post at the entrance, lining up along the wall with the other young valets.

As we entered, Miss Everett, Alice and I faced a crush of people already milling about, laughter, conversation and wine flowing. The room was a large and beautiful space; mirrors graced three of the walls from floor to ceiling, making it the perfect place to see and be seen. Down one side was a bar from which drinks and refreshments were served. Attached on either side of the room were a gentlemen's smoking room and a ladies' rest lounge. Everything seemed so comfortable here, it was a wonder anyone ever went back to see the second half of the show.

The room was filled with couples, primarily older men with young ladies on their arms. No matter how beautiful their own companions, the gentlemen appraised each new girl who came through the door. It felt like a hundred pairs of eyes were on me as we made our way into the room, and I forgot to pay attention to my train, which tangled around my feet and sent me sprawling.

Alice bent to help, but Miss Everett pulled her back. Women stared over the tops of their fans and men chuckled over the rims of their champagne glasses as I sat there stunned, struggling to free my feet from the mass of cloth.

I felt hands under my shoulder blades lifting me up: a gentleman kind enough to set me right again. When I turned to thank him, he was gone.

"You're to smile and act as if nothing's happened," Miss Everett hissed in my ear. "Keep hold of your train at all times if you must. I'll not have you embarrass me again." Going to Alice's side, she guided her to stand a slight distance away from me, the space between us the difference between favour and failure. I had been foolish to think I belonged here with them: I was a disaster.

Not knowing where to look or what to do, I was only saved by the approach of Mr. Dink himself, now dressed in a striped waistcoat and wearing a fragrant gardenia in his lapel. His chinstrap beard was trimmed neat along the edge of his jaw, and his eyes sparkled with interest and delight. No matter his height, I thought him a fine-looking gentleman.

He took Miss Everett's hand and kissed it. "My dear Emma," he said. "Welcome back."

"Mr. Dink," she said with a smile. "It's always such a pleasure."

Surveying Alice and me with bright eyes, he asked, "Are these the young ladies you spoke of when last we met?"

"They are, indeed," Miss Everett replied. "I give you Miss Alice Creaghan, and Miss Ada Fenwick."

Rose had mentioned that Mr. Dink kept company with Miss Everett from time to time, coming to the house late in the evening with a rose in his lapel and a bouquet of lilies in the crook of his arm. Lilies were Miss Everett's favourite flower.

"I think it's strange," Alice had said, shuddering to imagine Mr. Dink and Miss Everett together.

"It's just good business," Rose had said with a laugh. "There are three private boxes in Mr. Dink's concert hall forever reserved in Miss Everett's name. Why, just last week I saw *Uncle Tom's Cabin* there, while Miss Missouri Mills was making love to her gentleman *du jour* in the box below."

"Miss Fenwick," Mr. Dink said now, tilting his head and looking as if he were listening to some faraway sound. "What a lovely name."

Miss Everett nudged me with her elbow.

"Thank you, sir," I said, and for a moment I thought of bowing to him like Nestor had taught me to do when greeting Mrs. Wentworth, but I wasn't sure if Miss Everett would think it right. I folded my hands in front of me and looked down at the floor. To my great embarrassment, Mr. Dink stared at me for the longest time, stroking his beard and smiling.

"Forgive me," he said. "But you remind me of a young lady I once knew. Would you happen to be Black Dutch?"

"My mother was," I answered, thinking as soon as I'd said it that I should have lied.

Mr. Dink clapped his hands together with glee. "Aha! I knew it! The finest beauties in the world, they are, the Black Dutch girls . . ."

Bells rang from the hallway, and several people in the room began to move towards the door.

"I'm afraid that's my cue, dear ladies," Mr. Dink said. "Miss Everett, Miss Creaghan, it's been a pleasure." He bowed to them. "Miss Fen-wick," he said, lingering on my name and grinning. "I do hope we'll meet again someday soon."

As soon as he was gone, Miss Everett was at my side. "Well done," she said, as if my fall had never happened. Adjusting the back of my skirt where my train was still slightly askew, she took my arm to help guide me along.

Alice whispered in my other ear, "He liked you so well, I thought he might start purring like a cat."

As Cadet seated us again in our box, a group of minstrel singers performed a medley of songs in front of the curtain. Then Mr. Dink came out to announce the final act, the Ladies of the Tableaux Vivants. At first he spoke in the same boastful manner he had used to introduce all the earlier performers, but when he came to Miss Suzie Lowe, the tableau's premiere artiste, his voice became tender and reverent.

"Your heart will soar when you see her," he promised. "You'll be amazed."

As the curtain opened, there she was, naked and glorious, perched above the six other ladies in the tableau. She had one hand arched gracefully over her head and a knee turned gently to hide the curls between her legs.

The women stayed frozen for endless moments, as if a painter had captured them there. They were, to a one, perfect and lily-white, put there for us to stare at and think about and want. Miss Lowe was by far the loveliest, her chestnut hair flowing down to her hips, her mouth set in a perfect bow. Turning Rose's glasses to the side of the stage, I spied Mr. Dink watching her, nodding slowly, his lips parted, as if to say, *Yes, oh yes.* Looking back to Miss Lowe, I could've sworn I saw her smile, as if to say, *Perhaps.*

As the lights and scene changed, the women transformed themselves into new paintings, new pictures. They became goddesses, then swans, then angels, then saints. Each time they moved to a different pose, the music would swell and the crowd would shower them with applause. The more they changed, the greater the audience's appreciation. I sat with my hands to my heart, longing to be like them, to move with absolute surety, to change into whatever I wished.

Sometimes, for a moment, everything is just as you need it to be. The memories of such moments live in the heart, waiting for the time you need to think on them, if only to remind yourself that for a short while, everything had been fine, and might be so again. I didn't have many memories like that—Mama tying her scarf around her head, my father tipping his hat before he walked away,

Miss Keteltas' birds bowing and cooing to each other, Mrs. Wentworth's bracelet warm against my skin, the taste of sugary cake on my tongue in Miss Everett's parlour, the feel of Cadet's lips on mine, wet and sweet. No matter what might happen or what fate Miss Everett had in store for me, I now had the image of Miss Suzie Lowe to place alongside them. She would remind me that I was a girl who longed for things, a girl who wanted to become something more than she was seen to be.

21. Shall I soon be courted?

22. The gentleman that I am so glad to see, does he think of me?

23. Am I still thought a child?

24. Is his heart as affectionate as mine?

25. What must I do to please him?

26. Ought I answer the first letter?

27. What will happen if I go to the appointed meeting?

–from *The Ancient and Modern Ladies' Oracle*
by Mr. Cornelius Agrippa
(Infallible Prophet of the Male Sex)

XXIII.

When I lay in bed that night, even the vision of Miss Susie Lowe couldn't stop me from tossing and turning, and reliving the moment when I'd tripped and landed at the feet of all those gentlemen and their ladies.

Alice whispered to me in the dark, "Ada, are you all right?"

"Yes," I answered. "I'm fine."

"No you're not."

I went silent, hoping she'd leave well enough alone.

"You're not still fretting over your fall, are you?"

"Yes."

"Well, stop it. Miss Everett forgave you as soon as Mr. Dink appeared, I could tell.

Besides, you're the prettiest girl here by far. She'd be foolish to put you out over one tiny stumble."

"I'm not the prettiest."

"According to Rose you are. I heard her tell Miss Everett so, just yesterday. Mae heard her too—didn't you, Mae?"

Mae was sleeping like the dead.

"I know you wanted to help," I whispered to Alice, who was truly the sweetest-natured of us all. "Thank you."

"The gentleman who came to your aid was quite handsome," she said. "I believe he would have introduced himself had his lady companion not beckoned to him from across the room."

I wished it had been Cadet coming to my rescue instead, his hands wrapped around my waist, his breath warm on my neck. I knew such a thing would never happen, though, as it seemed he had no intention of ever looking at me again.

"Good night, Alice," I said.

"Good night, Ada."

Miss Everett came to my bedside the next morning and said, "Wear your dress that's meant for receiving visitors today. There's a gentleman who wishes to meet you."

"Yes, ma'am," I replied, wishing I could pull the quilt over my head and go back to sleep. After what had happened at the theatre, I couldn't see how Miss Everett would think I was ready to meet with a gentleman in private, but I wasn't about to question her orders—having tea with a man in the parlour was far better than being put out on the street.

When I got to the drawing room, Mr. Dink was there, sitting in one of Miss Everett's high-backed velvet chairs with a sturdy-looking wooden box at his feet. As I entered, he stood up from his chair and stepped onto the box to greet me.

"Miss Fenwick," he said, presenting me with a bouquet of scarlet roses that matched the bud tucked in his lapel. "It's lovely to see you again."

As I accepted the flowers, I couldn't help but think of Mr. Dink showering Miss Everett with lilies and affection, and the way Rose had insisted it was all for the sake of good business.

"And you as well," I replied.

Miss Everett, standing near the doorway, smiled at Mr. Dink. "Coffee or tea?" she asked.

"I'm afraid I've only time for business today."

"Very well," Miss Everett replied. "Shall we get on with it, then?" Taking a seat on the armchair opposite Mr. Dink, she motioned for me to settle myself on the couch.

I liked Mr. Dink well enough, I guessed. I supposed things could be worse.

"I'm quite impressed with you, Miss Fenwick," he began, stroking his beard as he had in the intermission room when we met. "Your graceful figure and humble nature are simply unforgettable."

I nodded to him, awkwardly, and the little man nodded back, grinning, then went on to explain that somewhere between the stroke of midnight and the break of dawn, it had occurred to him that our brief encounter might well lead to an arrangement of good fortune for us all.

Miss Everett was smiling now, nodding too.

I tried picturing myself with Mr. Dink–his hand on mine, his lips on my cheek–but the idea left me queasy and scared.

Bringing out a notebook from his pocket, he showed me a drawing he'd made of a well-dressed young lady standing in front of the entrance to Dink's Museum. He had figured onto the girl's skirt square after tiny square; a quiver's worth of arrows pointed out from them to a sign that read CARTES DE VISITE!

"You won't know this, my dear, but my museum also offers my patrons a bit of wonder and curiosity to take home with them–for a fair price," he said. "Such goods include, but are not limited to, vials of genuine pharaoh dust, mummy linen scraps, the teeth of any number of vicious creatures such as shark, wolf, hyena, bear and tiger; bird's-eye-view maps of this country's finest cities; real imitation shrunken heads; wax renderings of the bones of the inner ear; and a wide selection of *cartes de visite*."

"Unfortunately," he explained, "I only have a limited amount of space in which to display such cards: a single shelf behind the counter on which to fit one hundred generals, Indian chiefs, actresses, sideshow performers, and circus stars. My patrons often pass them over for other fare, or worse yet, they leave the shop without purchasing anything at all. This," he declared, "is an opportunity lost.

"The wealthiest tobacconists in the city always have a pretty shopgirl on hand to assist their customers. Hot-corn girls, although nowhere close to your station and manners, Miss Fenwick, tend to be comely young ladies overall. I could go on about the array of fresh faces behind every businessman's success in this town, but suffice it to say, gentlemen are far more eager to part with their money when a beautiful girl is involved."

As if he were about to bestow the title of princess or duchess or baroness upon me, he concluded, "To put it boldly and sincerely, I'd like you, Miss Fenwick, to be New York's first and only *cartes de visite* girl—"

"It's to be a limited engagement, of course," Miss Everett interrupted. "Until you've gotten your footing, so to speak, in the company of gentlemen."

Mr. Dink's proposition was as follows: each afternoon I was to stand in the entrance hall next to his curiosity shop and model *cartes de visite* for his patrons' viewing pleasure. Since all the museum-goers were men, I would have to be careful to be friendly with the customers, but not overly so, engaging them in conversation about the personages featured on the cards, the gentlemen's personal preferences in collecting them, and the weather. The men would choose the cards they wanted and purchase them from the shopkeeper. No money would pass through my hands, as my task was simply to entice.

The proposal came as a great relief. I wondered if it might even mean a chance for me to get out of my Sunday duties in the parlour. Afraid to put the question to Miss Everett, I looked to Mr. Dink and asked, "Would I be needed Sundays as well?"

"Of course," he answered with a smile. "It's our busiest day of the week."

After a round of yeses and handshaking, Mr. Dink left the house.

Then Miss Everett took me aside and said, "Not to worry,

Ada. More men than I can fit in a month of Sundays in the parlour will see you on display at Mr. Dink's."

At breakfast the next morning, Miss Everett told me that I was to go to Mr. Dink's place of business to be fitted for the dress I'd wear as his *cartes de visite* girl.

"Will Cadet be escorting me?" I asked, thinking I could get him to speak at least a few words to me on our way there and back.

"He's too busy," Miss Everett replied. "But don't fret. Dr. Sadie has agreed to escort you to and from the museum. She's been called to see to the well-being of one of Mr. Dink's players."

Alice, trying her best not to show any jealousy over my new position, wished me luck on my way out the door. "You're to tell me all when you return," she said.

"I will. I promise."

I hadn't told her that Miss Everett had relieved me from my Sunday duties in the parlour. No matter how strong our friendship, I knew she'd find it unfair, and I couldn't help but feel guilty.

The museum wasn't yet open when Dr. Sadie and I arrived. Leading me through a little side door at the back of the theatre, she turned a bell in another small wooden door and waited for an answer.

Before long, Mr. Dink opened up to us. "Miss Fenwick," he said, greeting me with a broad smile. Then, taking Dr. Sadie's hand in his, he said, "My dear doctress, it's so good of you to come on such short notice."

"Anything for you, Mr. Dink," she said, blushing.

It was strange to see her face turning pink at Mr. Dink's kindness, her eyes bright with their conversation. I'd come to think of Dr. Sadie as a woman who was, above all else, strong and sure of herself, immune to all weaknesses, struggles and charms.

"You know the way," Mr. Dink said, pointing to a stairway that led beneath the building.

"Of course," Dr. Sadie replied.

"I'll leave you to it, then." He bowed to both of us and took his leave.

Beneath the Palace of Illusions was an enormous den of rooms that seemed to have no end. This, Dr. Sadie said, was where the costumes for Mr. Dink's players were kept. Lights shone all along the stairway that led down to the vault, and as I descended into a world of flounces, frocks and magician's cloaks, I was smitten with the place.

We were soon met by a small, white-haired young woman whose pale skin glowed almost blue in the gaslight. I recognized her as the same lady who had assisted Mr. Dink's illusionist.

"Dr. Sadie," she said, smiling. "You look well."

"As do you," the doctor replied.

"And this must be Mr. Dink's little *cartes de visite* girl?" she asked.

"Indeed she is."

Turning to me, Dr. Sadie said, "Miss Fenwick, I give you the wise and all-seeing Miss Sylvia LeMar, the best fortune teller in all the boroughs."

"Pleased to meet you," I said.

"Of course you are," she replied.

As she and Dr. Sadie chatted, I reached to touch a garment on one of the many racks that filled the room.

"No touching," Miss LeMar scolded, without even looking at me. "No, no, no."

Just as I pulled my hand away, a second woman popped out from between the costumes, causing both Dr. Sadie and me to gasp in surprise.

"Good day," she cooed, peeking at us over her spread fan. Her dress sported several rows of ruffles that matched a spray of bright-coloured feathers in her hair. Snapping the fan shut, she revealed the whole of her face. One side was delicate and smooth like a lady's, the other half coarse and bearded like a man's.

"Oh!" I exclaimed.

In a deep, grumbling voice, she asked, "What's the matter, sweetheart, don't you like me anymore?" Batting her eyes, she tugged on the curl of her one-sided moustache and laughed.

Dr. Sadie laughed too. "Oh, Miss Eva, you're a naughty one."

I couldn't help but stare at her, wondering how many times she'd made a man's heart race while his belly turned, and just how much she'd enjoyed it.

"Miss Eva's an amazing sword swallower," Dr. Sadie said after their laughter had died away. "She and Miss LeMar are seamstresses by day and stars in the spectacles Mr. Dink puts on in his theatre by night."

"I'm afraid I won't be starring in the show anytime soon," Miss Eva complained, putting her hand to her neck. "I've got a terrible case of sword throat."

"How long has it been bothering you?"

"Three days," she moaned.

"Have you done anything different that might have caused it?"

Miss Eva stopped to think.

"She's been putting a dead soldier's sabre down her throat," Miss LeMar said, shaking her head. "I've told her to get rid of it. It's cursed."

Ignoring Miss LeMar, Miss Eva answered, "I've been adding more swords lately. I'd hoped to do seven at once by the end of the month."

Dr. Sadie frowned. "I see," she said. "Perhaps a little less ambition is in order," she suggested. "Along with hot tea with lemon and honey, and a week's rest."

"How about two days' rest?" Miss Eva wheedled. "Mr. Dink's got me on for Friday and Saturday nights."

"Three days, and I'll speak with Mr. Dink on your behalf."

While the doctor and Miss Eva were negotiating, Miss LeMar had gone about the task of searching for a dress that might suit me for my job. Reappearing from the racks, she brought out a sleek black dress with long sleeves and a high neck.

"Too plain," Miss Eva sighed, rolling her eyes with disapproval.

"You've no sense of propriety," Miss LeMar retorted, before disappearing again into a sea of silk and tulle.

The next dress had a large hoop skirt covered with bows.

"That one makes me sad," Miss Eva complained. "I cannot begin to tell you how much I detest it."

"You're impossible!" Miss LeMar cried.

"That *dress* is impossible . . ."

While the two women bickered, Mr. Dink arrived to check on my progress. Pulling out his notebook to show Dr. Sadie his sketch of the *cartes de visite* girl, he told her of his grand plans for me and his picture cards.

Staring at the sketch, considering, she leaned toward him to confide, "I think I have the perfect dress."

"And you're willing to lend it to the girl?" he asked.

"It's hers," Dr. Sadie replied.

We left Miss LeMar and Miss Eva to their argument, and followed Mr. Dink into a long corridor that stretched from a doorway in the back of the costume storeroom.

"Do you have time to see my latest acquisition?" he asked Dr. Sadie.

Her eyes grew wide with excitement. "It's arrived?"

"Oh yes." He grinned. "Miss Gertu is here."

Dr. Sadie fell in behind Mr. Dink, and I tagged along after the two of them through a series of tunnels that wound underneath the building and up to the main floor.

The museum was filled with glass cases and cabinets, stacked from floor to ceiling. Taxidermy specimens, arranged on stands with gilt-edged cards attached, were displayed in every corner—a golden eagle with its wings spread wide, a black jungle cat from Peru, a ferocious bear standing on its hind legs, and a brown-feathered chicken with four legs and three wings. Against the far wall was a cage containing a fat, lazy-looking snake. The creature, still very much alive, had reportedly devoured two chickens, a dog, a cat and a ten-month-old child in the space of one day.

126. Very fine dissection of the foot.

127–129. Brains of children—two, four and six months.

130. Monster child born in Bleecker Street; was
      exhibited in Broadway for twelve months; it lived
      fourteen months.

Most of Mr. Dink's curiosities seemed oddly familiar to me, bringing to mind things that had haunted the court-yards and curbs of Chrystie Street. Dead cats with their bellies blown open from rot. Jars of pickled somethings gone bad with the heat. Pensioner Pete's hero's stumps, shiny and covered with sores. The far-off stare of a child so thirsty she's about to drop. The whole slum had been one endless cabinet of horrors, only we had the smells and sounds of misery to go along with the sights.

We climbed a winding, gilt staircase to the waxworks. The place was windowless and dim, the gaslight turned down to a hazy glow, Mr. Dink explained, to preserve the integrity of the models, as they were susceptible to damage from the heat and light of the sun. The air in the room was close, and smelled sweet like honey.

204. THE MANIAC, a truthful portrayal of insanity.
205. The deathbed of ABRAHAM LINCOLN.
206. Execution of MARIE ANTOINETTE, with model of
      the guillotine.
207–209. Waxworks of CHARLES DICKENS, NAPOLEON,
      and WILLIAM TWEED.
210. EVE and the Apple.

In the centre of the room was the new attraction Mr. Dink had brought us to see, a life-size figure of a naked woman lying on a bed of pink satin. The top half of her body was whole and beautiful, her nipples like perfect little buttons, her eyes open just a glimmer, seeming to beg anyone who came near to take her home. Below her belly she'd been opened up to reveal her wormy insides and the mysteries of the female anatomy.

> 300. THE GREAT AND WORLD-RENOWNED GERTU, imported from Vienna by the proprietor, at a cost of $15,000. This has been pronounced by the many thousands who have seen it to be the very "Ne Plus Ultra" of feminine beauty, the development of all the organs are magnificent, and being life-size it is more than worthy of admiration.

"Isn't she divine?" Mr. Dink asked as Dr. Sadie approached the display.

"Indeed she is," she whispered, clearly fascinated.

Mr. Dink's desire to please Dr. Sadie, and the care she took with it was, to me, the most interesting curiosity of all.

My nose almost touching the glass, I stared at Miss Gertu. Her skin was dark, with a golden cast like Mama's. Standing there, I wondered if my mother had been aware of all the nights I'd lain awake beside her, trying to work out the arithmetic of my blood. My eyes, nose, voice and hair had all come from her, but it was the space between my front teeth, that pauper's share of my father, that made the sums in my head go wrong. It was a crack so small I couldn't even spit through it, but it made Mama frown every time I smiled.

That's not real, I heard Mama say in my head. *A belly and a slit is all there should be. That's all there is to a girl.*

Looking away from the figure, I noticed a doorway at the back of the room with a sign over it that read, THE WAGES OF SIN IS DEATH. As Mr. Dink and Dr. Sadie stood talking, I went through it.

One entire wall was filled with heads covered in boils, their noses sunken, their skin crumbling and dissolving away. Model after model of infected body parts was lined up, every last one disfigured by oozing chancres.

425. Very fine dissection of the penis and bladder.

426. Healthy genital organs of the male.

427. Half-dissection of the penis and bladder of a
      victim of self-abuse, showing the genital organs
      not fully developed.

450. Early circinated syphiloderma.

451. A waxwork of CUPID, suffering the ravages of the
      French Pox. "Love is Blind."

Gone was the beauty of Miss Gertu. All that was left was Mama's voice and the horror that I was seeing. I stared at the suffering CUPID, his mouth open with fear. Tongue dry, hands shaking, I turned and ran out the door.

A belly and slit is all you have, Moth. You must fill them as best you can.

Whistle, daughter, whistle
And you shall have a man.

Mother, I cannot whistle
But I'll do the best I can.

XXIV.

Before going back to Miss Everett's, Dr. Sadie took me to her rooms to see about the dress. She went straight to a trunk at the end of her bed and began pulling things from it–a pair of silk slippers, a couple of old tintypes, squares of half-finished needlework and a box full of letters. Finally, wrapped in the folds of a large white sheet, was the thing that she was after.

She cradled it in her arms, then she held it to her cheek, closed her eyes and smiled. "I wore this the night of my seventeenth birthday," she said. "There was a stone fountain in the middle of my aunt Charlotte's ballroom that had been shipped all the way from Paris, and an entire orchestra playing my favourite songs." Holding it out to me she said, "Here, try it on."

Its colour was deepest, emerald green, and the silk of the skirt was so soft and smooth I couldn't stop touching it, shushing the cloth between my fingers. The bell sleeves had embroidery stitched around them, rings of flowers and hearts covering every inch from cuff to shoulder. Although it wasn't in the current fashion, its quality was far above any

In the spring of 1836, Miss Helen Jewett, a wildly successful courtesan, was found murdered in her room on Thomas Street. The details of her death were gruesome—a scorned lover had taken up an axe to end the girl's life and then burned her body in her bed. When the accused gentleman was put on trial, a swell of sentimental support rose up among the young women of the city on behalf of Miss Jewett. Girls from all walks of life donned dresses of green (the colour of Miss Jewett's eyes) to parade in the streets outside the proceedings. For many years after Miss Jewett's death, debutantes wore green dresses for their entrance into society—most of them not knowing the reason why.

of the dresses, suits or gowns Miss Everett had given me. It was elegant, yet sweet, and I couldn't wait for it to be mine.

But when Dr. Sadie helped me lift it over my head to slip it on, it didn't fit. Too long and too loose, the tapered pleats of the neck fell off one shoulder, the cloth drooping across my chest. I tried to gather the fabric tight at my sides to make the gown stay in place, and insisted, "It's perfect."

Dr. Sadie just grinned at me. "Don't worry, I can fit it to you." She took my hand and helped me to stand on top of the trunk. Bringing out a sewing basket, she put pins between her lips, a thimble on her thumb, and set to work.

I watched my reflection in the dark of the window as she pinned the dress around me. Admiring myself, I held my hands up to my heart, just like the girl in the lodging house ladies' broadsheet I'd kept hidden in my crate on the roof on Chrystie Street.

Tugging at a sleeve, Dr. Sadie said, "Hold still."

I wasn't used to such thoughtful attention. Staring down at Dr. Sadie, I couldn't help but wonder what was in this for her. What did she want of me? Mrs. Wentworth, Miss Everett, even Mama had never given me anything without expecting something in return. Mrs. Riordan was the only person

I'd ever known to have a selfless heart. I figured the world simply couldn't afford to hold another woman like her in it. If I told Mr. Dink about Mrs. Riordan, he'd surely fetch her from Chrystie Street and put her on display.

"Did you dance in it?" I asked, wondering what secrets the dress might hold.

"Of course," she answered. "The more a girl dances in a dress, the more luck it brings."

"Do you think there's any luck left in this one?"

Nipping the shoulders up, pinning one side and then the other, she looked at me and said, "Yes, I'd say there's plenty."

That's good, I thought. *I'll need it.*

Honest and horrible all at once, those cankered, frightful models in the museum had held more than their share of truth about men. Even the parts of a gentleman shown in health looked strange to me, and I shuddered when I tried to imagine what it would be like to have a man's body naked and close to mine.

"What's it like to have relations with a gentleman?" I asked Dr. Sadie, daring to stutter out the question I'd had on my mind since we left the place.

Not looking up, she replied, "Surely Miss Everett's explained it to you, hasn't she?"

She hadn't, and I wasn't certain she ever would. I'd heard the sounds of Rose with the Chief of Detectives and spied Mama in her bed with Mr. Cowan, but those occasions, as real and shocking as they'd been, hadn't made things any clearer to me.

I'd never seen a wedding band or any rings on Dr. Sadie's fingers, but I assumed her profession didn't allow her to wear them. I couldn't tell if she'd ever been someone's wife or not. Like the dress, I guessed she had plenty of secrets.

"Is it always ugly, loud or awful?" I begged. "I want to know the truth."

Sighing, she motioned for me to turn so she could begin to pin one of the cuffs. "I certainly hope not."

"You don't know?"

"I can tell you of love, but outside of what's in my head from physiology texts, I'm afraid I know nothing of the other."

"You've never been married?"

"No."

"But you've been in love?"

"Yes."

"Are you still?"

"It's a difficult situation," she answered, closing her eyes for a moment as she worked to find the right words to say. "My choice of occupation is an embarrassment to my family. If I were to follow my heart in love as well, I'd wound them even more."

How had her being a doctor, as rare and strange a thing as it was for a woman, caused anyone any harm? As far as her being in love was concerned, I found it something of a relief to know that even the heart of a fine, educated woman could have trouble getting what it wanted.

"So you love him, even now?" I asked.

She looked up at me with sad eyes, colour fading from her cheeks. With great regret in her voice, she answered, "Yes."

By the time she'd finished making her tucks and darts, the dress clung to my skin like it was made for me. With proper petticoats and a modest hoop, it hid my too-small breasts, my memories of Mama and Mrs. Wentworth, and my worries over a man I was yet to meet.

Along with the dress, as it turned out, I was to wear a pair of angel's wings. They came from Mr. Dink, who said they'd appeared one morning, dangling from the museum's awning.

"It was a beautiful thing to find them there, all happy and white," he said. "It was like seeing a perfect Christmas goose in the butcher's window."

"You're a liar, Mr. Dink," I said, grinning at him.

Curling his finger, he motioned for me to come close. "I'll tell you the truth," he whispered. "They belonged to a girl I used to love. She kept track of the illusionist's rabbits and doves before Miss LeMar. Magnifico could make her disappear, right out of a box, wings and all."

It worried me to hear him say he used to love her, because I thought it meant they'd had a falling-out. Maybe he'd done something so bad that he didn't deserve to be loved any more.

"If she catches me with them, won't she want them back?" I asked.

"No," he said, looking sad. "She's dead and gone, my dear. Diphtheria."

I tried not to show him how much that relieved me. I didn't want him to think I was

Female physicians learn to suture in much the same way young girls learn to sew. We sit together in a circle, looking over each other's work, vying for the straightest, most pleasing stitch. There is friendship, of course, but competition too, and a shared pride in knowing that this aspect of medicine, so vital to the care of wounds, is best executed by nimble, feminine hands. Many a face in the slums of Manhattan has been made right by "women's work."

unkind. Still, I didn't mind that the wings had belonged to someone who was now dead. I felt bad for him, of course, but was happy to have them, and happier still to find that there was no one to get in the way of my keeping them.

From the place where I stood as the *cartes de visite* girl, I had a fair view out the museum's front windows, and could see much of the entrance hall as well.

Miss Eva Ivan sat at the ticket counter just inside the door. Holding her fan over half her face, she'd wink at the gentlemen patrons with the long, fluttery lashes of her right eye.

"Just the museum," she cooed at a young man who came in on my first day there. "Or are you staying for the show?"

The young man put a quarter on the wooden counter-top and slid it towards her.

She reached out and stroked his hand before giving him the ticket. "Enjoy yourself," she told him, and then snapped her fan shut to reveal the other side of her face.

"Shit," the young man cursed. "Holysaintoffuck, half of you's a man."

Miss Eva laughed, big and booming, dark and rough.

Shaking his head, the young man grabbed his ticket and shouldered his way into the museum. "Shit," he said again as he passed me. "Shitshitshit."

Miss Eva feathered out her fan and got ready for her next customer.

Nearly all of the gentlemen who came to the museum stopped to stare at my wares, many of them choosing to buy at least a card or two. The images of Mr. Dink's human oddities were quite popular with them. Legless wonders, lizard men, bearded ladies, dog-faced boys, and an entire family of albinos, including Miss Sylvia LeMar, entertained the men to no end.

But it was Mr. Dink's collection of exotic ladies from near and far that garnered the most attention. This was due, in no small part, to the fact that I kept them hidden away, to be viewed only by request. On Mr. Dink's request, Dr. Sadie had sewn a secret panel in my skirt, which could be revealed with the simple pull of a ribbon. The panel was lined with red silk and was the perfect place for such wonders to inhabit. "Men clamour for the unknown," Mr. Dink had said, knowingly.

One of the portraits featured Miss Suzie Lowe as Lady Godiva. She was sitting on top of a big, dark horse, her back turned to hide her breasts, her long hair flowing down around her shoulders. A large satin sheet was draped around her waist to hide anything else that might offend. She was looking over her shoulder, straight out of the picture like she shared a secret with only you.

My favourite of the hidden *cartes* was the Circassian Beauty, a young woman surrounded by tasselled cushions and Persian rugs. She was dressed in the costume of her native land, her skirt falling above her knee and the neck of her dress dipping temptingly low on her breasts. The most striking thing about her, however, was her hair. Unfettered by combs or ribbons, it graced her head like a lion's mane, the wonder of it threatening to escape the borders of the picture. She reminded me of Mama in better days, her proud, menacing expression daring anyone who crossed her path to try to bring her down.

Mr. Dink liked her best of all as well. "One of the biggest regrets of my life, she was," he confessed. "I let Mr. P.T. Barnum steal her right out from under my nose. Two thousand dollars he paid for her before I could even have my say. Then he told me I'd have to pay three thousand to win her back."

Mr. Dink himself had started out with Mr. Barnum: his parents had signed him over to be a sideshow attraction when he was only ten years old. When Mr. Dink attained the age of majority, he told Mr. Barnum he was leaving him. The showman had wished Mr. Dink well when they parted ways, but now there was a fair bit of competition between them. Miss Eva had defected to Mr. Dink's after the second of Mr. Barnum's great museum fires. Stealing away the Circassian Beauty had been Mr. Barnum's way of settling the score.

"Where did you get her in the first place?" I asked, wondering if there was some secret society that saw to the placement of sideshow performers. "The Circassian Beauty, I mean."

"Oh, she wasn't gotten, my dear girl," he said. "She was made."

He would say nothing else about her and I didn't press him on it. The wistful look that came across his face whenever he saw her card told me not to tread there.

In the hour before the museum opened each day, Mr. Dink would sit with me and teach me about the actresses and personalities on the cards as well as the various performers who inhabited his stage. It soon became my favourite part of the morning. His stories of the many performers he'd taken under his wing and the secrets he knew about their lives made me forget Miss Everett and everything that went on in her house. Mr. Dink said his business was also filled with a certain amount of scandal and struggle, but, he assured me, "we're just like family, only with more curious talents and ties."

He'd tell me which stars were currently favoured by the audience and which ones were fading fast. He said it was important that I commit their names and histories to memory so that when a gentleman approached, I'd have something to say.

The men frightened me at first with their eagerness. Respectable gentlemen with fancy watches, pockets full of money, and perhaps wives and even children who loved them at home, would look at me, biting their bottom lip or the inside of their cheeks, lust in their eyes. Like newsboys waiting for the confectioner to hand them a piece of taffy, their hands would tremble ever so slightly as they reached out to take Lady Godiva or one of the other exotic beauties from me, the bolder of them wishing to unpin the card from my skirts themselves.

In the safety of Mr. Dink's care, I soon learned to be a little cruel to them, taking my time to hand over the cards, waiting for them to turn red around the collar. I grew to want to make them blush. I wanted them to know that I was watching them just as closely as they were watching me.

AN ANGEL AT DINK'S MUSEUM

In the entrance hall of Dink's Dime Museum stands a young girl. A small, wooden pedestal is all that's under her feet but for this child's purposes it might as well be centre stage at the Academy of Music. Her dress– fashioned from the finest crepe, satin and embroidered silk–looks as if it came straight from Mrs. Demorest's closet. More impressive still are the two bright wings that arch, angelic, from her back. The illusion is so complete that children beg to pause in front of the museum window so they can peer inside to see if the wings are real. Even proper ladies–they who parade with purpose from house to carriage, from shop windows to their neighbours' sitting rooms–go out of their way to stare.

She doesn't shy away. She welcomes the attention, for she is the *cartes de visite* girl. Tied to her skirts with bright-coloured ribbons are photographic cards and pocket-sized looking-glasses. Scenic views and famous faces are on display, waiting for collectors and the curious to part with their money. When enough of a crowd gathers around her, she raises a hand for quiet, and sings a little song:

> *Cabinet cards or* cartes-de-visite
> *Find who's missing on your list.*
> *Sojourner Truth or Edwin Booth?*

Lotta Crabtree or Admiral Dot?
From Paris, France, to New York Harbor,
Fifteen Cents will buy you one –
Two for just a quarter!

November 23, 1871

I made a visit to Mr. Dink's on the Bowery as Miss Eva Ivan was complaining of "sword throat." It's a trouble she's had in the past, due to over-performing. This time, coupled with an eagerness to swallow multiple blades at once, she's made herself incredibly sore. I prescribed a therapeutic tea, and spoke with Mr. Dink about the matter. He is in agreement that Miss Eva is in need of patience and rest.

When she is well, I plan to approach her to ask if she is willing to allow me to try a new method of exploratory examination on her. Dr. K_. has been successful in placing a rigid metal tube down the throat of a sword swallower, and they have been touring together the past three years to demonstrate the technique to other physicians. The possibility of seeing down an esophagus clear to the fundus is quite exciting!

In my same visit to the museum, I believe I may have had a small victory with dear little Moth. I hope that I am not simply dreaming, but I can't help but think I have gained much ground with the girl. Winning her trust has felt akin to taming a cat. I try to tempt her with my warmth, my reliability, my concern. She is scared, I can tell, of what fate holds for her.

Mr. Dink has taken her on at the museum to help sell his collection of cabinet cards. While I'm unsure of the exact role Miss Everett is playing in all this, I am certain Mr. Dink possesses a good heart. At least Moth will now be away from that house more than she is in it.

S.F.

The New York Infirmary for
Indigent Women and Children
128 Second Avenue, New York, New York.
November 24, 1871

Mr. Thaddeus Dink
Dink's Museum and Palace of Illusions
The Bowery New York, New York

My dear Thaddeus,

You have always been good to me, our friendship strong, the trust between us unwavering. I will never forget the kindness you extended when we first met–how you took my hand in yours when the whole of polite society refused to touch me, how you gave me my first opportunity to practise medicine outside of the infirmary. Your generosity has been the source of countless good things in my life and I am forever grateful for it.

It is with great confidence in our friendship that I write to you now to ask a favour.

Please, as circumstances allow, watch over Miss Fenwick while she is in your care. She is, as you so wisely noted, a dear child of exceptional beauty.

While I understand you may have commitments to Miss Everett when it comes to the business of the theatre, I do hope that your commitment to being a gentleman allows you to see beyond business and into the heart of the matter.

I have reason to believe the girl is far more naïve than she makes herself out to be.

With greatest admiration and affection,

Sadie

When visiting the Gipsy's house, the stranger is admitted by a little girl. This girl was probably, a pure article of Gipsy herself originally, but had been so much adulterated by partial civilization that she combed her hair daily and submitted to shoes and stockings without a murmur. Ragged indeed was this reclaimed wanderer; saucy and dirty-faced was this sprouting young maiden, but she was sharp-witted, and scented money as quickly as if she had been the oldest hag in her tribe; so she asked her customer to walk upstairs, which he did. She herself went up stairs with a skip and a whirl, showed her visitor into the grand reception room with a gyrating flourish, and disappeared in a "courtesy" of so many complex and dizzy rotations that she seemed to the eyes of the bewildered traveller to evaporate in a red flannel mist.

–Q.K. Philander Doesticks,
The Witches of New York

XXV.

The man who'd accompanied Mae to the theatre the night of my first outing, a banker named Mr. Harris, had since come to the house to discuss a possible arrangement with Miss Everett. Mae's beauty, he'd told the madam, had been impossible for him to forget, and according to Mae, he'd told her outright that he had "a keen desire" to have her before any other man. "Rose better pack her bags," Mae bragged. "I'm on my way downstairs."

Mr. Greely had been equally eager to move things along with Alice. They'd shared tea in the parlour on several occasions, the grey-haired, red-faced, lanky gent talking loudly in Alice's ear and telling her he'd never seen a girl so pretty or heard a voice as lovely. He sang "Oh! Susanna" to her and squeezed her leg every time he got to the part about the banjo on his knee. Although she hated his singing and his forward ways, she'd come to regard Mr. Greely as a possible answer to her prayers.

Then, in a sudden turn, she'd ended their most recent meeting abruptly, and had run up the stairs crying bitter tears, all the way to our room.

"What's happened?" I asked, rushing to her side.

Throwing herself on her bed, she sobbed into her pillow and refused to answer.

"Did he hurt you? Are you unwell?"

My questions only served to make her wailing grow louder. Cadet soon came to the door to see what was wrong. Taking my place at the side of Alice's bed, he knelt to put a hand on her shoulder.

"It's all right," he said, his voice tender. "Whatever it is, it will be all right." He took a folded handkerchief from his pocket and slipped it into her hand.

"Thank you," she said, sitting up and looking at him with helpless eyes, tears still rolling down her cheeks. "But it's not going to be all right. He said to me, 'You'd better watch out, Miss Alice, I might just have to marry you.' So as soon as he was out the door, I took the good news to Miss Everett. She just laughed in my face. She said that Mr. Greely says that to all the girls. He has no intention of marrying me or anyone else, because he already has a wife."

Alice had pleaded with Miss Everett that she be allowed to turn Mr. Greely away in hopes of finding a better match. Miss Everett simply replied, "No, Alice. You've no choice in the matter."

As Alice began to sob again, Cadet moved to sit by her side and she buried her head in his chest. He looked at me as if to say *we don't need you here.* Putting his arm around Alice's shoulder, he told her again, "It's going to be all right."

I hated that he'd given her his attention so freely. The only things my tears had ever gotten me were a wet face and a scolding from Mama. I could never be like Alice. I couldn't match her sweetness or the graceful way she moved. Her blind devotion to all things bright and fair—even in the face of what was coming to her, to us—was beyond me. Watching her with Cadet, I was sure such ease and goodness was the sole property of girls born to true families in nice homes with both a mother and a father to adore them.

The women on the picture cards I kept hidden in my skirt at the museum didn't seem anything like Alice, yet gentlemen asked after them repeatedly, gazing on them, speaking of them as if they knew the ladies in the flesh. Demure or defiant, coy or come-hither, they all shared the same look of knowing in their eyes. It was now their confidence I was after.

Stealing a few *cartes* from Mr. Dink's collection for myself (Lady Godiva and the Circassian Beauty, among others), I pinned them to the wall of our room, hoping to make their power my own.

In the evenings, I'd sit at the dressing table, glancing back and forth between the cards and my reflection. I'd tilt my head, lower my eyes, and set my lips to try to match Miss Lotta Crabtree's pout. I'd found her expression to be more provocative than the others, and with practice, I soon mastered the sly, perfect pucker of her lips. I began to rouge my cheeks each morning and dot drops of Mae's neroli oil behind my ears. I tied the bow of my hat far to the right, like Rose, rather than making a homely, proper knot under my chin, like Alice.

I believed that everything would be easier—from standing in Mr. Dink's museum to lying down with a man—if I could become less myself and more like the women on those cards. *Miss Ada Fenwick—beautiful, tempting, in charge of her fate.*

Cadet's response to my efforts ended up being one more dagger in my heart. I'd breezed past him one afternoon with Alice, making sure I was close enough for him to catch the scent of my perfume. When he didn't speak to me, I smiled and said, "Good afternoon, Cadet."

When he didn't respond, I repeated my greeting. "Good afternoon—"

"Oh, I'm sorry, I thought you was Mae," he said, looking at me with a fair bit of spite.

Alice didn't speak until after he was gone. Then she said, "I'm not sure what came over him. He's usually quite gentlemanly."

"I suppose," I answered, realizing that any feelings Cadet might have had for me had been replaced by his fondness for Alice.

"Don't you favour him anymore?" she asked.

I'd seen her take the square of cotton that Cadet had lent her the day she'd fallen apart over Mr. Greely and tuck it under her pillow. I knew she had no intention of giving it back.

"No," I answered, taking her arm. "He's clearly got his eyes on someone else."

Blushing, she nodded.

Miss Everett, though, was quick to praise the change in me. "Your time with Mr. Dink has done wonders for you," she said. Handing me a small packet tied with ribbon, she added, "Here are a few of my calling cards to carry with you to the museum. Use them with discretion."

Miss Emma Everett

73 East Houston

Ladies' Boarding House

She instructed me to pay special attention to the quality of a man's suit, the shine of his shoes, the amount of wear on his hat. "The men who inhabit Mr. Dink's lobby might be looking to buy a few mementos to remind them of their time at the museum, but they also might be looking for a girl. If a man strikes you as exceptional, give him my card. I'll handle the rest. Mr. Dink need not be bothered with the details."

Standing in the entrance to the museum, I pictured myself in the arms of the various gentlemen who came to my side. It didn't take much imagination, as many of the men were bold, thinking, hoping, that I might be willing to offer more of myself to them if they asked. They called me *sweetheart* and *honey* and *darling girl*. They spoke of meeting at the concert hall or strolling in the park.

One man cheekily introduced himself to me as "Mr. Money."

I gave him a sigh in return.

"You're right, my dear, it's not," he said, feigning that I'd caught him out. Then, bringing out a fat clip of bills from his pocket, he said, "But you should know, I do have lots of it and I'd like nothing better than to spend it on a sweet little girl like you. What do you say we meet in the alley for a chat?"

"No thank you, sir," I replied, bidding him goodbye.

Another gentleman, who introduced himself as Mr. Wilson, visited three days in a row. He was an older man, who, like Mr. Birnbaum, had kind eyes that wrinkled at the corners when he smiled. He said I reminded him of a girl he once knew whose name was Helen. "She died before I could tell her that I loved her. She met with such a terrible end. It haunts me to this day."

Mr. Dink watched the proceedings from afar, greeting familiar patrons while keeping his eyes on me. He came to me now and again (especially when a gentleman got too close, or lingered too long) to ask if I was comfortable or if I might need to rest. "I can't have you fainting on the floor," he'd say, concern in his eyes. "You'll let me know if you need anything?"

"Yes, Mr. Dink. I will."

Miss Eva and Miss LeMar would sometimes come through the entrance hall to ask how many picture cards bearing their likenesses had been purchased that day. "You must lie to them every time," Mr. Dink had warned. "Or I'll be without a sword swallower or an albino, or quite possibly both. Tell them between fifteen and twenty-five, and Miss Eva's number must never exceed Miss LeMar's. Sylvia isn't one to tolerate losing."

Doing as Mr. Dink directed, I managed to keep peace between the two women. He was pleased with my efforts, and pulled me aside one day to say, "Should you ever find yourself through with Miss Everett, think of me, won't you? I'd be more than happy to have a *cartes de visite* girl as a permanent part of the Dink family. The pay would be a mere pittance compared to what the madam can offer, but it would be a wage, nonetheless."

I might have accepted his invitation on the spot, but visions of Miss Keteltas' house still haunted my dreams. The light through the windows now had a voice, low and throbbing like a heart. *Keep a fire in your belly, child. This will be yours. You must find a way.*

One day, I noticed a man circling, waiting for the moment when he might get a private look at my wares. Handsomely attired in frock coat and hat, he was, by far, the wealthiest-looking gentleman I'd ever seen. What struck me most about him, though, wasn't the quality of his attire, but his face. Although older, with more grey at his temples than when the artist had captured his likeness with oil paints and brush strokes, I recognized him in an instant. It was Mr. Wentworth.

My heart pounded at the sight of him, and with the wild

notion that Mrs. Wentworth was just outside the doors, waiting for her husband to drag me through the crush of dark-suited museum-goers and out to her carriage.

Glancing around, I checked to see where Mr. Dink was in case I needed him. When I spotted him standing at the ticket counter talking to Miss Eva, I gave him a little wave. He returned the gesture with a tip of his hat.

My stomach knotted as Mr. Wentworth approached. "Have you any Lady Godivas?" he asked in a proper, measured tone.

Nestor's voice sounded in my head. *You must hold back emotion, refuse impulse.*

Hands shaking, I reached to reveal the *cartes* in the hidden part of my skirt. "Yes, of course," I said, hoping he couldn't detect my anxiety.

He took his time with the cards, even taking a small magnifying glass from his pocket so he could carefully inspect each one. After gazing at the picture of Miss Suzie Lowe sitting on the back of her horse, he finally said, "She's just what I'm looking for."

The way he'd examined the cards brought me a great sense of relief. He was much like the other men who came to the museum. I was sure that he was there for himself and not his wife.

Remembering the album of tribal peoples I'd found in his study and the pictures of the young women who'd inhabited it, I pointed to the Circassian Beauty. "Perhaps you might also be interested in more exotic fare? The cards are two for a quarter."

"Perhaps I would," he said, reaching to caress the corner of the card with his thumb.

I'd looked upon his portrait so many times in the past that I found it hard not to act familiar with him or call him by his name. Not knowing the truth of his wife's wicked deed until Nestor revealed it to me, I'd often wondered where his sweet-faced dog had got to, and if the animal's absence had been ordered by his wife. I'd thought if he'd only been there to know me, he might have set me free himself.

After he'd chosen the Circassian Beauty too, I asked, "Anything else you're looking for?"

"That's all, I suppose," he said.

It occurred to me that the magic I'd done while fashioning a charm from paper and wishes had not only brought Mr. Wentworth home, it had somehow worked to deliver him to me. Taken with such a thought, I felt I couldn't let him get away so soon.

"Sir," I said, reaching for his arm and saying the first thing that came to mind. "I'm terribly sorry about your dog."

"Pardon me?" he said with a puzzled look on his face. "You must have me confused with someone else. I haven't any dog."

"I'm sure I've never seen you in my life, but I'm also certain that you had a dog—a white hound with a brown-speckled muzzle. A loyal friend, dearly missed."

Mr. Wentworth gave a nervous chuckle as he reached into his pocket and presented me with a nickel. "An astonishing parlour trick, dear girl. I did have just such a dog."

I refused to take the coin. "I can't accept your money."

Gazing at me with curiosity, he said, "I guess you're quite an exotic creature yourself, now, aren't you?"

Pleased with myself for holding his interest, I gave

him a look that would have made Miss Lotta Crabtree blush.

"Perhaps I could walk with you?" he asked, his voice hushed. "So we might speak in private?"

I looked again for Mr. Dink. He was on the other side of the entrance hall, engaged in a conversation with the two police officers he'd hired to stand out front on Saturday nights.

Reaching into my pocket, I pulled out one of Miss Everett's cards and handed it to him.

His eyes widened when he read what was printed on it. "Who shall I ask for when I make the arrangements?"

"Miss Fenwick," I said, my breathing shallow, my heart beating loud in my ears.

Putting his hand to his hat, he said, "Until we meet again, Miss Fenwick."

"Until then," I said.

Mrs. Wentworth returned to my dreams that night, stirring my emotions into a frightening mess. *Stealing my jewels wasn't enough for you?* she wailed as she came after me with her scissors.

Waking with a start, I imagined holding a knife to Mrs. Wentworth's throat while her husband looked on with a smile. I held tight to her fan as I lay sweating in my bed, wondering if I'd made a terrible mistake.

There was a little maid,
and she was afraid
That her sweetheart
would come unto her;
So she went to bed,
and covered up her head,
And fastened the door with a skewer.

XXVI.

The madam greeted Mr. Wentworth like an old friend. "It's been far too long," Miss Everett said, welcoming him with a kiss on both cheeks. "I was beginning to wonder if you'd fled the city forever."

"And leave behind the finest house with the fairest girls?" Mr. Wentworth teased.

Miss Everett allowed him to take me by the hand and lead me to sit next to him on her narrow couch in the parlour. He was so close I could feel the warmth of his leg through my skirts.

Dressed in a fine suit, much like the one he'd been wearing at the museum, his cuffs showed white out the ends of his coat sleeves. His collar was crisp and new, and the knot in his black silk tie was perfect. Cheeks ruddy, moustache neatly trimmed, he smelled as if a barber had just touched his temples with Macassar oil and smacked his neck with bay rum.

He grinned at Miss Everett as he recalled how we'd

met. "Your Miss Fenwick is a sly one," he said. "What a fun game she played with me at the museum–casting her witchery to keep me near, then slipping your card in my hand."

"Witchery?" Miss Everett said, giving me a surprised look.

"Oh yes," Mr. Wentworth replied. "She had me hanging on her every word. I dare say if I gave her my hand this instant, she could tell me my whole life's story."

"Why, Miss Fenwick," Miss Everett said with a smile. "I believe you've been keeping secrets from me. I'd no idea you had such talents."

Blushing, I said nothing. Unsure as to whether or not Miss Everett would approve of my using Mama's Gypsy ways on Mr. Wentworth, I thought it best not to admit anything.

She'd been beside herself after he made the arrangements for the visit, telling me more than once, "If he chooses you, you'll be a very lucky girl." Her excitement over his interest was evident even now: her lips had turned up in a smile that seldom left her face, and she nodded in agreement at his every word.

"Excuse me, won't you, Mr. Wentworth. I must go to the kitchen to see about our tea," she finally said.

"Yes, of course, Emma," he replied, staring intently at me.

Once she was gone, he eagerly asked, "Will you share your gift with me now, girl? Surely your sight can be given to a bit of palmistry." Holding out his hands, he said, "Tell me what you see."

Left for a lady, right for a man, Mama always said.

I pulled off my gloves and took hold of his right hand, cradling it in mine, bringing it to rest in my lap. With my other hand, I stroked his palm, ran my fingers down the length of it, then traced its lines one by one. If he was all that Miss Everett said he was, I would do everything I could to win him over.

"You've the touch of an angel," he said with a sigh.

"Shh. You mustn't speak."

His palm was broad and wide, his fingers thick. Lines cutting deep, thumbnail bitten to a ragged edge, I might have mistaken him for a working man if it weren't for the softness of his skin. Ink stained his middle finger where I guessed he held his pen.

"You've a keen mind for business," I began. "Good with numbers and words, you never spare the details. People say it's to your credit and your benefit."

Nodding at me, his eyes widening, he said, "Go on."

Caressing the fleshy mound at the base of his thumb, I glanced at his face. I could feel his hand was swollen there, and when I kneaded at the muscle, he made a slight scowl.

"I see you're a man of large appetites," I said with a grin.

Biting his lip, he replied, "Indeed."

"A drinker of fine brandy, perhaps?"

"Right again," he whispered, shaking his head in disbelief.

I would've gone on with it, gladly walking the line between Mama's wisdom and my memories of his house, but Miss Everett returned. As she rolled the tea cart into the room, I let go of Mr. Wentworth's hand.

"Please, don't let me interrupt you," she said, pouring a cup of tea for each of us.

Mr. Wentworth gave me a wink, as if to say that what we'd just shared was to remain a secret.

Between sips of tea and bites of cake, he talked of his

travels and of the rigours of the social season in New York. His words washed in and out of my hearing, as I thought of things I might tell him the next time we were alone. Seeing him rapt over the bit of theatre I'd performed felt better than any revenge I'd ever imagined on his wife.

When it came time for him to leave, he took hold of my chin and tried to kiss me.

Damn you, Miss Fenwick, give me my husband back, you whore.

Surprised by his boldness, I pulled away.

"Perhaps next time," he said, letting me go.

Miss Everett looked at me and frowned.

He came to see me the next day, and the day after that, each time growing more intent on winning my affection. Miss Everett was so sure of Mr. Wentworth's intentions that she sent word to Mr. Dink to say he should start looking for a new girl to stand in his lobby and sell his cards. She didn't even let me go to the museum to say goodbye.

She left Mr. Wentworth and me alone for much of our meetings, so I filled our time together smoothing my fingers over his palm and telling him of a business agreement that was about to succeed, and how he was also quite close to capturing the heart of a "true Gypsy girl."

At the end of his third visit, he presented me with a gold locket that opened up to reveal a lock of his hair. Strung on a velvet ribbon, it was a lovely thing, the front of it engraved with a bouquet of forget-me-nots. As I tied it around my neck, he put his hands around my waist, determined to finally kiss me.

Holding my breath, I let him do as he wished. I thought of Cadet as he came near. Mr. Wentworth's kisses weren't anything like his. They were bold, and searching, and left my mouth sore from his eagerness.

Mama had been right about boys' kisses. Sweet as they were, they held no promise of anything past the moment they were given. Mr. Wentworth's most certainly did.

"You've got him, Ada," Miss Everett said, coming to me in the parlour that day after he left. "He's asked to take you to the theatre."

Rose said her goodbyes the day I was to go out with Mr. Wentworth. She showered all the girls in the house with clothes and trinkets she didn't need any more along with good-natured teasing and advice. Then she called me into her room for a private word.

"I hear you've got yourself a man," she said as she tucked the last of her things in a large trunk.

"Yes," I replied.

"It's going to be all right, you know."

Sitting on the edge of her bed, I thought of my first night in the house and the kindness she'd shown me. I wished things could go back to the way they'd been then, when I'd been glad simply to be clean, and safe and fed, with Rose caring for me like a dear, older sister.

"Your first time with a man is just one night," she said. "Like Sunday morning standing in front of gentlemen with your dress around your ankles—it's there, and then it's gone."

She went on to tell me, with a great deal of pride, that the apartment Mr. Chief of Detectives had arranged for her had a parlour, bedchamber, dressing room, bathroom, and water closet—each room furnished with the finest trappings money could buy. The hotel's marble halls contained any kind of shop you could imagine, including a twenty-four-hour hairdresser and a dining room with waiters who had nothing better to do than serve a person's every whim. Once Rose got there, she joked, she need never go outside again.

Sitting next to me, she put her hand on my knee. "The trick to getting what you want," she said, "is to make duty seem as easy as desire."

I liked Rose. I looked up to her and hoped to follow in her footsteps. I thought that if she could make it from Miss Everett's to a private suite in the Fifth Avenue Hotel, I could very well end up with everything *I* wanted. I swore I'd do my best to take her words to heart.

THE PLAY THAT SWEPT PARIS IS HERE!

NOBODY'S FOOL

BETRAYAL. SECRETS. BLOOD.

Featuring **Miss Suzie Lowe, Miss Kitty Swift**
and the **Zuppa Circus Players**

Tuesday – Sunday 7pm (no matinees)

The Palace of Illusions

The Bowery

XXVII.

"What a lovely gift Mr. Wentworth has given you," Miss Everett said as she fastened the locket he'd presented to me around my neck. Her lips curled into a satisfied smile. "If all goes well tonight, I'm certain he'll make an offer."

Pinning roses in my hair, she gave me specific instructions on how to act with him, explaining that he would be a different sort of man in public than he'd been in the parlour. "Tonight you can expect courtesy and flirtation rather than advances."

Alice and Mae were to be seated in the same box with Mr. Wentworth and me, along with Mr. Greely and Mr. Harris. Miss Everett was quick to say that we each would have different paths to follow with our gentlemen. "Mae can be quite forward, as we all know, and Mr. Harris only hopes she'll be more so with him this time than last. Alice, of course, will win the day by her sweetness, and you, my dear, must stay a course that's true for you and Mr. Wentworth."

"Are you sure he won't expect to carry on as he did in the parlour?"

"No, my dear. His expectations are merely to have a pleasant night out, and that's all. He's a gentleman of the highest sort."

For Mae, the evening could only have one end—it was to be her first night with a man. Mr. Harris had at last made a generous offer for Mae's maidenhood, and Miss Everett had gladly accepted it. As soon as Rose walked out the door, Miss Everett brought in fresh flowers and new bedding to dress her room, and Mae carried her personal effects down from our quarters. She put her best ribbons on the dressing table and draped her favourite silk shawl over the back of the chair. It was a bright shade of blue, which looked striking when next to her red hair. Dr. Sadie had agreed to be waiting at the house when we got back. As soon as the deed was finished and Mr. Harris gone home, she'd check

Evening Toilette–This graceful toilette is of salmon-coloured faille. The skirt, without flounces or overskirt, has an elaborate trimming of white chenille balls, imitating pearls. The low square corsage is edged with point lace, and has lace frills across the back and front; also swinging chains of balls fall from the shoulders. The necklace and coiffure are also of chenille. Pink and yellow roses are suggested as decorations for the hair.

on Mae's well-being and assist her with the important tasks that came after a girl's deflowering.

On our way out of the house, Mae gave Miss Everett a winning smile and said, "I won't let you down."

Giving her a short nod in return, Miss Everett replied, "See that you don't."

Cadet travelled with us, pushed to the corner of the cab once again by the ruffles and flounces of our gowns, only this time he sat next to Alice. Watching the way he looked after her now was almost more than I could bear.

Alice was stunning, the cut and fabric of her gown far better than either Mae's or mine. It had belonged to Rose and was made from row after row of ivory-coloured French lace. The difference between her dress and Mae's was so great that Mae had pouted over it, begging Alice to trade. Miss Everett had put an end to Mae's nagging, saying, "The colour suits Alice better." Mae had let it go without further argument, but stayed silent the entire way to the theatre.

Mr. Wentworth was the first of the gentlemen to arrive in our box.

"What a lovely gown," he commented after we'd gotten settled next to each other.

"Thank you," I said, putting my hand to the locket to see that it was still securely fastened around my neck.

"Is the view to your liking?" he asked, with an intent stare.

"Yes," I replied, hoping he was pleased that I'd worn his gift.

My bare arm brushed against his sleeve and he took it as an invitation to put his hand on mine. In an instant I pulled my hand away and folded my hands in my lap. My nerves had gotten the best of me. For one brief moment I'd worried that his wife might spy us from another box and come raging after me in her madness. Looking to Mr. Wentworth and seeing the calm expression on his face, I determined to put my fears to rest.

The play that evening starred Miss Suzie Lowe and another actress from Mr. Dink's *cartes de visite* collection, Miss Kitty Swift. One fair, one dark, they played sisters who were in love with the same man. It was a blood and thunder tale, where everyone booed and hissed at the villains and yelled "Balderdash!" at the top of their lungs.

Eventually Kitty found Suzie dallying with the man in question, a gentleman farmer named Tom. Poor Kitty watched from behind a haystack as Suzie sang a song to her lover.

In the dark of the box, I could feel Mr. Wentworth's shoulder against mine, hear his breathing rise and fall as he listened to Miss Lowe sing of forbidden kisses and Tom's sweet embrace. And as the curtain closed on the scene, I noticed a wistful look on his face.

Right or wrong, I knew that most of his desire for me arose from his wanting to have something he shouldn't.

At the intermission, Mae managed to free herself of Mr. Harris almost as soon as they arrived in the reception hall. The next time I spotted her, she was standing near the bar, talking to two young men, one of whom I was sure was the gentleman she'd flirted with on the horsecar all those days ago. Alice was at her side, no sign of Mr. Greely.

Each time Alice laughed at something one of the men said, Mae would take hold of her arm like they were the dearest of friends. It seemed a strange turn to me, considering the way she'd acted towards Alice over the dress. Mae had never been one to easily let go of a grudge.

When I saw them slip into the ladies' lounge, I excused myself from Mr. Wentworth and followed them.

Alice ran to me as soon as I came in. I'd been too busy with my own gentleman to notice, but she told me that she'd spent most of the first half of the evening politely avoiding Mr. Greely's advances.

"He started out just calling me 'sweetheart' and 'darling,'" she moaned. "But then he put my hand between his legs."

The horrified look on her face set Mae to laughing. "If you want the man to lose interest, you should've followed my lead," she teased. "Acting coy drives Mr. Greely mad. It only serves to pulls him closer."

"I wasn't acting coy," Alice insisted. "I just don't feel the same towards him is all."

Cheeks ruddy with the heat of the room and the glass of champagne Mae had given her, Alice told me that she'd met Mae's handsome young clerk, the one she'd been sneaking out to meet at the concert hall.

Mae interjected, "And his friend, Mr. Samuels, was very glad to meet you, Alice."

Alice blushed at Mae's words, and I could imagine how it might please her to be the object of the attentions of someone who seemed to like her without knowing what she was. "They want Mae and me to go with them to the concert hall . . . just for a little bit."

I frowned at her and shook my head.

Seeing my look she said, "The theatre is so crowded and close tonight, and Mae says we could be back well before the last act. The concert saloon is only half a block away."

"You told them no, of course?" I asked.

Alice put her hand to her mouth and giggled. "Mae says I should see it once before everything changes. Before Mr. Greely decides he needs me to be his, and before she has to give herself to Mr. Harris."

"Hush," Mae whispered behind her gloved hand. "You've given our plan away."

Alice pouted at Mae. "Ada won't tell." Looking at me with all the innocence of a child, she asked, "Will you, Ada?"

"We won't be long," Mae said, not waiting for my answer. "Our gents will barely notice we're late, I promise."

Although Alice had scolded Mae time and again for sneaking out, I'd seen her twirling around our room, imagining how it might feel to float across the dance floor in a gentleman's arms. Holding a feathered fan to her face, she'd gracefully glided past me, saying, "What a night this is. Isn't it grand?"

As the bells chimed to announce the call to the second half, Mae turned to me and said, "Just tell them Alice was feeling faint and that I decided to stay with her a while longer. I'll do the same for you next time, I swear."

"Please," Alice begged.

"I'll see you soon," I told Alice, and then left her in Mae's hands.

Mr. Wentworth offered me his arm as we made our way back to the box.

If Mr. Wentworth chooses you, you'll be a very lucky girl.

Cadet, who'd taken up his post outside the box, pulled me aside when we arrived. "Where's Alice?" he asked.

"She's with Mae," I answered, not wanting to lie.

"I see," he said. "I'll go back to the reception room and wait for them."

"All right," I replied, feeling awful for not telling him everything.

I smiled at Mr. Harris and Mr. Greely as the band played the actors on. "Miss Creaghan was feeling light-headed," I whispered to Mr. Greely. "Miss O'Rourke stayed behind to assist her," I told Mr. Harris. I hoped my performance was as convincing as the one taking place on the stage.

The second half of the play was taken up with Kitty going after Suzie to exact her revenge. She purchased a knife from an old witch, played by Miss LeMar. She poisoned the blade by rubbing it with the leaves from an enchanted tree, played by Mr. Dink's long-legged illusionist. Telling Suzie an evil lie, Kitty got the young woman alone. I watched as she plunged the blade into Miss Susie Lowe's heart and I gasped when Suzie cried out, "Dear God! This is the end of me!"

As she died her terrible death, Mr. Wentworth took my hand and held it tight. This time, I didn't take it back. Alice and Mae might have chosen to escape Miss Everett's expectations one last time, but I had chosen to meet them.

Slumber, my darling, thy mother is near,
Guarding thy dreams from all terror and fear.
Sunlight has pass'd and the twilight has gone.
Slumber, my darling, the night's coming on.

Sweet visions attend thy sleep,
Fondest, dearest to me,
While others their revels keep,
I will watch over thee.

XXVIII.

There was no sign of Alice, Mae or Cadet for the rest of the performance. The other gentlemen, clearly displeased, left right after the curtain, but Mr. Wentworth stayed with me while I waited for Cadet to reappear. Seeing the worry on my face, he said, "You mentioned that one of the young ladies was under the weather. Do you suppose she is in need of a physician?"

"I'm sure Cadet has seen to her care. That's probably what's keeping him."

Nodding in agreement, he was more than glad to take my words as a reassurance, and quickly went back to wooing me. "I'd thought you were the sweetest girl I'd ever met," he said while gazing into my eyes. "And after tonight, I'm sure of it. Please say you'll see me again, Miss Fenwick?"

His attention felt out of place in light of the uncertainty I was feeling over Alice and Mae, but I did my best to respond to it with as much flirtatious enthusiasm as possible. "It would be my pleasure, Mr. Wentworth. I was praying all night for you to ask."

As soon as I'd given my reply, Cadet appeared. He gave a short nod to Mr. Wentworth, but I could tell he was only pretending to be calm.

"Good night, Miss Fenwick," Mr. Wentworth said. "Keep safe until we meet again."

"Until then, Mr. Wentworth," I replied.

"Until then."

Cadet waited for the man to move out of earshot and then turned to me, his voice frantic. "I've looked everywhere, even backstage and outside in the alleys around the theatre," he said. "I couldn't find them."

"Did you think to check the concert hall," I asked, pretending not to know exactly where they'd gone.

The way he stared at me then made me feel horrible and small. The look on his face said he was sure I'd conspired again to fool him, maybe even cost him his job.

And so I confessed. "Mae intended to go there with a young beau she's been seeing, a Mr. Vaughn. She enticed Alice to come along as a partner for his friend."

Cadet took my arm and held it fast as we came out of the theatre into the cold night. "Watch your step," he said as we came to a curb, alerting me to a wide gap in the stones that surely would have tripped me.

Sticking two fingers between his teeth, he gave three sharp whistles. The signal brought a gang of boys from the shadows. There were seven of them, wiry and dirty, their eyes shining out from their grimy faces as they looked to Cadet.

"Have you seen two girls in gowns with two dandies on their arms?" he asked them.

I quickly added, "One was fair and pretty, and the other had red curls."

"Girls go by here all the time," one of the boys said, shrugging, staring at the locket around my neck.

He was bigger than the others, and from the way they were watching him, I guessed that he was their leader. It was clear he wasn't going to lend his assistance without getting something in return.

Unfastening the locket, I held it out to him. "Help us find them."

The boy snatched it from my hand and shoved it in the pocket of his sack coat. He nodded to the rest of the guttersnipes and they fell in behind Cadet.

"Is there gonna be a fight?" one of them asked.

When Cadet didn't answer, another boy said, "I'd say that's a yes."

A pair of dandies were in the next alley over, playing cruel tricks on a ten-cent whore. Shirt tails untucked from their pants, it looked as if they'd had their way with her and were now offering to pay a penny for this, a nickel for that in an attempt to see if they could strip away what little remained of her dignity.

"Will you eat horse shit for a penny?"

"No, you asses."

"Will you eat it for a nickel?"

"Sure, a bite."

"Will you put a bottle in your hole?"

"Which one, front or back?"

"A nickel if you do both."

"Fuck you."

"A nickel each?"

"All right."

A couple of the boys in the gang scurried down the length of the alley and back again. I sighed with relief when they returned, shaking their heads at Cadet. "No girls here," one of them reported, so we moved on.

The gang's leader and another lad ran ahead, searching. I looked all around as we followed, constantly turning to glance behind me, hoping to catch sight of Alice and Mae. I thought if we could find them now, there might be time to concoct a lie that would save us all from Miss Everett's anger. Hearing a young woman's laugh, I stopped short, only to find that it was a lady being helped into a nearby carriage. Her night was ending in the sort of happiness I'd pictured for Alice, Mae and me.

As we neared the door of the concert saloon, a whistle like the one Cadet had used to signal the guttersnipes rang out from the entrance to the alley just past the hall. "Stay here," Cadet ordered, breaking away from me to investigate what was going on. Ignoring his words, I chose to follow him. "I'm coming with you."

The voices of men grew louder as we approached. They were shouting orders and howling with approval.

"Get it in her!"

"Fuck her again!"

"I'll pay you fifty cents if you let me have a go."

Another man's voice sneered, "She's *my* cherry. I paid for her fair and square."

When we reached the alley we were met with a terrible sight. Three drunken sporting men were standing over a fourth man who had a girl pinned to the ground. The girl's skirts were pulled up past her middle and all but covered her face. The man was on top of her, thrusting his hips hard against her body and holding her pale arms down to the filthy pavers of the alley. The men watching were moving, stepping around the pair, making it difficult at first to see who the girl was. One of the men had a torch and was holding it above his head. Another torch was propped on the stones near his feet. The smell of burning pitch stuck in the back of my throat as I thought, *No, no, no.*

"Please stop," I heard the girl weakly plead. My heart fell at the sound of her voice.

"Get away from her!" Cadet shouted, flashing a knife at the men as he lunged towards them. The gang of boys advanced with him, holding hunks of brick and broken glass.

The sporting men staggered back with fear in their eyes and then quickly disappeared from the alley.

Alice was still trapped in Mr. Samuel's grasp. Paying no attention to what was going on around him, he grabbed her by the hair and hit her head hard against the ground. "That's for soiling my coat sleeves, you little bitch," he growled.

Alice's head lolled to the side.

Cadet grabbed the man by the collar, pulled him away from Alice, and shoved him against the side of the building. Mr. Samuels tried to wrestle free, but Cadet punched him in the gut and then dragged him out of the alley, the gang of guttersnipes trailing behind them.

I ran to Alice and knelt next her, gently bringing her head to rest into my lap. Her hair had fallen out of its combs and her curls were covered in muck. The beautiful dress Rose had given her was now soiled and torn. Even in the dusky alley, her face looked pale and ashen. Eyes shut tight, she was breathing, but her body felt heavy and limp against mine.

"Alice," I called to her, "I'm here. It's me, Ada." The wet of the puddles and filth beneath me seeped through my dress and my underskirts, soaking all the way to my skin. As terrified as I was of what I'd seen, my only thought was of protecting Alice and making sure she would be all right. Reaching out for a broken bottle that was lying near, I brought it close, ready to lash out at anyone who dared bother us.

Stroking her cheek, I spoke to her again, "Alice–."

Finally opening her eyes, she looked up at me, tears rolling down her face, but didn't speak.

"All will be well," I told her. "I promise."

Cadet and the boys were near enough that if I turned, I could see them out on the sidewalk, half in shadow, half in the light of a street lamp, pushing and pulling at Mr. Samuels. They'd emptied his pockets and taken most of his clothes. The punishment they were heaping upon him now was gruesome and loud. Their boots and bare feet cracked and smacked and pounded at the man. Every so often Cadet would give a shout, and they would all stop, waiting for Mr. Samuels to beg for mercy. When he began to moan and plead, they'd all go at it again.

A crowd soon gathered, but no one dared to stop them.

I turned my attention back to Alice, and before long Mae was standing at my side.

"What's happened?" she asked, staring down at us.

I felt the heat of anger rush through me. I blamed Mae for everything that had happened. "She was attacked," I answered, imagining her arm in arm with Mr. Vaughn, her laugh echoing off the bricks as she left Alice to fend for herself with Mr. Samuels in the alley. Not wanting to upset Alice any further, I bit my tongue and stopped myself from saying more.

"We were in the concert hall together, and then she was gone," Mae said, her excuse small and worthless. "I thought she'd just stepped out to get some air."

Cadet and the gang of boys were now moving towards us. The crowd had departed, leaving Mr. Samuels on the sidewalk in a bloody mess.

One hand swollen and cut, his clothes dishevelled, Cadet bent down to take Alice into his arms. He whispered to her, "You're safe now. I'll get you home."

She whimpered a quiet "thank you."

The leader of the guttersnipes stepped forward to bid us good bye, Mr. Samuels' hat now perched on his head. "You want his waistcoat?" he asked, holding the garment out in front of him and offering it to Cadet.

"No," Cadet answered. "It's yours."

As Cadet made his way out of the alley with Alice, Mae and I followed, lifting our skirts with every step. It felt wrong to care about whether my dress would snag on the brick or if the heel of my slipper might catch on the curb, but these were the only thoughts I could manage without falling apart. I'd been too late to save Alice, and neither my sadness nor my guilt was going to do her any good.

On any given day, acts of kindness occur all across the city. Someone gives up their bed so someone else can rest their tired, aching bones. Someone hands a bit of change to a stranger. There's hot soup and good fortune, soft words and bread.

Then there are the cruel things that happen, the worst that you can imagine. Heaven help you if even one of them finds you. The memory of it will never let you alone.

December 12, 1871.   THE EVENING STAR

MAN SEEKS SHELTER AFTER GUTTERSNIPE ATTACK

As most New Yorkers know, patrons of the Bowery Concert Hall come from a variety of walks of life–from men in uniform to Wall Street gents to notable figures like Mr. William Tweed. Anyone who walks through the door is free to join the rest of those gathered for an evening of drink and dance and song.

Last night, just past the hour of nine o'clock, a gentleman came through the door of the establishment in need of more than the concert saloon's usual fare of ale and good cheer. Exhausted, bruised and badly beaten, Mr. Charles Samuels could barely make his way without assistance and came to the place seeking refuge.

Mr. Samuels, son of well-known financier Mr. Alistair Samuels, claimed that he had been attacked by a gang of boys in an alley near the corner of Houston Street and the Bowery. After the man gave up all valuables and money in his possession (a gold watch and chain, over one hundred and fifty dollars in cash, and an impressive gold ring given to Mr. Samuels by his mother), the group of Street Arabs threatened the man's life and demanded he dispense with his clothing.

An Isolated Incident

An alarm was put out and Officers Fuller and Knox, special to the Palace of Illusions, were called to the scene to investigate, but the attackers were not to be found. Mr. Samuels said the boys were of a tender age, but were so many in number (perhaps a dozen or more) that the harm they inflicted on his person through biting, kicking and punching was substantial. Although the boys are not known to Mr. Samuels, it is believed that they frequent the area.

Officer Fuller claims it was an unusual crime for December, as this kind of attack most often occurs during the summer months. Because of this, Fuller believes that it was an isolated incident. He went on to say it should be noted that such a crime is, however, representative of a larger problem plaguing the city— namely that of the burgeoning number of children taking to our streets and running wild.

Mr. Samuels went on record as saying, "Those guttersnipes are not children. They are filthy, untamed animals, and should be treated as such. I will not rest until they are punished for their barbaric deeds."

The Evening Star does wonder if this startling event will lead those who run our fair city to finally take steps towards correcting Gotham's growing orphan problem.

Little girl, little girl, don't lie to me –
Tell me where did you sleep last night?

In the pines, in the pines, where the sun never
*   shines,*
And you shiver when the cold wind blows.

XXIX.

There was much confusion when Cadet brought Alice through the door. She was weepy and frightened. "I cried out for help," she said over and over again. "He said he would slit my throat."

Miss Everett rushed to meet us, Dr. Sadie close behind. She had been waiting in the parlour, expecting to tend to Mae later that night. It was a bitter surprise for her to have to care for Alice's ruined, weeping self.

"What's happened?" Dr. Sadie asked, trying to look Alice over even while Cadet still had her in his arms.

"A man attacked her," I said.

Miss Everett looked to me, her eyes flashing, and then ordered Cadet to take Alice to our room. "The doctor will see to her there."

As we went up the stairs, I could hear sounds coming from both Missouri's and Emily's rooms. Laughter and low talk came from under their doors, the girls and their gentleman callers clueless as to what was happening on the other side.

Cadet placed Alice on her bed and then turned to leave the room, tears in his eyes. It broke my heart to see him like that, his true feelings only daring to come out as he left her behind. *How could this have happened to beautiful, sweet Alice.*

Miss Everett stopped Cadet before he could leave the room. "Wait for me in the parlour, I'd like to speak with you."

Alice pulled herself into a ball and went silent.

"The man can't hurt you now," Dr. Sadie reassured her.

"You girls go to the kitchen," Miss Everett said to Mae and me. "Warm up by the stove and have some hot milk. There's no need for you here."

Mae left the room, but as I made to follow her, Dr. Sadie put her hand on my arm to hold me back. "I'd like you to stay." Then turning to Miss Everett she said, "I'll need a hand with things. She's been with me on rounds. She knows how to help."

"Very well," Miss Everett said with a nod, now heading to the door as well. "I'll be in the parlour should you need me."

Motioning for me to help, Dr. Sadie told Alice, "We need to undress you now so I can see to your care."

"All right," Alice replied, sniffing back tears.

As I unfastened the buttons on Alice's gown, I thought of how lovely she'd looked earlier that night. The prettiest girl in the theatre by far, the ribbons in her hair had perfectly matched the trim on her collar, and her dress had shimmered in the house lights.

"Lay your head on your pillow," Dr. Sadie instructed, before she moved to examine Alice's wounds. Draping a sheet over the top half of Alice's body, she put her hand on the girl's knee. "I'll be as gentle as I can."

Closing her eyes tight, Alice said, "He bragged about what he did. He said making me bleed would give him the virgin cure."

Dr. Sadie shuddered, and I could tell that it was all she could do to carry on with her work. "Fetch the bowl from the washbasin," she said to me as she examined the bruises and blood between Alice's legs. "Fill it halfway with water."

When I brought it to her, she took a bottle and packet of powders from her bag, poured their contents into the basin and mixed them with the water.

"I have to clean your wounds, inside and out, Alice," Dr. Sadie said. "It will burn, but I've no choice."

Alice grimaced, holding her knees together.

"The sooner I see to it, the sooner it will be done."

She nodded to Dr. Sadie and then turned her head to face me. "Hold my hand?" she asked.

I gave her my hand and she squeezed it tight.

While Alice cried through this new pain, I couldn't stop thinking that what had happened was partly my fault. I could have stood up to Mae and told her that this time she wasn't going to get her way. If I had a heart like Alice's I would've knelt by her side and prayed for God to heal her, but I felt I had no words to give except to tell her, "I'm sorry."

Even in her distress, Alice gave me a tearful smile.

When Dr. Sadie was finished, she gave Alice three spoonfuls of brandy to help her rest.

"Why don't you join Mae and have Mrs. Coyne fix you some warm milk in the kitchen," she suggested to me. "It's time for Alice to get some sleep."

Pale and exhausted, Alice had finally stopped crying. She was now covered with a quilt, her head resting on her pillow. I tucked a stray curl behind her ear and said, "I'll be back soon."

She gave me a tired nod and closed her eyes.

As I reached the foot of the stairs, I could hear Miss Everett's voice coming from the parlour even though the door was shut. She wasn't with Cadet, but with Mae.

"I did nothing wrong," I heard Mae say.

"You've ruined a whole night's business for me," Miss Everett replied. "Every appointment was put off or interrupted by your folly."

"I'm not to blame," Mae protested.

"I've heard otherwise," Miss Everett said. "Turn out your pockets and your reticule."

"I don't understand."

"Do it."

Through the crack where I'd pressed my ear I heard coins hitting the floor, so many of them I lost count.

"What have you done?" Miss Everett threatened. "Where did a girl like you get so much money, and all in one night!"

There was a shuffling about, and then the sound of a hard slap. "That's mine!" Mae wailed. "You can't have it."

"You've cost me enough."

"I'm not to blame."

"Aren't you now? I wager you knew exactly what you were doing, and had been planning it for some time."

Mae's voice was strong now, her words indignant. "I brought you two girls, just as you asked, and I've never gotten what I was promised."

"You would've gotten your reward after tonight."

"Before you sent me away?"

Miss Everett did not respond.

"I knew you were meaning to keep Alice," Mae complained. "Missouri told me so herself."

"Foolish girl." Miss Everett's voice did not soften. "I meant to keep you both."

Footsteps came near, and I rushed away down the hall. When the parlour door flew open, I turned to see Miss Everett holding Mae by the arm, her face angry and tight.

"Cadet!" the madam called.

He appeared in an instant from his post outside the front door.

"Put this one out in the street," Miss Everett said through her teeth.

Wailing, Mae begged Miss Everett to let her stay.

"I don't wish to look on you again," the madam said.

Mae spotted me and cried, "Ada, tell her I've done nothing wrong!"

I stared at her in disbelief. She'd ruined Alice for her own profit, and she might well have been planning to do the same to me. The girl I'd thought had rescued me from the street had only been out for her own gain. I watched with sadness and relief as Cadet finally took her out the door.

Miss Everett came to me the next day and said that Mr. Wentworth had sent word to say he'd enjoyed our evening at the theatre and wished to move things forward with me in the near future. "He's had to leave town for a holiday retreat, but he's assured me that he'll be back to see you before the first of the year." This time, Miss Everett explained, there would be no going to the theatre. The evening was to begin and end in Rose's room.

"He's offered a substantial reward for you, my dear," she said with a smile.

"How much?" I asked, wanting desperately to know.

"I don't discuss the exact sum with my girls," she said, wagging a finger at me. "It makes for bad blood between you."

I thought of the night Mrs. Wentworth came to Chrystie Street and the small purse she dropped on the table for Mama. The question of how many coins it contained had stayed with me all this time. No matter Miss Everett's reasons for not sharing Mr. Wentworth's offer with me, I wasn't about to be left wondering.

"I won't go with him unless you tell me," I said, challenging her.

"Don't be foolish, Ada. Knowing that he's willing to pay what I think you're worth should be enough."

"Please, I want to know."

She finally said, "It's more than Rose fetched, and until now, her bounty was the highest prize I'd ever been offered for a girl's first time. Don't you dare mention this to anyone else."

"I won't."

"You'll never fetch this much again in one night, but if all goes well, he'll favour you and there will be gifts and perhaps a future with him, and that will make it all worthwhile."

Two weeks after Alice was attacked, a chancre appeared where Mr. Samuels had forced himself on her. It blossomed into a shiny button of a sore. Wearing rubber gloves, Dr. Sadie applied a calomel salve to help it go away.

"I'm afraid things will only get worse from here," she confided to me. She'd been expecting a chancre might appear and was now certain a fever would soon follow. "She'll break out in a terrible rash that covers her whole body, even the palms of her hands and the soles of her feet." Dr. Sadie had been stubborn about Alice's care from the start, coming nearly every day to bring her medicine, comfort and sympathy. "There's not much more I can do."

Christmas came soon after that, and Miss Everett, in an attempt to return a sense of rightness to the house, made certain that the day was not forgotten. She postponed all regular business and turned the front parlour into a banquet hall, everything sparkling from top to bottom. Even the fruit on the table—the apples, pears, grapes and persimmons—glittered with sugar and candlelight.

Rose made a surprise visit from the Fifth Avenue Hotel, dressed in sable and diamonds, and both Missouri and Emily fawned over her, begging for the details of her new life. At dinner, Cadet, being the only gentleman in the house, sat at the head of the table, carving knife in hand.

Alice took it in with wide-eyed wonder, her eyes welling up with tears.

The day after Christmas, Miss Everett and Dr. Sadie went round and round about what should be done with Alice. Dr. Sadie had wanted to take her to the infirmary on Second Avenue, but there were no beds there for those with such diseases. The madam complained that she'd already let Alice stay at the house longer than she felt she should. She was worried that if anyone were to get word of the girl's condition, her business would be ruined. In the end, Dr. Sadie dressed Alice in cloak and veil and took her from the house in the middle of the night, escorting her on the long trip to Charity Hospital on Blackwell's Island. Cadet went along to say his goodbyes.

I was not allowed to go with them, so I bid Alice farewell at the door.

"Take care," I said, my own eyes wet.

"Be well for both of us," she replied.

Dr. Sadie accompanied me the following day on a walk to the pharmacy on Thirteenth Street.

"She'll live, won't she?" I asked her.

"Yes, most likely."

"Will she ever be well?"

"No, not completely. You remember Miss Tully, don't you?"

"Yes," I answered, wanting her to leave it at that.

In an attempt to cheer me, she took my arm and told me that Mr. Hetherington had a new perfume oil I might like to try.

"And have you seen his fish?" she asked. "If you haven't, you really should."

Mr. Hetherington and Dr. Sadie lingered, chatting at the counter of the shop for at least an hour. He explained the qualities of this oil or that powder, while Dr. Sadie perched on a stool, listening raptly. I stood quietly looking at a fish as the two of them moved on to talk about how much each of them liked to think about thinking. Mr. Hetherington said he did his best thinking after. "After the bolt's been thrown in the door . . . after I've turned the sign in the window so the world's closed and I'm open."

Dr. Sadie said she was much the same, and that every evening she'd ponder such things as recipes, measurements and infusions, honesty, and good scientific practices. "I believe every thought, like the leaves of a plant, holds the essence of truth somewhere inside it."

Mr. Hetherington beamed at her. "Of course, sometimes I think about things too much and that leads to terrible trouble in my brain. I've had to stop going to the Sunday afternoon magic shows at Mr. Dink's Palace of Illusions because every time I go there, I come away feeling crazy over some trick I've seen. I stay up for days at a time, struggling to figure out how it's done."

Pulling a jar from under the counter, he presented it to Dr. Sadie. "But lately I've been thinking about your carbolic problem and how you said it leaves your hands so dry . . ."

Dr. Sadie looked at her red fingers and blushed.

"You should give this a try," he said, opening the jar and holding it out to her. "It might help."

I could smell the scent of the salve from where I was standing. It reminded me of the cakes from Mueller's bakery that Miss Everett piled high on her tea cart in the afternoons.

"Thank you," Dr. Sadie said, dipping her fingers into the jar and then rubbing some of the mixture over her hands. "I'm afraid being devoted to Dr. Lister's antiseptic practices does take its toll." She stopped for a moment to examine her skin and then nodded to Mr. Hetherington with approval. "This is wonderful. It's making a difference already. What's in it?"

"Almond oil," he whispered as if to keep it a secret between them. "And calendula and beeswax as well. Working the ingredients together was something of a challenge, but I think it came out all right, don't you?"

"Oh yes," she said, admiring the jar before setting it down in the middle of the counter.

Mr. Hetherington pushed the jar back towards her. "It's for you."

"I couldn't." Dr. Sadie shook her head.

"I insist," Mr. Hetherington replied. "You were my muse, after all."

She closed her eyes, her face flushing. She looked just like Mama did when she was remembering how my father had stolen her away on the back of my grandfather's horse.

As soon as we were out of the shop I asked, "Why can't you be with him?"

"Who?" she replied.

"Mr. Hetherington. It's plain to see he's the man you love."

She didn't bother to deny it. Standing under the awning, looking to where a few stray snowflakes had appeared in the sky, she said, "Mr. Hetherington has a wife."

"Oh."

She explained that Mrs. Hetherington had been ill for some time with consumption. Dr. Sadie had tried everything she could to help her, but it was a difficult case and the woman was wasting away a little more every day. She and the apothecary had first started spending time together in an effort to find ways to help his wife, but as time passed and her condition worsened, Dr. Sadie had begun to feel drawn to cure the sadness of the husband. It was a constant struggle for her and for Mr. Hetherington as well.

"There's nothing to be done . . . for either of us," she said.

"Perhaps when Mrs. Hetherington is gone . . ."

"Shh, Moth. That's enough."

Waiting at the corner till it was safe to cross the street, Dr. Sadie traced the edge of a low tree-stump with the toe of her boot. "I asked the old pear tree a question once, when it was still standing here," she said.

"The pear tree?" I asked, my heart racing.

"My father brought me here to see it when I was young," she said. "Mr. Huber was the apothecary then, and his kindness towards me was part of the reason why I chose to become a doctor. On the first Sunday in June, people came from all over the city, old Dutchmen like my father, mostly, to tie their wishes to the tree's branches. It was such a shame when the tree came down."

All the times I'd pictured the tree, it was thriving, older and wiser than ever, still giving magic to anyone who dared to ask for it. I'd hoped one day to stand in the spot my father had stood in with Mama and ask it a few questions of my own.

When the leaves of a pear tree emerge in the spring, they bear much the same colouration as the fruit. Yellow-green, with a blush of pink around the edges, they serve as messengers of the sweet reward warm days and gentle rains are sure to bring.

"Did you get an answer?" I asked.

"I did," she replied, and then said nothing more.

Crouching close to the stump, I hoped the tree's voice might come up from the ground. People were passing by on all sides, busy with getting where they needed to go.

"I'm here," I told it. "It's me, Moth." I wanted the dusty, worn-down stump to know me, to welcome me back, to tell me that my father was waiting for me somewhere.

"Come live with me, Moth," Dr. Sadie said, now holding out her hand to help me up. "I'll make room for you in my garret, and you won't have to worry about a thing."

If it had been her, instead of Mae, who'd saved me from Mr. Cowan, we might already be keeping house together, singing songs as we darned socks or telling stories in the dark at the end of the day. But I knew Miss Everett would make me honour my commitment to her, and I couldn't ask Dr. Sadie to buy me out—how would she ever afford it? I had no choice but to follow through with Miss Everett's plan.

"I know what's fair and right isn't the same for everyone," she continued. "And compared to the many other fates a girl in your circumstances might meet, what Miss Everett has offered you must seem better by far. But after everything that's happened with Alice, I needed to put this to you, to offer my assistance once more. I can't keep every girl from the terrible, dark things that happen in the city, but I could help you, I could see that you lead a happy, more forgiving life—"

"I can't," I said, stopping her from going on. "Miss Everett has made an agreement for me."

"I see," she said, frowning.

Looking to comfort her in some small way, I said, "It's my best chance."

"I hope it is, Moth," she replied. "I truly hope it is."

In 1854 Dr. Elizabeth Blackwell, founder of the New York Infirmary for Women and Children, went out to Randall's Island and adopted a young girl named Katherine "Kitty" Barry. "When I took her to live with me, she was about seven and a half years old. I desperately needed the change of thought she compelled me to give her. It was a dark time, and she did me good. Her genial, loyal Irish temperament suited me."

December 27, 1871

I have put poor Alice Creaghan in the Charity Hospital on Blackwell's Island. There are more young girls there, in her same condition, than I dared imagine. Few doctors or hospitals will care for unmarried and fallen women, no matter their malady, and the island was the only place I could find for her.

It is sickening to find that with this disease, this great pretender, most physicians of note still swear it is an illness that only dwells among the morally corrupt. Girls from polite homes, bearing every symptom, are hidden away, their persecution never mentioned. Their parents point fingers at one another behind closed doors, but in the end, they settle on a story of "bad blood" that was passed on from some wayward relative through the family tree. Science be damned, social standing preserved.

Miss Everett was no less offensive in the way she handled the situation. When I suggested we should go to the police over it, she argued it would do no good. "Cadet took care of it in his own way."

I asked her what good is it for her to pay for police protection and to cater to the Chief of Detectives if they can't provide assistance when she most needs it, but she was adamant in her refusal. "The father of the young man in question is a valued client. It wouldn't do for me to go after his son."

"This happens every day, all over the city. It needs to be stopped."

"It was a regrettable incident. We must leave it at that."

Today I had the notion that I might still be able to convince Moth to leave Miss Everett's house. She refused me yet again and I fear there's nothing more I can do. In a desperate attempt, I went straight to Miss Everett and demanded to know what it would cost to buy the girl myself.

"You can't afford her."

"How much?"

"It's not just her first time you'd be paying for, but the entire life of a whore."

It was one of the few times I've regretted how far I've fallen out with my family. There is money enough in my mother's jewellery box alone to buy Moth a thousand times over, yet I know if I went to her on the girl's behalf she'd refuse to hear me out. Nothing upsets her more than talk of poverty and prostitutes.

I have informed Miss Everett that I will be excusing myself from her house once Miss Fenwick has gone through her first encounter. I'd hoped the threat of my departure might change her mind about the girl, but it did not. She ended our conversation with a curt "So be it."

On the night in question, I will pick up the pieces for Moth as best I can. I will once again extend an open invitation to her, telling her that she may come to me whenever she may need to, but as for Miss Everett and the rest of the house, I am finished.

S.F.

For one Circassian, a sweet girl, were given,
Warranted virgin. Beauty's brightest colours
Had decked her out in all the hues of heaven.
Her sale sent home some disappointed bawlers,
Who bade on till the hundreds reached the eleven,
But when the offer went beyond, they knew
'Twas for the Sultan and at once withdrew.

—*Don Juan*, canto IV, verse 114, Byron

XXX.

A pair of sisters moved into the quarters upstairs, Fannie and Jane Byrne from Boston. They'd been sent to Miss Everett by one of her former girls, a Miss Nadine Bix. Having started a house of her own in Boston's North End, Miss Bix had requested Miss Everett train the Byrne sisters up to be proper whores for her. Miss Everett was to receive the bounty from selling their maidenhood and Miss Bix and the Byrne sisters would then reap the rewards of their having had a thorough education.

The day Mr. Wentworth was to make his return, Dr. Sadie came to examine the girls and to meet with me as well. "Have you any questions concerning the arrangement Miss Everett's made for you?" she asked.

"No," I answered, and I met her eye as steadily as I could.

"Please promise me you'll look the man over as best you can," she said, barely able to meet my gaze in return. "You know from Alice the signs of disease. If he shows any hint of illness or bears any indication that he's using mercury to fight it, you must refuse him at once. Miss Everett is in agreement. Cadet will be waiting outside the door."

"Don't the men who come here give Miss Everett proof of their being clean?"

"You must be vigilant too," Dr. Sadie said, reaching out to touch my wrist. "If a man is willing to pay a large sum for a girl who hasn't been touched, then he's certainly got enough money to pay whatever it takes to get a doctor to sign his bill of health."

Miss Everett too had advice for me. "There's an art to it," she said as she readied me for the night, "especially the first time. There are rules to follow, expectations to be met, and, perhaps, if you're lucky, enjoyment to be had. You can stumble a bit now and then, so long as you're graceful about it—you're young, after all. There will be time for knowing in your actions and your countenance later, your innocence is your greatest asset your first time out. He must have no reason to question it."

Mr. Wentworth had sent a bouquet of roses earlier in the day, so I put them in a vase on the dressing table along with a brush and comb Rose had given me before she left the house. I pinned my collection of *cartes de visite* on the wall next to the mirror. After turning the quilts down, I picked up a large box that had been delivered along with the flowers and I placed it on the bed. Tucked under the twine that was tied around the package was a note.

For my Gypsy girl.

The box contained a white chemise, a velvet hair ribbon and a skirt made from lavender-coloured gauze. The chemise had delicate gathers around the neck and when I slipped it over my head it sat gracefully on the edges of my shoulders and dipped low at my breasts. I looked at myself in the many mirrors on the wall as I tied the ribbon in my hair. While not nearly as long as it once had been, it had at last grown past my shoulders. Playing the part Mr. Wentworth desired, I would leave it down and put my combs aside for the night.

I took Mrs. Wentworth's fan out from under my pillow and spread it open in front of my face. I imagined sitting with Mr. Wentworth, flicking the fan open and shut as I told him of his wife's cruelty. "Let me tell you a story, Mr. Wentworth," I'd begin. Then, in the middle of my tale about a poor girl held captive by a horrid woman, he'd recognize the fan, and promise to make amends and take care of me forever.

Touching the fan's silk to my cheek, I had to admit to myself that I'd captured Mr. Wentworth by knowing when to leave the truth alone. Any justice I might gain would have to come that same way. The task of turning the tables in his house, if I ever found my way to it, would have to be done without my past being known.

He'd already chosen the order of our night from a list of services Miss Everett had presented to him. Upon his arrival I was to give him a delicate undressing, followed by a hot bath. Oil rubdowns were popular with many men, as were ticklings with feather fans. Although these things seemed to have been arranged for the gentleman's pleasure only, Dr. Sadie had encouraged me to use them as an opportunity to get a look at Mr. Wentworth to make sure he showed no signs of disease.

Cadet grumbled as he came in carrying heated water from Mrs. Coyne's stove. Steam rose to his face as he tipped the bucket into the copper tub. Rose had left it behind because she had a bigger, better tub waiting for her at the hotel.

"Thank you," I said, tucking Mrs. Wentworth's fan into my dressing table drawer.

Nodding to me, he left the room to fetch more water.

He hadn't been the same since the night of Alice's undoing. I'd often catch him holding a lace handkerchief that she'd given him before she'd gone away. No matter how sorry I felt for him, we'd never really been friends, at least not the sort who might lean on each other in times of trouble, so I let him go about his work and left him alone with his regrets.

The water was warm and the fire bright when Mr. Wentworth arrived. He nodded his approval when he saw I was wearing the clothes he'd sent. Setting his hat and gloves on my dressing table, he asked, "Shall we begin?"

I knew I should feel lucky that I'd not gone the way of Mae and Alice, but I was still fearful of what lay ahead. Playing to his wish to have a true Gypsy girl, I tried to put him off a bit longer. I reached out and took his hand in mine.

"Would you like me to read your palm first?"

"Later, my dear girl," he said. Dipping his fingers in the waiting tub, he flicked several droplets onto the water's surface. "For now, you're to undress me, then bathe me, then take me to bed. Understand?"

Nervous, I nodded.

"I'd like you to keep your clothes on," he instructed with a smile. Then gazing up and down the length of me he asked, "Are those pantaloons under your skirt?"

"Yes."

"I'd prefer it if you removed them."

I started to go behind the dressing screen to take them off, but he stopped me. "Lift up your skirt and get rid of them here, please. I want to see you do it."

Fumbling with the ties of my pantaloons, I finally got them loose and let them fall to the floor.

"Show me your front," he ordered. And so I lifted my skirt. After taking a long look at me without his eyes ever meeting mine, he said, "Now turn around and show me your backside, sweet Gypsy."

I did, shamed and frightened despite my vows not to be, and even though he showed no signs of intending to be rough or mean.

Loosening the silk tie around his collar, he gestured for me to undress him. Rather than bearing the clean, fresh scent he'd had during our meetings in the parlour, he smelled of cigars and liquor. As I slipped his jacket from his shoulders and began to unbutton his waistcoat, I thought of the attention and care I'd shown his wife while I lived under his roof. I tried to be confident with my touch, but when I got to his trousers my hands were shaking.

"Go on," he coaxed. "It doesn't bite."

Cadet will be outside the door.

Trousers at his feet, facing me with his naked body, he took my hand and put it on his cock. I wanted to pull away, but knew he wouldn't allow it. Kneading himself with my hand under his, what seemed soft and harmless at first soon changed into something quite different. The thought of having that thing, that Roger, pecker, dick, rod, whatever anyone chose to call it, inside me made no sense, even if I could convince myself I was willing.

"No one's had you before, my sweet?" he asked, even though he knew the answer.

"No," I said, and he let me take back my hand. "Perhaps you're ready for your bath?" Moving towards the tub, I wished I was less afraid. "I wouldn't want the water to get cold."

"Of course," he said, taking my cue and stepping into the tub.

I washed every inch of him, thinking, *yet another Wentworth under my sponge.* He stared at me, much as his wife once had, looking at my face, my shoulders, my breasts as I worked. I wasn't sure, now, which one of them, husband or wife, I feared more. I went slowly, trying, as Dr. Sadie had suggested, to get a good look at him. I squeezed the sponge out time and again, over his neck, his chest, his back.

At last he grew impatient. "That's enough. Go to the bed, dear girl. Lie on your back," he ordered as he rose from the bath and dried himself with the large white towel I'd set on a chair.

I did as I was told.

"Spread your legs, little Gypsy," he said, and lay down beside me, pulling up my skirt and putting a hand between my thighs. He never put his lips to mine or even tried to steal a kiss. All his effort, instead, went into pushing his fingers as far inside me as they would go.

Holding my breath against the pain, I thought of what Rose had told me to think about the first time I lay down with a man.

You must make duty seem as easy as desire.

"You're good and tight," he said with a grin. "I see you

haven't lied." Then he rolled on top of me, using one knee to push my legs farther apart.

I tensed and put my hands on his shoulders in an effort to slow him down, but it was no use—he was stronger than me by far.

"No . . ." I begged.

Grabbing my wrists and holding my arms down, he stared into my eyes and smiled. Then, in an instant, he was forcing himself inside me, grunting as he pushed.

Racked with pain, I turned my head, just as Mama had done with Mr. Cowan. I closed my eyes, squinting back the tears.

When he was finished, he got up from the bed, wiped himself down and dressed without saying a word. It was just as Rose had said: *It's there and then it's gone.*

Curled in the quilts, blood sticky between my legs, I felt the hurt of what had happened as a throbbing ache.

"It's been a pleasure, Miss Fenwick," he said, looking back to me as I lay on the bed.

The ribbon had fallen out of my hair and was lying on the floor. He spotted it and picked it up, but rather than giving it to me, he slipped it into his pocket, yet another memory for him to keep in his desk drawer.

"Aren't you forgetting your fortune, Mr. Wentworth?" I managed to ask before he reached the door. He'd gotten what he wanted. It was my turn to take something from him.

"Oh, my dear child, you don't need to bother."

"No, please, I insist."

Giving me a polite smile, he came and sat on the edge of the bed.

I took his hand in mine and began tracing the lines of his palm. "I see a house divided," I began. "A large house with a troubled wife. Angels of light watch over her as she walks, they stand guard at your stairs."

"What are you playing at?" he said, eyes growing hard.

Holding his hand fast, I would not stop. "A man with a scarred face lives there too. He knows your secrets."

Mr. Wentworth's hand jerked, and he said, "I'm quite frightened of you now, Miss Fenwick. You must stop."

"I told you I have a gift. My mother was a witch. I'm bound by her blood to tell you what I see."

"I'll have no more of this—"

"Ill will is in your house, Mr. Wentworth," I hissed. "It has cast a terrible shadow over you. Great harm will soon come to your person. You are in danger, Mr. Wentworth—"

Grabbing my other arm he dug his fingers into my flesh. "By whose hand?" he growled. "My wife's? Nestor's?"

I yanked my arm out of his grip. I stared at the marks his hand had left behind on my skin and then at him. "I'm sorry, Mr. Wentworth. I'm afraid the vision is gone."

"You must tell me," he begged, every trace of smugness and surety gone from his face. "It's clear you know my fate."

"You've exhausted me, Mr. Wentworth. I can't go on. It will have to wait until next time."

Swallowing hard, sweat coming to his brow, he said, "Until then, Miss Fenwick."

"Yes, Mr. Wentworth, until then."

When Dr. Sadie came to my side, I crawled into her arms and at last let myself cry. She pulled me close, but didn't say a word.

I'd thought becoming Miss Everett's girl would settle everything for me. I'd thought it would make me feel like I was worth something, even if it came along with the title of "whore." I'd thought it would make me forget Mama, and Chrystie Street, and all the fears I'd ever had—of being poor, of Mr. Cowan catching me, of not having a home. But it had done none of these things.

Through my tears I tried to tell Dr. Sadie what I thought she'd want to hear. "I did just what you said. I looked him over as best I could. I think he was clean—"

"Shh, stop, Moth," she said, stroking my hair. "You needn't say a word."

She could have seen to Miss Everett's bidding and been done with me. I wouldn't have blamed her if she'd thought me a foolish girl who'd just gotten what I deserved. Her kindness towards me had been constant from the start and I'd pushed it away, time and again. All my dreams of having a full belly, of sleeping in a fine, feather bed, of hearing Miss Keteltas' birds singing in my ear, now seemed like they belonged to someone else.

"I'm so sorry," she said, pulling a quilt around my shoulders and drying my tears with the cuff of her sleeve.

Leaning my head on her shoulder, I began to cry again, this time thinking I might never stop.

My beloved mother,
I bring you gifts from life into death.
Commune with me,
make yourself known . . .

XXXI.

The next morning, Miss Everett woke me. Regarding me dryly, she reached out a hand to touch my swollen eyes. "Tea compresses will take care of those," she said, "along with a little more sleep. I don't mind if you stay in bed this morning, you'll need your rest—he'll be calling on you again tonight."

"So soon?" I asked, hardly believing what I was hearing.

"Yes, my dear. You've managed to please the gentleman beyond measure. He's eager to keep you for himself."

Three sets of undergarments, seven pairs of stockings,
two day dresses with petticoats, a pair of boots,
a soft bustle and a corset.
One bottle of Circassian hair oil—large.
One pen, one bottle of ink, two packets of paper, and
        a five-cent stamp.
One silk walking suit, with matching hat, gloves and
        boots.
Two evening gowns—one with a train, one without . . .

"Does that mean my debts are paid?"

"Close to it, I'd say, perhaps one dress shy, but I'll gladly gift it to you." Turning to me on her way out the door, she said, "The room is yours."

Catching sight of myself in the many mirrors on Rose's wall, I felt the urge to break them all. She was a perfect, beautiful whore in every sense but I was not. No matter how hard I tried, I knew it could never be that easy and right for me.

"Why did you sell me away, Mama?" I asked, calling my mother's ghost. "Why didn't you love me?"

I remembered Mama at her table, glass sliding under her fingers, messages from spirits hissing out between her lips. Taking a sheet of paper from my dressing table, I scrawled inky, dark letters across the page. I wanted Mama's spirit to crawl into my hands and spell out a message for me.

I picked up a penny that must've fallen out of Mr. Wentworth's pocket and placed it in the centre of the page. Putting my finger lightly on it, I waited for her to make it move.

Come to me, Mama. Make yourself known.

I made several attempts to draw her spirit near, but I didn't sense a thing. Moving the penny across the paper on my own, I spelled out, *I-k-n-o-w-w-h-a-t-y-o-u-d-i-d*.

By my will or Mama's ghost, the penny at last began to move on its own, tracing out the letters *M-o-t-h-w-a-n-t-s-t-o-r-u-n-a-w-a-y*.

I got dressed in my lilac walking suit, my favourite of all the clothes Miss Everett had given me. I took a pillowcase off one of the pillows on the bed and pushed my belongings into it—a half-empty bottle of hair oil, the brush and comb Rose had given me, stockings and a clean petticoat, my collection of picture cards, and my dear Miss Sweet. Leaving the rest of the dresses and gowns behind, I headed for the door.

"Ada?" Miss Everett called to me from down the hall. "Where are you going?"

I didn't answer.

Cadet was standing at his post. He took my arm and held it fast.

Praying he'd take pity on me, I whispered, "Please, let me go."

"Make it seem a struggle," he whispered back.

As Miss Everett came down the long corridor towards us, I worked to get out of his grasp, wondering if he really meant to keep me from going.

"Give me a kick," he said.

I cracked his shin with the toe of my boot, and he let go of me.

"I'm sorry," I called, before shoving through the front door. I raced down the steps and broke into a run. I ran all the way to Second Avenue.

Dr. Sadie told me to make myself at home.

"Thank you," I said, hoping I could keep myself from starting to cry again.

There was snow that evening and church bells rang from down the street. "It's New Year's Eve," Dr. Sadie said as I stood at the window, watching revellers below get an early start. The holiday had never been anything special when I lived with Mama, but the week after New Year's was her favourite time of year. She did some of her best business then, women calling on her in hopes that she could peer into the coming months to see what was in store for them. She found wealth for nearly every soul inside her crystal ball. Holding out her hand to receive her share, she'd say, "A Gypsy's blessing to you and a very happy New Year too."

After we'd eaten a meal of meat pies and stewed apples, Dr. Sadie went to where my pillowcase was sitting and asked, "Have you things to put away?"

I nodded. "I suppose."

She didn't bother to ask how long I might be staying or what I planned to do next. She simply opened the trunk at the end of her bed and said, "You can put your things in here for now."

Peering inside the trunk I saw the dress she'd given me to wear at Mr. Dink's. I'd made a practice of leaving it at the museum each day, as it had been too difficult a task to take the cards on and off of it. Miss Everett had never liked the looks of the dress. She said it was out of fashion and that she didn't approve of me wearing it on the street.

"I'm glad it's here," I told Dr. Sadie, stroking the soft folds.

"Mr. Dink returned it to me a little while ago." she said. "He was terribly sad when Miss Everett sent word you wouldn't be coming back to the museum."

> The Circassian Beauty is a creation of her own making. Rinsing her hair with copious amounts of beer, she lets the frothy liquid dry in her tresses and then combs it into the messy, unkempt style that is the hallmark of her appearance.
>
> Tossing aside her given name (which is often as simple as her origins) she replaces it with a moniker such as Zoe, or Zelda, or some other name more fitting for a woman of myth, magic and wonder.

I'd often wondered if he really meant what he'd said about taking me on as one of his own. I couldn't imagine that he'd have me now that I'd actually become a whore. Even if he was willing to take me back, after what had happened with Mr. Wentworth I wasn't sure I could stand there each day, with so many men near to me.

"He's a thoughtful man," I told Dr. Sadie.

"One of the best I've ever known," she agreed.

Taking the picture cards one by one from the bottom of my pillowcase, I laid them on top of the dress. When I got to the Circassian Beauty, I stared at the card, wondering if the woman was as strong and defiant as she seemed.

Curly locks, Curly locks,
Will you be mine?
You shall not wash dishes
Nor yet feed the swine;
But sit on a cushion
And sew a fine seam,
And feed upon strawberries,
Sugar and cream.

XXXII.

For weeks I did little but sit by myself and try to forget. I slept each night in a cot Dr. Sadie had borrowed from the infirmary and set close to her own bed. She cooked simple meals for us—soup and bread, eggs and sausage, porridge with milk and honey.

My body healed where Mr. Wentworth's lust had made me bleed and where he'd dug his fingers into my arms. My spirit, however, was slow to mend, and my memories were bleak. Some small consolation came from finding he hadn't left me with any illness or disease.

"You're a good, beautiful girl," Dr. Sadie said time and again. "A girl with much promise."

She made mention of a school nearby where I could take lessons in arithmetic, literature and penmanship, but I told her I wasn't interested.

"I understand," she said as she mended the string on one of her aprons, letting the idea fade into the quiet of the evening.

Some days I went with her on her rounds, but most days I didn't. When she asked if I'd like to pay a visit to Miss Tully, I declined. I knew it was wrong of me, but I couldn't bring myself to go with her.

"I'll be home soon," she said, and then left me to mind the fire.

I wondered how she could be so patient with me. Sitting there alone, I also wondered, as I had many times in the past days and weeks, why Miss Everett hadn't come to Dr. Sadie's door and insisted on taking me back. Dr. Sadie had told me that I was safe with her and that I would never have to see Miss Everett again, but in all the times she'd reassured me, she'd never bothered to explain why she was so certain of it.

After Dr. Sadie changed the calendar on her wall to a bright, unmarked FEBRUARY 1872, I decided I would go to see Mr. Dink. Worried that I had overstayed my welcome in the good doctor's home, I wanted to speak with him about gaining a position at the museum, perhaps assisting Miss LeMar and Miss Eva with the costumes in the rooms under the theatre. Even with Mr. Dink watching over me, I didn't want to risk Mr. Wentworth seeing me there.

"Do you think he'll have me?" I asked Dr. Sadie, hoping she might put in a good word on my behalf.

"I do," she said. "But I'd like you to let me dress you for the occasion."

Thinking my walking suit better than any other choice she might have in mind, I said, "I'm not sure I understand."

"Do you trust me?" she asked.

"Yes," I said.

As soon as I'd given her my reply, she sat down at her desk to pen a letter, sending word to Miss LeMar and Miss Eva Ivan to ask if the two ladies might be willing to "assist a young girl in making a bit of magic."

"Two thousand dollars," I said, looking across the table at Mr. Dink.

Deep in thought, he stroked his chin.

I was about to take it back and tell him he could make me an offer instead, but Miss LeMar, who was sitting to my right, gave me a stern look as if to say *hold your ground*. Miss Eva, who was on my left, did the same.

My costume was made from fine, embroidered silk. The skirt had several rows of ruffles, and I wore a robe that went all the way down to the floor. The sideshow ladies had used beer to fashion my already unruly hair into the full mane of a "moss-haired girl." I was now a Circassian Beauty.

"Seventeen hundred," Mr. Dink countered.

"That's an insult," Miss Eva said, crossing her arms. Miss LeMar whispered, "Tell him you'll go to Barnum."

"Two thousand and not a penny less," I said. "Any respectable impresario or curiosity hunter will offer me at least that."

"That's highway robbery, my dear girl!" he exclaimed.

"Two thousand," I repeated to Mr. Dink with a smile. "And you'll also have my undying loyalty."

He gave me a big grin and stuck out his hand. "It's only because you remind me of a girl I once knew," he said as we shook to seal the bargain. "Miss Fenwick I believe was her name," he added with a wink.

After discussing a few more details, he said I'd need to get my picture taken as soon as possible, so he could put my image on a *carte de visite*. "Mr. Sarony is a magician with that camera of his," Mr. Dink said. "He makes stars out of sunshine, silver nitrate and glass."

The photographer's studio was in the top of a building on Union Square. All the notable actors and actresses of the day went to see Mr. Sarony there: Mr. Joseph Jackson, Miss Lotta Crabtree, Mr. George Fox, Miss Susie Lowe. Mr. Dink said that their fame had come soon after Mr. Sarony made their portraits and that he expected the same would happen to me.

He arranged for me to stay at the Astor Place Hotel the night before I was to see the photographer. He said it was important that I feel comfortable and have all the necessities at my disposal. "Please think nothing of the cost."

Dr. Sadie stayed with me in the suite, and we ordered milk and cakes to be sent to our room before bedtime. I called for the maid three times more, just so I could have three extra pillows for my head. I didn't want my curls to lose their shape overnight.

In the morning Mr. Dink and I travelled by private carriage to the studio. Mr. Sarony's reception room was filled with all sorts of unusual things, almost as strange as those Mr. Dink had in his museum. There were paintings and pictures hung all over, of angels and saints and ladies with nothing but flowers in their hair. There were shields and swords leaning along the walls, and animal heads, open-mouthed and staring from every corner.

A crocodile, just as pale and white as Miss LeMar, was suspended from the ceiling.

Before long, a lovely woman with a long striped scarf around her head came down the stairs. She motioned for me to follow her. As I approached the staircase, I made room for an earlier client, a gentleman, who was making his way out carrying another man on his back. The second man had his arms draped over the first man's shoulders and was holding tight as the first gentleman took one careful step at a time. As they passed me, I could see that the man being carried had no legs.

Both stopped to look at me and smile. "He's Jerome," the first man said of the man on his back. "He don't speak."

Jerome had dark eyes that made me think of Cadet and I hoped that he might be set to appear at Mr. Dink's, and that I'd see him again.

"Mr. Dink's beauty to see you, sir," the woman said when we finally entered the studio.

Hearing her words, I found it wonderful, even unbelievable, that she could be referring to me.

Mr. Sarony was something of a spectacle himself. Dressed in a bright red jacket, he wore a soft velvet fez on his head. His hands moved constantly as he talked and every so often he'd reach up to his head and take the fat tassel that was hanging from his fez and flip it over to the other side.

"I've been waiting for you!" he cried as he took my hand and kissed it. "This is your first picture ever?"

"Yes."

"Good," he said, looking me up and down, tilting his head back and forth.

The sun was filling the room through a large slanted skylight, making the blue paint on the walls appear to glow. Mr. Sarony hurried to the corner of the room closest to the window and began moving things around. After spreading out a beautiful rug woven with patterns of ribbons and flowers, he brought out several vases, a large stringed instrument and six tambourines. In the middle of all that, he put a chair. It was covered in green velvet and the wood on the arms and legs had been carved into lovely flowing scrolls.

Patting the cushion, he said, "Please, come sit."

After I was seated, he came to me with a mirror in his hand. "What do you want people to see?" he asked, putting the mirror in front of my face.

"I don't know. I thought that was up to you."

"No, no, no," he said, shaking his head so hard he set the tassel on his hat to swinging. "You can't leave that up to me. When I look through my box, you're far away, upside down. It's you who has to make the picture. You decide."

I paused for a moment, but nothing came to mind. "I can't think of anything," I replied, wondering if I'd come so far only to disappoint Mr. Dink, and myself.

"Lady Mephistopheles," he said, making more gestures with his hands. "She thinks of fire, of course. Miss Suzie Lowe, she thinks of love. Miss Lotta Crabtree, she won't say, she keeps it a secret. You see?"

"I think so," I said, still without any idea of what to hold in my thoughts while he was behind the camera.

Bringing three metal contraptions over to me, he said, "Head and arm clamps. They keep you still while I take the picture. It takes a bit of time."

Ether is used by both physicians and photographers alike. Known for its sweet, medicinal scent, it can have an intoxicating effect when used in confined spaces.

I pulled away as he stretched the clamp for my head up the length of my back and nestled its cold tines against the back of my skull.

"You must relax," he scolded.

I tried my best not to flinch as he worked to get me into the position he wanted. As I breathed in, I could smell lavender oil mixed with the strong sweet stink of something else I couldn't name. It reminded me of Dr. Sadie and the way she sometimes smelled after coming back from the infirmary. I wondered to myself what Mr. Sarony would think if I asked him to take the lady doctor's portrait with her skeleton.

At last, he walked away to fetch his weighty monster of a camera. Slipping underneath a long black cloak, he looked like he was attached to the thing, his legs set wide apart, his head and torso replaced by a box with four eyes and a sliding glass-plate heart.

He called to me, his voice muffled under the cloth. "I almost have you now. Five, four, three, two, one–think." One hand reached out and took the cover away from the lenses.

I held as still as I could, searching for the answer to Mr. Sarony's question. Memories came together in my mind and heart–Cadet kissing me, Dr. Sadie wiping away my tears, Mr. Dink stroking his beard, Mama holding her chin high as she tied her scarf around her head at the start of each day. Sitting there, with all the trappings of a life I'd never imagined, it came to me. No matter what the title read at the bottom of the card, or whatever name Mr. Dink might give me, I wanted the person holding it to see me–Moth, a girl from Chrystie Street.

A TRUE CIRCASSIAN BEAUTY

Mr. Thaddeus Dink of Dink's Museum and Palace of Illusions recently announced the arrival of his newest performer, Miss Zula Moth.

A true Circassian Beauty, the young lady's story is filled with interest and intrigue. The daughter of a prince from the mountainous region of the Black Sea, she was stolen away from her home by brute force. Born of Circassian blood, she is of the lineage of women said to be the most beautiful on Earth. Prized by Turkish sultans for their harems, these Circassian beauties are sold to the highest bidder and taken away for a nightmarish life of sexual servitude.

A Daring Rescue

The slave markets of Turkey have long been an emporium for the sale of these delicate, unfortunate creatures. Held captive by the Turks in order to be sold for the gratification of their men, Miss Zula Moth was rescued from one such slave market in the darkest heart of Constantinople.

To the men who rescued her, she is forever grateful. "The people of America are the most prosperous and free in the world. I am fortunate to now call your country my home."

In her next breath, she laments the fate of her less-fortunate sisters of Circassia. "Girls as young as twelve years old are disposed of every day by their families.

They are sent for sale at Stamboul as their grand settlement in life."

She says that the hardest lot falls to the women there, who in consequence become wrinkled and aged before their time. Mothers launch their daughters upon the market, anxious to discover the amount that a commodity so useless to them will bring.

Her memories of her homeland are like an imperfect and confused dream, causing her to lose the command of her native tongue. Remarkably, she has taken to the language of her adopted home with ease. Her ability to adapt and learn may be attributed partly to the keen powers of her mind, for she has many talents in the realm of spiritual intuition, including palm reading, crystal gazing, and communing with spirits.

Sometimes known as a "moss-haired girl," Miss Moth is the ideal of feminine beauty. Her skin is pure as cream, her voice as sweet as an angel's, and her manners as genteel as the princess she is. Dressed in the garb of the Orient, she is the picture of loveliness in silks and lace. Her hair, fashioned in the style of her native Circassia, is wildly lush and dark.

"Among the most charming attractions offered to the people of New York today as a most delicate curiosity is a young and beautiful native of Circassia," says Mr. Thaddeus Dink.

What more can be said on behalf of this lovely Circassian girl?

(Exclusive to Dink's Museum, Miss Zula Moth appears six days a week, by appointment only.)

EPILOGUE

I live in a house on Gramercy Park with two pug dogs, a pair of lovebirds and an ever-changing cast of maids. Tomorrow I'll turn nineteen.

Between a doctor's garret and theatre lights I was raised to be a sideshow belle. Pretending came naturally to me. I'm my mother's daughter after all.

Miss LeMar trained me in the ways of soothsayers, and was a far better fortune teller than Mama had ever been. Miss Eva refused to teach me to swallow swords, saying she didn't want me to risk my beautiful throat. Shortly after I turned thirteen, Mr. Dink started a travelling circus. For six summers I boarded a train and journeyed to Cincinnati, Indianapolis, Chicago, St. Louis and all the towns between. Each September, tired of strangers, I came back to the city and embraced my dear New York.

The demand for Circassian Beauties waned over time, but fortunately people still continue to yearn for a glimpse of the future. These days I spend less time in the theatre and the museum and more hours in private consultation with Mrs. Astor's four hundred. The ladies of society wish to know if they've made right choices–in evening gowns and china patterns, in friendships and in lovers. Their gentleman husbands, having held on during the dark years, want to know which stocks will rise and fall, which ventures will return high yields. The excitement of a lucky guess has caused me to fall into the arms of a banker, and a broker or two, but these transgressions were by choice and delicate negotiation, not for my survival.

Miss Everett goes on the same as always; she's as much an institution in this town as Wall Street or the Metropolitan Bank.

Dr. Sadie goes on as well, now married to Mr. Hetherington and living in New Jersey, her spirit renewed by the birth of their first child, a little girl. She holds meetings of the SPCC in her home, her babe in her arms, telling other mothers of the darkness she's seen. I go as myself, modestly dressed, my hair pulled back, and tell them my share of the story. When the women ask what they can do, I tell them, "Teach your children to be honest; teach your daughters to be strong."

There is a new time ahead, Dr. Sadie says. I hope that she is right.

I write these things from my sitting room, a place with a window so wide I can nearly see the whole of the park below. It's surrounded by a tall iron fence to which only a chosen few hold the key. I wear mine on a chain around my neck, dangling down my back like a true Gypsy girl.

Walking the perimeter of the park every day, I look for a weakness, a space wide enough for a child to crawl through. So far, it has not appeared. I prefer to promenade on the outside of the gardens because I find it hard to sit inside the park. The walkways are perfect, every shrub, flower and bench beautiful and right. Even the houses the gardener built for the birds are palaces of safety and shelter. But shutting the gate doesn't suit me. The moment it clangs, I'm left wishing I could leave it open as an invitation to some poor child walking by, the ghost of my younger self.

Requiring a lady's maid, I opened my door to a girl six months ago, hoping to find such a ghost. Miss Maggie Harlow came to me from Forsyth Street, just steps away from where I once lived with Mama. She is a child with spirit, and eyes shining with pride.

In the afternoons we wander Broadway and Sixth Avenue along with all the other ladies of the mile. From Stewart's to Stern's we promenade with purpose, the city pulsing with our stride. At Tiffany's on Union Square we stop to sift through jewels and gems, looking for the perfect stones to match our eyes. Every clerk and shopkeeper is happy to see us, knowing that our dreams, our wishes, our secrets are what hold up the buildings that now fill Manhattan's sky.

As I close the pages on this tale, it is summer. Shoots are coming up from the stump of my father's pear tree—I saw them only yesterday. Mr. Hetherington says that it happens every year: the tree tries hard to come back before Mr. Huber, in a rare appearance, comes to cut down its tender growth. One of these years Mr. Huber won't come, and the tree will make a defiant return.

Miss Harlow went about the duty of dressing me this morning, but she has since gone to the train station with my best wishes and a hundred-dollar bill. A wonderful child with ambition enough to take her anywhere she wishes to go, I hadn't the heart to hold her back. I filled her pockets with money and set her free.

She is steaming towards California to find her way.

I must find another girl.

HELP WANTED.

A lady of good standing and personal means
Seeks a girl to serve as her maid.
Skill with needle and thread desired.
Preference shown to girls from below Houston Street.

AUTHOR'S NOTE

It started with an old painting, a long lost relative, and a little girl who once lived on the streets of New York.

When I was young, I used to sit and stare at a portrait that was hanging above our piano, a beautiful painting of a woman and a young girl. The woman, dressed in black taffeta, was seated in profile as she watched over the little girl who was at her knee. The child, looking as if she'd been allowed to play dress-up in her mother's clothes, stared out of the painting with contentment, a loose fitting dressing gown the same shade of blue as the sky in the artist's background draped around her, a large silver bracelet on her wrist. Her dark hair was held away from her face with a red ribbon, and I'd often beg my mother to fix my hair the same way. Every time I asked her to tell me about the two sitters in the portrait, she'd patiently explain, "The woman is your great-great-grandmother. I was named after her, and she was a lady doctor. The child is her daughter."

My desire to learn more about "Dr. Sadie" followed me throughout my life. I begged all the information I could from my grandmother and other relatives, but family papers, journals and letters had been lost over the years, leaving me with little more than a few names and dates. In 2007, my mother passed away after a long battle with colorectal cancer. In the months that followed, I decided that it was time to uncover Sadie's past for myself. I went back to notes I had taken several years before and began to piece her life together, one clue at a time.

It was a journey filled with serendipitous twists and turns. An envelope given to me by a medical historian led me to a woman who held a personal archive of letters written to and received from a young female medical student who happened to be a contemporary of my great-great-grandmother's. Second-hand books as well as books and ephemera from the shelves of the New-York Historical Society Museum & Library helped me to understand what the city was like in the late 1800s (*The Nether Side of New York: Or, the Vice, Crime and Poverty of the Great Metropolis; Sunshine and Shadow in New York; Darkness and Daylight in New York: Or, Lights and Shadows of New York Life; a pictorial record of personal experiences by day and night in the great metropolis*, a "gentleman's directory," and a catalogue of exhibits at an anatomical museum, to name but a few.) Another trip led me to Dr. Steven G. Friedman of the New York Downtown Hospital, which celebrated its 150th anniversary in 2007. In his office I held in my hand an official historical document naming my great-great-grandmother as one of the first graduates of the Women's Medical College of the New York Infirmary for Indigent Women and Children. I realized then that I had stumbled on a tale much larger than the one I had first set out to uncover, a tale that needed to be told.

In 1870, over thirty thousand children lived on the streets of New York City and many more wandered in and out of cellars and tenements as their families struggled to scrape together enough income to put food on the table.

Under the mentorship of sister physicians Drs. Elizabeth and Emily Blackwell, Sadie and her classmates worked tirelessly to care for such children. They faced fierce opposition from the medical establishment as well as from society. People sometimes rioted outside the doors of the infirmary, and funding was difficult to obtain. It was their mission to give health care to all women and children, no matter what their station or income might be. As the population of the city rose at an unprecedented rate, the ravages of disease were felt most keenly on the Lower East Side. Outbreaks of typhoid, diphtheria and smallpox rose alongside the continuous spread of tuberculosis and sexually transmitted diseases such as gonorrhea and syphilis. As the "lady doctors" of the infirmary worked to increase awareness of the plight of the city's poor, the young boys of the tenements were shoved out the door to find work, and little girls became a commodity.

Sold into prostitution at a young age, many girls from poor families were brokered by madams (or even their own parents) as "fresh maids." Men paid the highest price for girls who had been "certified" as virgins.

At this same time in New York, syphilis was an overwhelming, widespread puzzle of a disease with no remedy and it was this taboo topic that my great-great-grandmother chose as the subject of her graduation thesis. In her day, there continued to be much argument over how the disease was spread and there were many unsuccessful (and often destructive) forms of treatment. An even greater tragedy than the human wreckage resulting from this disease was a deadly myth that preyed upon young girls. The myth of "the virgin cure"–the belief that a man with syphilis could "cleanse his blood" by deflowering a virgin–was without social borders and was acted out in every socio-economic class in some form or another. In fact, the more money a man had, the easier it would have been for him to procure a young girl for this unthinkable act.

As one physician of the time stated, "I have been surprised at discovering the existence of this belief [the virgin cure] in people generally well informed as well as among the comparatively illiterate. I have tried to find evidence for the theory that it is a belief traceable to certain districts but I have discovered it among people of different places and of different occupations–so different that now I should scarcely be surprised to come across it anywhere."

Originally I thought that the narrative voice of *The Virgin Cure* would be Sadie's, but as I searched for the best way to write the story I wanted to tell, I discovered that it wasn't to be found in her voice after all. I spent hours walking the streets and sidewalks that had once been travelled by my great-great-grandmother in her work as a medical student and physician in the late 1800s. As I walked, I tried to conjure up the memory of her life and the women and children she had served. On Second Avenue, I stared at the place where the New York Infirmary for Indigent Women and Children once stood. I went to Pear Tree Corner to see where Peter Stuyvesant's great pear tree had lived for over two hundred years. I visited the Lower East Side Tenement Museum and looked into the small, dark rooms of the past. On those streets, I found my answer. I found the voice I'd been waiting for, the voice of a twelve-year-old street girl named Moth.

ACKNOWLEDGEMENTS

I am indebted to the following people for their tremendous efforts and their contributions to this book.

To my family and friends near and far–thanks for the encouragement and for listening.

To my parents, who are with me always.

To my amazing agent, Helen Heller, for sharing her wisdom and expertise (and for reminding me to follow my gut).

To Anne Collins, for her editorial prowess and elegant touch.

To Allyson Latta, for her keen eyes and for asking all the right questions.

To Kelly Hill, who continues to make my words look like magic.

To Deirdre Molina and Nicola Makoway, for their great skill in making sense of things.

To Diane Martin and Angelika Glover, for their enthusiasm and support.

To Chris O'Neill of the Ross Creek Centre for the Arts and Ken Schwartz of Two Planks and a Passion Theatre–your friendship in life and art means the world to me.

To the Zuppa Theatre Co. players and the cast and crew of *Jerome*–muses all!

To the 2010 Creeklings–Rebecca, Ruby, Ivy, Mariah and Ainslee, and honorary Creeklings past, Caitlin, Sarah and Aliah. You, my dear girls, will take the world by storm.

To the staff of the New-York Historical Society Museum & Library, for following through on my countless questions and queries.

To Dr. Steven G. Friedman of the New York Downtown Hospital, for opening his office and helping me find a page from my great-great-grandmother's life.

To Milly Riley, for your willingness to share pieces of your family's past.

And, to the three who are my everything–my sons Ian and Jonah, and my partner in life and poetry, my husband Ian. *Du meine Seele, du mein Herz.*

The
Virgin
Cure

READING GROUP NOTES

ABOUT THE AUTHOR

Ami McKay's debut novel, *The Birth House* was a number-one bestseller in Canada, winner of three CBA Libris Awards, nominated for the International IMPAC Dublin Literary Award, and a book club favourite around the world. Previously a music teacher in Chicago, Ami's literary career started moving forward with an enforced career break whilst waiting for residency papers after her move to Nova Scotia. She decided that 2000 would be the year of writing thank-you notes to people she didn't know and now every day is a writing day. Born and raised in Indiana, Ami now lives in Nova Scotia.

In Conversation with Ami McKay

Q Why did you feel that Sadie's wasn't the narrative voice for this story?

A My first draft of the novel was from Sadie's point of view, but the more I wrote about Moth, the more she pushed her way to the front of my writing, her voice nagging in my head saying, "Get out of the way and let me tell the tale." Once I started writing from her perspective, everything made sense. I couldn't wait to get back to my desk each day to see where she would take me.

Q Whilst a sense of authenticity is crucial to a novel like *The Virgin Cure*, is absolute historical accuracy also needed, or can it hinder?

A One thing I've learned from years of sleuthing around libraries and archives is that the historical record is far from perfect. I do my best to honour the past in my writing while keeping a close eye on the story I want to tell. There comes a point when the research reaches critical mass and the writing takes over. When the desire to create my own story trumps everything else, I know it's time to take all the bits and pieces I've gathered and make something new.

Q How did you physically write *The Virgin Cure*, and why?

A I write first drafts with fountain pen in notebooks, doodling in the margins or creating collages on some of the pages as I go. I love how it feels to put pen to paper and the fact that there's no "delete" unless I throw the pages in the fire. Typing the text into my computer comes later and is part of my editing process.

Q Which character in the novel are you most like?

A As much as I adore Moth, I'm more like Sadie. She's based on my great-great-grandmother, so I became quite attached to her during the writing process. Her history was a bit of a grand puzzle for me to solve, and her character contains a mixture of traits from the women that followed her in my family tree.

Q Your entrance into Moth's world began with a painting – how important is it to create vivid images in the minds of your readers, and how did you set about doing it?

A Scenes tend to run through my mind as I'm writing, and I "hear" the dialogue in my head. I suppose you could say that I've got a cinematic imagination. I do my best to capture what's in there and put it on the page.

Q What authors do you admire and why?

A While writing *The Virgin Cure* I reread several Charles Dickens and Edith Wharton novels I'd read when I was in my teens. It was amazing to see how much of their work had stayed with me over the years and how their words had influenced the story I wanted to tell. Both authors had the ability to bring a city to life on the page, (London and New York respectively) without ever losing track of plot or their characters' hearts.

Q Silence or music while you write? If music – who do you listen to?

A There's always music. The soundtrack for *The Virgin Cure* included Alicia Keys, Sarah Slean, Adele, Laura Nyro and Alison Krauss. The novel seemed to flow best to female songwriters with incredible talent and haunting voices.

Q Where did the idea for the visual structure of *The Virgin Cure* come from?

A While researching the book, I fell in love with the look and feel of 19th-century newspapers – the fonts, the ads, the cadence of the writing. I wanted to capture some of those elements in the layout of the novel. I also wanted to include voices other than Moth's in the narrative, sort of like instruments in a musical score. Sadie's voice is heard through sidebars and journal entries. The voice of New York is heard through the articles from the *Evening Star*, a fictional newspaper I invented for the book.

Q What's your most treasured possession?

A My life.

Q Is it important to educate your readers as well as entertain them?

A No. What's most important to me is to stay true to the tale. *The Virgin Cure* led me to ask lots of questions of the past and the present, setting me on a chase through history to try to find answers. Some of those questions are answered in the novel, while others are still on my mind waiting for me to pursue them. Readers will have their own journeys in reading the book and I respect that. What they take away from the novel is theirs alone.

Q What single thing about you would surprise us the most?

A I used to teach music at a high school in Chicago.

Q Has life on those streets changed so very much over the years for girls like Moth?

A While the streets where Moth lived may be safer in our time, and girls like her are better protected by the law, there are parts of the world today that are just as dangerous as the 19th-century slums of Chrystie Street. Sadly, the myth of *The Virgin Cure* is alive and thriving in many Third World countries. Child prostitution and rape are problems we still need to solve.

Q What's your most vivid memory?

A My earliest memory was the day the piano was delivered to my childhood home. I was just a toddler at the time, so it's quite remarkable that I remember it at all, but I can still recall the big black boots of the delivery men and the way the piano keys felt smooth and cool as I stroked them with my fingers.

Q Any clues about your next book – any snippets for us?

A It's something of a sequel to *The Virgin Cure*, taking place in 1881 and still following the life of Moth. She's joined by a few new characters this time around, and that's all I'm willing to share at the moment. (I tend to be superstitious about works in progress.) The title is *The Witches of New York*.

FOR DISCUSSION

- How does the author set the scene?

- What does it mean to be an 'American girl'?

- 'I knew when it came to love or bruises, nothing was ever simple.' What does this tell us about Moth?

- 'Even at her lowest, she knew who she was. In that way, we were more alike than different.' To what extent is the sense of identity a central theme of *The Virgin Cure*?

- 'A girl should command attention, not suffer it.' To what extent is this still relevant today?

- 'Given the choice between wooden slats or feather beds, which would you choose?' What about you – which would you choose?

- 'Words are an unreliable way to measure the heart.' True, do you think?

- How does the author demonstrate the similarities and differences between Moth and Dr Sadie?

- 'Sometimes, for a moment, everything is just as you need it to be.' What does Moth really need?

- How does the author contrast the living conditions of 19th-century New York?

- 'The trick of getting what you want . . . is to make duty seem as easy as desire.' Is Rose right?

- What devices has the author used to make *The Virgin Cure* seem like a period memoir?

Suggested Further Reading

The Crimson Petal and the White by Michel Faber

The House of Mirth by Edith Wharton

Oliver Twist by Charles Dickens

Maggie: A Girl of the Streets by Stephen Crane

The Morgesons by Elizabeth Stoddard

The Excellent Doctor Blackwell:
  The Life of the First Woman Physician by Julia Boyd